A SYSTEM SO MAGNIFICENT
IT IS BLINDING

A SYSTEM SO MAGNIFICENT IT IS BLINDING

AMANDA SVENSSON

TRANSLATED BY NICHOLA SMALLEY

SCRIBE

Melbourne • London

Scribe Publications
2 John St, Clerkenwell, London, WC1N 2ES, United Kingdom
18–20 Edward St, Brunswick, Victoria 3056, Australia
3754 Pleasant Ave, Suite 100, Minneapolis, Minnesota 55409, USA

Ett system så magnifikt att det bländar © Amanda Svensson, first published by Norstedts,
Sweden, in 2019.

Published by Scribe 2022
Published by agreement with Norstedts Agency

Copyright © Amanda Svensson 2019
Translation copyright © Nichola Smalley 2022

'Landlocked Blues': words and music by Conor Oberst © 2005, reproduced by permission of
Bedrooms & Spiders Ltd/Sony Music Publishing, London W1T 3LP.
Excerpts from 'The Building' and 'This Be The Verse' from *The Complete Poems by Philip Larkin*
© Philip Larkin, reproduced with kind permission of Faber and Faber Ltd.
Excerpts from 'Am I Unto Death Quite Worn' by Harriet Löwenhjelm translated by
Anne-Charlotte Hanes Harvey © Anne-Charlotte Hanes Harvey.

Typeset in Adobe Garamond Pro by the publishers

Printed and bound in the UK by CPI Group (UK) Ltd, Croydon CR0 4YY

Scribe is committed to the sustainable use of natural resources and the use of paper products made
responsibly from those resources.

978 1 913348 04 5 (UK edition)
978 1 925849 93 6 (Australian edition)
978 1 957363 11 0 (US edition)
978 1 922586 54 4 (ebook)

Catalogue records for this book are available from the National Library of Australia
and the British Library.

The cost of this translation was defrayed by a subsidy from the Swedish Arts Council,
gratefully acknowledged.

scribepublications.co.uk
scribepublications.com.au
scribepublications.com

The baby blues came quickly to the triplets' mother. But before that, the babies, of course. Sebastian was first, then Clara, then Matilda. Or perhaps the order was different — afterwards no one could really be sure because then came pandemonium, as one of the newborns' heartbeats, and then breathing, went awry. A doctor rushed into the room. A baby was borne out at lightning speed and in its place was brought a tray bearing open sandwiches, cordial, and three little Swedish flags (bad timing, obviously), and a father — the triplets' father — was suddenly left empty-handed with not a clue what to do. He picked up a cheese sandwich while his wife, with the two remaining babies clutched one to each breast, delivered the afterbirth.

It wasn't until afterwards that he realised what he ought to have done was run after the doctor who'd gone to try to revive his child. Perhaps he was in shock — that's what his wife would think later — and in any case the baby was soon back again: suddenly there it was, lying in its father's arms, tiny, wrinkly, and gulping for breath, but quite clearly alive. It was like getting a second chance, the father thought, looking down at his newborn's fluffy head — and he decided to take it. The triplets' father wasn't stupid, and even the first time he stuck his hand down his dental hygienist's knickers he'd understood two things. One: that he didn't have strong enough nerves to maintain a double life indefinitely and would therefore be forced, sooner or later, to admit his affair to his wife — who he actually loved very deeply, or at least had a very deep dependency on, which, the father reasoned, was essentially the same thing. And two: that the best time to do this would be at the exact moment she'd become responsible for not one but *three* children, making it unlikely she'd be able to manage on her own, and consequently, unlikely she'd throw him out.

This turned out to be a wholly correct assessment. In the jittery moments after her three children had been borne into this world on a wave of blood and pain, the triplets' mother, a priest at All Saints Parish in Lund, experienced a fear of the future that was so intense it caused her very belief in God to evade her mockingly. The fact that one of her babies had almost perished from what the doctors would later call *spontaneous asphyxia neonatorum with no lasting complications* unsurprisingly exacerbated this fear. For the ten minutes during which, instead of the three babies whose soft feet she'd for months felt pressing against her hands through her abdominal wall, she'd suddenly only had two, she experienced a sorrow so cruel and bottomless that all the sorrow that was to come, including that inflicted by her own spouse, paled into insignificance. For those ten minutes she'd felt ready to throw God out with the babies' first bathwater — for what God could tear a newborn baby from its mother's arms before she'd even had the chance to touch its wrinkly little hand?

Compared to this divine betrayal, the betrayal of the man who'd stood there, mouth full of Gouda and fluffy white bread, solemnly swearing to stand by the babies and her, if she'd only overlook his dalliances with the dental hygienist, appeared little more than a trifle.

That's not to say she didn't cry.

That's not to say she forgave the guy.

But she was happy, she was happy all the same. So dizzyingly, joyously happy about the babies, about suddenly having a family, even if it was somewhat skewed and scuffed and a bit of a sham. Suddenly the gold in the world stood out so brightly all around her: the coffee, the clementines, the fluttering hospital curtains on that unusually warm, sunny autumn day, as finicky little Sebastian finally latched on to the breast in exactly the right way and took a full feed for the very first time. Everything tasted heavenly. All the colours were vivid. Every bodily sensation, even the painful ones, took on a new, almost erotic dimension. In a meadow of powerfully scented flowers — since flowers were still allowed on labour wards in the late eighties — over the week she stayed in the hospital with her three rather underweight little babies, the triplets' mother slowly but surely regained her faith in God and divine love, of which the children were unquestionably a part.

Things were undeniably less certain regarding her earthly love for their father, and yet she endured for more than two further decades.

There were other things to think about. Feeding schedules. The cost of music lessons. Secrets.

But of course, the marriage was bound to crumble in the end.

First came the triplets, then the drama and the tears, and the drama again. Then almost twenty-three years' ceasefire. But the day finally came when the last of the triplets left home: the first-born, Sebastian, who, perhaps because he'd been the first to leave the womb, had the most difficulty flying the nest, even though he flew no further than to a room in the local student halls. The same day, their father moved into a single room at the local hotel. It didn't even have a minibar, but there were stars outside the window — indeed, the whole universe. He looked out of the window and for the first time in his life it struck him that the universe was very, very big and that a person, in comparison, was very, very small.

This happened in 2012 — making the triplets' birth year 1989, in October. For Christmas the same year, their father gave their mother a piece of the Berlin Wall he'd bought from a street-hawker outside the supermarket. It was supposed to symbolise reconciliation. She threw it at the kitchen wall and went on breastfeeding.

In the summer of 1994, southern Skåne was swarming with ladybirds. Small red dots everywhere, even in the dog's fur. All three siblings remembered it, even though they'd never talked about it.

In the summer of 1999, the dog died and was seamlessly replaced by another. It was a Newfoundland just like the first and they called it Bernarda. It had nothing to do with García Lorca.

1994 was also the year Sebastian wet the bed an average of 3.2 nights a week.

In October 1989, a girl who came to be christened Violetta was born in the same hospital. Her eyes were remarkably blue, her limbs remarkably thin, and her breathing notably laboured.

In the spring of 1995, Clara learned to ride a bike, but not Sebastian or Matilda. This was balanced out by the fact that both Sebastian and Matilda learned to swim that summer, but not Clara. The question of whose motor skills were the most advanced therefore went mercifully unanswered.

In 2016, Sebastian travelled to London, Clara to Easter Island, and Matilda to Västerbotten, in Northern Sweden. After that, none of them were the same. That year, their mother got an allotment in St Månslyckan. There, one frosty morning in February, she met a badger whose pungent scent and sharp claws made her think for a moment she'd come eye-to-eye with the devil, just like Luther in the Wartburg Castle. After that she started calling the allotment Fright-Delight, a name that made her feel alive. It was also the catalyst for a new-found desire to become completely pure in the eyes of the Saviour, which, over the coming months, would turn her children's already somewhat complicated lives upside down.

In 2004, both Clara and Matilda got their first periods, in January and February respectively. Sebastian got a PlayStation 2.

I
LONDON

All love stories, no matter how twisted they become in the end, have an innocent beginning, and this was Sebastian and Laura's.

Him saying: Laura Kadinsky?

And her saying: Here.

The human brain is both more and less complex than the average person thinks. The brain isn't a machine: it bears only a fleeting resemblance to a computer processor; it encompasses much more than the Chinese room. If you rolled out your neurones on the ground they would stretch three times round the equator. If we assume that the average person covers roughly ten kilometres a day on foot then it would take almost half a lifetime to go just one circuit around your own head, and that's not taking into account the fact that at a fleeting glance, the brain is something of a labyrinth. In reality, though, it's so simple you could compare it to the veins on a leaf. Picture the spine as a stalk, and the mind as a leaf in the palm of your hand. Then imagine your life as water, your soul as sugars and chlorophyll. Some spiders' brains are distributed throughout their bodies, and the leech has thirty-seven brains. In the human intestinal cavity there are as many neurones as in the head of a cat, though not many people are prepared to acknowledge this.

All vertebrates have a brain, but not all brains are created equal. The human brain, for example, consists of three distinct and well-studied parts — the cerebellum, the cerebrum, and the brain stem — while the giant squid's brain most closely resembles a rubber ring, through the opening of which it forces the food it has chewed into its body. But the thing that most distinguishes humans from less complex beings is a thin but very compact outer layer, a gold plating to the cerebral cortex known as the neocortex. It is present in many mammals: when humans see a dolphin pretending to have fun at the aquarium, it's the neocortex's shiny surface they're seeing themselves reflected in. But in any case, the human neocortex is something quite apart. Together with our opposable thumbs it's what has made the human race king of the castle, the jewel in the crown of creation, the only species on earth incapable of being completely satisfied.

The price of this dubious privilege is primarily paid by women and their fragile perineum, the pressure on the bladder caused by the human infant's outsized head. Sebastian Isaksson — twenty-six years old, blond, blue-eyed, clinically depressed even though he himself wasn't aware of it, son of a priest in the Swedish Church and an administrator at the Swedish Tax Agency, and the brother of two women who didn't speak to each other, currently residing in a miserable studio flat in London's southern suburbs — had always thought of the biblical story of the fall of man as a metaphor for the origination of the human brain's grotesquely oversized neocortex. Eve, he thought, was striving for a cognitive ability beyond what she saw in Adam, her lifelong comrade and only stimulus, happy as he was as a pig in muck. She reached with evolutionary instinct for the apple and God said: Eve, I'm going to give you a brain with capabilities you can't even imagine in your present half-vegetative state; I'm going to give you gifts called abstract thought, spatial awareness, a sense of time, consciousness of death, generalised anxiety; I shall give you everything you're asking for and a little extra; and all this shall spring forth from something I shall call NEOCORTEX!

And Eve said: Sounds good.

And God said: To fit all this into your skull I have to make it swell like a sourdough to twice its size, and the same shall apply to your offspring, but just to be difficult I'm not going to expand your pelvis and your birth canal.

And Eve said: Okay. Fine. Whatevs.

And God said: Because you're still unable to think logically, you're not able to put these two facts together, but I can tell you that the consequence will be that you and all women after you will give birth to your children in horrific pain.

And Eve said: I'm not afraid.

Though in reality she was shit-scared.

And thereby, with her pluck and her pride, proved herself worthy of both gift and punishment.

Truth be told, the neocortex isn't the only thing inside the skull that directs human behaviour. You can think of the brain as an advanced Ancient Roman delicacy, a Russian doll made of more and more complicated animals: a mouse inside a pheasant inside a pig. On the outside, a golden casing of milk and honey, and in the very centre a terrified little bird, encapsulated in an egg. Without all that meat in the middle, the casing would fall in upon itself. There's a brain stem, without which we'd be unable to breathe or swallow, without which the heart would be unable to beat. There's a little lump above the neck without which we'd be unable to stand up or run a finger across someone else's cheek. There's a middle layer of functions without which human existence would be completely meaningless: the hippocampus (memory), the olfactory bulb (scent), the ventricles (waste disposal). But you can go on all you like about the basic functions, it's still from the neocortex that the most human of human traits arise, which you could say has gone to its head somewhat. The neocortex is poised at the top of the pyramid. The neocortex is the best-compensated part of the brain system, taking 80 per cent of all the energy. The neocortex makes weird mistakes at work but blames its underlings. In other words, the neocortex is boss.

Not entirely unexpectedly, the brain's hierarchical structure is reflected in the physical world it's played a part in shaping. From woodland and wetland, muddy waterways and half-decayed stegosaurus bones, have risen skyscrapers and signposts, clock towers and cranes, everything that is tall and beautiful and functional. Man has built the world from the bottom up, because that's how he has built himself. So it's only natural that the London Institute of Cognitive Science (LICS) — one of the world's leading centres for research into everything from our senses to our synapses, right at the cutting edge of cognitive science — was organised according to the same model as the one found inside the human cranium.

The Institute was in the heart of London, a city that had, at one time at least, had a claim to being the centre of the world. The building in itself, a charming brick edifice which over time had been extended upwards and outwards with nothing but layers of concrete and metal, had an internal structure that was as strictly hierarchical as it was complex. Furthest down in the basement were the animals, in a literal sense, with the workers — in other words, Sebastian and his colleagues

— on the many intermediate floors. Visitors were admitted through the doors facing the street and then shunted at lightning speed between floors via a complicated system of lifts and stairs. It was said that many never made it out again, that they burned up like short-circuited nerve cells and disappeared.

Right at the top and right at the front, with a view out over historic Russell Square, in the building's equivalent of the prefrontal cortex, the Institute's directors had their offices, neatly ordered by seniority. It was outside the third door from the end that Sebastian Isaksson found himself standing one pallid morning in January, trying to smooth his hair into something resembling decorum across his sweaty forehead. After failing multiple times, a fact remarked upon by a passing cleaner, he gave up and knocked on the door with trembling knuckles.

Why was Sebastian so nervous? It was partly, if not wholly, a result of the fact that this was the first time he was meeting his boss. Throughout the recruitment process at LICS Sebastian had dealt with many people, from the academic talent scout who'd been in the canteen at Lund University's medical faculty one day, holding a sign with his name on, just like the kind pre-booked taxi drivers have when they're waiting for business passengers at airports, to the researcher who welcomed him on his first day at the Institute, but the actual director of the place had only communicated with him via the building's pneumatic postal system. The fact that his boss was the only one at the Institute who still used the old system — instead of just expelling little puffs of information into the much-vaunted 'cloud' — had made Sebastian suspect that his superior was of the eccentric type not completely uncommon among men of talent. This anticipated eccentricity was the other reason Sebastian was nervous — a lifetime surrounded by eccentric women had taught him it was a most overrated character trait.

The door flew open.

'So, we meet at last, my young friend! Take a seat, I don't bite,' thundered Rudolph Corrigan, the towering red-headed man with a strong American accent who reared up in the doorway. He stepped to one side and pointed to a chair. The hand that pointed was as big as the scalp of an average-sized Scandinavian two-year-old and Sebastian obeyed, suddenly filled with the striking sense of wellbeing that arises when you've thrown yourself into a situation you've been dreading, only to realise you're probably going to survive after all.

'So … Sebastian Isaksson. From Lund University.'

'That's correct, sir.'

'Venerable seat of learning, n'est-ce pas? Not quite Cambridge, mind you, but the best you have in Sweden, I understand?' said Corrigan when he'd cast himself down behind his desk.

'Sadly, I have to confess that Lund is mainly known for the humanities. The best medical research takes place at the Karolinska Institute in Stockholm.'

'So why haven't you found your way there?'

'Personal reasons, sir.'

'Love?'

'Fear.'

The forbidden word slid out of Sebastian before he had time to stop it; slippery as an eel, it wriggled across the room, floated down into Corrigan's postal tube, and out into the building's synapse system, soon reaching every lobe, every person, sending a cold shiver down the spine of each and every one, because that's how it is with certain words, they ought never to be spoken aloud except in a psychologist's office. However, Rudolph Corrigan was a gentleman. Not for nothing had he spent twelve years eating apple pie, practising French conversation, and ironing his school uniform at an exclusive prep school in New Hampshire. He let Sebastian's faux pas pass and changed the subject.

'How are you finding it here with us? It must be coming up for a month since you arrived?'

'Very well, sir. I'm very grateful for the opportunity.'

'Are you?'

'Yes. Or, what I mean is, I'm sure I'm going to be very grateful once I understand what this opportunity means. Which I must admit I don't quite. Yet. But I'm sure it's wonderful. The opportunity, I mean.'

'Yes, it's something of a mystery, isn't it?'

'I'm not quite sure I follow you, sir.'

'What you're doing here, Sebastian. It's a mystery, right?'

'I don't know if I'd use a word as strong as mystery. But I have to admit it's a little unclear.'

'It's clear as day to me.'

'Yes, I hope so,' Sebastian said, allowing himself a smile he hoped would be interpreted as jovial, or even collegial. Corrigan didn't take the bait.

'This is how it is, Sebastian, now listen good, because I'll say this once and once only. The days when brain research was a marginal field of medicine, aimed at curing disease and solving little everyday mysteries such as why some people become homosexual or others depressed, are over. We're on the brink of a paradigm shift. The nature of which I imagine you're aware of.'

(Sebastian wasn't.)

'That's why I think you also understand that there's a need to keep information where it belongs.'

(He didn't understand this either, just as you can't understand an equation in which the basic denominator is unknown.)

'In other words, it's not for nothing that I use this reliable old system.'

Corrigan stroked the pneumatic post apparatus fondly and leaned back in his black leather office chair.

'We live in a surveillance society, Sebastian. I'm no dinosaur — as you know, you can't be in this field — but I believe in a certain degree of integrity, both personal and professional. In vain I've sought to convince those higher up to realise this and stop their blind belief in this "cloud" business, but what can you do. Fundamentally, everyone here on the top floor is agreed that we need to maintain confidentiality. That's why the Institute is no longer a proponent of transparency; quite the opposite, we're in the midst of a restructuring process according to a model well tested by criminal networks and terrorists. Not because we're criminals, mind you, but because, in spite of everything, they've proved themselves extremely effective when it comes to minimising the risk of leaks. I'm talking, you see, about a division into cells, in which each cell holds only the information needed to undertake the tasks delegated to that cell. In the event of, say, bugging, kidnapping, or similar, the damage would be limited because a member of a given cell would hold only one or possibly two pieces of the puzzle that makes up the bigger picture. Are you with me?'

'Yes, sir.'

'And you understand that we're talking about a puzzle with thousands of pieces? Because to be as frank as I can without undermining the model I've just described to you: I can't tell you exactly why we've recruited you, Sebastian. Bearing in mind that you accepted our offer in spite of this, I can only conclude that this neither deters nor particularly surprises you. Am I right?'

'Yes, sir.'

(Of course, this was no more true than it was untrue. Due to the situation Sebastian found himself in when he was approached by the Institute's talent scout and offered the post, it was all the same to him what it involved, in the same way it had been all the same to him whether the sun would rise the following day or not. He would have said yes to any offer that got him out of Lund. Because there was nothing left for him in Lund, and in some ways, having nothing is less painful in a new environment. Or at any rate, it's painful in a different way.)

'Bien!'

Corrigan clapped his hands cheerfully before digging around in a heap of papers on his desk.

'I have a few reports here from Barázza … he says you're getting along very well. You and Barázza are in the same cell, perhaps you were aware of that? On the basis of his praise, one might imagine you were a Multi-talent! But of course, he's temperamental, Barázza …'

'A Multi-talent, sir?'

'Our most valuable employees, Sebastian — the diamonds, the cherries on the cake, the Nobel Prize–winners–in–waiting. It's no secret who they are, or that they have a salary that's more or less precisely 4.3 times higher than yours. Childs, Harvey, Misomoto, Benutti, Jensen … myself, naturally. And Travis, of course, the delightful Jennifer Travis! And what do I know, Sebastian, perhaps you're sitting on talents we've not yet discovered, it's certainly possible. Though I doubt it, to be quite honest.'

'No, probably not, sir.'

'In any case: Barázza has written here that you seem to be a fast learner, cooperative, and most of all, that your judgement of the sample material seems to be very accurate. To quote: "An initial degree of uncertainty seems to have been replaced by an uncommon clarity as concerns diagnosis, cataloguing, and proposed measures for those cases of abnormal cerebral process previously observed by Cell 12 in the referred subjects. I recommend *with burning passion* that Isaksson's areas of responsibility be expanded to include, alongside diagnostic assessments, follow-up, investigation, and — if desired — initial treatment of some of the future subjects in Cell 14's test groups 3A, 3B, and 3C. It is proposed that this should occur under the supervision of the undersigned." Et voilà, Sebastian! With this little scribble from me, your first promotion is authorised ...'

With the kind of flourish typical of those accustomed to power, Corrigan signed the piece of paper he'd just read from and pushed it across to Sebastian, who, without knowing what he was supposed to do with it, picked it up and just sort of held it there in mid-air. Corrigan jerked the sheet of paper out of his hand, folded it, and once again pushed it across the desk to Sebastian.

'Take this and give it to Barázza. He'll inform you of your new tasks and the level of confidentiality applicable to the results generated. Well, what do you say, shall we celebrate?'

From a desk drawer, Corrigan pulled out a thermos and a packet of Jaffa cakes. Sebastian — who, during his weeks in England, had developed a certain fondness for Jaffa cakes — identified them as a more expensive kind than the ones he tended to indulge in, and discovered to his surprise — and unformulated terror — how a wave of hunger for life, and for these specific Jaffa cakes with their promise of higher-than-average cocoa content and bitter rather than sweet orange filling, tickled his waistline. Was it really that easy? Was that all that was needed to break the emotional fast he'd imposed since *what happened happened* — a little praise, fat, and sugar?

'Well, help yourself!' Corrigan roared, waving the pack of biscuits under Sebastian's nose. 'Or are you one of those fanatics who think sugar is comparable to speed? As someone with significant experience of both substances, I can tell you: IT IS NOT.'

'Of course not, sir,' Sebastian said, picking up one Jaffa cake in each hand. Their scent was intoxicating, like the scent of a woman's thighs rubbing against each other as she walks by. With horror, Sebastian realised he was on the verge of tears, whether from gratitude or sorrow was hard to say, but it was embarrassing in any case, and he was forced to stuff his mouth full in order to swallow the lump in his throat before it tore him asunder across Corrigan's desk.

'And how're things going with the monkey?' his boss asked, tipping his office chair back to a suitable angle from which to conduct an apparently relaxed conversation with an underling.

'Good,' Sebastian managed to stammer once the mass of biscuit had cleared his gullet and his tear ducts.

'Bear in mind, Sebastian, that this is a very special monkey.'

'I realise that, sir.'

'I really don't think you do,' said Corrigan.

'I mean, she's very intelligent. Almost like a human.'

'Not at all! She's not at all like a human, Sebastian! I'm disappointed in you. I really am, I have to say.'

Corrigan pulled a lever on his chair, making the seat back fly forward with a pop. Suddenly the distance between his face and Sebastian's was uncomfortably small.

'This is the deal, Sebastian: the monkey you've been entrusted with caring for is interesting because — despite her obvious, if not unique, level of intelligence — she exhibits clear signs of a trait quite alien to human nature. You see, she has a moral compass, this monkey.'

'Many monkeys —'

'Yeah, yeah, yeah, I know. But you're not hearing me: this is a *very* moral monkey. She has her rules, you see, and she never wavers. I mean, *never*! That's a level of consistency I'm sure you'll agree no human on the planet can boast. Most of us think, for example, that you shouldn't, say, eat people. And yet: imagine you're stuck on a desert island with no food, together with an old lady who's had two hip replacements, with cataracts, diabetes, and what have you. I'm sure that if you got hungry enough, you'd kill the old dear and eat her, wouldn't you?'

'No. Well. Maybe. Maybe I would. I don't know.'

'You see?' Corrigan said merrily. 'Nothing's really sacred for us humans, not even the widely accepted rule that individuals from our own species have an inviolable right to life, you know? But this monkey, she *never* wavers on *anything*.'

'But, what kinds of rules are we talking about?' Sebastian asked, genuinely curious.

'The monkey came to us from the philosophy department at UCL. They'd used her in some kind of morality experiment, you see, trained her to decode human expressions as they were confronted with various classic moral dilemmas. And she seems to possess a set of moral rules based upon a kind of average Western, Judeo-Christian viewpoint. Thou shalt not kill, thou shalt not steal, thou shalt not covet thy neighbour's wife, and so on. The difference being that she follows them slavishly. I myself was tasked with her care for a while, but I couldn't take the pressure. I'm going to be honest with you, Sebastian: I like women. Pretty much all women. Don't misunderstand me, I'm happily married to an exceptional woman, but we have an open marriage. And I've tried to explain this to the monkey. Many times. But she fails to see my side of the story.'

In his head, Sebastian saw Corrigan and the monkey in the grip of an animated sign language conversation in which the same obscene gesture was repeated time and time again until Corrigan was tearing his red hair out.

'Me and Temple — you know, Tiffany from the admin department — we tend to meet once a week or so and, well, enjoy each other's company. Nothing wrong with that, in my eyes, quite within the regulations seeing as the secretaries work in a separate cell structure over which I have no jurisdiction of any kind, so what's the problem?' At this, Corrigan paused as though expecting a reply. Sebastian, whose sex life had been beset by every kind of problem, could come up with at least a dozen but refrained from spelling them out. Instead he asked:

'So what did she do, then?'

'Temple? Well, you can hardly expect me to tell you that, are you crazy? I repeat, Isaksson, one must keep information where it belongs.'

'No, the monkey, sir, I meant the monkey! What did the monkey do?'

'Exactly what you're doing now.'

'I'm not doing anything. What am I doing?'

'Your eyes, Sebastian. I could see it in her eyes every time Tiffany'd been to visit. She couldn't look me in the eye. Refused her afternoon snack, kept throwing pieces of cucumber at my head instead. Classic monkeying around, nothing particularly refined. But still, it hurt.'

'How do you know her agitation was of the moral variety? Perhaps she was just jealous?' asked Sebastian.

'I've thought about that, of course. But no. She has nothing against my wife, for instance. It's definitely a moral standpoint.'

· 'What are you going to do with her, then? The monkey, not Temple.'

'I'm afraid I can't tell you that. You don't have clearance to access that information. Your duty is to feed her and make sure she stays in a good mood. That's all. Then we'll see, then we'll see. If the day were to come, well …'

Corrigan let his gaze drift mysteriously out through the window, and Sebastian did the same. From up here, the dark water of the river looked like a line drawn with a paintbrush, the buildings like piles of ash. It wasn't beautiful, but it could make a grown man cry: how delicately the milky air quivered, how a single sunbeam could split it into a thousand golden shards of smog, ready to dissolve before you'd even had a chance to register their existence.

For a few seconds, Sebastian got the sense that he and Corrigan, united in pale grey silence with their eyes turned towards the city's formless body, were having what the girls in his high-school class used to call a *moment*: a flash of wordless understanding, of shared terror and joy at being alive. This was implausible, Sebastian soon realised, as it dawned on him that he had absolutely no damn clue what Corrigan was thinking, making it impossible to speak of any genuine understanding. Of course, that wasn't unique to this situation — indeed, thought Sebastian, the chimera of genuine understanding was a fact of human life, which could only occasionally be surmounted by true and eternal love and its defiance of all worldly laws. And if Corrigan and Sebastian hadn't just fallen deeply and irrevocably in love, it was hardly a tragedy. But still. The realisation that they were, in spite of everything, still just two strangers who happened to be sitting there staring out at the same magically tragic view suddenly made Sebastian feel very, very alone.

Which was exactly what he was, and in a certain sense what he always had been.

'Well,' said Corrigan, pressing his broad hands against the table. 'Don't look so scared, young man. I believe in you. You'll be alright on the night. Otherwise you wouldn't be here.'

Sebastian swallowed. To his ears that sounded more like a jibe than an encouragement.

'Begone!' bellowed Corrigan, and Sebastian rose without a word and left the room to return to his office, more uncertain than ever about what he was actually doing there.

It didn't matter that it wasn't beautiful. The building itself, for example, wasn't beautiful; it blended in, grey against grey, as though it were one with the sky. The birds certainly seemed to think it was the sky: they crashed into the concrete facade on a daily basis, falling like snow to the ground. The shredded plumage looked like icing sugar.

It was later that afternoon, and Sebastian was standing in his office leaning his forehead against the window. He thought he'd probably get used to it — the dying birds, the fright-delight, the sound of the birds' speed through the air — impossible for the human ear to register before the blow comes, the blow that brings everything to an abrupt end — the sense of complete identification with the birds, when the feeling of intoxicating freedom and the feeling of paralysing sorrow reach a person at exactly the same moment, awakening every part of the emotional spectrum. He'd get used to it, he thought, because that's what you do. Get used to things. You could get used to almost anything, the taste of spinach, the taste of blood, the taste of freedom and loss. The taste of ruin. It was just a consequence of the brain's plasticity.

It didn't matter that it wasn't beautiful, he thought soberly, writing a name in the fog from his breath, because beauty never lasts. That was what the birds reminded him of, of how fleeting everything was, how quickly everything you'd built up could be torn down. Bang! The feathers flew into the air just like the flour from a dropped packet. And then, in the dawn, men and women in orange hi-vis came and swept up the traces from the ground, and life was reborn somewhere else, the leaves crunched under the wellington-shod feet of children, the breakfast queue at the sandwich place round the corner lurched forward, and a new working day began at the Institute.

In this context it didn't matter that the building he found himself in from nine to five every day was the same colour as the ashen face of death. After all, there was table tennis in the basement, and Klimt reproductions in the canteen. There were monkeys and there were fish, and tapeworms, and reptiles with Alzheimer's whose brain tissue was like crinkly cellophane, all within the building's impenetrable walls. There were stem cells. There was work organised in the same way as terror cells. There was the only thing research, just like life, really needed: forward progress, cyclical progress, any kind of progress that death couldn't touch. He thought this was what he wanted, and even if it wasn't, then at least it was what he needed.

It was now more than three weeks since Sebastian, an emotional amputee with a brand-new PhD, had left the Institute of Neuroscience at Lund University for this junior post at LICS. But it had been three weeks stretched like an elastic band, to breaking point; where every second was at once significant — and completely meaningless. Three weeks and an ocean of low-level anxiety, full of the navigational obstacles of working life. His slender shoulders had taken on so much more responsibility, bowed by the weight even as it made him walk taller. And he was tall as it was, six foot two, and as beautiful as Susanna at her bath. Admittedly, it was his mother the priest who'd paid him this last compliment, but others thought Sebastian was beautiful too. That had got them nowhere. Sebastian had come to London for several reasons, but only one bore a woman's name, and that name was literally carved in stone.

Sighing inwardly, Sebastian turned from the window and went back to his desk where his promotion letter was staring at him from beside a pile of half-completed anamneses. He wasn't all that glad to have risen among the ranks. It was hard enough just conducting the interviews with potential subjects. Having actual responsibility for them was more than he was confident of managing.

The gigantic and rather vague research project Sebastian was employed on included an extensive and ever-growing group of volunteers — most of them ill in some way — who had to be interviewed, assessed, and then given an in-depth examination using both fMRI and an individually tailored, experimental set of tests. As the most recently appointed talent at the Institute, and also one of the youngest, it had fallen to Sebastian to undertake many of the initial diagnostic interviews with the would-be research subjects. Or, that wasn't actually true, the very first screening of volunteers was done by a general psychologist by the name of Dr Benedict Katz, who had a rudimentary grounding in neuroscience. It was the managers' opinion, Sebastian had understood from conversations with his supervisor Barázza, that this preliminary work involved little more than a kind of conveyor-belt categorisation to separate the attention-seekers and general chatterboxes from the genuinely neurologically damaged, and fob them off. In this research institute people in need of talking therapies were not wanted; what was required were defective brains, fantastic brains, brains that behaved differently in ways that were light-years away from what the standard brain was capable of.

So it wasn't until Benedict had cut out around 95 per cent of the corpus of applicants that Sebastian met the remaining 5 per cent for an initial diagnostic interview. This was all new to Sebastian, who'd previously kept a respectful distance from the interpersonal dimension which is occasionally to be found even in the hardest of the natural sciences. There had been a time, as in the life of every youngster in Lund, when Sebastian had dreamed of becoming a doctor — a dream he'd nurtured tenderly during his early teens with the same blind desperation as someone watering a plant whose root system has long since dried out. It wasn't until he saw an episode of the wildly popular mid-noughties show *Grey's Anatomy* that he realised the medical profession, as it had developed during the twentieth century, was as much about tending souls as diagnosing bodies. Sebastian didn't want to tend souls at work, that much he'd realised at seventeen — he had enough of it in his personal life, with one sister who had a loyalty card with the local child psychiatrist, another who was afraid of her own shadow, and a girlfriend who insisted on only eating on odd days of the month. He didn't want to comfort anxious relatives, because he himself was an anxious relative in need of comfort.

So he decided on another path — instead of brain surgery, he would dedicate himself to brain research. If he'd grown up in any other town in Sweden, he probably would have been laughed at for his new dream career — a fantasy career; he might as well have said he wanted to become an astronaut, a lion tamer, an investigative journalist. But Lund was different:

it was a city of learning, a city of science, a city of pretensions and professors collecting their pensions, a city where the sons and daughters of academics and architects ate waffles on the roof of the observatory or lay in piles of leaves under the plane trees, rubbing their cheeks against each other's soft woolly jumpers and whispering, 'When we graduate from high school I'm going to become a neuroscientist and you'll be a poet, we'll have babies and dogs and honorary doctorates and nothing bad will ever happen to us, as long as we live on the right side of the tracks.' That's what the youngsters whispered, and, far from being met with ridicule or class analysis, they encountered instead a gentle smile, a fingertip on the cheek, and a hoarse yet resonant: 'Sebastian, I think I love you.'

In other words: teenage Sebastian had had the support of those around him in his new life goal, most of all his mother and father, since his sisters had much less ambitious natures — from Sebastian's perspective, it had seemed as though Clara and Matilda spent most of their time longing to escape, energy Sebastian thought would be better spent actually trying to go somewhere else, if that was what they really wanted (and in time they managed it, too — after a few years as an aid worker in Bangladesh, Matilda finally settled down in Berlin, and Clara had long since lived in Stockholm). But he'd never wanted anything but to stay in Lund for the rest of his life. To be moderately successful in his career, get married, and have his own old-before-their-years children.

But of course, things turned out differently, after *what happened happened.*

It's well known that traumatic experiences can redraw our inner landscapes — that is, the brain's spiderweb of impulses and emotions — in the most dramatic way. Sebastian knew that what had happened to him was the sort of life event that could explode a brain like dynamite, requiring a person to carefully piece it back together again afterwards. Most people spent their years of bereavement trying to rebuild the person they'd once been, but it didn't have to be that way. You could also try to build something new out of the remains. The thing in Sebastian's life that looked like a catastrophe, and without a doubt was, would perhaps also — since nothing in life was just one thing — turn out to be a catalyst. With many of his brain's synapses burned out by grief, he might be able to become a different person to the one he'd previously been: a person who lived wholly for his work, for science, for the things that death couldn't touch.

Every morning, before Sebastian left his room in Tulse Hill, he stood in front of his shaving mirror and recited a mantra based on hard facts that he'd decided would be the guiding light of his new life:

REMEMBER
THAT THE BRAIN IS PLASTIC
THAT MEANS IT IS POSSIBLE
TO LEARN AND RELEARN
THROUGHOUT YOUR LIFE

THAT MEANS
THERE'S NO DAMAGE
THAT CAN'T BE UNDONE

THERE'S NO CHARACTER TRAIT
THAT CAN'T BE TURNED INTO ITS OPPOSITE

THERE'S NO FEAR
THAT CAN'T BE CHECKED
AND LIFE LIVED
DIFFERENTLY

But every day it ended with him laughing at himself in the mirror, turning away, and going on with his life exactly as before, in other words, fumblingly. The brain could be retrained, but that didn't mean it was easy.

In spite of his dread of social interaction, the diagnostic interviews had, to Sebastian's great relief, got easier each time. It was a victory, albeit a small one, a step on the way to becoming someone who was not affected by other people as anything more than mere objects of study. He no longer vomited with nerves every time a new person put their mind in his hands and asked him to judge whether it was healthy or sick, normal or abnormal, beautiful or grotesque. That's not to say he found it fun or even rewarding. He longed to be down in the basement, among the machines, among the images of walnuts bursting with all the colours of the rainbow, those maps of the innermost, of the uppermost, the answers to those elusive questions about what a human being really is; the brains, he longed for the *brains*, disconnected from the makeweight of the human enigma: the bodies, the hands, the sweat, the voices, the eyes, the desires, the fears, and the demands.

Now Sebastian sat down at his desk and looked unhappily at his promotion letter. The thing he should have realised from the very beginning had just occurred to him: that the latter, i.e. the scientific study of brains, didn't exclude the former, i.e. the interpersonal contact and feeling of responsibility for the people whose brains he was tasked with examining. In his new post he'd finally get into the lab, but he'd also be binding these unlucky people closer to him. They would think he could help them, and only he — as well as, perhaps, the very moral monkey, who really was very perceptive — would know it wasn't possible.

He was roused from his melancholic slumber by a beep from the intercom system (another of Corrigan's innovations).

'Isaksson,' Sebastian said.

'Tiffany from admin here. I've been notified from on high that you're henceforth to be responsible for Subject 3A16:1?'

Sebastian looked at the clock. His promotion had been in effect for exactly two hours and seven minutes.

'Yeah, hmm, that sounds about right. If you say so. Who is it?'

Tiffany lowered her voice. 'I'm not actually allowed to say things like this, but I was there when Benno did the interview and bloody hell, this one's a real nutjob.'

Sebastian fixed his gaze on the ceiling. Am I unto death quite worn.

'Dr Isaksson? Should I send up the notes?'

'Yeah,' Sebastian replied with a sigh. 'Send them up in the chute.'

Subject 3A16:1, known as 'Toilet Baby' (TB)
Interview with Benedict Katz, PsyD (BK), 7 January 2016
Transcription: Tiffany Temple, med. sec.

TB: I dreamed I gave birth to a premature baby in my toilet. You know, like some chicks you read about sometimes: 'WENT TO TOILET — GAVE BIRTH: Fat turned out to be foetus' and you're just like, what fucking state of denial has that girl been living in? How can you not notice you're preggers for nine months? And then the obligatory picture of the girl in the hospital bed with a smile like a fucking banana from ear to ear and this unexpected surprise of a kid in her arms, and though she says stuff like, 'Course it was a bit of a shock, but I mean, the first time I looked into his eyes there on the floor of the toilet at the Fox and Bullhorn I felt this love I'd never felt before, it was totally magical and I'm so happy,' you can see from her eyes that she's flippin' well scared to death and thinks, like, if I hadn't been so idiotically terrified of confrontation then I would have discovered, like, eight months ago that I was pregnant and then I could have aborted this little monster, but now I'm here and I'm tabloid material and the best thing I can do is hope Huggies will find my story scintillating and want to be my nappy sponsor. So yeah, in my dream I was, like, that kind of girl. Went into the loo with a bit of a tummy ache thinking I was in for a real squitfest, and what happens? I feel something sort of wriggling out of me like an eel, all slimy and cold. And then I look down into the toilet and there it is, and I realise it's a foetus, so I get up because I can't handle seeing it, but then I change my mind, you know, I've never seen a miscarriage, I've never even had an abortion, believe it or not. And what do I see but the little brat moving about down there in the water! Waving its little arms and legs and opening and closing its mouth like a fish. And I'm just like, shit, it's alive, so I reach down into the toilet bowl and pick it up. It's really little, maybe a foot long, and skinny as hell but, like, its face is totally fine, you know, the way babies look in nappy adverts, and I'm just like, I almost can't say it, but like, what I felt was … love. Not disgust, even though the kid was dripping with toilet water and, like, blood, but love. And there I stood, rocking the fucking kid even though I hadn't even known I'd been carrying it inside me, and for a few short moments before I woke up, life was completely perfect.

BK: I'm not quite sure what you think I —

TB: But, like, what the hell does it mean? I normally dream about dolphins.

BK: I can't answer that. We don't do psychoanalysis here, I'm sorry if you've misunderstood. We work with neurological problems on a strictly physiological basis; for anything to do with — god, I can barely bring myself to say it — 'the subconscious', you'll have to go elsewhere.

TB: Actually, no, I haven't misunderstood. I know what you do here. Scanning and stuff. That's what I want.

BK: The question is not really what you want, but what you have to offer the Institute. We only study subjects, sorry, *people* — with very specific symptoms. I'm talking about actual, statistically significant deviations from the norm.

TB: But you haven't heard the whole story yet! This thing about the dream was just a colourful introduction.

BK: Okay?

TB: This thing about abilities, yeah, recently I've been totally awesome.

BK: Can you be a little more precise?

TB: So, like, I don't know how to explain it.

BK: But can you give me some example of your sudden ... awesomeness?

TB: Okay, I'll just come right out with it: I've turned into a fucking Picasso. I mean an artist. I mean a really fucking good artist. I mean, like, a genius artist. I mean —

BK: I get the message. When did this happen?

TB: After the dream! That was what I was getting to. I had that crazy dream, and the next day I trashed every single one of my lip pencils and the white feature wall in my bedroom. Just, like, drawing, you get me? I haven't drawn since I went to nursery.

BK: What did you draw?

TB: Art, for god's sake.

BK: Can you be more specific? You talked about Picasso — would you describe the art as cubist? Or more classic, are we talking about impressionism, expressionism, what?

TB: Who cares? The point is: it was great art. I could hardly draw a stick man before. Before this dream. You get what I'm saying? That it kind of symbolised something that was happening to me. The kid was like my inner talent being born there on the toilet. And I'm thinking maybe I've always had this inside me but never been able to see it, you get me, just like those girls who are like: pregnant, what, me? And that something kind of happened in my brain that triggered all this stuff. And I was thinking maybe it would be interesting for you, that I could, like, do my bit for science, like a service, but okay, if it doesn't suit you I can go. I've got some new paints being delivered this afternoon and I'd like to get going with them.

BK: Oil paints?

TB: Finger paints. I'm not made of money. Yet. My dealer says he can make me rich and famous. Until then I'm painting with my nephew's messy play equipment; he's only interested in computer games anyway. My sister reckons he's autistic, but I think we've got a bit of a case of pot-kettle in that family, if you know what I mean.

BK: You have a dealer? So this new talent has been confirmed by others? Experts?

TB: Yes, for Christ's sake! My mum, my sister, my neighbour, my boyfriend, they're all like: shit, you're totally awesome! So I rang this guy I used to sleep with ages ago who studies at Goldsmiths, okay, so I swear, when I used to fuck him he was totally normal, that was when we were, like, fourteen, then he became gay and started studying art. Whatever, I rang him and he was just like: shit, you're absolutely awesome! And so he rang his professor who rang some dealer, and, yeah, they said the same thing.

BK: That overnight you'd become awesome at … art?

TB: Fuck, you don't believe me. I can see it. Wait a sec, I'll —

BK: What are you doing? That's my research report you're doodling on.

TB: Not anymore. Now it's art.

BK: Holy shit.

For assessment and resolution see Appendix 11b.x: Additional investigations by diagnosing party.

'You want to go out? Is that what you mean?'

The monkey looked at Sebastian with a smile plastered across her hairy little face and raised one shoulder to her ear; in the six weeks since he'd taken over care of the monkey, Sebastian had learned this movement meant 'thanks' (the monkey was, of course, very polite).

'Just take a look at this first,' Sebastian said, pointing at the computer screen with a pen. 'Can you see how much activity she's got going on in her parietal lobe? That's not normal in a resting state. Not at all.' He noticed he was almost getting excited. It was now nearly a month since he'd been promoted to a real research position and assigned Esmeralda Lundy, aka Subject 3A16:1, or 'Toilet Baby', as his first proper patient. Three days previously, he'd finally managed to get her in the scanner — she'd been remarkably resistant. Sebastian couldn't understand why. He would have been happy for anyone at all to have looked in his head, seeing as he already knew what was there: a gaping hole shaped like a 'y', toes pointing to the underworld.

The monkey said nothing. When Sebastian tore his gaze from the computer screen and looked down at her, she was sitting with her face averted demonstratively. Sebastian had forgotten himself — the monkey respected the integrity of strangers. The permission form Ms Lundy had signed, giving Sebastian the right to peer into the innermost recesses of her person, hadn't said anything about a monkey. With a sigh, Sebastian closed the images and logged out, got up from his desk, and reached for the lead he kept in one of the desk drawers. He had a strange feeling in his chest. It wasn't until he stepped into the lift with the monkey on his arm, and caught sight of his drawn face in the mirror — grotesquely angular beside the monkey's rounded calm — that he realised he was longing to speak to someone. A human, ideally.

The disadvantage of having a monkey to take care of, rather than Nedjelko's roundworms or Travis's cicadas, was that the monkey demanded significantly more attention. Generally she had free run of

Sebastian's office, aside from when he was undertaking consultations and she was required to stay in her cage for safety reasons, but of course she had to be walked every day. Corrigan had implied the walking wasn't all that important, but it was clear to Sebastian that the monkey wasn't happy on the days she didn't get to go out. She was too like him in that respect, or perhaps it was the other way round, he wasn't sure. He only knew those days tended to end with them both sitting in silence, staring at the wall.

Normally they would stop at the little turning circle of tarmac and rubbish bins behind the Institute. A monkey in town was an attention-grabbing sight even in London, and Sebastian wanted to avoid close contact with strangers, so they tended to keep themselves to themselves. Today, however, Sebastian decided without further ado that the monkey needed a change of scenery. Over the past few days, he'd been thinking she seemed understimulated. So, with the monkey scuttering after him on the lead, he headed out through the main entrance, crossed the street, and went into the park in the middle of Russell Square. It was an uncommonly beautiful day for February in London — little wispy clouds in the sky, little chubby children playing with nannies, and scooters around the fountains and under the ash trees. Selfie sticks, UCL students with their heads crowded over books and tablets, a waitress brushing crumbs from a cafe table. He did a circuit of the park with the monkey scampering around his feet. Many people looked at him, but no one spoke to him. He was both relieved and disappointed.

After a while he sat down on a bench by the gravel path and let the lead out to its full length so the monkey could have some climbing time. He tried, as was his wont, to think of nothing in particular. It didn't go too well. He'd happened to position himself in such a way that he had a view of what appeared to be a well-mannered little family out for a picnic. He thought they must be tourists, otherwise the parents would probably be at work. They didn't look unemployed. They looked happy. Mother, father, only child: neat jackets done all the way up, each with a plastic bag under their behinds — they obviously hadn't expected the weather to be good enough for sitting out on the grass. Both the mother and daughter wore berets, and the father removed his brown leather gloves finger by finger before opening the packaging of his triangle-cut sandwich. Sebastian thought from a distance that it looked like egg and cress, but he couldn't say for certain. Perhaps it was more a feeling he had. The girl was eating pieces of mango from a pot with just her fingers. Her mother was trying to get her to use a wooden fork, but she flatly refused and the father laughed, pulling off her beret to ruffle her hair. The mother gave up and leaned back on her elbows. She had an upturned nose, she was beautiful, she seemed happy. The child ate her last piece of mango and jumped on her mother. They engaged in some sort of middle ground between wrestling and cuddling. Sebastian looked at the monkey, who'd climbed onto the lowest branch of a tree. He realised that deep down what he wanted was for the monkey to come down and attract the child's attention. But perhaps the child wouldn't be the slightest bit interested. She appeared to have everything she needed right there.

When he was growing up, Sebastian had thought a lot about what it meant to be an only child, which was clearly what this child was. There were a few in his class at school, and it had always bewildered Sebastian that they didn't seem the slightest bit lonely, unlike Sebastian, who not only had two sisters but two *triplet sisters*. On the contrary, their inviolable position as the only child in their families seemed to make them very much the centre of attention, for parents and relatives, of course, but also for other children — as though the mere words 'only child' were a cry for help so loud that help was never needed. The parents of only children all seemed to be so afraid of the possibility that their child would view themselves as solitary that they went through fire and water to make him or her socially attractive to other children. Partly with the help of various status symbols, of course, but mainly by imparting in the child a healthy appetite for new people and human contact. As an adult Sebastian realised that the only child had to learn early on what he had only come to understand when he met Violetta — that people need other people, that contact with others is something that can't be taken for granted, something you have to fight for with everything you have, even if you don't have anything.

Sebastian's family was large and noisy, but it was questionable whether it was a happy family. It certainly wasn't a particularly well-functioning one. It was only a few years since his parents' marriage had finally gone to pieces, but it had been cracked for as long as Sebastian could remember. Since his father had moved out, Sebastian had heard from him only sporadically, often on Sebastian's own dutiful initiative.

His father hadn't been very good at being a father. It was no coincidence he worked as a tax inspector, and expected things — you might call it an occupational injury — to add up. Unfortunately, people, and children in particular, didn't work that way. Sebastian's father was a methodical person who always had a plan. If that plan went belly-up, he would quickly fix something new and regain his feeling of control. The fact that his children often behaved in a way he regarded as completely irrational made him nervous and irritable around them, and more often than not he avoided family life, instead spending his time with marginal tax rate tables or — something Sebastian had only recently realised, when his significantly more perceptive sister Matilda had told him — one of his less complicated mistresses.

But he hadn't been an equally bad father to all his children — Sebastian had the sense that his father had the hardest time with him in particular, which was inexplicable given that Sebastian was the sibling who acted most rationally and who, moreover, was his father's only son. But aside from the odd round of ping pong at Gerdahallen sports centre, Sebastian never felt he got any special treatment from his father; quite the reverse: watching Sunday night TV on the sofa, there was space for one child under each of Papa's arms, and it was always for Clara and Matilda. Sebastian sat with Mama.

As for the relationship between Sebastian and his two sisters, he couldn't with any certainty say whether it was good or bad, close or distant. He'd always functioned as a shock absorber between his sisters' clashing temperaments. Matilda was outgoing and aggressive, Clara thoughtful and reserved. In relation to these poles, Sebastian thought his own personality rather wan, and it had always seemed to him that Clara and Matilda had, through their rather antagonistic relationship, a special and unassailable bond.

Like his own to Violetta, from the day she came into the picture until *what happened* finally happened.

During his years with Violetta, Sebastian had spent more and more time with her family, and less and less with his own. Perhaps it was easier to belong in a context where belonging was less a matter of course. Violetta was also an only child. She'd learned at an early age to demand the love Sebastian had taken for granted — to stop at nothing to get it.

Sebastian felt restless. The apparently very happy little family was preparing to go. Sebastian wondered where they were headed. Probably to the British Museum to look at mummified cats. Sebastian sometimes went there himself after work. He liked artefacts, the older the better. There was something touching, he thought, in how desperately people sought to preserve things that were really transient. He liked the Eskimo jacket made of seal guts, so delicate it would fall apart were it not enclosed in a hermetically sealed glass case; the stone statue saved from some distant island, which would never be allowed to weather again; the broken vases that had been painstakingly glued together and restored, placed on pedestals. One lonely Saturday, Sebastian had taken a bus to the Horniman Museum in Forest Hill to look at row upon row of butterflies pinned in a glass cabinet. It was fantastic, he thought, that it was possible to handle something so delicate with so much care and so much cruelty.

Sebastian had, however, strenuously avoided the art galleries. Art, in his bitter experience, could have a destructive influence on fragile people. To be fair, he didn't consider himself that fragile, not really, but it was best not to take the risk.

The family stood up and brushed themselves down, carefully tidying away their rubbish into one of the plastic bags and looking at the ground about them for things they might have forgotten. The girl skipped off towards the fountains; the adults turned their backs on Sebastian and started walking, calling the girl's name: Chloe! The woman tripped, perhaps on a branch, and the man caught her by the arm. She laughed.

None of them looked around again. They were gone, without even having seemed to have noticed Sebastian.

He got out his telephone, felt its weight in his hand. He considered ringing his mother. Since his move to London, he'd hardly heard from anyone in his family apart from Matilda. She wrote cheerful emails from Berlin, full of anecdotes about the tribulations of life as a stepmother, her plans to spend the summer in Västerbotten, and the importance of breathing from the root chakra. Sebastian was ashamed to admit it but sometimes he did no more than skim the emails, counting the words to reassure himself Matilda was only chatty, not manic, before quickly but dutifully replying, answering one or other of the many questions Matilda had asked, and pressing send. It wasn't that he didn't want to communicate with her, not really, no — it was just that it made him feel so tired, all this obvious vitality his sister had, when he himself felt quite dead. And maybe it made him jealous, the life she'd apparently managed to create for herself in spite of the obstacles along the way.

Matilda was the only one of the siblings who had her own family, even though in a way it was a family she'd stolen from someone else. No, not stolen, that was the wrong word. Inherited, perhaps. The man she lived with had, if Sebastian understood correctly, already been divorced from the child's mother when they met, so morally it was all fair and square — even the very moral monkey agreed with that (Sebastian, unsure himself, had asked). If Matilda had had a choice, there probably wouldn't have been a child included in the package, that was what Sebastian had concluded from his analysis, but he had to admit he wasn't sure. When Matilda wrote or talked about Siri it was always in the same cynically joking tone she used when talking about herself; she spoke about the child as though she were an adult whose virtues and shortcomings could be measured on the same terms. It was an alien perspective to Sebastian, who viewed children as mysterious — with good reason, he thought, since he actually had an insight into the tumultuous processes a child's brain goes through up to their late teens. Sometimes Matilda wrote about Clara, too — she wanted to know if he'd heard from her, if he knew when Clara intended to start replying to Matilda's emails. Because the answer to both questions was no, Sebastian tended to avoid them (he wasn't someone who liked saying no). He hadn't heard from Clara in many months, except via occasional reports from their mother. And Sebastian had only spoken to her — their mother, that is — a few times since his move. There was something in her voice he couldn't handle. She'd been different ever since she'd kicked out their father four years previously, more demanding in some way, a little jagged, but it wasn't until *what happened happened* that she'd really started putting Sebastian in a bad mood. He felt as though she wanted something from him, something he couldn't give her because he didn't know what it was. And even if he had known, he thought, there was no saying whether he'd have wanted to give it to her. As always, it was easier to say nothing than to say no.

The monkey had climbed down out of the tree and came scuttering towards Sebastian with her hand outstretched. Relieved, he let his phone slide back into his pocket and fished out a pack of dried banana, peeling off a few slices and putting them into the monkey's palm. She drew her shoulder up to her ear. Then his phone rang in his pocket. Astonished, Sebastian pulled it out.

'Mama? I was just thinking of ringing you,' Sebastian said, which was of course true. In a way. The monkey didn't react in any case.

'Sebastian! You know what, I could feel it. Like telepathy.'

'Telepathy doesn't exist, you know that. There's absolutely no evidence for it,' Sebastian said out of pure habit, even if a few of the things he'd heard about since coming to the Institute had, quite frankly, made him doubt almost everything he knew about the human brain's abilities.

'No, perhaps not,' his mother said merrily. 'But I'm not so fastidious when it comes to proving God exists, as you know. How are things, my love? I haven't heard from you in, well, I don't know how long! Does it cost a lot to call?'

Sebastian gave the monkey a few more pieces of banana and folded the bag down into his pocket.

'Everything's fine. I'm fine. Lots on at work, but it's exciting. I've had my area of responsibility expanded, you could say.'

He pictured his mother clapping her hand over her mouth delightedly, even though he couldn't actually see her.

'Sebastian! I'm so proud of you. What is it you actually do, then? I might not understand, but I'll try!'

'I … I don't have permission to tell you.'

'Do you mean it's secret?'

'In a way. I think?'

'You think?'

'Yeah,' Sebastian said, briefly. 'How are things with you? Are your plants growing well?'

'Oh silly,' his mother said, laughing. 'The season hasn't started yet, you know that. But I've got some lovely little tomato seedlings on the windowsill.'

'Mmm, tomatoes.'

There was silence on the line. Sebastian waited for his mother to say something, but she stayed quiet. It was this silence, he thought, that he'd been fearing. He knew the point was that he should say something, but for his life he couldn't think what. He'd already asked about the garden.

'So, have you spoken to Papa lately?' his mother said at last.

'No, why?'

'Oh well, no, nothing. Clara and Tilda?'

'Er,' Sebastian replied, evasively. If the mostly unanswered emails from Matilda counted, he had. The monkey obviously didn't agree. She started climbing Sebastian's leg pointedly. He tried to shake her off as he searched his exhausted brain for something to say about Matilda. He'd been sleeping badly lately.

'Tilda's got very good at the crow.'

'What kind of crow?'

'It's a yoga pose, I think. A hard one.'

'Oh right. Well, I've started Zumba. At Gerdahallen.'

'The prices are good there.'

'Yeah. Are you making do?'

'Huh?'

'With money, I mean. London's expensive.'

'I don't need any money, Mama. I have a job.'

'Yes, poor Clara,' his mother sighed. Sebastian tried in vain to remember if he knew what she was talking about. Involuntarily he noticed his gaze being drawn to the monkey's, as though she could help. She stared back, uncooperative, like a block of granite. His mother was silent at the other end. After a while Sebastian could no longer resist. He couldn't hear someone being pitied without asking why; it was against his nature.

'What's up with Clara, Mama?'

He heard his mother sigh disappointedly.

'So she hasn't told you? It's several weeks since it happened.'

'I've been pretty busy,' Sebastian said. That wasn't really a lie either. 'We haven't spoken for … a while.'

'She got the sack! From the paper. Restructuring, they said. Soon they'll restructure away the paper they print on,' his mother said, disillusioned. Sebastian didn't have the heart to tell her this had, in principle, already happened. Instead he made an indignant noise, while making a mental note to get in touch with his sister. With both his sisters. That evening. Or as soon as he could manage it. As soon as the evenings got lighter and the nights quieter. As soon as he got some of his emotions back, any at all, apart from the guilt.

'Are they speaking to each other?' his mother said suddenly.

Sebastian was so surprised he didn't understand what she meant at first. 'Who?'

'Clara and Tilda.'

'Er, yeah … well, er …' The monkey dug her claws into the leg of his jeans. 'What do you mean?'

'You don't need to pretend, Sebastian,' his mother said, earnestly. 'Tilda keeps trying to brush it off, and Clara's saying nothing at all, but I know they fell out after Violetta's funeral and they don't appear to have got over it yet. And it's really been quite a long time now. Almost a whole year. It pains me, Sebastian. As their mother. They think I haven't realised but I have; nothing passes me by.'

Sebastian wasn't so sure. Something had happened between Clara and Matilda at the funeral, that much he knew too, but the falling out had happened long before. If it was even possible to speak of a falling out, since they'd never really been 'in'.

Sebastian fastened his gaze on a nearby tree. He didn't know what kind of tree it was. Clara would know. She knew the names of all living things. She used to call it a safety measure. She said things became less dangerous if you could name them. This tree appeared to have flowers. It was covered in small, pale pink buds, no larger than his little fingernail. And there, right at the top, one had opened. Fat little birds on every branch, a bumblebee hanging upside down in the ruffled blossom. It made Sebastian feel uncomfortable, in a way he couldn't at first understand. Then he realised it was February. It felt somehow unwholesome. Unnatural. But also beautiful, almost painful.

'Sebastian?'

'Yes, Mama?'

'You haven't spoken to Papa?'

Sebastian came to and sat up on the bench.

'No? You already asked that. What's up with Papa?'

'Did I? Crazy,' his mother tittered. 'This old dear's going senile. Soon it'll be me getting fired! Anyway, my boy. I'll let you get back to your work. You are at work, I take it?'

Sebastian looked at the monkey, who'd wandered away the full five metres the lead allowed and seemed to be completely immersed in gazing at her distorted image mirrored in the water of the fountains.

'Yes, I'm at work.'

'Then I won't hold you up. You'll give me a call soon? Let me know how you're doing?'

'Will do,' lied Sebastian.

'Okay.' There was silence at the other end of the line. Sebastian waited for his mother to hang up so he wouldn't have to.

In the end he said: 'Take care.' There was a sound as though someone who'd held their breath a very long time finally exhaled.

'Bye, sweetheart.' And then a click.

The monkey had tired of her mirror game by the fountains and slowly came scooting back to Sebastian. He lifted her under the arms and put her beside him on the bench. He had a definite feeling she wanted something from him, and that it wasn't a piece of dried banana. He tried anyway. She threw it on the gravel.

'I don't know what she wants,' Sebastian said. 'Mama.'

The monkey yelped in irritation. Two elderly gentlemen just passing on the other side of the fountains turned and stared. Sebastian shushed the monkey, but she went on yelping.

'Okay, okay,' Sebastian whispered. 'I know she wants me to take care of this family. Because she thinks I'm the only one who can. That's what she wants, okay, I do know. But what can I do, do you think? Hey?'

The monkey didn't answer. Of course. However intelligent she was, she couldn't speak so a human would understand. It was frustrating, obviously, but also nice in some way — a simpler form of communication, stripped of any expectation of transparency. Sebastian's earlier wish to speak to a human being was a distant memory.

'And you know what?' Sebastian went on angrily. 'Maybe that's what I ought to do, but it's not what I want, you know? I don't want anything. Anything at all.'

The monkey cocked her head. Her eyes were shining, as if she were about to cry. Sebastian didn't know whether monkeys cried or if tears were something humans had come up with all on their own.

'You don't believe me?' Sebastian said quietly.

The monkey rubbed her head against his shoulder.

'I'm so worn out,' Sebastian said to the monkey, to no one at all. Am I unto death quite worn, he heard in his head all of a sudden, a line from a poem he barely remembered. Was it Mama who used to hum it, in the evenings, when the mountain of dirty dishes towered up towards the ceiling and Papa was nowhere to be seen, when Matilda was chasing Clara through the garden with a slimy black slug between her fingers, and Sebastian sat curled up on the sofa with a *Donald Duck* book, the only one there to hear his mother's resigned laughter?

'Am I unto death quite worn, sick and worn and lonely,' he murmured now. The monkey put her arms around his neck, something she'd never done before. 'Say, where is my little friend, special friend, only friend, in the whole wide world?'

The image, such as it was, as it hung on the wall of the museum of his memory: she was called Violetta. That was her name. She was his girlfriend for nine years. What happened was that she died.

In a sense it was his fault.

But before that, love.

See the soap bubble.

Laura Kadinsky was, just like all human beings, three-dimensional. She was quite aware of this fact, beyond any reasonable doubt. If she put her hand around her thigh, her hand bent, like light in a tunnel, like space-time curves around mass. And if she put her finger to her ear, to the exact epicentre of the whorls, her finger fell inwards. There was depth, and she knew it.

And yet the doubt came back every time she looked at herself in the mirror.

It didn't help that Laura Kadinsky had an essentially aesthetic, in other words, unrealistic, sensibility. She'd always seen her body as being like Nike of Samothrace's, plus arms, of course — and those she thought of as borrowed from one of the mannequins in the glittering windows of Selfridges. In other words, she viewed it as a beautiful body, a body of both weight and volume; in yet other words, as a real body, the curves of which could be seen and held in the hand. Like most women, Laura had spent aeons face to face with herself. Nowadays, when she looked at herself in the mirror each morning, she therefore knew with total certainty that something decisive had changed in her face, just as she knew the precise coordinates of the moles on her daughter's back, and immediately noticed if the sun had coaxed forth a new one. But what was it that was eluding her, what actually was it that caused her to rest her forehead against the mirror's cool glass with increasing regularity, staring into her own eyes as though they were crystal balls full of foreboding? She didn't really know, but she often found herself thinking of her honeymoon in Paris, and how one evening in Montmartre, her husband had insisted on getting one of the two-bit artists in the Place du Tertre to carve a silhouette of her profile into shiny black cardboard. And how when they came home, he'd immediately hung the silhouette on the wall of his office, and had so far spent more of their marriage with the silhouette than with her real face.

Then came the day when a vague suspicion was replaced by something that at least superficially resembled certainty. Laura had dropped Chloe, livid as per usual, at her Montessori school and was on her way out through the gates with the child's anger still bobbing in her ears — she always thought of children's crying in that way, that it bobbed like a boat, free and rebellious, intoxicated. It had been raining. Just outside the gates a puddle had formed, and Laura stopped to look at her reflection in the water, to look at her short, childish nose and her dark bob, the freckles that were unusual for her complexion, and the rather oversized mouth that didn't quite look real.

Her husband tended to say her face looked like a collage pinned to the wall of a teenage girl's bedroom — which made her think, that teenage girl was me.

I made that face for men like you.

People think you get the face you're given, and that's that, your genes are what they are. But it's not true. Humans are like plants, they seek survival through fertilisation, by becoming fruit that gets picked, eaten, shat out. Different species have different preferences: some love sweet things, others sour, and some, like Laura's husband, love girls with bodies like Greek statues, but faces like paintings from Picasso's cubist period. Every teenage girl who's ever sat with a pair of scissors and a fashion magazine, playing with pictures of women she could maybe one day be, knows this. Every girl who's played with her face like with a puppy or a pot plant, nurturing the features that will attract the men she wants, petting her Bambi eyes, watering her cocker spaniel locks; and who in the same way has erased the things that don't fit, starving her cheeks, closing or opening gaps between her front teeth (that dividing line, that magical dividing line which splits humanity in two: for or against a gap between the teeth — of course, Laura's husband was all for it, just as he was for wonkiness in general, except in the soul); and who, in the end, when all is done and dusted, walks out into the world and waves her petals, pistils, all that is scented and sparkling.

It was that face Laura saw mirrored in the puddle, crowned with a grey knitted beret. And under the face: the lily-white throat, the brown marl knitted sweater and the well-cut coat, the narrow jeans, the shiny galoshes that were only visible as a ripple in the water. This face-on-demand she'd worked seventeen years to shape, then another seventeen to conserve and refine — suddenly she couldn't tear her eyes from it.

According to basic mathematics, then, Laura was thirty-four years old, no longer a dew-kissed morning rose, but a showy dahlia somewhere between lunch and an early afternoon tea. It was a good age to be as a woman; you could wear lipstick during the day without looking like a harlot and could finally (if you'd made a little effort) afford good-quality tights, the kind that gave off a sheen rather than a cloud of dust when a ray of sun caught them through the bus window. Laura took the bus every day, from Chloe's school in Camden to the theatre in Spitalfields where she worked as a production designer. It was a journey that took exactly fifty-three minutes in rush-hour traffic, and it gave Laura plenty of time to consider a dilemma that had become a personal tradition, whether she actually preferred Goya or Velázquez, and which of Philip Larkin's poems she'd want her husband to refrain from reading at her funeral. Her husband, as it happens, was also called Philip, a name she liked — it was both domesticated and stylish, a name for a man who valued his family and his career in equal measure, and who shaved neatly every day except on Sundays, when he made French toast instead.

And indeed, her Philip was, on the whole, such a man. But like most men, he couldn't be content with that; like most men, he'd never had to learn to stay within the bounds of his given role, he simply had to be contrary. First there was this thing with shaving: he often stopped shaving during periods of intense work, he called it 'the artist's prerogative', and it made no difference how many times Laura pointed out that there was no contradiction between a creative temperament and well-shaven cheeks, just look at your great idol Philip Larkin! He still did what he wanted. What's more, when it came to their sex life, he really did leave a lot to be desired — he was nowhere near as virile as a man of his attributes ought to be, and as Laura still deep down hoped he would someday become. In the sex-impoverished years with Philip, Laura's skin had taken on a kind of electric charge that never really left her. Even when he'd just made love to her and gone whistling out into the kitchen to gobble a chilli — one of his more eccentric habits — a gentle sense of longing still hummed under Laura's soft skin.

Sometimes she thought perhaps it wasn't about sex at all but something else, another insufficiency — perhaps calcium, perhaps sunlight, perhaps catastrophes and cliff edges. But no. What form would that take, anyway? There was nothing to be afraid of. She had a child, she loved her child, she had expensive galoshes, she loved her galoshes, she had a face that was reflected in a puddle, Philip loved that face, and she loved his. There was nothing to hanker for, no hunger that could never be sated, no thirst that could never be quenched with salt.

Laura knew she should be hurrying to get to the bus stop, that today of all days it was important not to arrive last at the theatre. That evening was to be the first night of a new play by Marius von Mayenburg, and Laura had certain concerns about the scenography. There were a few things that weren't quite right and which might need to be corrected. Truth be told, it was the director and the theatre manager who had concerns, not Laura, but whatever. She was sensitive enough that she'd be able to move the cross if it became necessary at short notice. But still, time was of the essence. So why was she finding it so difficult to let go of her own face? What was wrong? There was nothing to be afraid of, so why was she seeing fear in those watery eyes?

Carefully, Laura crouched down to get closer to herself, stretching out a hand to poke her mirror image — not so much to touch it as to destroy it, to break the trance, to be free from this foreboding sense of non-existence. Water is merciful in that way; it arranges itself neatly only momentarily, a tentative reality, renegotiable. She reached out her hand, her finger, and then suddenly she realised what the problem was.

She'd actually become flat.

Completely flat.

She looked at her hand and it existed in only two dimensions — it looked like the hand of a paper doll — admittedly very neatly cut out, perhaps with the very finest nail scissors, borrowed from a mother's bedside table, but still: *not real*. What she'd seen a hint of in the mirror over the last few months had finally come true. The smoothness, evenness, and reasonableness which the nostrils and temples had somehow taken on had now taken over the whole of her body, and strangely enough she didn't feel surprised, only terrified.

On an impulse, she shook her hand, as you do when you wake up with pins and needles in your fingers after a night of deep, corpse-like sleep. She shook her hand two, three, four times and each time it seemed to regain more of its natural contours. Thumb, index finger, middle finger, *daddy finger, daddy finger, where are you? Here I am, here I am, how do you do?* She held her hand up in front of her face, studying each finger with the same curiosity as a four-month-old baby would have done.

It was normal again, her arm too, and though the reflection in the puddle was still flat, like reflections always are, that peculiar absence of shadow which had been there before — the thing that Laura realised, now the shadows were back again, had appeared so *unheimlich*, a term she remembered very vaguely from her university studies, and which came to her now as an echo from the innermost recesses of her brain, those two almond-shaped cabinets of curiosity deeply embedded in the limbic system's porous tissue — this absence was now absent, in other words the shadows were present, and Laura could finally stand up from the puddle, somewhat shaken and a little embarrassed, as is always the case after a momentary confusion of the senses, where the impossible suddenly seems not only possible, but tangibly real.

To think she'd become flat!

Ridiculous and impossible.

Laura Kadinsky, a paper doll!

A bizarre thought, of course. Her brain had probably just been playing tricks on her, like when you get déjà vu, maybe, that must have been it. And as Laura finally made her way to the bus stop and the first night of Marius von Mayenburg's new play, she thought about the bakery on her old street in Dalston, which was called the Déjà Vu Bakery, and the way she and Philip always laughed at it when they went past, *Haven't I seen that teacake before? No, wait — it must be déjà vu!* She couldn't help laughing at the memory, though on closer consideration she wasn't sure if it was real or imagined.

★

Sebastian lay in bed, not really awake yet, and cried like a child. Like a child because he was a child, with a child's wet sheets wrapped around his almost hairless legs. Violetta had always teased him for that, lovingly, the fact that he had about as much body hair as a five-year-old.

She, on the other hand, grew as downy as a peach over time. Then she grew interested in black-and-white art photography from the sixties and seventies. Then she died. End of story.

Epilogue: Sebastian moved to London and woke one night having wet the bed.

When he awoke for the second time it was in the bathtub. At first, he didn't know where he was. Perhaps he was dead. It was a thought that occurred to him almost every morning, and it was with a certain degree of laconic sorrow that he concluded it wouldn't have been the end of the world. Sometimes, when he dwelt on it a little longer, he would end up thinking it might actually be a rather positive thing, to wake and find oneself dead — not only for him personally, but quite generally, as an experience. The fear of dying, after all, was nothing more than the fear of one's consciousness being extinguished. All humans know deep down that that's what happens, that there's no life after this one, no consciousness after death. To wake up and realise one was dead, in other words, would be the same as waking and realising one was immortal. He didn't think all that this morning; instead, his train of thought resembled a picture in a picture in a picture. He thought: *Where am I? Am I dead? No. Bathroom. Why am I lying here? Where do I turn the light on? It smells of wee. It's me that smells of wee. I'm lying here because I wet the bed. I wet the bed because I dreamed I was five years old and needed the toilet and dreamed I was five years old and needed the toilet and dreamed I was five years old and needed the toilet and so on for all eternity but somewhere in the distance where that eternity ends I really was five years old needing the toilet and dreaming I was five years old and needing the toilet and I found a summer meadow and took a wee in it, but when I woke I was a five-year-old who'd wet the bed because he'd dreamed he was a five-year-old who'd wet the bed, and so on ... And when I'd finally worked my way through the whole thing my mother came along and changed the sheets and lifted me up and took me to the big bed and my sisters too, both of them, because you have to treat everyone fairly otherwise before you know it you'll have three bed-wetters instead of one and of course this was the end of the dream, because at that point I woke up, and naturally there was neither mother nor sisters, and yet I was crying, wasn't that strange, I was crying as though someone could hear me ...*

A spider was sitting on the hasp of the little bathroom window. It was, as far as Sebastian could make out, the only living thing in that sad little studio flat of his — his for the time being, at least (though of course that could be said of everything we think belongs to us, even life itself). Not even a mouse seemed to want to live here, not even pot plants or blooms of mould. The lack of moisture was very unusual for London flats in this price band, he'd come to understand, or to be quite honest, for London flats full stop.

As a concession to his mother, Sebastian had transported a mother-in-law's tongue all the way from Lund, but it had already dried up, a fascinating achievement bearing in mind its waxy, fluid-filled leaves. He still hadn't told his mother about it. She would ask: *How's my little plant doing?* And he would have to say: *She's dead.*

Sebastian hadn't spoken to his mother since she'd rung him in the park a few weeks earlier. That wasn't down to his mother, who'd been ringing on an almost daily basis. It was down to Sebastian, who hadn't been answering. Neither had he, in spite of his promises to himself and — indirectly — to the very moral monkey, been in touch with either of his sisters. He did his utmost to avoid having a bad conscience about this. After all, wasn't it a choice he'd made, part of his strategy, to renounce responsibility for the living so as not to be touched by death? Yes, it was. Was it a morally correct choice? Probably not. Definitely not. But it was a necessary choice. He had things to concentrate on that were of a more urgent nature, perhaps also a more significant nature — at present it was still hard to say.

If Sebastian had thought his promotion would mean he'd get a clearer sense of the activities that took place at LICS — and he probably had — he was quickly proved wrong. He still had no idea what the intended outcome of the research was, beyond itself. Knowledge for knowledge's sake. The gathering, organising, and structuring of information. The systematisation of unknown variables. It was beautiful, but also frightening.

Somewhere within Sebastian, there was a sense that all was not as it should be at the Institute, that something sinister was going on behind the scenes which he didn't grasp, couldn't have grasped even if he'd tried. So he didn't try. He merely observed events, the research subjects who came and went, the animals shrieking in their cages, the sealed documents shooting up and down the pneumatic postal system; tried to do his work as well as he could, make do with that. It was a strategy that worked, at least in the sense that it kept him too occupied to answer the phone.

After a while Sebastian hauled himself out of the bath, washed, and put on his trousers. It was a work day. In other words, he had to go to his workplace. In yet other words, he had to shave. While he stood with the razor against his throat it occurred to him that something unexpected had happened the night before: Clara had emailed. Clara. From whom, in contrast to his mother and Matilda, he hadn't heard so much as a peep since leaving Sweden. Could it really be true? He couldn't actually remember; the shift from day to night had been too blurry. But yes. An email had come from Clara, an email he hadn't opened. He'd seen it just before the drug-induced sleep had taken him, his phone had slipped from his hand just as he'd registered the words GOOD // BYE in the subject line.

As he dried his cheeks with the only towel he owned — a threadbare bath sheet with a faded parrot print some previous tenant had left neatly folded in the flat's solitary Billy shelf unit, as though it were an essential part of the inventory, which absolutely must not be absent when the next tenant moved in — he walked over to his bed and bent down. The phone lay there as anticipated: dark, silent, and flat like a very small, desecrated gravestone. He picked it up, holding it between his teeth as he pulled on his last clean T-shirt and lay down on the tatty divan, the room's only large piece of furniture besides the bed. With the phone hovering above his face like a flying saucer he opened the email. It wasn't a choice he made. It was just something he did, because he couldn't not.

SUBJECT: GOOD // BYE

Clara Isaksson clara__isaksson@koolaid.com

Sebastian,

How are things over there anyway? Sorry I've not been in touch, but you know I'm not the type to be in touch. As Mama's probably told you, I got the sack. Instead I'm going to South America, or to Easter Island to be precise, to do a story on consumerism, environmental destruction and the end of the world, and how modern civilisation is to blame. That's why I'm writing, I want you to know. In case I don't come back I wanted a chance to say bye too.

I know what you're thinking. You're thinking I'm being ridiculously dramatic. I just mean you never know. If I had someone who needed me, I would have got life insurance. Planes disappear and are never found, and then if they are found the black box is gone, and relatives are left to live the rest of their lives in uncertainty verging on terror. People go falling over cliff edges and break their legs, and no matter how loud they shout no one ever hears them because the wind is blowing too hard in the wrong direction, and they die there, with broken legs, and their hands all shredded with no nails left, like in some Elizabeth George thriller. Not to mention cars, crime, and obscure tropical diseases.

You know what though, I'm going to spend two days in Santiago in Chile. I know nothing about Santiago apart from the fact that Pablo Neruda had like seventeen houses there, and I can barely speak a word of Spanish. I might walk into a deathtrap, maybe cunningly disguised as one of Pablo Neruda's houses, with no idea what awaits me until I'm stabbed in the stomach with a machete. Okay, I know it's mostly in Colombia that people die from drug-related violent crime, but still. And speaking of drugs, I can't rule out the possibility of being charmed by a charismatic young man with unnaturally white teeth who'll ask me to take a little package to his dying sister in Münster, and then doing it, against my better judgement, and ending up in some dingy prison like in *Brokedown Palace*, and the Ministry for Foreign Affairs will pretend to be pulling their hair out and tell the media they're doing all they can to get me out, but actually they'll just be glad to have one less unemployed citizen on their hands.

Anyway, as I said, I got the sack. Or rather I was forced out, you could say: the paper wanted to put me on some crazy project, like cataloguing letters from the Swedish Scientology movement or something, and I thought, I'm not going to stand for it. Which was of course what they wanted me to think. So I decided not to think that at all, truth be told. I said yes and spent a while in a Shurgard self-storage unit in the suburbs. But anyway, now I'm freelance. Have you heard from Mama lately? Or Papa? Matilda? Is she still with that guy with the kid? I mean, call me a cynic, but I don't think children are the future, I really don't. They'll grow up too, sooner or later, and then what's the point?

Speak sometime,
Clara

Sebastian closed the email and searched for Easter Island. He hadn't thought it was a place that really existed, outside of *Donald Duck*. But sure enough, there it was, on the map at least. It was shaped a bit like a pasty. Or an upside-down pelvis, where the crests were formed by two — volcanoes? Sebastian pondered this, letting the hand holding the telephone sink onto his belly. The fact that Clara was voluntarily taking herself off to a volcanic island 3,500 kilometres from the mainland was either a sign of unprecedented personal development, or full-fledged insanity. He hoped it was the former, but considering the Isaksson family's collective contribution to the history of madness, the latter unfortunately seemed more plausible.

Though what did Sebastian actually know about Clara's life these days? He hadn't seen her for a whole year, not since the funeral. Maybe she'd finally decided to tackle her phobias, including her fear of flying, fear of isolated places, fear of being near the equator (even Clara agreed that one was completely illogical), fear of volcanoes, and fear of embarrassing situations caused by linguistic misunderstandings. It was obvious she hadn't totally got over her fear of getting banged up for being a drug mule, but Sebastian knew better than many others that the brain was a stubborn creature which couldn't be tamed with a wave of the hand. You had to take it one step at a time.

He lifted the telephone again and looked at the clock, realising he didn't have any more time to dwell on things. He had to get to LICS — he had a monkey to feed.

That it was her fault? No. That didn't feel fair, though Laura had to admit the von Mayenburg wasn't her most accomplished work. She could see now that there were, so to speak, things that had got in the way throughout the whole process, both personal and professional — the exact location of the line between these two domains was never easy to pinpoint when it came to art. But still, there had been problems, with Philip, with Chloe, with her colleagues, with Marius von Mayenburg himself and his beautifully glossy paper face, his puppy-dog eyes looking down at her from a poster day after day and week after week, making it hard for her to concentrate on anything but casually sinful fantasies. And then, of course, these problems with her vision and the world, which she now realised had been going on for some time, longer than she'd wanted to admit to herself there by the puddle.

I'm sorry, but the whole world has gone flat.

She could hardly say that. No, she really couldn't, in spite of the accusations being levelled at her by Karen Buller, the theatre's artistic director, who was sitting on Laura's work desk, tossing her raven-black hair.

'This has been a complete fiasco, without a doubt. We can forget being invited to Edinburgh Arts this year — and that, I have to say, is very, very worrying. Very, Laura.'

It was two weeks since the opening night, an opening night that had gone so badly they'd had to cancel the production after just ten performances.

'With all due respect, Karen, I don't think this all came down to me. It was a bad production, full stop; we were all part of it. We're a team, after all.'

Karen Buller swung her Prada-shod foot.

'Absolutely, Laura, absolutely. I'm glad to hear you say that: as you know, there's nothing I value more than collaboration. But still, Laura, I have to say, even if it pains me to do so, I am your manager, and that carries certain obligations, not least with regard to our generous funders …'

'You think I did a bad job — just say it, Karen. I know it wasn't exactly first class, I know that, so you don't need to tiptoe around the issue. I … I've been having a few problems recently, personal problems, and it's possible they've had a knock-on effect on my work. But it will improve, I can promise you that; this von Horváth play, it's really inspiring, it puts me in mind of Kokoschka, don't you think?'

'No, I can't say it does. But anyway. I really must stress —'

'I mean in terms of the colour palette. I'm thinking blues. Cobalt. Klimt! Every shade you can imagine. Expressive, like the sea.'

'Laura, please, let's not dodge the issue. It's painful taking criticism, I know that, I've just been with Leonard from fundraising and it would be fair to say he gave me hell. A certain lady who you know gives us significant sums every year was very, very dissatisfied with — and I quote — "the quite incomprehensibly clumsy performance of Marius von Mayenburg's new play".'

'Once again, Karen, with all due respect, if the company put on a — and I quote — "clumsy performance", I can hardly be blamed. You should speak with Kevin. He was the one who tripped over the cross every night, and if you ask me, the lady in question is mainly upset about Kevin embarrassing himself, because she likes it when he takes her from behind.'

'Laura!'

'It's true!'

'That has nothing to do with it. Yes, Kevin had a major problem with that cross, it's true. Him falling into the prompter's hatch on opening night was unfortunate, to say the least. And I've talked to Kevin about his coordination issues —'

'His alcoholism.'

'His coordination issues. But Laura, you know it wasn't just Kevin. Everyone kept tripping over the damn cross. And Masja walked into the pulpit in at least half the performances. And those tubs of water, what were you thinking? The audience got splashed every time someone flung out their arms, and you know as well as I do that when you're doing German drama you fling out your arms every ten minutes! It's really no coincidence, no coincidence at all, that no one could focus on delivering the text properly when they were forced to navigate that minefield of a set.'

'I do agree with you that it wasn't an optimal set design —'

'Not optimal? It was a fucking deathtrap! We have to count ourselves lucky no one was seriously injured. What I don't understand, Laura, is why you didn't listen to Lawrence during the rehearsals; I know he spoke to you about synchronising the set and the direction multiple times, and asked you to move the cross, for example —'

'And I did!'

'But not where he asked you to, am I right?'

'Perhaps.'

'I can't think of any other way to interpret this car crash than that you chose to ignore Lawrence and the company's input so as to push your own aesthetic agenda, and that won't wash, Laura. It really won't. Good god, not even after the opening night debacle did you do anything about the problem!'

Laura swallowed. This really wasn't fair.

'I tried,' she said, tersely.

'You tried?'

'Yes, I tried. But it turned out wrong.'

'And how, precisely, did that happen? And then why didn't you try again?'

'It ... I ... I don't know what else I can say, Karen. It turned out wrong, and I'm sorry about that. I promise not to build any deathtraps into the set of the next production. Nothing you can trip on or dislodge or walk into. It will be a completely empty stage, I promise. Blue. Like cobalt.'

Karen Buller looked displeased.

'I think that sounds rather underwhelming, Laura. To be frank. It would be better if you just learned to be guided by the director. That's not so difficult, is it?'

'Of course not,' mumbled Laura.

'I hope not. Because I have to say, Laura, that even though we've been very, very glad to have had you here over the past year, you know just as well as I do that it's not customary to have a production designer on permanent staff. I'm absolutely not saying this to put you under pressure, but, well. You understand. It's important that it turns out well, this Horváth thing.'

'Otherwise I'll get the boot.'

'I haven't said that.'

'But it's what you mean.'

'It's first read-through tomorrow morning. If I were you I'd make sure I was there on time.'

Anger coursed through her all the way home. It wasn't enough that she'd had to answer to Karen Buller, no, that bitch seemed to have been going around talking to the whole theatre about her, if the way they stared at Laura as soon as she set foot in the corridor was anything to go by. It stung Laura; their pity burned like chilli-fingers on her nose and genitals. BAH! She decided to ditch the bus home and walk instead. She was afraid of being so close to all those strangers, afraid of what she might feel the urge to do to them, and this anger needed to burn out before she got home or she'd never be able to toss spinach and marinate chickpeas with a smile on her lips.

It wasn't fair, it really wasn't. Nothing at all, and in particular this thing she was suffering from, this strange illness, this disability — what did Karen Buller know about fear? The fear that rose in Laura's throat each time it happened. When the world became nothing more than a screen and suddenly she didn't know whether it was real any more, assuming it ever had been.

Laura thought about the day two weeks before, when she'd been caught up by the puddle outside the school, and later that evening when it had happened again. Philip, who for once had sought out her body in the night, lifted and parted her legs. She'd stretched them over his shoulders and suddenly she saw it in the strip of light from the full moon

— her paper doll's feet dancing like two flat shapes behind the dark shadow of Philip's thrusting body — the way she'd screamed, and how he'd thought it was from pleasure when it was actually from terror.

Now she wished she'd been right. That it had only been her that had become flat. *I could have lived as a paper doll, it wouldn't have been that different to how things were now,* she thought, *but I can't live in a world without depth and shadow, I can't live in a world without beauty and space, I just can't, they have to be able to fix it, it must be something to do with my eyes. Maybe I'm going blind?* No!

She stopped, heart in mouth, and realised she'd more or less run the whole way to Old Street and that, despite the distance not being particularly great, she was exhausted — her legs were shaking and she could barely raise her arm to wave for the bus that was appearing by the roundabout. Having boarded and sunk down onto a seat, Laura realised the rage had run out of her and been replaced by a phenomenon quite unknown to her: soul-searching. Suddenly she didn't feel angry with Karen Buller any more, just tired. It was obvious she'd had to put Laura straight, good lord, the set had been hopeless. And it was true, Lawrence had repeatedly asked Laura to make changes so the stage would be more playable, and Laura had tried, she really had, but how could Lawrence and Karen understand how hard it was to move a chair half a foot backwards when backwards no longer existed? How it was virtually impossible to mark out positions with tape on a floor that kept moving? How would she even be able to get them to understand without immediately losing her job, being made to go on sick leave, being left for dead? So yeah, of course Karen thought she was insubordinate or, even worse, just generally clodhopping; of course she had to put her heels on and clip-clop into Laura's office to put her to rights. And of course Laura needed to pull herself together and get a few answers from that goddamn eye doctor and their goddamn waiting list, otherwise her career would be over whatever happened, and just as Laura was thinking this, that she was damn well going to get a grip on this and get her life back on track again, just as she stepped determinedly off the bus on Parkway and crossed the rain-soaked street without tripping or getting run over, she felt the doubt niggle away at the soles of her feet, seeming to take root and grow up through her legs like the root-threads of a parasitic fungus — what were they called again? Mycelia? Muesli, she needed to buy muesli, they'd almost run out this morning, it would last until tomorrow morning, but no longer, and if she didn't buy Chloe any muesli the nanny would complain there wasn't anything to give Chloe for her afternoon snack tomorrow, and then she'd go out and buy it herself and she'd buy Cheerios since that's what Chloe would ask for, and the nanny would go along with it just to get on Laura's nerves. Laura knew Giselle thought her stance on sugar was over the top, but Giselle's own children were so round they might as well have been beach balls, Laura had seen for herself in photos, so who was in the wrong there? Laura headed for Whole Foods and went in, grabbed a basket and a mango and a pack of black quinoa and a bottle of organic Bordeaux on special offer and as she was walking towards the muesli it happened again, the world flattened out into a photograph and she realised too late: she walked right into the muesli stand, which was much closer to her than she'd realised, gouging a chunk out of her knee so that blood started dripping across the floor as she tried to grab all the boxes of Dorset Cereals falling through her arms.

Outside Whole Foods she sat down and cried. She thought about her home, which she suddenly lacked the strength to walk to, the beauty that gradually seemed to be losing all depth and meaning. She thought about the pillar candle in the window, which Giselle had probably already lit; it had already been dark an hour and she was probably sitting there waiting, wondering when she'd get to go home to her own children. Laura knew it was awful of her to be sitting here, but she just had to go through it all first, to make a list, before it disappeared.

It was happening more and more often, several times a day now. How could life change so fast? Sometimes it went on for several hours; she could no longer pretend it was just a migraine. So she made a list of everything that had been lovely and round and alive. Chloe's cheeks when she was born, much too late and much too big, 4.4 kilos with cheeks like oranges. The view from Primrose Hill, the city spreading out beneath one's feet, so far in each direction you could believe it never ended. Maybe there was still time; she could go there tomorrow, if she had a stable period, see it one last time! How long could it be before it became permanent — weeks? Months? And then, would it get worse? Would she go blind? The pavement's moisture soaked up through her skirt and the tears tickled her cheeks. Dusk and darkness, tights with a hole in the knee, and blood coagulating on her boots, no one asked if she was okay, and why should they? Yumchaa was still open and it was nicer to have a cup of tea.

She got up and walked home slowly. Stood outside the gate and looked at her house, the candle flickering in the living room window, the trees stretching their ghostly fingers towards the sky. Spring would come soon, putting pale pink buds on the magnolia's knotty branches. How she'd loved that magnolia, how she loved it still. She would do her best to see it, the fat, dripping buds, to really see them when they burst.

The present table was quite grotesque. Laura lost count at twenty, just like with her own birthdays — what was she even, thirty-three? Thirty-four? Thirty-four, because she was twenty-seven when Chloe was born, and today Chloe was turning seven. Her hair, which was the same colour as melted butter, was brushed smooth and plaited into two just-messy-enough plaits, and she had a new dress, one with polka dots, which Philip had bought, as was their custom. He always bought Chloe's birthday dresses, because he'd got the idea it was something fathers did, just as they opened savings accounts for the kid as soon as the umbilical cord was cut.

When did that rule of only buying one present when you went to a child's birthday party end? When did people start bringing two, or even three gifts for the birthday child, and flowers or wine for the hosting couple on top of that? Laura didn't quite know, but there had been more presents every year, despite the fact that the number of children invited — eleven — had been the same since Philip had determinedly announced, ahead of Chloe's first birthday, that there were to be precisely twelve children, including his daughter, at the party, neither more nor less, because twelve is a magical, lucky number and therefore the best — crunch — Philip had bitten into a chilli and started writing out invites. Laura pictured it with a glow in her heart — it had been a wonderful day, Chloe's first birthday. Philip had put on a thirty-minute puppet-theatre version of *Peter and the Wolf* for all the babies, and refused to give up before the end, even though the kids were all crawling round like epileptic slime fungi, not the slightest bit interested, of course, and all the parents were shuffling uncomfortably on the hard but very elegant chairs. That was back when Laura still believed that Philip did things like that to amuse (her) and provoke (everyone else), before she realised that Philip didn't do anything for anyone else, either good or bad, only for himself. Even the things that appeared considerate, like the eternal birthday dresses, were actually just part of his ongoing self-fulfilment project, him fleeing from his poverty-stricken roots.

'So, where are you hiding Philip, then?' Arthur's mum, Emma, asked, tilting her head gently to one side, obviously to make her hair fall at a flattering angle across her face and its put-on empathetic expression. 'James had so much going on at work, you know, they're in the middle of reorganising the whole editorial structure at Channel 4, so I said, it's fine if you can't make it, James, it's not your child's birthday, right? But he insisted. Oh — but what am I saying, I didn't mean —'

Emma quickly covered her mouth with her hand.

'No, no, of course not!' Laura said. 'God, no … Well, Philip, you know, he has his phases. Of inspiration, I mean, and he goes right into it. But then, when he's not working, he's absolutely fantastic with Chloe. Yeah, you know, he's always picking her up from school, even though we have Giselle —'

'Oh god, yeah, so often!' said Emma, laying her hand reassuringly on Laura's arm and stroking it a little, as though spreading butter on bread, which Laura was sure Emma hadn't done for many years, if ever. In contrast to most of Philip and Laura's friends, Emma and James didn't even make a pretence of being in touch with what constituted economic reality for the majority of those in the cultural class they identified with. Laura admired them a little for that but hated them at the same time, and for the same reason, because Laura, in spite of everything, was of the opinion so widely held among well-off bohemians that poverty was ennobling, not in the long term, of course (in that case it makes you fat, UKIP-voting, and unashamed of screaming hysterically at your children in public), but as a brief and finite part of your life experience. Laura had been poor, and probably still would be if she hadn't married Philip, and even Philip had been until 2002 when, aged just twenty-eight, he'd in one and the same golden breath got his breakthrough at the Royal Albert Hall with the opera *Laika in Cyberspace* — for which he'd written not only the music but also the (even Laura was forced to admit) incredibly touching and dramatically accomplished libretto — and made the first of several successful property deals, as he sold the run-down flat he'd bought five years previously in the then extremely shabby

London Fields for seven times the price. In addition, that year, he'd finished his biography of Philip Larkin — no cash cow in sales terms, of course, but the generous stipend it had generated from a philanthropic shipping widow from Hull had been better than a punch in the face. It was doubtful whether Philip's character had really been refined by the poverty that had marked his upbringing and young adulthood, and which, in contrast to Laura's, hadn't been relative but absolute to the extent that it had involved free school meals, home visits from social workers, and shoes stuffed with newspaper. It was more likely that it had contributed to his latent but incurable egotism, his sense of himself as a 'self-made man', which meant that today he'd gone out on one of his decidedly rare runs an hour before the party was to begin, and still hadn't returned two hours in, despite his promise to be standing freshly shaven and scented at his wife's side as the first guests arrived.

Emma cast a look at the children, who — tired and bloated after mini-hamburgers, mini-pizzas, mini-pancakes, and a large quantity of similarly diminutive baked goods, followed by a contrastingly gigantic bombe glacée (children react positively to contrasts, at least that's what they said at the Montessori school) — were reclining on the living room floor watching the hired balloon artist, who, with growing panic in his eyes, was trying to satisfy their ever more complicated requests. They seemed to see it as some kind of competition, and why shouldn't they, thought Laura, they were seven years old, old enough to be starting to get used to the idea that life was little more than a string of successful or unsuccessful performances. Chloe's bestie Margoe asked resolutely for an okapi and laughed cruelly when the balloon artist was forced to ask her what such an animal looked like. Emma turned to Laura again and held out her glass to get a top-up of the G&T Laura had mixed in carafes so the children wouldn't know the adults were drinking alcohol.

'Well, I know all about inspiration, I get full tunnel vision when I get into a new project. I've been given a commission by the Royal Academy of Arts, have I mentioned it? I can't tell you who it is, it's rather sensitive, political, I mean, ah, you can probably guess who it is anyway, can you?' Emma said.

'Yes, well, one has one's suspicions. Exciting.'

'If everything goes according to plan … Yes, it will be *amazing*. Quite amazing. Actually, I'm working on another exhibition at the same time; you'll never guess what a ridiculous story it is. The artist is a pure savant. In any case, that's what her dealer says, but what do I know. Storytelling and so on, you can't really rely on people in these post-post-post-modern times, can you? It's rather sad, I think. There's no authenticity, it's almost become a dirty word. But this girl, she's had almost zero formal training, at least that's what they claim. And of course you don't need it, some people are just gifted, it's not hard to imagine a completely untrained performance artist who just has it, you know, anyone can have ideas, but the thing with this girl is that she's old-school. I mean, like Caravaggio. Like Rubens. Like fucking Rembrandt. It's almost … scary. If such people really exist.'

'It has to be a bluff,' Laura said, as it occurred to her that she'd become a little intoxicated. Her vision was slightly blurred around the edges, but it didn't feel threatening, in the way what she'd come to think of as her *auras* did; instead it felt familiar and comforting, like an old friend, like a well-known body in the dark, one that, despite all its faults and insufficiencies, makes you feel protected from the world outside. She fished the cucumber out of her glass — you have to have cucumber with Hendrick's, otherwise you might as well buy any old shit — and started nibbling it listlessly. Out of the corner of her eye she saw James and one of the school mums whose name Laura was always forgetting — Siobhan? Sheila? Cheryl? — sitting a little too close to each other on the sofa while looking at something on James's phone. Their knees were touching. Involuntarily, Laura felt herself getting a little turned on. As though she were somehow involved in their sinful little game, had a role to play just by standing there diverting the attention of the wife, who was far from done talking about her peculiar new charge.

'I really don't think she is a bluff, Laura, I really don't think she is. Of course, we've investigated, as thoroughly as we can. She hasn't studied at any of the two hundred biggest art schools in the country, at least not under the name she uses now, which I know is her real one, I've seen all her papers. And to be honest, it didn't surprise me, when I saw it in black and white. How can I put it, she's … from another world. Socially, I mean. I can't imagine how she could have been through an art education and still be as … unrefined as she is. Perhaps it's not politically correct to say so, but that's the way it is.'

'Uh-huh,' murmured Laura, trying to stop looking at James and Charlie — that was her name, Laura suddenly remembered, or at least the name she wanted to be known by, actually her name must have been Charlotte, like all princesses — and imagining the saliva flowing in their mouths as they looked at each other like that. Of course, nothing would happen between them, life's not a soap opera, after all, and many fewer people than you'd think have enough energy and guts and fear of dying to actually be unfaithful: Laura had looked at the statistics and found it simultaneously reassuring and disheartening. But anyway. She couldn't stop picturing them sneaking out into the garden with the excuse that they were going to smoke e-cigarettes (Philip only allowed the smoking of real tobacco in the house, and then only before eleven in the morning; it was a matter of principle), then seeing how James opened the door of the garden shed and slid his fingers up Charlie's cunt even before they'd managed to shut the door behind themselves and the spiders, and how a spider started crawling up Charlie's leg, still half-covered by her Chantelle tights, tickling the inside of her thighs at the same moment James …

'Laura?'

'Hmm?'

Emma tapped her on the arm.

'You vanished,' she said, offended.

'Oh, sorry,' Laura said, and placed — gingerly — her hand on Emma's shoulder.

'Where did you say you found that artist?'

'It's actually a funny story,' Emma said. 'She went looking for help, you know. At a research institute. On Russell Square, I think? She thought something weird was going on with her brain. Which was true. I know someone who works there, one of the managers of the whole shebang, actually; he rang me. You have to have contacts in this line of work.'

'A research institute?' Laura said. 'That researches … what?'

She wanted to hear more about this place where they dealt in weird brains, but she didn't have time to ask Emma more, and it was probably good she didn't, since Emma was a real gossip. In any case, at that moment, the door of the Kadinsky family's three-storey Victorian terrace flew open, and Philip strode into the hallway. Laura heard him cross it in three long strides, before he appeared, standing at the entrance to the living room.

'Ladies and gentlemen!' Philip called, waving two Punch and Judy puppets that looked like they could have been borrowed from the Victoria and Albert Museum, which Laura couldn't completely rule out. 'Anyone for a little theatre?'

Subject 3A16:2, known as 'Woman Without Depth' (WWD)
Interview with Benedict Katz, PsyD (BK), 4 March 2016
Transcription: Tiffany Temple, med. sec.

WWD: I like to practise on Hampstead Heath. Right in the wildest parts, where not even any joggers go. It has to be perfectly silent and still, otherwise I lose focus. It's like those 3D images they used to put on boxes of sweets when we grew up — we must be about the same age, you and I? Do you remember them? The boxes of pastilles with 3D pictures on the back? It's more or less the same thing I have to do with my eyes. Stare, kind of, really focused, but at the same time not stare, more like a kind of release for the eyes. As though my eyes are floating in the air in front of me, just attached to my head by two small threads. Slowly but surely, I can make my eyes come together, overlap, or I guess it's actually the image that overlaps, I don't know? In any case, if I can get myself to that point, I can see them: the trees, how they are in relation to one another; that is, suddenly I can see that one is in front of the other, which is in front of another, and so on. Otherwise I have to rely on the size, but, of course, that can be deceptive. A little tree can be in front of a big tree, I mean, size isn't always to do with perspective.

BK: Drat, and here I was, trying to convince my wife!

WWD: You think it's funny? Because it's not. I'm trapped in a permanent trompe l'oeil. The world is like a tapestry to me.

BK: No, no, I get that it's problematic. Can you tell me more about your experiments in the forest? How long are you able to maintain your depth perception?

WWD: It depends. Sometimes as long as a few minutes, but mostly just a few seconds. It's about concentration; it's so easily broken. A bird flutters, or my phone rings, or I start thinking about something ultra-stressful, like I realise I forgot to pack my daughter's wet-weather gear when she went to school, or that my husband's gone Philip Larkin–

crazy — again — and now I'm not going to be able to reach him for months, and then who's going to make sure I don't go crazy? And bang, everything's back to normal again, I mean, back to my current normal. Everything's flat. Totally flat. Like the Bayeux tapestry. Metre after metre of stylised trees against a sky that has no space.

BK: I'm going to be honest with you: I've been at the Institute a very long time but I've never heard of a case like this. I'd guess it had something to do with disturbances in your prefrontal cortex, but as to what's causing that … I'm at a loss … which, of course, on the other hand, is good news for us. There are few things that make us happier, here at LICS, than someone with a thoroughly abnormal set of symptoms stepping into the office and offering up their brain in the service of science. And that's got to be something, right?

WWD: He doesn't know anything. My husband, I mean.

BK: How you manage your private life is something I honestly can't express an opinion on, it's totally against regulations.

WWD: Do you understand how difficult it is to pack wet-weather gear when you can't tell where things are in relation to one another? Just putting my hand into the drawer is a challenge. It's like putting a glass of water on a table with your eyes closed. However careful you are, the contact with the table's surface is always a shock. If you ask me, I should be signed off work, but I can't lose my job, I just can't. It's the only thing stopping me from going nuts. And my husband has always wanted me to stay home with Chloe, actually, but he can't say it out loud because it's not, shall we say, socially acceptable in the circles we move in, to want your wife to stay home, I mean. But give him a reason, and …

BK: Can I just ask — if you'll excuse my interruption — what is it you're hoping to contribute to our research?

WWD: Your research? I don't give a shit about your research, I just want to see my magnolia opening.

For assessment and resolution see Appendix 11b.x: Additional diagnostic report.

Him saying: Laura Kadinsky?
And her saying: Here.

She liked his voice and his scent. For women it can be as simple as that — everyone who's ever read a teen magazine or fallen in love with their nursery friend's dad at an embarrassingly young age just because his voice reminded them so much of Tom Jones knows that. Attraction works totally differently for men and women; it's something to do with the brain, of course, Laura had read about it in *National Geographic*, and to do with Evolution, and the Survival of the Species, and Animality. Men judge women's attractiveness on a visual level — the shine and condition of her hair, the size of her bust, the width of her pelvis in relation to stated bust size and the length of her legs, all to optimise the chances that the woman he sleeps with will be able to bear healthy children with strong teeth, then feed those children, and survive to bear more.

The way a woman smells is, quite frankly, irrelevant from an evolutionary perspective; it gives no indication whatsoever of her general health — and anyway, sooner or later her scent is going to be drowned out by the most desirable one of all, that scent of milk and honey, the thick yellow and thin white, the toffee-scented discharge and everything else that is sweet and life-giving. For that reason, it's no wonder that women at their most fertile age, in the event they even care about smelling of anything in particular, often choose sweet scents like vanilla, coconut, and peach, like a taste, so to speak, of what's to come.

Women, on the other hand, look for things other than strictly visual delectation, the *National Geographic* article had said that too — confirming something Laura already knew instinctively, namely, that a man's true nature makes itself known in his armpits and there alone. It's from here that the highest concentration of pheromones issues, that testosterone-laden declaration of health which says everything about a man's strength, vitality, and sperm quality. Men must know this somehow — how else to explain their constant need to work out in public? Why all these football players throwing their strips up into the stands, rock stars doing the same into a swirling sea of fans? Why else would they put their hands behind their heads and lean back in their chairs when there's a woman in the room? Why, it's nothing more than mating rituals and content declaration.

But the young doctor didn't do this. He sat quite still behind his desk, leaning slightly over Laura's notes, drumming the fingers of one hand on the desk's smooth surface. He had unattractively shiny nails, like a classical guitarist — through her spouse, Laura had met a whole heap of classical guitarists and found them, as a type of man, rather repulsive — and eyes of an unclear, murky colour. In all other respects, however, he was very, very beautiful. Or perhaps it was just that he *wasn't ugly*, Laura couldn't really decide. That is, she thought he was beautiful, insanely beautiful, but she hadn't seen him until *after* the first time he'd said her name — and by that point it was all over, so to speak, the impulses had already gone from her brain to her frayed nerves, right down into that pocket in her ribcage where it always starting aching the second before she fell irredeemably in love. It hadn't happened that many times, perhaps three or four instances in her life — the Tom Jones dad, and her husband, of course, and in between, when she was in college, a pair of twins with essentially identical voices and the same captivating speech defect, a kind of reined-in stammer (and consequently, Laura had never really been able to decide which of them she was in love with, which resulted in an embarrassing *arrangement* — as the more dramatically inclined twin had put it — followed by a very physically pleasant, but spiritually corrosive, erotic experiment; summa summarum, whether the twin fixation could be counted as one or two went undecided) — but this was, as Laura very well knew, a reason to retain a certain scepticism towards her aesthetic judgement of the object of her infatuation. It was quite possible, even probable, that her assessment of his appearance was deeply coloured by her already intense attraction to the terribly young man with the remarkably beautiful forearms who at that moment was sitting opposite her, sucking on his bottom lip like the male prostitutes on Dalston Junction.

'How old are you?' Laura asked finally, since he wasn't saying anything.

'Twenty-six.'

'You look younger.'

'I've just shaved.'

'Just? As in just now?'

'Yes. I don't have any hot water at home. I live in Tulse Hill.'

'I live in Camden. By Mornington Crescent. We have lots of hot water.'

'Sounds lovely.'

'You have very well-kept teeth. I've never seen anything like it.'

'Swedish dental care is among the best in the world,' the doctor said, running his tongue over his front teeth.

'I thought you might be Scandinavian.'

'I'm a visiting researcher, from Lund. Do you know Lund? It's in southern Sweden. To tell you the truth, the Swedish dental success story started in Lund, at the so-called Vipeholm Asylum. At the beginning of the last century, the Swedish populace had terrible teeth; a survey of army conscripts showed that 99.9 per cent of them suffered from severe caries, barely a single tooth without decay could be found in any of the mouths examined. So an investigation was launched to find out what caused dental decay. One theory suggested the problem was sugar. They created the so-called Vipeholm toffee, a toffee that was hard as stone and sticky as superglue, and then they gave limitless quantities of it to the mentally deficient patients at the Vipeholm Asylum, in the belief that they were too stupid to feel pain. A kind of animal testing, actually, the researchers probably thought of them as animals. Of course they weren't; they got holes as big as moon craters, and suffered horrendous pain. The sugar industry was unhappy, naturally; they'd invested large sums of money in the experiment, to absolve themselves, so to speak, and that was the outcome. A rather illustrative bit of scientific history, I think.'

The young doctor let his gaze drift out of the window.

'Shall we maybe talk about me a little now?' said Laura.

He looked at her again.

'Of course. Laura Kadinsky ...'

'That's my name,' Laura said curtly, all too aware that if he said her name again with that soulful vibrato, she would lean forward over the desk and stroke his golden-brown arm — the same colour as a freshly baked sponge cake, and god knows Laura loved sponge cake — and that such an occurrence would be extremely difficult to explain away, and therefore extremely embarrassing, to tell the truth, probably ruinous, since in order to defuse the situation, she'd be forced to incorporate the pawing into her description of her symptoms, which would of course lead to a misdiagnosis by the young doctor, and so the whole visit would have been a waste of time. To have laid hands on heaven wouldn't make up for continuing to live like this, it really wouldn't, or would it, she didn't know, she was almost about to do it, but then he said:

'I've read your notes, but I'd like you to tell me, in your own words, why you're here.'

Laura breathed out and moved further back in her chair.

'I've lost the ability to see in three dimensions. To put it plainly.'

'Hmm,' the doctor replied, furrowing his brow in a manner Laura couldn't help finding a little theatrical. It was oddly touching, the way he seemed to be putting it on for her sake. 'When did this start?'

'Hard to say. I suppose it's crept up on me,' Laura said. 'First it was just fleeting moments, unreal, like when you get déjà vu. Then they came more and more often and grew longer and longer, and then, of course, I started to worry. But I don't know. I suppose I thought it was stress.'

'Stress?'

'Everything's about stress these days. You can even get cancer from stress.'

'Are you stressed?'

'No,' said Laura.

'I see,' said the doctor.

'Anyway. It's just getting worse and worse.'

'The stress?'

'No, the problem with my vision! Or whatever it is. I thought it was something to do with my eyes, so I went to an ophthalmologist. But she said they were perfect. My eyes. "The truth is I've never seen such extraordinarily well-formed vitreous bodies," she said. About my eyes.

And there wasn't anything pressing on a nerve or anything like that.'

'They're brown …' said the doctor, and looked Laura in the eye more deeply than anyone had since Chloe — newly born, covered in vernix, placed at Laura's breast — for the first time looked up at her mother and saw what she would believe, for a few short weeks, was the entire world.

'Yes?' said Laura.

'Your eyes. In Sweden, 60 per cent of people have eyes that could, in sweeping terms, be called blue. Though in truth, they're generally towards the grey end, few are lucky enough to have truly blue eyes, like cornflowers or the summer sky. In all my life I've only met one such person. And funnily enough, her name was Violetta. But of course, her eyes were blue, not purple.'

'Why must you always be so eccentric?' Laura asked in an attempt to defend herself.

'Who?'

'Talented men. I assume you're talented, since you're sitting here. Though you can barely be older than my daughter.'

'How old is your daughter?'

'Seven.'

'I'm twenty-six.'

'You know what I mean. My husband's just the same. Insanely talented. He's a pianist. A composer, too. And a literary critic and a property magnate. And frightfully eccentric. I suppose it's charming to begin with, but you soon tire of it.'

'I'm not eccentric. Not at all. I'm just nervous.'

He actually did look very nervous. That too was touching.

'That's decidedly odd, you being nervous. I'm the one who's sick, after all.'

'I didn't mean any offence when I mentioned your eyes, Mrs Kadinsky.'

'No, I should hope not,' Laura said. 'As I said, they're extraordinary, if my ophthalmologist is to be believed. But what help is that, if my brain's falling apart?'

A glittering tear, no larger than a pinhead, welled up uninvited in

Laura's left eye and spread tremulously along her bottom lashes. For a moment the young doctor looked as though he was about to reach out and wipe it away. A little twitch of the hand.

But instead he said:

'No, Mrs Kadinsky, what help is it? Not a damn bit, I imagine.'

'You can call me Laura,' she said, and heard how it sounded like a plea.

Five minutes later, while Sebastian fetched a glass of water, Laura Kadinsky had dried her tears and, Sebastian noticed, touched up the concealer under her eyes. He placed the glass on the desk in front of her and nodded at her encouragingly, then sat down and waited for her to take a sip so the interview could continue.

Sebastian wasn't normally a particularly talkative person. He was a listener. His sudden outbursts about Swedish dental history and eye-colour statistics had to be understood as an indicator that he was not unmoved by the person sitting opposite him. He wasn't sure if it was due to Laura's relative beauty (her face looked like a collage! And the gap between her teeth!) or if it was actually because she reminded him of the Bright Eyes song 'Laura Laurent', which he used to listen to every night before he went to sleep during the greater part, if not the whole, of his time in high school. Or were these two things really one and the same, her actual face and her pop-heroine face, making the attraction something that arose somewhere in the vibrating string of electrical impulses which traced this connection in his brain? Since Sebastian had become interested in neuroscience he'd become increasingly convinced that everything significant happens in the gaps, in the bridges between one thought and another, between one signal and another.

And, not least, between one life and another.

Perhaps that was why, instead of immediately taking up the conversation again, he was content to sit opposite her in silence, to sit there and observe her while she fumblingly reached for the glass, and he, in his mind, reached with his whole being towards this woman whose cumulative associations were too much for his (fairly) young brain to bear.

You shouldn't make fun of that. You should never, never make fun of love.

Minutes ticked by, and Laura Kadinsky, despite repeated attempts, still hadn't managed to get her hand around the glass. Sebastian thought he could see the concentration floating around her dark hair like a halo, a force field, and yet her fingers still scrabbled in vain, first to the right, then to the left, first a few centimetres in front of or behind the glass, like a very young child's. The hopeless efforts of her slim fingers almost brought Sebastian to the verge of tears; in the end he was forced to lift his own hand and give the glass a gentle, well-aimed shove so it met hers. Her fingers closed around the glass and for a moment it was as though he himself could sense how it felt — the cold, convex form in his own hand instead of in hers, no, *at the same time* as it was in hers. He'd read a lot about this. It's called mirror-touch synaesthesia — the brain cross-connects the senses and makes you experience the thing you see happening to someone else's skin as happening to your own. A few people live with it, anyone else can only understand it in abstract form — perhaps as an especially deep form of empathic ability, and empathy born of the flesh rather than the intellect. If you suffer, I suffer. If you experience pleasure, I experience pleasure. For Sebastian the experience came as a sensory shock, not unlike the one following his first real orgasm. Just as suddenly, it too rang off, leaving the palm of his hand tender and bereft.

It was a kind of loneliness, of absence, that he'd never expected to experience again.

He cleared his throat and spun around on his chair. Once he'd returned to his original position, Laura Kadinsky sat with the edge of the glass pressed against her lips and her eyes locked on him, statue-still. He grabbed the edge of the desk to stop himself, embarrassed at his spontaneous frivolity. He wasn't a frivolous person. He hoped she understood that. Slowly, Laura took the glass from her lips — she hadn't drunk anything, he noticed — and lifted it towards the light.

'It's worst with glass,' she said. 'Transparent things. Without depth, you know what's left? Just shadows, nothing more, shadows to chase on the wing.'

'Would you say you have issues with colour vision?' Sebastian asked, grabbing his notebook.

'No, that's not what I mean,' said the woman who wanted him to call her Laura. He thought she sounded disappointed. Disappointed in him? The thought was more than he could bear, so he dropped it.

'Good,' he said. 'Difficulty recognising faces, even those belonging to people close to you?'

'No.'

'Flashes of light? Flickering? Sudden blackouts? Reduced peripheral vision? Blind spots, and so on?'

'No.'

'Short-term memory?'

'Good.'

'And long-term memory?'

'Also good.'

'Headaches?'

'On and off.'

'More on or more off?'

'Off. Roughly as much as before.'

'Nerve pain?'

'What, in my eyes?'

'Anywhere.'

'No. No, I don't think so. How does it differ from other types of pain?'

'Tingling.'

'No, there's no tingling.'

'Burning? Stinging? Chafing?'

'Sometimes it feels like I don't fit in my own clothes.'

'Hmm.'

Sebastian leaned back in his seat the way he'd seen his colleagues do when trying to inspire trust. He cast a look at his computer, unsure as to whether he was following what Barázza called 'the diagnostic routine' to any degree. He wasn't. Laura Kadinsky was admittedly only his third subject, but with the previous two he'd thought he was in control of things: asked all the questions in the right order, created a neat little set of notes, drew up a plan of action in less than an hour. He didn't understand what the difference was this time. That he thought Laura beautiful was certainly true, but so too was the woman who worked in the off-licence by his house, and who beckoned him into the shop every morning when he was on the way to the bus stop, to give him a peach without a word. And that didn't make him nervous or distracted. The fact was that the world was full of beautiful women, and until now, only one had ever made him fail to do what he'd set out to.

And as we know, she had died.

That didn't bode well for Laura Kadinsky, or for Sebastian.

One hour and many questions later, the consultation was over, and Laura had been escorted out into the corridor by an assistant. Sebastian was left in his office, at a loss. His normally efficient attitude to his work had been thrown out by the confusing — or, to be frank, *erotic* — atmosphere pervading his meeting with Laura. For Sebastian, it must be said, confusion and eroticism were not two separate things; in fact, they were tightly interwoven. Both in the sense that he found the erotic confusing, but also in the sense that, as a fundamentally rational person with rational interests, he found few things so erotically loaded as chaos and uncertainty, especially when these manifested as a very beautiful woman. Perhaps it was all just early conditioning. Perhaps it was unhealthy. It was obviously unhealthy. He knew that, just as he knew that right at this moment, he ought to be entering his observations into Laura's notes and moving on to the rest of the day's tasks. But he couldn't do it. In the end he gave up trying to rid his mind of Laura's image under his own steam, and decided instead to replace it with a less dangerous face. He threw his notes in a drawer, and made his way down to the basement.

The cicadas' song buzzed in his ears. It wasn't a figment of his imagination, but real cicadas from the small-invertebrates lab on the other side of the corridor. There were animals distributed throughout the Institute — an absolute time suck, according to the staff who, quite rightly, would have wished to have them all in one lab, catalogued according to the Laika system so well established in animal testing. With the animals spread across twelve floors, and with an — apparently — randomly scheduled rotation of the animals, it was naturally impossible for anyone to keep track of them, leading to a whole lot of hither and thither in stairwells and lifts. According to the research director — that is to say, Corrigan — these rotations were the result of a directive from the very top; it was a *staff wellness initiative*, exercise being the *very foundation* of a well-functioning brain and, consequently, exemplary research outcomes.

There was no definite consensus at the Institute on whether the rotation of the animals was really random, though many factors pointed to this being the case. From the faction who believed in a higher order — consisting primarily of the British staff members as well as the Japanese and Korean visiting researchers — the argument was often put forward that randomness was such a foreign concept to the rule-driven Brits that this kind of randomly orchestrated animal circus was absolutely unthinkable. The unanimously elected leader of this faction (dubbed Team Bletchley after the finest hour of the British penchant for order) was Jennifer Travis, great-niece on her mother's side to the mathematician Alan Turing, who undoubtedly — according to the faction's internal ranking system — had come closest to breaking the code behind the rotations. Among those who, on the other hand, believed in the randomness of the rotations, there was, of course, no elected leader, which undeniably led to a more fragmented line of argument. But that wasn't a problem. The non-existence of a pattern is impossible to prove conclusively, as long as the pattern's sequence has not been ruled out, which freed Team Gödel from any attempts to do just that, something one of the faction's more devoted affiliates — the Spanish visiting professor Álvaro Barázza — would chucklingly conclude every time the issue was raised in the cafeteria, which was on an almost daily basis.

'Travis?'

Sebastian walked along the basement corridor, swiped open the door of the small-invertebrates lab, and called out Travis's name multiple times in order to be heard above the song of thousands of cicadas.

The cicadas were Travis's very own project. As one of the Institute's most prominent Multi-talents she had certain privileges, of which the cicadas were one. Travis's work with the cicadas was generally viewed as an eccentricity, a Sisyphean task, or even a Frankensteinian one. This was because, from a neurological point of view, cicadas are uninteresting in every way — they lack the refinement of the primate, the potential of the roundworm, and the convenience of the fruit fly, so what's the point of studying them? Jennifer Travis didn't agree, an opinion that had very little to do with empiricism but all the more to do with theory, and, perhaps most important of all, with Travis's fear of not being quite as brilliant as everyone believed her to be.

To begin with, Travis had been given licence to keep a hundred specimens of all in all a dozen species, but as the insects mated, very rapidly and determinedly, as insects are wont to, their number was now beginning to approach the unmanageable. Travis was constantly having to increase the number of terrariums in order to house them, at the cost of other insects. This had naturally led to a level of irritation among the other research groups, but no one wanted to be the one to snitch, and soon enough it would probably be time for a rotation again, at which point Travis's inability to limit the fecundity of her cicadas would become more widely known and be stopped. Until then, her colleagues had an unspoken agreement to let her be, partly out of respect for her Multi-talent, and possibly also partly due to a healthy fear of the abyss in Travis's psyche, which had generated her fixation on these insects. As far as Sebastian had hitherto understood from occasional scraps of gossip, her obsession was rooted in a psychological cluster of problems centred on a task that Travis had failed at multiple times, something their colleagues referred to simply as 'the puzzle', in half-whispered tales along the lines of: 'She's never really been herself since that first go at the puzzle …' or 'Just wait until the puzzle comes round again, she'll forget everything else.'

When Sebastian finally found Travis in the furthest corner of the laboratory, she appeared, in any case, to be in a very harmonious state. With neon-pink ear defenders on her ears and a soft glow in her eyes, she was bent over a terrarium observing two cicadas of a larger model, who appeared to be in the process of mating. Sebastian cleared his throat and tapped his feet a little to draw her attention from an appropriate distance, though he knew he should just go over and take her ear defenders off. Travis was perhaps the least easily frightened person in the universe, at least when it came to the kind of external stimuli that trigger the amygdala in most people: sudden noises, unexpected physical contact, shadows on the path. It could have had something to do with her obvious lack of surprise about trivial changes in her environment, a consequence of a similarly obvious lack of interest in them. The fact that Sebastian had come into the lab surprised her no more than if he hadn't done so, and therefore didn't trigger any kind of irrational fear. When she turned around and caught sight of him standing there toing and froing, she just beamed and took off her ear defenders.

'Sebastian!'

'Travis,' said Sebastian, in accordance with the unwritten rule asserting that the Institute's male employees should be addressed by their first names, but the female employees only by surname, in order not to undermine their already inherently fragile authority, a rule he had understood was extra important when addressing those female colleagues who, like Jennifer Travis, had looks going for them, that is — in an academic context — going against them.

'Come and look at B2 and B14. They're so beautiful when they make love,' Travis said, tucking her wisps of blonde hair behind her ears. When Sebastian didn't react, she reached out her hand and pulled him towards her. Lab coat against lab coat, Sebastian could feel the warmth of her body, but it left him unmoved. The soft breasts, the round, broad hips that stretched the unisex lab coat to breaking point, her spearmint-scented breath — none of Travis's many feminine charms succeeded in driving Laura Kadinsky from his thoughts. He hadn't imagined they would either, but somehow he must have hoped, when he sought Travis out here in the cellar, that it would be possible to drive out one woman with another, to balance the forces, so to speak. He had neither the time, the desire, nor the emotional energy to fall in love, but were it to happen regardless, anyone would be a better object than a very sorrowful, married woman who was also his patient — this he felt instinctively.

Jennifer Travis, as always, was in her own world.

'I suppose one shouldn't have favourites,' she said, with cheeks as rosy as toffee apples, 'but I can't help it if I enjoy this. *Cyclochila australasiae*. One of the loudest insects in the world. You should have heard him shrieking earlier, B2, but he's happy now. Soon B14 will burrow into that branch right there and lay eggs. Hundreds. And when all the young come out of their cocoons, in about fourteen days, it's gonna be one hell of a noise in here. Then I'll take a couple of hundred and cut their heads open, if I can bring myself to. You could almost be fooled into thinking I've grown fond of them!'

Travis laughed out loud and nudged him in the arm with her head before throwing a little food down to the post-coital Australian cicadas and moving on to the next unit.

'What are you up to, then, Sebastian? Have you got the hang of things yet? Have you seen this, by the way? *Megapomponia imperatoria* … Aren't they magnificent? U3 over there has a wingspan of twenty centimetres; I measured it.'

'I just had a woman in for her first consultation,' Sebastian said, feeling a compulsive urge to talk about Laura. 'She can only see in two dimensions. It's really strange. I think it's something to do with a problem in V2, but I'm far from certain.'

'I don't know how you have the energy to deal with people,' Travis sighed. 'Much too much fuss, and all for nothing.'

'For nothing?' he said. 'But isn't that what it's all about? I mean, people. Human existence, that's why we're doing what we're doing, isn't it? Whatever that is … Actually, now we're on the subject, I've been meaning to ask you, since you've been here longer than me and so on —'

Travis held up one hand to interrupt him. She stuck the other into the terrarium and pulled out one of the grotesquely large cicadas — perhaps the famed U3, but that was more than Sebastian could determine — and let it fly towards the ceiling.

The wingspan was indeed impressive; the shimmering brown wings were like a book being opened as they unfurled under the strip light. Jennifer Travis followed it with her gaze as though she really were trying to read it.

'Sebastian, the brain is a hierarchical structure. As you know, of course. The stuff at the top is a result of the stuff at the bottom, not the other way around.'

'Yes …' he said cautiously, unsure what she was getting at.

'But we so dearly want the human brain to be a mystery, right? As researchers, we want it to stay like that too, even if we might insist on the reverse. We want to work our way up to a point we can't get beyond, where we can say: okay, here it is, the outermost boundary, the mystery, the golden egg, the ultimate enigma, the unique thing, the *soul* itself. So we dig around in the abnormal, in the exceptions, the things that contradict everything we actually already know about the brain: that it's logical, structured, that it's an equation. A pretty complex equation, sure, but an equation nonetheless. That's what a human is. A puzzle with a limited number of pieces. They fit together with no need for a sticky soul to glue them together.'

She shrugged, reaching up a palm. The enormous cicada landed on it, like a pet.

'It sounds so ordinary when you put it like that,' Sebastian said.

'Of course you think that, my friend,' Travis sniggered and tweaked Sebastian's nose with her free hand. 'Of course you do. You're a *human*.'

Sebastian must have looked worried, because Travis softened a little, tilting her head to one side.

'There's a system in the madness, Sebastian, that's all I'm saying. A system so magnificent it blinds us.'

And with those words, she turned her back on Sebastian and began to hum a song he thought he recognised as the rather macabre nursery rhyme 'Ring a Ring o' Roses'. With an unexpected, overpowering feeling of being blinded by her impeccably white back, Sebastian backed out of the laboratory, out into the corridor, and found himself forced, momentarily, to rest his head against the subterraneanly cool wall.

Less than a week had passed since the appointment, when Laura Kadinsky literally ran headlong into the young Dr Isaksson in the rose garden in Regent's Park. Laura was upset because she'd just had an argument with Philip on the telephone. They rarely argued — it was remarkable, Laura thought, that someone like Philip, who was so extraordinarily good at almost everything, could be so bad at fighting — and when they did, in nine out of ten cases it was about trivialities. Today's bout had begun with Philip calling and informing her that he was planning to leave work early and take Chloe to see a silent film at Hackney Picturehouse. Laura had asked if it was a film for children. Of course not, Philip had said. It was a Lois Weber. Laura had just caught sight of an extraordinarily beautiful rose, had seen the cupped hand of its petals, and let the matter go. But then Philip started talking about some research he'd read that said milk was bad for children. Laura had said that if there was one thing in the world on which there was consensus, it was surely that milk was good for children. Philip had persisted, saying that the report had shown that milk, contrary to everything previously thought, didn't lead to strong bones, but to brittle ones. The calcium in milk was of no use, quite the opposite, Philip had said (and these were his exact words): 'Milk sucks calcium out of your bones.' From now on, Philip thought Chloe should have almond milk on her Cheerios, or better still, oat milk. Ideally home-made. He'd already been and bought two kilos of almonds and a nut milk bag from Borough Market, and was planning a first attempt that evening. Laura — who absolutely didn't want Chloe to grow accustomed to something so complicated, something that it would, in the long term, fall to Laura to provide — had informed him that anything that was good enough to nourish a calf was good enough to nourish her daughter.

It had just gone downhill from there.

Laura had been on her way home from work when Philip rang. His decision to spend the evening with Chloe instead of with Larkin (he was in the middle of translating *The Whitsun Weddings* into Farsi, something that wasn't much discussed in their marriage, since Philip's knowledge of Farsi was a direct consequence of a three-year relationship he'd had with an Iranian beauty before Laura) meant that Laura was suddenly free to do what she wanted with her afternoon and evening. The feeling of freedom was intoxicating, though not in the word's normal, positive sense — instead of elated and hellraising, Laura felt tired, listless, and vaguely nauseous, like when she'd drunk two glasses of wine on an empty stomach and then dropped the salt cellar in the Le Creuset just as dinner was ready. She sat down on the nearest bench and grasped a rose between her thumb and forefinger. It was an Ingrid Bergman, with petals red as blood and delicate as the fingernails of a newborn. Laura remembered how she used to bite off Chloe's nails with her teeth when she was a baby, how she'd bend over her crib in the darkness so the child, sheltered by sleep, wouldn't notice. Nowadays, Chloe bit her own nails, in spite of Giselle's scolding. Laura guessed it was some kind of original sin. Deep down she felt consoled by the fact that her daughter was still an animal, an animal just like she was. Consoled, and somehow triumphant.

Laura often walked through Queen Mary's Rose Garden on her way home, even though it was out of her way. She liked it best in the winter, when you could see all the thorns, the glossy rosehips which would never perform, since roses, like apples, have to be grafted in order to generate worthy progeny. And sometimes, miraculously (though really, thought Laura, it was just the greenhouse effect), you'd catch sight of a solitary rose blooming wildly, almost desperately, dangling at the very end of an unpruned branch or hunched with crossed legs on a pergola. Laura's self-image was sufficiently atomised that she was able to identify with these survivors, as well as the dead seed heads and thorns.

Now it was spring, and the roses were fighting for space on the branches, late tulips turned their club-like hands towards the sun, and the stone statues crouched demurely on their plinths, as though to protect their nakedness from the steady stream of selfie-mad tourists. Laura let go of Ingrid Bergman, but could still feel the flower's weight in her hand. However, she didn't have time to register the fact that she'd actually managed to reach for it and grasp its stalk, precisely and without difficulty — something she wouldn't have believed herself capable of if she'd thought about it — before she caught sight of something strange: in a tangle of foaming white clematis further along the gravel path, something glimmered like gold, something that was buzzing and moving about. A fly? Too big. A dragonfly? Too loud. An exotic bird, with a golden beak and a plume on its head? But then where was the plume? Surprised by her own curiosity, this sudden attack of childish inquisitiveness, Laura found herself bouncing up from the bench and setting a course for the clematis and the golden insect, if that was what it was. The thought did cross Laura's mind that it was an optical illusion, just a tear-soaked blot on her cornea, a new nail driven between the two sides of her brain. But before she reached the clematis arch, the insect had flown away; she saw it sweep through the grass, rise up towards the sky, dive down into a creamy white English rose, hover up again, and disappear off to where the path deviated around a ball of box topiary. She ran after it and actually managed to catch sight of it one last time — a little golden speck right in line with her eyelashes — before she ran headlong into another person.

A while later Sebastian, to his surprise and terror, was sitting with Laura Kadinsky outside the rose garden's only servery: a glorified hotdog stand known as Regent's Pork. Exactly how they'd ended up there was not wholly clear to Sebastian; it may have been him who took the initiative (it was — but he'd done it so subtly that both of them would later come to think of their first meeting in the outside world as almost predestined). He hadn't thought he'd see Laura again before it was time for her first fMRI, but now here they were, sitting side by side under a green-and-white-striped parasol, about to eat sausages. They'd each ordered one — the same kind, rosemary and truffle oil, to avoid having to exchange pleasantries about each other's culinary experiences once the sausages had arrived and been sampled — and were talking, as they waited, about the Windsors, settling on the Queen Mother.

'I think she probably was a real bitch,' said Laura Kadinsky. 'Just like most mothers forced to live in a man's shadow.'

'Not mine,' said Sebastian. 'My dad was a very successful tax auditor but my mum was still a really kind woman.'

Laura laughed. It was the first time he'd heard her laugh, and he'd made it happen. Was it that easy to make women laugh? It had always been a struggle with Violetta. But if Laura Kadinsky was happy, why did her laughter sound like rain against a dirty pane of glass?

'Do you have any siblings, Doctor?' Laura said, her fingers creeping across the table towards her beer glass.

'Two. Two sisters,' Sebastian said.

'Younger or older, or one of each?'

'The same age, actually. The same age as me.'

Laura stopped and her beautiful brow creased, as though that required careful thought. Sebastian was used to that reaction. People always seemed to have difficulty making the genetics stack up, which Sebastian thought must be because he and his sisters were of different genders. When people thought of triplets, they thought of Huey, Dewey, and Louis, a homogenous little band of individuals, impossible to differentiate from one another. They never thought of Sebastian, Matilda, and Clara.

'We're triplets,' Sebastian said. 'Two-egg. It's actually not that complicated, biologically speaking.'

'It sounds ever so complicated,' Laura said. 'Psychologically speaking.'

Sebastian coughed. His beer had gone down the wrong way. Laura stretched out a hand and thumped him on the back. His central nervous system was unprepared for this physical contact from the most beautiful woman in the world (yes, he'd concluded a few moments earlier, as she licked a drop of beer from her extraordinary, pillowy upper lip, she was without doubt the most beautiful woman in the world, perhaps the saddest too, perhaps they were the same thing). All his nerves went into overdrive, a wave of heat flooded his body, and he was forced to cross his legs under the table.

'Was that a little blunt?' Laura asked, placing her hand back on the table. Sebastian noticed that her small fingernails were bitten to the quick and that a tiny drop of blood had accumulated at the edge of one.

'I'd like to say it was unintentional, but that would probably be a lie. Perhaps it's because I'm going to die soon, but I've begun to find small talk intolerable. You might as well get straight to the nitty-gritty.'

'You're not going to die, are you?' said Sebastian, aghast. 'I mean, not right now.'

'No, I'm probably not going to die today,' Laura said cheerfully. 'But maybe tomorrow. Tell me honestly — do you think it's a tumour?'

'I hope not.'

'But do you think so?'

'No,' Sebastian said truthfully. 'I don't think so. But it's hard to say before we've done an initial fMRI. Actually, I'm surprised you've not sought medical help. I'm not really a doctor, you know.'

'Perhaps it's not a doctor I want,' said Laura. 'I've met a lot of doctors in my life; my husband knows a whole shift's worth. But I can tell you this: not a single one of them has been interested in my brain.'

And Sebastian thought: right now your brain is the only thing in the world that interests me.

It was quiet in the house on Mornington Terrace when Laura finally got home that evening. Philip was asleep. Chloe was asleep. They looked to her like Raphael's cherubim. Philip had shaved. His cheeks shone like hand-polished crystal glasses. Chloe's cheeks were as rosy as. As. As. As the rosy cheeks of a child. There was no more accurate way to describe them, since nothing is rosier than the rosy cheeks of a child, not even a rose, it's the Waterloo of comparisons, a child is a child and can be described in no other terms. Everything about a child comes straight from the world of Ideas; you can't get closer to heaven no matter how many fancy words you use.

Laura wanted to touch her daughter's cheek, but was scared to, in case it turned out to be cold and flat. They lay beside each other on the sofa, her husband and Chloe, the television screen frozen on an image of Winnie-the-Pooh dangling from a bright red balloon. Laura looked from the TV to her family, back and forth, to try to discern a difference between the frozen fiction and the real world. But both lacked depth. She contemplated Winnie the Pooh as though he were her child. She contemplated her husband as though he were Winnie the Pooh. Then she turned and went out into the kitchen.

It took her a while to get down the tea caddy. She put her hand flat against its surface and carefully moved it around the corner of the caddy, finger by finger, until she was able to grasp the golden edges and lift it down. Then she had to locate the curved handle of the drawer, repeating the same tentative procedure. After that it was the handle of the kettle she had to find, and the tap, then slowly positioning the kettle under the stream of water, because if she did it too quickly, there was a looming risk that she would miss, banging the kettle right against the wall. And there would be a crash, possibly a crack in the glazed surface, and maybe Philip would wake up, come out into the kitchen and see it, the crack.

While the water was boiling she went to check on Chloe's hamster. Philip was always forgetting to feed it, perhaps because he hated it, and

Chloe was a child, after all, with a child's natural tendency towards neglect, not through cruelty, of course, but due to a fundamental inability to distinguish living things from toys. Neither was Philip's hatred of Essie the Escapist (for that was the hamster's name) an expression of any inherent evil in him. He was only human, after all, a human with perfect pitch, and Essie the Escapist's squeak was out of tune, badly out of tune. According to him, her squeak was somewhere between a C and a D, and instead of steadily occupying a reasonably comfortable half-tone, it wavered irregularly between the two notes in a way that could only be described as intolerable — to a gifted ear like his, in any case.

Essie's squeak was a particular problem at night, when the rest of the house was silent. So Essie's cage was carried down into the cellar every evening when Chloe had gone to bed, only to be brought up to her room again before she woke in the morning: a complicated procedure of which Chloe was kept mercifully unaware. To Chloe's mind, not even a toy belonged in the cellar, the most terrifying place on earth.

It seemed unlikely to Laura that the hamster had already been moved down into the cellar, since Philip appeared to have fallen asleep at the same time as Chloe. So it was to her daughter's room that she went in search of the little bronze ball of fur known as Essie the Escapist — so called for her ability to break out of her cage at least twice a week. Not, in classic small rodent style, by squeezing between the bars, but by opening the little wire door and jumping out, without further ado. How she managed it was a mystery, only surmounted by the fact that, once out, she seemed to have absolutely no interest in hiding or running away. She just ran a few laps around the outside of the cage, before calmly and collectedly lying down nearby to consider her new-found freedom. Laura could make no sense of it. If she'd been a hamster with the world at her tiny feet — well, no fucking way would she be sitting there waiting to be locked up again.

And indeed, there was the cage, in its place by the window, on a yellow table decorated with a home-made paper banner on which Chloe, with Laura's help, had spelled out ESSIE'S HOUSE in coloured pens and with a double exclamation mark. The cage seemed to Laura as flat as the rest of the room, the hastily made bed with its pale yellow cover, the model dinosaurs on the bookshelf. And yet she still had a slight attack of vertigo as she approached it, because in front of, or maybe behind, or possibly even inside the cage, Essie was running around in all her three-dimensional glory. Laura approached her with caution, not daring to take her eyes off her. But yes, Essie was three-dimensional to the highest degree. Astonished, Laura knelt down in front of the cage, opened the door, and carefully put in her hand. She fumbled around in the cage for a moment — as usual, it was like running her hand over a piece of paper — before getting hold of the hamster's soft body. She took Essie out, cupped her hands around her, and devoured her curves with her eyes.

'I can see you,' Laura whispered to the hamster. 'I can see you as you really are. It's just like with the doctor … Sebastian.'

And the hamster looked at her with her beady eyes, quizzically, because she didn't know who Sebastian was. Perhaps she wondered why Laura was crying and pressing her so tenderly to her chest.

Subject 3A16:7, known as 'The Blind Photographer' (TBP)
Interview with Benedict Katz, PsyD (BK), 11 December 2015
Transcription: Tiffany Temple, med. sec.

TBP: First of all, I want to say I have diabetes.

BK: Would you mind putting down the camera?

TBP: Do I have to?

BK: Yes.

TBP: I don't like it when people tell me what to do.

BK: Hmm, that's a problem many young people have. But I need to be able to see your face.

TBP: It's an ugly face.

BK: That's not for me to judge. From Germany, you say? You've come a long way.

TBP: Bremen. But it's not an issue, the travelling, I mean. I've been travelling constantly since it started. I want to see as much as possible.

BK: And when did it start exactly?

TBP: Two years ago. When I took my *Abitur*. The blindness started then. The visions came later, perhaps a year after that.

BK: I see. Since then, have you sought psychiat—

TBP: I'm here because of the visions I've been having, not the blindness. The blindness is caused by diabetes.

BK: I see.

TBP: And it's not total. Yet. I can see you.

BK: That's good. But, look here, can I ask —

TBP: I just took a picture of you.

BK: For Facebook or something, eh? Ha ha.

TBP: Are you crazy?

BK: Funny you should mention that word —

TBP: I just want to know what's causing it. The fact that I see things that are going to happen, and then they happen. The first time, it was snow falling in clumps as big as stars. That was in April. And then the following day it started snowing.

BK: You know what they say about the weather these days — unpredictable! Soon we'll be growing grapevines along Hadrian's Wall. But do you know what, they did that in Roman times too — do you think the Romans would have cared about Scotland otherwise?! Most things have a natural explanation, that's our firm conviction here at the London Institute of Cognitive Science.

TBP: I saw my sister having a miscarriage, then she had a miscarriage.

BK: Very common in early pregnancy.

TBP: She was at week 27.

BK: Placental abruption?

TBP: I don't know. I have pictures of her belly while there was still a baby inside. She doesn't want to see them.

BK: What else, then? What else have you seen that has come true, so to speak?

TBP: I've lost count. Mostly it's things that are about to happen, as though there's a time lag, but in the wrong direction. Like déjà vu but more drawn out and on a bigger scale. But it's bigger things, too, further in the future.

BK: Hmm. Tell me, young man, have you always taken photographs?

TBP: No. Or, well, yes. Everyone takes photos all the time these days. With their phones and so on. But no one sees anything.

BK: But you see things.

TBP: I see more than I want to.

BK: And what do you see that worries you so?

TBP: I see a fire. There's going to be a fire, it's going to be immense. And I see a girl who'll come back from the dead.

Diagnosis and recommendation: Raving mad youth. Since the man is an adult and a foreign citizen, psychiatric referral not required. Possible flag to National Counter Terrorism Security Office.

Sebastian was wandering around a room in the Institute's radiography department. He looked at the clock — Laura Kadinsky wouldn't arrive for almost an hour. He wondered what she was doing at that precise moment, if she was sitting on the Tube or the bus, if she was sauntering through Regent's Park, if she'd stopped for a tiny little coffee in a tiny little white espresso cup in some Italian cafe-bar — in Marylebone, for instance — if her husband was driving her somewhere in their car, if they had one, and whether it was a Volkswagen if so. He wondered what she looked like naked, by which he meant inside her skull — oh god, no, of course not — of course he really meant her body, but her brain too: what colour it was, whether it would shine silver or glisten green under his fingers. He wondered about that and he wondered what he should do with his time until Laura turned up; he sat down on an uncomfortable armchair with a fuzzy, dark green cushion, and went on waiting. Perhaps he should take this opportunity to look in on the monkey, but he was too restless to do anything but pull bobbles off the arms of the chair and run his fingers through his hair over and over again.

When there were thirty-seven minutes left to wait, Sebastian's phone started vibrating in his pocket. He was so startled he pulled it out and swiped right without even checking who it was.

'Isaksson speaking,' he said.

There was a short silence on the other end.

'Basse? Fuck, I didn't think you'd answer.'

'Tilda?'

'Yes. Fucking hell.'

'Don't call me Basse.'

'Okay. What are you doing?'

Sebastian cast his eyes around the fluorescent room. In front of him was the bed on which Laura's body would soon rest, an undulating hillscape against a sharp, sharp sky, like a sacrifice on an altar. There was a murmuring sound from the tunnel he was about to send her into.

'I'm at work.'

'Shame. I'm in the middle of booking tickets to Sweden, but the website went down. So I'm ringing you instead.'

'You going home? How come?'

Against his will, Sebastian grew uneasy. It would be typical of their mother to fall down the stairs just as Sebastian had found a tiny sliver of beauty in his life.

'Nah, not to Lund. Billy's family have a summer house in Norrland. Västerbotten. He takes Siri there every summer. He wants her to feel close to the bears and the wolves.'

'Huh?'

'You've never seen the bear, but the bear has seen you. That's what he always says. I tell him that Siri has seen bears, at the zoo. But apparently that's not enough.'

Sebastian looked at the clock. Thirty-one minutes. There was no reason not to take this opportunity to speak to Matilda. He could tell the monkey later. She'd be glad, and maybe not pay so much attention to his less than Christian feelings about Laura Kadinsky's naked brain.

'You're bad at responding to emails, Basse. Really, really bad. The only person worse than you is Clara. I've written about seventeen emails to her this last month and she hasn't replied to a single one. Do you think she's dead?'

'I think she's on Easter Island.'

'Easter Island? Are you kidding? Where even is that?'

'The Pacific Ocean.'

'Fucking hell. No one ever tells me anything. She's angry with me, for some reason. I've tried to apologise, for everything I could think of, but it doesn't seem to help. So she talks to you, then?'

'Very little. I got one email.'

'God.' Matilda fell silent. Sebastian heard her inhale through her nose and then exhale in a single long, even stream. Just when he thought she was going to say something, she did it again.

'Kathleen always says life is a watercourse that flows around our feet. It never stands still, not even when we think it does.'

Kathleen was, if Sebastian remembered correctly, Matilda's yoga instructor.

'Okay,' said Sebastian.

'I mean that you have to make the most of that energy,' Matilda said. 'You and Clara ... you're the same. You keep all the hard stuff inside your bodies instead of letting go of it. That can't be fucking healthy. To be honest, it can drive you crazy.'

Sebastian pointed out that the only one of them who'd spent time in closed psychiatric facilities was actually Matilda.

'In any case,' his sister went on, 'I wasn't ringing for Clara's sake, or yours. You are the way you are. Jeez, sometimes it feels like I'm not even related to the two of you. I just wanted to know what you think about Mama.'

'What about Mama?'

'Something's going on with her, you must have noticed? Or don't you speak to her either?'

'Yeaahh ... maybe a couple of weeks ago?'

'Did she ask you about Papa?'

'Yes, yeah. Like, twice.'

'Hmm!' Matilda burst out, almost triumphant. 'She seems a bit muddled too, I think.'

'She's always been muddled,' Sebastian began. 'And it's probably a bit strange for her, being on her own and everything. Since I left, I mean.'

'That's exactly what I mean,' Matilda said. 'I'm scared she wants Papa back, which would be a really bad idea.'

Sebastian had to laugh.

'Papa and Mama? Back together? I don't think so. I really don't.'

Matilda didn't seem convinced. Sebastian had a feeling her jollity was actually there to conceal her anxiety, but maybe that was just because the conversation had ended up being about their mother — it reminded him so much of the conversation he'd not so long ago had with their mother that it gave him an unpleasant feeling of déjà vu.

'Tilda, are you okay?'

'Of course! Just doing some deep breathing.'

'Okay.' Sebastian looked at the clock again. Seventeen minutes left. He suddenly felt nauseous.

'I kind of have to go now. I have a meeting. You could say.'

'Is it a woman?'

Sebastian leapt up from his chair. Matilda laughed, but her nose whistled sadly.

'Basse …' she said, sounding suddenly like a child confiding a secret. 'You know this thing with colours — synaesthesia, I mean. Okay, so, hypothetically speaking, what's actually normal, should it get better or worse with age? Or, like, stay the same?'

'Hypothetically speaking,' Sebastian said (fourteen minutes), 'I have no idea. I don't think it's possible to say. Why do you ask?'

Matilda snorted.

'None of your bloody business, you little twerp. Oof, so, shall we hang up? I have to pack Siri's stuff so she can go to her mother's and Billy seems to think she's old enough to do it herself though she can't even put her knickers on the right way around.'

Sebastian had a distinct sense there was something he ought to ask, but he couldn't for the life of him get it together to figure out what it was. This whole conversation with his sister already felt like a dream, even before it had ended. Twelve minutes. His groin was sweating.

'Okay, bye then, Tilda. Speak soon, yeah? Speak to you soon.'

'Yeah. And hey …'

'Yeah?'

'If you speak to Clara can you tell her to sort it out. I want to be friends. Kathleen always says —'

Sebastian didn't hear any more, because suddenly Laura Kadinsky was standing in the doorway. He hung up and dropped the phone into his pocket.

'Sebastian?'

'Yes, Mrs Kadinsky?'

'Call me Laura. Please, call me Laura.'

'Laura. Are you nervous?'

Sebastian looked down at Laura lying on the bed, dressed head-to-toe in white, ready to let herself be conveyed into the thundering arch of the MRI scanner. Such trust, thought Sebastian. How would he ever live up to it.

'No,' Laura answered. 'Of course not. But I want to tell you something. Before you send me into that thing. Before you get a look at it.'

'At what?'

'My sick little soul. Or whatever it is.'

She lifted her arm and rapped herself on the forehead.

'Soul ...' said Sebastian. 'That's a word we don't often hear within these walls.'

And it was true. The question of the soul's existence, a person's quintessence, which transcends and permeates the body, is the neuroscience equivalent of theology's dispute about the doctrine of transubstantiation. As Sebastian had previously implied to Jennifer Travis, he belonged, perhaps as a result of his religious upbringing, to that ever-shrinking faction unable to get away from the idea that the human self must contain something that can't be measured: call it consciousness, call it a soul, call it a spirit. He did his best to cast off this old-fashioned mindset, and for the most part he succeeded. When he didn't succeed he would console himself with the thought that it is doubt that defines consciousness — anyone who doesn't doubt their own beliefs from time to time is, with almost 100 per cent certainty, both blind and deaf in the face of reason. And yet his heart still fluttered when Laura said that forbidden word. A flutter of unease, a butterfly's measure of unbelief, over how Laura so openly, and somehow so touchingly, assumed that both he and science were capable of seeing what they really couldn't: the soul and its contours.

Beneath him, Laura moistened her lips with her tongue. Her head was fastened to the trolley and her eyes were fixed on his. Suddenly he realised she was lying. She was nervous, after all. Not just nervous: she was boltingly, wildly terrified. Of what? He couldn't tell, nor could he ask. He put his hand beside her body on the trolley and hummed. She turned her gaze towards his hand.

'Has anyone told you that you have really beautiful hands?' she said. 'And arms. You have very beautiful forearms, if you'll forgive my saying so.'

That fluttering again, this time inside his ribs, and behind his knees, and in the folds of his trousers around his groin, and finally in the hand that Laura had made beautiful. This too was a kind of transubstantiation, thought Sebastian.

'Sebastian?'

'Mmm?'

Laura Kadinsky raised her eyebrows entreatingly.

'As I said, there was something I wanted to tell you. Are you listening?'

Sebastian blushed.

'Of course. Of course. What did you want to tell me?'

'I've realised something. It's about you. And my daughter's hamster, but mostly about you.'

'About me?'

Laura Kadinsky nodded earnestly, or at least she tried to — her head was still strapped down, making the movement stiff, curtailed.

'There's something special about you. I wasn't sure at first, I thought it was just a coincidence, but now I'm almost convinced. It's the same with Essie the Escapist!' Laura said.

'Essie the what?'

'Chloe's hamster. My daughter. I can see her too, properly. I mean the hamster. Not Chloe, more's the pity.'

'I'm not sure I follow,' Sebastian mumbled, searching for something his gaze could settle on that wasn't Laura's eyes, large and moist and hungry. He tried to think about the very moral monkey. For a moment he wished she could have been there. You couldn't have lab animals in a clinical environment such as this, of course, but if you could — the monkey would have put her foot down, naturally. He himself couldn't. Words became flesh, and the flesh was weak. He looked at his hands. Beautiful. He looked at Laura. Beautiful.

'I can see you, Sebastian. I can see you, properly, the whole of you. That was what I wanted to say.'

'Laura ... Mrs Kadinsky ...'

Sebastian was having difficulty speaking; his throat felt as if it had swollen up.

'What do you think it means?' said Laura excitedly.

'What do I think it means?'

'That whatever's going wrong in my head doesn't apply to *you*. My husband is always completely flat, it's been several weeks since I last saw him properly, and Chloe ... But you're like a clear spot in my vision, you're like the only actor in front of a flat backdrop. I've only met you three times, and yet it feels like you're the only person in the world who truly exists.'

'And the hamster, right?' Sebastian said slowly.

'Yeah. Isn't it funny?'

'From a neurological perspective, quite inexplicable.'

Sebastian stared down into his notebook. He was pretending to make notes in order to avoid looking at Laura's beseeching face. She wanted him to be able to explain it but he couldn't, in the same way he couldn't explain to himself why the mystical trinity she'd traced between herself, him, and the hamster felt so natural.

'You know what,' Laura went on, 'when Philip and Chloe have gone to sleep I creep down to the cellar where Essie spends the night and hold her in my hands. Sometimes I let her run around and then I catch her, just to feel that perfect connection between what I see and what I touch. That the world is whole, if you see what I mean? I think you see. You have to see.'

And there it was again, the fear, or whatever it was — the need — in her eyes. She needed him to see, but he didn't, not really. On the other hand, he could see that Laura Kadinsky needed him, had appointed him as her saviour. But from what? Hard to say. Perhaps a hypothesis would become possible once he'd got these first images of the convolutions of her brain.

'Are you ready?' he asked with a nod at the machine. An ambiguous smile spread across Laura's lopsided face. Then she reached out her hand and laid it almost reverently around his left forearm. Her fingers were cold and slightly clammy, like a nicotine addict's.

For a fraction of a second, the memory of another touch flared — Violetta's fingers, which had been similarly cold and clammy the last time they'd seen each other. She'd been stick-thin then, living on cigarettes and echinacea effervescents. It was outside the Wrangel Library. She was studying art history, but wasn't really interested in the course, she said, it was mostly to pass the time. She was fiddling with the threadbare measuring tape she'd started carrying everywhere with her. He'd asked her why, of course, he'd asked her numerous times, but she'd just shrugged and laughed her new laugh, bright as a brass button. It wasn't until after *what happened happened* that he remembered how she used to wind it round her wrist and read it, the way others look at their watch. But that last time they saw each other, outside the Wrangel, just as the lilacs were coming into bloom and the winter fell away, she didn't measure her own ever-shrinking circumference, but his. She bound his hands with the measuring tape before placing her cold fingers on his cheek. 'Never stop measuring the world, Sebastian,' she said. Then she kissed him on the mouth and left. For some reason he didn't follow her, didn't even call after her. Perhaps because for once, she seemed happy.

'Do you believe in kindred spirits?'

Sebastian jumped. Laura Kadinsky had lifted her fingers from his arm. Suddenly he realised she'd been holding him hard, so hard a pattern glowed white for a few moments where her fingers had been. It was in the shape of a pasty, or possibly an upside-down pelvis with volcanoes for hips.

'Easter Island,' Sebastian said, pointing at his arm.

Laura laughed. Rain on a window. Cat on a hot tin roof.

'Don't dodge the issue. Answer me,' she said.

'In some ways yes, in some ways no,' Sebastian said.

'A very unsatisfying reply,' Laura said.

He shrugged.

'I think it's time to take a look at your soul, Mrs Kadinsky.'

'Say my name,' she said. 'Say my whole name.'

He hesitated a moment.

'Laura,' he said then. 'Laura Kadinsky.'

'Thank you,' she said, and closed her eyes on everything that lay beyond: the hunger and the damnation and, perhaps — even though Sebastian very much doubted it — the salvation.

He walked over to the control panel to check the settings. Then he took out a pair of headphones and put them over Laura's head, taking care not to accidentally touch her cheek. She smiled wanly from behind closed eyes.

'Twenty minutes,' he said, going into the control room. Once he'd come in and turned on the machine, he realised she wouldn't have been able to hear what he said. Trust, he thought again. Such a beautiful, dangerous, seductive thing to have in one's hands, one's beautiful hands. Through the glass he saw Laura moving slowly into the white tunnel, like a corpse being shunted into a crematorium oven. It was a comparison that occurred to him every time he saw someone being channelled into the scanner, and in occasional moments of doubt he would think about how the comparison arose not only from the visual similarity of those two situations, but also went deeper, to the very quaking heart of the issue, to matter and anti-matter and the borderline between them.

This too was one of Sebastian's forbidden doubts: that knowing more doesn't always make us wiser.

He looked at Laura Kadinsky, her irregular little head on its way into the great, perfectly circular tunnel. He leaned his forehead on the glass and listened to the noise. It sounded like the sea.

There was a fervent atmosphere in the Institute staff canteen. It was Friday, a week or so after Laura had touched Sebastian's arm and asked him to say her name. He'd said it thousands of times since then, but only in his head. Still, he knew it was dangerous. There are few things that twine neurones together as hard as verbal statements, and anyone who inscribes another person's name into their neural networks will never forget that person. Faces dissolve and ebb away, but names are like bedrock and scar tissue, indelible.

Sebastian took a tray, filled it with food, and looked around for a place to sit where no one would mind if he didn't talk. He didn't dislike his colleagues, but he felt strange and insufficient, full to the brim with worries big and small, which he was fearful he might air if he opened his mouth. There was Laura, of course, whose sparkling brain he'd analysed for the past week without becoming any the wiser, just more and more convinced it was his responsibility and salvation, at once a prize and a punishment. There was the monkey, who seemed to think everything he did was contemptible. There was the Institute itself, its mysterious machinery, its cogs and levers, the half-articulated threats and promises he couldn't tell apart, the feeling that something was going on right before his eyes, which he was too tired or cowardly or stupid to see. There was the pain and the memory, the dangling toes, the bluest eyes in the world, the ten thousand lightbulbs that had exploded in his chest. And there was his family, the insoluble puzzle that seemed to lack any limits. Matilda had rung again, several times; she refused to leave him in peace. She talked about tiny blue frogs at the Berlin Zoo, and about a film she'd seen starring the former child actor Dakota Fanning, about the world's biggest cheese slicer, which was apparently located in Västerbotten, and about their father, who wasn't answering the phone. Why Matilda had even bothered to ring their father was something Sebastian couldn't bring himself to contemplate.

Sebastian soon realised that the commotion in the canteen had something to do with the ongoing factionalism between Team Bletchley and Team Gödel — several of the most prominent voices on each side were echoing around the room, and Sebastian caught phrases such as 'reductio ad absurdum' and 'Hilbert's second problem'. The only person who didn't seem particularly worked up was Jennifer Travis. She smelled of Pears glycerine soap and marmalade and wet woollen socks, and looked, if anything, bored, as she sat there at a table, noisily slurping tea and twisting a lock of hair round her finger. There was something oracle-esque about her appearance, something wise and self-sufficient.

He sat down at her table.

'Jaffa?'

Travis pushed a plate across and peered at him from beneath her damp fringe.

'What's wrong, Sebastian?'

He hunched his shoulders right up to his ears and looked up at the ceiling. Sighed and dropped his gaze to Travis again. Someone asking him what was wrong, someone to whom he didn't owe anything, someone who wouldn't demand anything, someone he couldn't hurt no matter what he said. He couldn't resist.

'It's my family,' he said hesitantly. 'They want so much from me that I'm not sure I can give. Do you have family?'

Travis let her head fall onto the table, and her broad forehead hit it with a thud. When she lifted it, Sebastian couldn't tell whether the look she fixed him with was amused, irritated, or just confused.

'Sorry,' said Travis, tilting her head. 'I should've been clearer. I didn't mean what's wrong with you. I'm sure there's something wrong with you, there is with most people. I meant, can you see what's wrong with their argument?'

She gestured towards Childs, Jensen, and the others in Team Bletchley, who'd now finished screaming themselves hoarse at Team Gödel and had instead withdrawn to a separate table, where they were in the midst of animatedly drawing up some kind of flowchart on the table with ketchup. Sebastian couldn't make out what it was; more than anything it looked like a Joan Miró drawing, but Travis shook her head suspiciously.

'They haven't got a snowball's chance in hell.'

'I thought you agreed with them that there was a pattern?' Sebastian said.

Travis pouted.

'Oh,' she said. 'There is. Of course there is. But they're using *odd* dates over there. They haven't realised that the relocations that happen on odd dates have quite arbitrary displacement patterns. It's only the relocations on *even* dates that are statistically significant. I figured that out long ago.'

'Aren't you going to tell them, then?' Sebastian asked, casting an anxious gaze over at their table.

Travis looked genuinely surprised.

'Why would I do that?'

'To help them out?'

'Aha, I get it. But they need something to do. Otherwise they'll get restless.'

Travis took a Jaffa cake and nibbled it carefully. Sebastian half expected her to go back to his family now the subject of Team Bletchley seemed all tied up, but she didn't. Sebastian realised, of course, that Jennifer Travis didn't always react the way you might expect a person to, but he still hadn't got used to it. He tried another tack.

'Is it true Alan Turing was your uncle?'

'My dad's uncle. How old do you think I am? But yeah. Though he was already dead when I was born — Alan, I mean. I think we would have got along dreadfully, don't you? You know — he was obsessed with proving that things were unprovable.'

Travis blew a lock of hair out of her face.

'Anyway, he would've detested this place, it's all far too chaotic,' she said, looking as though she were about to get up and go. Sebastian reached out a hand and took hold of her wrist, suddenly convinced that Travis, even if she had no intention of listening to his family problems, would at least be able to clarify a few other things he'd been mulling over. Travis looked at his hand gripping her wrist, but showed no sign of disgruntlement. Sebastian let go, leaning forward to whisper:

'Hey, there's something I've been wondering. I mean, a few things. The others say you're close to Corrigan and so on. I mean, I've been thinking maybe you know … what it's all about. This whole thing.'

'What do you mean?' Travis asked, looking at him suspiciously.

'Well, you know … the work.'

'The work?' Travis cast her eyes around the room cautiously. 'You know we're not supposed to communicate between cells,' she whispered.

'But why not?' Sebastian said. 'It's ridiculous. All research is about sharing results. This seems totally backwards. Actually, this whole place seems totally backwards.' Travis looked at him and bit her lower lip. 'Just don't say anything to Corrigan, okay?' Sebastian added. 'I mean, it's not that I don't appreciate the opportunity to get some proper experience.'

'But experience of what?' Travis said, very, very quietly. 'You're absolutely right, that's the real question. Can I trust you, Sebastian?'

Sebastian nodded cautiously, even though it had been a long time since he'd last thought of himself as a trustworthy person.

'Give me your phone. Come now, hand it over.'

He dug his phone out of his pocket, unlocked it with his thumb, and passed it to Travis. She started jabbing away at it, fast as lightning. They sat quietly for a few minutes as her fingers fluttered.

'I just love Candy Crush, don't you?' Travis said loudly as she kicked him in the shin. 'You're right, Level 372 *is* hard, but … there we go!'

With a grin she passed back the phone. 'I always help Corrigan out with that, he's useless.'

Sebastian looked at the handset he was holding. On the screen was a short note in the memo app: KEEP QUIET. PROB. BUGGED. DUNNO Y BUT STH SHADY AS THEY SAY. CICADAS R THE ANSWER. AWAIT FURTHER INSTR. DON'T CALL ME I'LL CALL U. PS. YOU RLY SUCK AT CANDY CRUSH. PPS. DELETE THIS.

Sebastian looked up at Travis who was standing with her tray. He could have been mistaken, but he thought she looked kind of energised.

'By the way,' Travis said, nodding at the phone. 'You just got an email from your mum. Seems like your dad's gone missing? You should probably read it yourself, it was really hard to understand with Google Translate.'

Sebastian looked down at his phone, which had gone to sleep, dark and dead as a flat black stain on the white Formica table.

'My mum? What? You read it? How —'

Travis shrugged, adjusted her lab coat, and screwed up her nose in distaste.

'They talk about the singularity, but all I can say is that as long as people keep on communicating with this thing we call "language", algorithms are going to have problems.'

And with that, she left Sebastian alone with the latest dispatch from his mother.

SUBJECT: 'Let the children come unto me' (re: your father)
annika.isaksson@svenskakyrkan.se

Dearest son,

I'm going to get right to the point: your father is missing. I wouldn't be too worried if I were you, as we know, he's capricious by nature. You probably don't know this, but he has a woman in Berlin. A younger woman, I should add, though I don't know how many decades younger. She's a drinker, which could go some way to explaining it. In my experience as a tender of souls, women with alcohol problems tend to have very complicated relationships with their own fathers.

In any case, Sebastian, I haven't been able to get hold of him for several weeks and Our Good Lord knows I've tried. There's something I've been meaning to raise with him, something about you and your sisters. I don't want to sound overly dramatic, but it's hard to avoid, since the thing I would have liked to talk to you and him about is of a rather dramatic nature.

He knows what this is concerning, has always known — so we're both equally to blame. Though sometimes I wonder if he's not even more so. I've wanted to speak to you about this matter ever since you've been old enough to understand it, but he's always said no. And I let him decide. Maybe because I thought he was right. Or maybe I was just a coward — if that's the case, I'm the one who's most to blame. I choose to believe he meant well, that he thought it was for the best the way it turned out. I, on the other hand, have always been convinced that we did the wrong thing. But now I'm waffling! You must think your mother's taken leave of her senses. I can assure you that's not the case. In fact, I'm slowly but surely regaining them.

Having children, Sebastian, is like becoming an animal. All the values, all the moral principles you've previously held in high regard are subjugated to this one thing: protecting your children from all harm. It's a paradox, because when you renounce something you know deep inside is right, you yourself become the source of harm. I know you've had a peculiar upbringing, I see it in the people you've become and the problems you've struggled with. Matilda and Clara are clearly not harmonious people, but I want you to know I've seen it in you too, my son — the wildness, that thirst for security. Your relationship with Violetta wasn't healthy. I know you won't like my saying so, but it's true. You gave her everything without getting anything in return, and I let it happen because I didn't have the heart to put a stop to it. Truth be told, I didn't want to be separated from her either. I ached for her, almost like a mother. Somewhere I guess I've always hoped you'd find what you were seeking in Jesus, just like I did.

Have you talked to your sisters yet? Clara tells me she's on Easter Island. Easter Island! It surprises me — she's always been so timid. And Matilda's having a lovely time in Berlin, as far as I can make out. Billy seems to be good for her, and she actually seems to enjoy being a stepmother. You never cease to surprise me, my wonderful children.

I've dabbled with the idea of asking Matilda to track your father down there in Berlin, but it feels futile — I don't even know what this new woman is called, and anyway, I've already made my decision. He's forced me to keep my mouth shut for twenty-six years, but now I've had enough. Oof, now I'm getting all dramatic again! But that's life, I guess — dramatic, dirty, and sometimes dreadfully chaotic. The true sinner is the one who refuses to admit their sin.

I've been thinking a lot about Luther lately — the centenary is just around the corner, and I had the strangest thing happen at the allotment the other day. I'll tell you more another time. But it brought to mind that story about the inkwell, that the devil left Luther's chamber as soon as Luther acknowledged his existence: when he looked up from his scripts, looked him in the eye, and threw an inkwell at his evil figure. I think this email, even though it's written in ones and zeros rather than with a quill, can serve as my inkwell. I'm going to write to your sisters as well, but I wanted to write to you first, so you can help me convince them to speak to each other, and with you, and with me. I know they've not always got along, and I'm worried that what I have to tell you will make the situation even worse. They're going to need your calm.

Of course I know it's futile to think I might be able to gather you all here with me, even if it's what I really want. But with three children on different sides of the planet I realise we'll have to use modern means. I've learned to use Skype, you see — it's very practical when you have to account for souls as far afield as Torna Hällestad. So I propose we meet in a group chat as soon as possible. You can add me using my email address, but I suppose you already know that. I understand your beautiful head must be awhirl with questions right now, but you must understand I can't say any more in writing. Please respond and let me know when you can talk, but don't ask any questions — I don't yet quite understand how I'm going to be able to answer them. On this matter and more, I'm going to pray over the coming days.

Remember that God loves you unreservedly, as does

Your mother

PS. This thing about Clara and Easter Island is truly incredible. I can't for the life of me understand what she's doing there.

II
EASTER ISLAND

Easter Island. The loneliest place on earth. A triangle of volcanoes and dragonflies, located 3,501 kilometres from the Chilean mainland, 2,075 kilometres from the nearest inhabited landmass. Considering that the speed of sound in sea air is somewhere between 330 and 340 metres per second depending on air temperature, you can calculate, with simple arithmetic, that a cry for help from the rocky coast of Easter Island would reach the mainland in around three hours. By that point it would most likely be too late to catch the person falling.

There are also 887 gigantic stone statues on the island, each with eye-holes as large as heavenly bodies. A few centuries ago, the islanders decided to build the statues instead of finding food, and then fill their empty stomachs with nonsense. There were gods involved, and obsession, belief in a higher order. Unsurprisingly, the islanders all died.

EVERY LAST ONE!

Apart from maybe three or four.

They had babies who had babies who grew up only to see the statues wither and fall apart. And then? You can read the rest on Wikipedia. That was what Clara Isaksson did the same evening she got the sack, she read until her eyes shrivelled up like raisins. Then she cried until they regained their lustre, and booked some flights: Stockholm–Frankfurt–Buenos Aires–Santiago–Rapa Nui. A week in Buenos Aires, to acclimatise, two days in Santiago, then three weeks in the loneliest place on earth, where not too many years ago the sun was eclipsed for thirty long minutes, and tourism boomed like never before.

Few things attract tourists as much as the promise of a foretaste of the apocalypse.

There's a single conurbation on Easter Island, and it's called Hanga Roa. Six thousand people live there, and it's also the location of the airport: the damp fog, the weak lights along the landing strip like fireflies, their little glowing behinds.

From above, the landing strip looked like a strip of tape marking off the south-western tip of the island. Clara Isaksson — twenty-six years old, dark-haired, blue-eyed, afraid of everything and very much aware of it, the sister of a sister who wasn't much of a sister, and of a brother who was the centre of the world, currently on the run from a life that wasn't much of a life — pressed her nose against the window and tried to see what was beyond the broad brushstroke of the landing strip, but she couldn't see anything.

Just black.

When Clara stepped into the harsh light of the arrivals hall, she was struck — not for the first time and definitely not for the last — by a strong sense of alienation from her fellow humans. In this case, from her fellow passengers, who were few — most of them clearly hardened backpackers with whom Clara had absolutely no way of identifying. It smelled of air freshener and the cold tile floor had been scrubbed clean, even the crumbling grouting, but still, the floor wasn't clean, not really. Because it was moving. The floor was shape-shifting under a carpet of cockroach-like beetles, bronze-coloured and leisurely and everywhere, a moving carpet of vermin. Clara blinked, started sweating, blinked again. How was this possible? It wasn't possible, but it was true. Of course, before coming here she'd had nightmares about all kinds of vermin, parasites, and spiders as big as your palms with rustling pipe-cleaner legs, of course she'd read everything there was to read about snake bites and what to do if you were surrounded by a troupe of ferocious monkeys, of course she'd been vaccinated against TB and Hep B and a few diseases she couldn't even pronounce, but this inferno, so soon? And why was she the only one reacting?

Clara stood stock-still just inside the swing doors that led into the arrivals hall and searched vainly for a path through the sea of insects. She breathed through her nose, just like she'd learned from Matilda, before Matilda stopped talking to her and fled to the other side of the world to teach the girls of the future to read instead. Sebastian always said you could teach the brain to unlearn anything, not least panic attacks, which, after all, were nothing more than a physical reaction to a destructive cognitive pattern, so Clara breathed through her nose and thought constructive thoughts, like how a vibrant insect life was a natural and crucial part of a functioning ecosystem and therefore something to be happy about, and really, we should be delighted by this apparently vigorous species of … What was it actually? Clara tentatively opened her eyes again, trying to focus on a single individual in the muddle of beetles, but it was almost impossible, they were absolutely everywhere. Their fragile little feet against the ground — thousands upon thousands of them — howled like the wind. They piled up in drifts under chairs, carried each other involuntarily on their backs, fondling flip-flopped feet and trainers.

'Señora?'

Clara shrieked as a hand landed on her shoulder.

'Señora, is there a problem?'

Beside her stood a man in uniform. It looked like a military uniform, and Clara didn't like the military; she was a pacifist except possibly in times of extreme crisis. Was this a time of extreme crisis?

Her heart said yes, but her heart was a treacherous thing.

'No,' Clara whispered. 'No, no problem.'

'Why is the señora just standing here?' the uniformed man said in Spanish. Clara wasn't good at Spanish, but still managed to stammer out a comprehensible and, to her own mind, feasible explanation.

'I … I'm waiting for bags.'

'The bags have arrived,' said the uniformed man sharply and jerked his head towards one of the arrivals hall's two luggage carousels. He had the beginnings of a pate, and evil eyes, observed Clara, then she felt bad. Maybe they weren't evil, maybe they were just intense.

'Of course, yes,' Clara mumbled and stood up straighter, sweeping her sweaty locks from her forehead. 'Muchas gracias.'

The security guard, or whatever he was, murmured doubtfully and backed away, but he didn't take his eyes off Clara. It was clear she had no choice but to move. Tentatively she took a first step forward. The beetle sea parted, but didn't go away. Cautiously she took another step, searching for human eyes that could confirm these creatures existed and that they were an anomaly, something to be surprised and revolted by, but in vain; everyone else just went on walking towards the exit, towards the cafe, they ordered café con leche in little white paper mugs and dry sandwiches in several layers of plastic, they drank the coffee and unwrapped the sandwiches and ate, talking, then dropped the plastic on the floor, turned their phones on, dug around in their bags, as if the floor was just a floor and not an inferno. So Clara carried on. She walked so fast the beetles had no time to get out of the way, and were crushed under her feet, crunching in confirmation that they really existed, which was something of a relief. She was many things — scared stiff by almost everything, including beetles, men in uniform, professional humiliation, steady relationships, the end of the world, and all kinds of extreme weather — but at least she wasn't psychotic. Almost triumphantly, Clara yanked her rucksack off the baggage reclaim, hoisted it onto her shoulder and began, with the biggest strides possible, to make her way towards the exit. The doors were open to the sultry, dark night, heavy with the scent of the sea and moist vegetation and a hint of rubbish, and the beetle carpet continued out through the doors, not stopping until nature, the unknown, took over. Clara was already regretting having come here, but there was no space, no time, for regret.

Clara had, in spite of everything, one trait that could be called a strength, and that was that she always finished what she started. Actually, it wasn't so much a strength as a survival strategy. Those naturally prone to anxiety and vacillation, among whose number Clara had counted herself since childhood, don't have the luxury of changing their minds or compromising, because if they did, they'd never do anything but change their minds and compromise for all eternity, and that's no way to live. Clara knew that if she didn't see *everything* through, she'd never see anything through. This knowledge had led to her doing all kinds of rash things over the years, not least this trip, not least the time she'd laid down on a bed of glass and let a quack fakir stand on her head, not least the time she'd dived into the quarry at Dalby Stenbrott, or all the terrible sex she'd had with potential carriers of sexually transmitted diseases just because she'd glimpsed a pair of beautiful eyes and immediately decided they were going to see her naked.

She took a deep breath and walked through the doors.

That was when she felt an itch on her neck. Or perhaps not an itch, but a creeping, a tip-tap-tip-tap-tippy-tappy-tip-tap, from her shoulder, along her neck and up behind her ear. It was no more than a second from perception to realisation to reaction. Clara tore off her rucksack and threw it on the ground, flailing at her neck, throat, head, face, body, flailing until her palms burned. It didn't help, something was still moving on her skin, under her top now. She didn't stop to think, just tore it off, throwing it on the floor alongside her rucksack. She could no longer breathe the way Matilda had taught her, she was breathing the way blind fear had taught her — hard, fast, shallow. The oxygen got no further than the top of her ribs, hovering there and bubbling while her head swelled and other parts of her body grew shaky. And she could still feel it moving, now she could see it, the insect, as it crept under her bra strap, on its way round to her back. It must have been inside her rucksack, perhaps there were more in there, she took a quick look down at her few possessions, the only things she had to hold on to in this strange new place, and realised she was lost, that she no longer had anything, because she'd dropped her top and her rucksack on the ground, and now they belonged to that scuttling mass of legs and shells that surged over every nook and cranny. Clara scratched herself on the back and opened her mouth to scream, but no scream came out, and at that moment the hand landed on her shoulder again, like a raven, the fingers boring into the hollow between her collarbone and her shoulder, she couldn't escape.

'Señora, señora?'

A slap in the face.

'Señora, you on drugs? Narcotics? Señora, you have to come with.'

Clara shook her head in confusion. The uniformed man with black eyes had loosened his grip on her shoulder, but only so he could turn her around. Now he took hold of both her shoulders instead, trying to read her face as though he were solving a sudoku.

'Señora, look me in the eye. You okay?'

'No, no,' was all Clara could manage.

'You on drugs, right? We don't accept drugs. You come with me now.'

'No drugs, just bugs. Cucaracha, no se? Cucaracha?'

Clara's breathing was still laboured, and she gestured at the floor as well as she could. She could still feel her skin crawling, but she was held in the strange man's grasp as securely as in a rollercoaster, she couldn't get her arms round to her back.

The guard pouted and shook his head suspiciously, glancing at the floor and kicking vaguely at a few insects. 'No cucaracha. They're cicadas. It's their mating season. But these ones are dead, you see that, no? No flying, no singing. No one knows why. They just die. Big problem.'

Now there was no time for Clara to process this, because the guard had taken a hard grip on her arm and was leading her to a door bearing the words *ADUANAS — CUSTOMS*.

Clara was struck by a terrible thought.

What if there actually *were* drugs in her bag? How could she be sure? Wasn't it possible, or even likely, in light of this guard's absurd interest in her, that the whole thing was a charade, that something had been planted in her bag by, say, a Chilean customs official in cahoots with the police so they could have a crackdown and dress up their statistics? Oh good god. Clara felt herself starting to sweat, a trickle ran down her jaw, another between her breasts, oh good lord, she was half naked from the waist up, how had that happened? She'd taken her top off. What kind of idiot takes off their top at a South American airport, what kind of idiot loses their head over a layer (admittedly a thick layer) of dead insects on the ground? What kind of idiot travels alone to the loneliest place on earth and lets themselves be taken into police custody?

'You don't understand,' she stammered in English through chattering teeth, 'I have panic attacks, it's medical, okay? Not drugs. I am fine now, I am fine, please. Please!'

The guard didn't answer, just pushed open the door. Clara caught a glimpse of the room within: it was empty and bare, with pale blue walls cracked with damp, a rickety table with a melamine top, a bulky computer and a coffee machine, a poster of a solitary moai statue, the nose broad, the nipples two protruding knobs. Clara pulled her arm automatically across her chest, trying to conceal her breasts and the flight of her heart. What was going to happen? Would she be put in prison or just deported, would she be raped? The thought stopped Clara in her tracks. A life lived in preventative fear had prepared her for many things, but weirdly enough, sexual violence had never figured that prominently in her nightmares. Maybe, she said to herself as she tried to tear her eyes away from the moai's emphatically bulging nipples, she'd thought of it as too banal. Too predictable. Unimaginative. She'd never walked home from the station at night with her keys tucked between her knuckles. She'd never got nervous about male taxi drivers or felt compelled to turn around in the stairwell and check to make sure no one had forced a size-eight-or-larger foot in between the door and its frame. She'd never even been afraid of being mugged in the Shurgard units during that depressing week in the suburbs.

And now here was her punishment.

'Please …' she whimpered one last time, before the guard shoved her through the door. She closed her eyes and saw her own naked ribcage before her, her bra ripped off, ribcage ripped open; she saw her ribcage like a prison corridor, door after door slamming shut in a claustrophobic darkness without end, and how she would have to wander that corridor every day for the rest of her life.

But no door slammed shut. Instead she heard a voice that was neither hers nor the guard's. An American voice, deep and hoarse, like an old-fashioned film star's. She couldn't tell if it belonged to a man or a woman.

'Mister? Wait a second. Wait a second. I know this woman.'

Clara felt the guard's grip on her arm relax a fraction. It was enough to allow her to twist her torso and catch a glimpse of this person who was no more than a metre away but had still managed to mistake her for somebody else. Clara was annoyed. She had no desire to wait for the catastrophe that now seemed unavoidable.

'Excuse me?' the guard said. 'This woman belong to you?'

'Well, I wouldn't say she *belongs* to me,' the person said (Clara was now fairly sure it was a woman) and smiled wonkily with bright red lips. 'I don't own anyone. But she's my friend. What's the problem?'

Clara tried to make eye contact with the stranger, but failed. She was wearing impenetrable sunglasses of the old Hollywood style, and was lounging on one hip, sharp as an elbow. Her arms and legs were long and made Clara think of cold, soggy French fries; they were kind of slippery and had a sickly yellow-blue pallor, so thin they looked like they would flutter up at the merest breath of wind. Her head was wreathed with shiny black curls, apparently well massaged with argan oil. Her brow was high and white, her cheeks powder-pink. Her shoulders were as broad as a man's, but her hands as small as a child's.

The guard cast a confused look at Clara and then back to the stranger.

'What is your name, señor ... a?'

'Elif.'

'Is that first or last name? What is your friend's name?'

Clara swallowed. She wondered whether it was possible that this Elif was under the influence herself. Otherwise you'd think that by this point she'd have figured out she had the wrong person. Of course, Clara didn't have extensive experience of people high on drugs, but she was a journalist — wearing sunglasses indoors was a hallmark of users everywhere.

Instead of answering the guard's question, the woman took a step towards Clara and reached out her hand, put it on her shoulder and smiled broadly.

'Honey, why don't you tell the gentleman your name?'

Clara flinched in surprise at the touch, but soon felt a peculiar calm spreading through her body, from the shoulder in question and out into each of her unfeasibly tense limbs. She opened her mouth like a fish and out tumbled her name.

'Clara. Clara Isaksson.'

Elif turned back to the guard. Now she suddenly started speaking Spanish, a fluent, rattling Spanish far beyond the basic conversation Clara could muster.

'You see, señor, my friend is having a panic attack. There's no danger, she's never violent, just scared. She has a phobia of insects, too, and when she saw all these … cicadas, they are cicadas, right? Thought so. When she saw all these cicadas it triggered an attack. But as you can see, she's calmed down now. We're going to our hotel. We're staying at EcoVillage, you know the place, señor? Lovely spot, a really lovely spot. My name is Elif, Elif DeSanto. Perhaps you've heard of me? Seen some of my films? I'm here to film a music video, Clara's keeping me company, we've been friends since childhood, I know her better than anyone —'

'She seems to be high on drugs, señora.'

'No, no, not Clara. Claralita, are you on drugs?'

Clara automatically shook her head.

'She would never,' Elif went on, as she too shook her head emphatically. 'You see, her brother …' Elif drew her finger across her narrow throat.

The guard squirmed awkwardly. Elif would have been half a foot taller than him even without shoes, but in her high stilettos she could have rested her chin on the man's head. Clara saw her dig her hand into the pocket of her stonewashed denim shorts, and with a studied discretion, pull something out which she handed to the guard, concealed in her palm.

'We're in a bit of a rush; I'd appreciate it if you'd let my friend go. Where's her bag?'

The guard put out his hand to take Elif's. His was large and clumsy, Elif's little, and she laid her other hand over his so it was completely enclosed, and shook it heartily.

'Muchas gracias, señor. I promise my friend won't cause any trouble.'

The guard swiftly lowered his hand and stuffed it into his pocket with a rustle. He wrinkled his nose and gave Clara a quick nod.

'Señora, you can go with your friend. Put a shirt on.'

Clara didn't move. The strange woman held out her hand as if to a child.

'Come on, Clara. Let's go to the hotel. I guarantee you it will be insect-free, or you'd hope so, given the price!'

Elif gave a short laugh, linked arms with Clara, and pulled her towards the exit.

'My bags …' Clara whispered.

Elif gestured towards a baggage trolley. On it, Clara's rucksack and top were arranged neatly above three suitcases bearing the distinctive Louis Vuitton logo. They got to the trolley and Clara snatched her top, too confused to even shake it before putting it on.

'Don't worry, it's been sanitised,' Elif said, shifting her bony hip. For the first time, her unknown benefactor seemed to look right at her, even if it was hard to tell through the sunglasses.

'Can you take off your sunglasses? It's bad manners not to look the person you're talking to in the eye,' said Clara.

'But I can look you in the eye perfectly well,' Elif replied and tilted her head. 'If anything, you're the one showing bad manners by not looking into mine. But let's not argue now, my dear, we've only just met.'

Clara followed Elif out of the terminal building and looked on as she lit a cigarette.

'Thanks,' Clara said, inhaling the humid evening air, the cigarette smoke, and the song of those cicadas still living. 'How much did you pay him? I can pay you back. I think.'

Elif laughed and sat down on a stone bench.

'Don't worry, sister. I'm rich.'

'Are you really an actor?'

'You can't tell? I'm almost hurt.'

Clara looked out into the darkness. A few taxis crept along the road; it was gravel, and seemed to glow in the moonlight.

'Why did you help me?'

Elif put out her cigarette against the bench.

'I've seen my fair share of panic attacks, and I know when people start throwing their clothes on the ground, things are really bad. Plus, I like buying things. Freedom is a commodity like any other.'

'I thought he was going to rape me,' Clara said.

Elif shrugged.

'Very possible. Probably not, but it would have meant hassle and delays and calls to ambassadors and paperwork and so on, that's bad enough. Where are you from?'

'Sweden.'

'Exotic.'

'To some, maybe.'

'To an American, everything's exotic. Are you staying at EcoVillage?'

'No,' Clara said, not even knowing what it was. 'Just some hotel, I can't remember what it's called. I'll get a taxi now, I think. Thanks again. For … saving me, or whatever.' She realised that sounded cold, so she added: 'I mean it. It was a lovely thing to do.'

'Even ugly girls do good things sometimes. Shall we share a cab? I've ordered a car, it should be here any minute.'

But Clara was already making for a taxi. She shook her head without turning around and jumped in.

She'd booked the cheapest hotel she could find. Still, it was beautiful, at least from a distance, if you squinted in the dim evening light and came from a country where everything wreathed in warm darkness is considered beautiful. When Clara got out of the taxi the ground was solid and still. No insects, alive or dead. The palms swayed and the white-washed walls swayed, a pool shone turquoise in the light from a clutch of coloured bulbs, and a tourist was lying knocked-out on a sun lounger, looking decadent and innocent all at once: classic alcohol-induced slumber. Inside the low hotel building it smelled strongly of chlorine from the cold clinker floors. Clara counted ten little imitation moai in the reception alone — at least, she assumed it was the reception, based on the small brass bell on the counter, and the open mini-refrigerator full of beer and toothpaste that was behind it. Clara rang the bell, and realised as she did so that her hand was still shaking — and suddenly she saw all the cracks in the walls, the hotel's thin varnish coming away like day-old nail polish, the ants travelling along the seams in the clinker despite the bleach, the patches of mould that bloomed on the receptionist's cheeks as she slowly came shuffling out from behind the faded drapes.

We each create our own hell, Matilda had said once, sitting by the kitchen window in the yellow house in Professorsstaden. She seemed to mean it. Matilda had always been of the opinion that you reap what you sow, that once you've made your bed you must lie in it, that karma was something to be mindful of, and that the external world was really just a physical manifestation of our inner one. This, according to Matilda, explained how people could have such different understandings of the world. 'Objectively speaking,' she'd said, taking a drag on her American Spirit, 'we're all living in different worlds. It's up to each of us to decide what form that world takes.' Sebastian, who'd been a little tipsy that evening, had been trying to do tricks on his skateboard, but had fallen in a heap on the floor. 'That doesn't sound the slightest bit objective,' he'd said. 'That sounds like horseshit. It sounds like the most unscientific drivel I've heard in my life.' But he'd laughed, and Matilda had laughed, and they'd eaten Wall's vanilla right out of the tub and smoked the last of Matilda's cigarettes, Matilda and Clara top and tailing on the kitchen bench, and Sebastian perched on the oven, already so tall he had to hunch over to avoid catching his hair on the extractor fan. They were sixteen, home alone for a whole weekend while their mother was at camp with her confirmands and their father was 'at a conference' with a red-haired German Shepherd breeder from the Söderslätt region, and Clara often thought they'd probably never been so close before or since, and that maybe, if it hadn't been for everything that had happened later, if it hadn't been for Violetta and for Matilda's loyalty card at the psych ward, and for Clara herself — if she hadn't created her own personal hell — then maybe they would still have been able to sit there together, just being, more or less. Instead: email and smoke signals, deciphering signs in coffee grounds and internet histories. Instead: Easter Island, this hotel, Clara's very own personal hell. She felt more and more certain of it as she followed the sullen receptionist along a dark corridor with flickering lightbulbs.

She complained her way to a room change three times. Since her Spanish was pretty ropey and the receptionist spoke terrible English, it went a little like this: Clara — after stepping into her allotted room and suffering another, if milder, panic attack from the heavy scent of mould — would rush out into the corridor and gesticulate at the doors to other rooms. The receptionist — who seemed used to this reaction — would trudge off to another room, whereupon the procedure was repeated. This happened twice more, until Clara acknowledged defeat with a nod, and let the receptionist tuck the key into her pocket and pat her on the cheek with a dry, wrinkled hand, which was surprisingly reassuring.

After that, Clara, now truly alone, squatted on the floor and cried. She dared not lie down, since the floor was striped with filth and black mould. She knew this wouldn't have bothered her sister in the slightest. Matilda had spent two years in Bangladesh and lived in worse conditions than these. She'd gone without washing for days at a time, been a mosquito net away from dying of dengue fever, and found a scorpion in the pocket of her dress. Clara knew all this, because even though she never replied, she read Matilda's emails with almost pious exactitude. She knew everything about the man Matilda had loved and betrayed, about her departure from Bangladesh, the move to Berlin, the new man, the stepchild, the cafe job, the electric-blue frogs at Berlin Zoo, and the brightly coloured paper kites at Tempelhof. She followed her sister's life like a soap opera, but she wanted nothing to do with it, not really. Being here was enough, with the shadow of a letter in the palm of her hand. J. J for joker, J for it's just the end of the world, J for Jesus Christ, help me.

J for Jordan.

In the end she got cramp in her thighs and tear ducts. Clara stood up, wiped away her snot with her sleeve, and resolved to pull herself together. She wasn't Matilda, but goddamn it, she was a journalist. Journalists love penury and personal privations. The sound of bombs falling outside their hotel window sends life pulsing through journalists' veins; a little filth here and there can't touch them. With her jaw locked and her eyes wide, Clara pushed open the door to the little toilet, inspected dispassionately the verdigris-coated bathtub and the shower in the form of a mouldy hose with no shower head, the unemptied bin from which there issued a stench she suspected was the product of someone else's menstruation, and the inauspicious crack in the mirror which split her face in two. She washed her face in a chlorine haze that made her nostrils numb, brushed her teeth with lukewarm mineral water, and went to get into bed. It was here that her courage failed her for a moment, and she lay down on top of the quilt. Before she fell asleep, the thought she'd been anticipating popped into her head: *What am I doing here?* The fear didn't really take hold of her until she realised that *here* didn't refer to the place, Easter Island, or the hotel from hell, but to life in a very general sense.

And that was when she heard the rat. Or what, given the sound, must have been a rat, even if she didn't see it. Clara respected rats' right to exist, she really did, but she didn't want to sleep in a room with them. Without any actual conscious decision, she jumped out of the bed, grabbed her scarf, and ran out into the corridor, out through the door, around the building to the pool area where the drunk man was still sleeping like an exhausted angel on his sun lounger. She carefully stroked his stubbly cheek before lying down on the next lounger. In the morning, she thought, the sun will rise and everything will be washed clean in the blinding daylight. In the morning she'd find someone who was more frightened than she was, who maybe had or maybe hadn't lost the same thing she had. She fell asleep, clutching the scarf like a comfort blanket under her chin.

The following morning, she was woken by the pling of a text. Her brain reacted to the sound like a new mother fished out of sleep by her child's cry, conditioned by equal parts fear and compulsive love. Maybe that's how all modern humans operated, but, though she couldn't be sure, she suspected it probably had more to do with all those years of disasters popping up on her phone at frequent but irregular intervals, almost always originating from her mother, almost always concerning Matilda, and if not Matilda, then Sebastian or his wisp of a girlfriend.

She sat up groggily and looked around. The night-time drunk was gone; she was alone with the pool's muddy mirror. She pressed her scarf against her nose and breathed in the scent. It already smelled less like her, more like sun cream and sweat and lukewarm spilt milk. On the way, she'd stayed her seven days in Buenos Aires as planned, then the three in Santiago, a total of ten days of Casa Rosada and café con leche and late, solitary nights on hotel balconies. She'd seen Pablo Neruda's house La Chascona, and the complex layout had made her dizzy. She'd drunk pisco sours and hidden from a stray dog. And now here she was. Her first long trip ever, and she'd chosen as her destination the end of the world, for the sole reason that the world was ending and she wanted someone who knew her sister to hold her hand while it did.

With a sigh, Clara fished her phone out of the tote bag she'd stowed under one arm while she slept. She took a deep breath before activating the screen. She could relax, it wasn't from home. *Sry but got to take care of someth. Same time tomorrow? X Jordan.* Clara's stomach ache came right back. The only thing she liked less than interviewing people was the dread of interviewing them. Now she had a whole twenty-four hours before she could put this meeting behind her. Not that there was any hurry, but still. And anyway, she didn't like people who were inconsistent in their text abbreviations; it seemed simultaneously affected and lazy, as if they were making an effort to seem nonchalant but hadn't realised they actually didn't need to make an effort, because their inability to see the charade through attested to their extreme nonchalance. Clara texted back a short okay and dropped her phone into her bag. Another day of solitude.

Clara had got the sack just before Christmas. It wasn't only the planet that was in a precarious state — the news media was also under constant existential threat. That was the (unspoken) reason why Clara, along with a third of the staff at the paper where she worked, was asked to clear her desk and join the growing freelance precariat, to do her bit to save the imperilled world of journalism from certain destruction.

'You understand, of course ...' her manager had said, the manager who didn't look like one, because in this new media landscape all the managers were just that: managers, not journalists; correspondingly, they had to make an extra effort not to look like what they really were, that is, managers brought in from the business world to carve gold with their butcher's knives. 'You understand, of course,' her manager said, 'that we can't afford to go on producing quality journalism if that means we have to pay a load of people to produce it?'

The most tragic part was that Clara actually had understood. Maybe not that particular example, but the principle, the need for a *cost-benefit analysis* — at the point where costs exceed income, the risks also exceed the opportunities, and risks must be handled with the greatest of care. You have to handle them with kid gloves — or ideally not at all. The manager had therefore decided not to take the risk to the paper's future survival, which Clara and her mediocre efforts as an all-round reporter constituted. That had been deeply wounding and worrying as concerned her private finances, of course, but it hadn't upset Clara's principles. 'We have a responsibility to our readers, I'm sure you'll agree, to go on fighting for our survival in this infantilised landscape of fake news and ten-a-penny blogs,' the manager had said, stroking his beard. After that he talked for a while about how the paper needed to expand its vision, in these hard times, as to what journalism was and could be. Who was a journalist? Did it necessarily have to be someone who'd studied journalism, or could it be a bold young haircare entrepreneur with a burning passion for consumer rights? Perhaps it could be a child, with a child's natural curiosity and inclination to ask 'But why?' 'Forgive me for getting a bit philosophical,' said her manager, 'but don't the words "journalist" and "human being" really mean the same thing? Shouldn't everyone with a brain and a heart be able to call themselves a journalist?'

Clara didn't think so, not at all, but what could she say? She hummed in agreement and was given a choice: either she'd resign voluntarily, or she would be relocated to a new project outside of editorial. The aim of this project was to digitise all the unprinted letters to the editor dating 1972–2002 that had been stored in the paper's physical archive. These decades-old letters and poison-pens from Scientologists, know-it-alls, and alleged Olof Palme murderers would then be used to create everything from clickbait quizzes to podcasts and supplements. 'Because madness,' the manager said, 'sells just as well as sex, if not better.' The work was expected to take between twelve and eighteen months, and would be carried out in the four Shurgard storage units in Kungens Kurva Retail Park that the paper had been using as a slush pile since 2003. Of course, there was no pressure to accept this task, if, for some strange reason, the prospect didn't appeal. If she wanted to go on with the day-to-day journalistic work that 'would always be at the heart of the paper', the possibility was always there — as a freelancer.

Of the seventy-two employees who'd been threatened with relocation to Kungens Kurva, seventy-one had said no, and thereby quit. One said yes, and that was Clara. Partly, this was because she was scared stiff of freelance life, and partly it was because she was genuinely fascinated by the mad and the obsessed. But after a week, she could stand no more of Kungens Kurva. Too many shadows in the corners, too much asbestos dust in her nose, too few escape routes should the ceiling collapse. She'd gone to the manager and let him kick her out, out and down the hallway. Then she'd made up her mind. She had her very own conspiracy theorist to take on, her own fate to follow, her own rabbit hole to fling herself down.

Clara resisted the impulse to sneak over to the place where she knew the camp was and spy, and instead spent the day wandering around Hanga Roa. If she got caught, she'd be seen as nosy and disrespectful, and that was no way to form a rapport with these people. That was what Clara told herself — actually, it was probably just like most things, that she wanted to avoid any chance of interpersonal confrontation.

Some people would have described Clara as brusque, but it was more a case of poorly concealed shyness. Clara didn't like new people, or maybe she just didn't like people, plain and simple, she wasn't sure. The problem with not liking (new) people was that it got pretty lonely in the long run. Unless you had pets, but Clara didn't like animals either. She liked plants, but that was as far as she would stretch. She liked the sea, the trees, stones and minerals. The big movements, continental plates, the world as a system, an immortal organism.

And now it was going to die. The earth. It was impossible to ignore. Or rather, it was possible, many people did, that was the problem. But Clara couldn't. Ecological collapse was, in fierce competition, her biggest sore point, her hardest tension knot, the little chunk of frozen ground which — in contrast to Siberia's permafrost — never thawed completely. She wasn't sure when it had started, it had always been there in some form, but it had escalated over the last few years, ever since she first saw the patch — the patch of blue below Greenland. Blue was the most beautiful colour, thought Clara, but there were rules for where it was and wasn't allowed to be — on the rounded belly of a bird, yes, in the fine veins on the inside of a beautiful man's wrist, absolutely. But not in the middle of the Gulf Stream. And yet that was where it had been found, the mysterious blue patch that wasn't actually blue, not really — just on the diagrams of increases in global temperatures. Everywhere glowed red, because, of course, the world was getting warmer; that was old news. But there, below Greenland, the sea had actually got colder. Good news? Of course not. It was terrible news, because it could only mean one thing: that the glaciers had melted so much and so quickly that the meltwater flowing off them had affected the complex system of undersea currents, meaning the Gulf Stream itself had grown colder.

It was as she was compulsively googling the blue patch that she came into contact with Jordan for the first time. He had a blog, like it was still 2007 (he also had a MySpace page, so maybe his clock had stopped sometime around then, or maybe it was some kind of anachronistic protest), where he wrote about the end of the world. Not really with those words — he expressed himself more elegantly than that — but that was the essence. He wrote about the fear, the grief, how difficult it was to reconcile yourself to the idea that the natural world was dying. Clara had read a lot about this stuff, more than was healthy: she'd read everything worth reading about the Anthropocene and the seventh mass extinction and bee colony collapse and the brand-new continent made up of plastic waste that was floating around in the Pacific Ocean. But she'd never read anything like this, anything so resigned, so raw, so totally lacking in purpose, if by purpose you expected something relating to environmental issues to be at least a little hopeful and constructive.

This guy Jordan believed, apparently, that it was already too late, that no so-called climate solutions would be able to halt the catastrophe, that tech optimism and rolled-up sleeves were just a new phase of the same illusion that had brought the human race to this very point: the conviction that humans had power, when actually, they were, and always had been, totally powerless. The human race's sole distinguishing feature was, in Jordan's eyes, the ability to deceive itself. That was a strength, but also a weakness. Jordan claimed to love this weakness and to disdain it. He'd seen it in himself, during his years as an environmental activist and aid worker, and in the end he couldn't take it any more. He'd given up. All he wanted now was to come to terms with his own fears, his own grief. He wanted to be close to nature on a small scale, not because it would make any difference to the planet, but because it was the only worthy end he could imagine. The battle was lost, and so it was better to stop and enjoy the view rather than to keep fighting. So he went to live in a cabin in Vermont, he wrote his blog, he brewed his tea over a wood stove and learned the names of all the fish in the stream. He baited his lines with worms and slept under the stars. He was a Thoreau without ideals or hopes for the future, a preacher without promises, an apostle of dread. And it wasn't only Clara who seemed to find a certain comfort in this comfortless existence — his blog had a small but loyal following with whom he sporadically interacted.

Clara had followed Jordan's blog for a little over a year when three things happened. The first was that Jordan left the States. The reason why was never really explained, but Clara read between the lines that it had something to do with tax debts (not for nothing was she a taxman's daughter). In the same instant, the blog vanished. Clara hadn't realised how much she needed it until it was gone, but after three weeks the sense of loss had grown so powerful that she'd taken a gamble and emailed the address she'd found at the bottom of a screengrab of an entry about uprooted trees — and he'd responded. They'd corresponded. She'd told him she was a journalist, because she didn't know what else to say, why she'd got in contact, what she wanted from him. It was true, of course: she was a journalist. It was also true that she was alone and scared and had a strong suspicion that this wasn't the only thing tying her own, pathetic life to Jordan's. She'd told him she wanted to interview him. He'd said okay, but she'd have to come to him.

He was on Easter Island and he wasn't alone.

She'd told him that was impossible. But then the second thing happened: Clara got the sack. And then the third: she got an email from Matilda, more urgent than any that had come before: *Now it's damn well time we made peace. Come to Berlin, or I'll come find you in Stockholm.*

But Clara wasn't ready to make peace. Maybe she never would be. The fact was that she was pretty convinced that battle was lost, so to speak. Better to look at the view than to fight on, better to come to terms with your grief: look that which scares you in the face.

She could have gone to Berlin to meet her sister. Instead she went to Easter Island to look for her in the resigned eyes of a stranger.

Hanga Roa was like nowhere Clara had ever seen, but then she hadn't seen that much. Lund, Stockholm. Paris, once. The peak of Kebnekaise, in her dreams. The Bhairab River and the Spree, on the internet.

London, on the internet.

In none of these places had Clara seen a church painted in leopard print. In none of these places had she seen great cupped flowers as big as the palm of your hand and a deep nail-varnish pink. In none of these places had the air tasted of grilled chicken and Coca-Cola, salt water and passion fruit. At lunchtime Clara discovered that there was more than one type of passion fruit. She'd had no idea. Towards the afternoon she discovered it was really quite exciting to go down streets without knowing where they led.

But towards the evening she realised she was scared, still. Scared, and alone. She thought about the email she'd sent to Sebastian before she left. She'd tried to stay jokey, but she had a feeling the anxiety peeped through, unfortunately. She didn't want to lay it on Sebastian, she never had done. In contrast to Matilda, she'd never tried to lay claim to Sebastian's attention. So she'd left him in peace, ever since *what happened happened*. He had enough of his own sorrow; if he needed Clara, he'd get in touch. That was how it was.

Except, of course, that wasn't how it was at all.

Clara was scared.

Of the sorrow in Sebastian, of the sorrow in herself.

So she'd run away, to Stockholm, to Easter Island.

When it got dark, Clara went down to the sea. The jellyfish were glimmering. It looked as though someone had poured a bucket of stars into the sea. Clara mumbled the words to herself, mumbled them many times, as though to hypnotise herself into feeling confident. It didn't go so well. She knew all too well that the stars were actually jellyfish giving her the evils. She thought about the time she'd fallen asleep on the beach at Falsterbo — they were maybe twelve or thirteen, the hormones were making her tired, the growing, all those new cells being made, those muscles getting stretched out — and then up came Matilda, it must have been Matilda, even if she'd never admitted it, not even as an adult, and put them there, one jellyfish inside each of the triangles of cloth on her chest. She ran off, quick as could be, and when Clara came to, awoken by the slimy chill of the jellyfish that had made her nipples stiffen (a shame which in its prepubescent intensity was worse than both the fear and the disgust), there was no one there. Only Mama and Papa and a thousand other holidaymakers all wondering why she was screaming so hysterically.

She wasn't screaming now. She could see that it was beautiful, too. Beautiful and terrifying, and in that sense the star comparison wasn't all that far-fetched, after all, as every intelligent person knows, there's nothing more fantastic and terrifying than the thought of the stars' vast distance from one another. She also knew from experience that you had to be sparing with your screams. Otherwise you might not have any left when real fear rapped on your skull and wanted to come in. Then you'd have to resign yourself to letting it in without a word, to feel it tearing your mind to shreds without even the simplest attempt at communication with the outside world, the very simplest cry for help, managing to escape your chapped lips. When it was done with your mind it would take the rest of your body. Your arms, legs, throat, heart. Everything broken down into the tiniest pieces. She knew it was known as a panic attack and that it wasn't dangerous. But what does danger mean? Who gets to decide?

There is danger, too, in that which doesn't kill you. Ask a cripple. Ask the deaf and the blind and the dumb. Ask the ugly and the poor. Ask the lonely and the all-round wretched. Ask the grieving. Ask those who've been forced to give birth to a dead baby. Ask those with post-traumatic stress. Ask the raped and the rejected. Ask those who love someone they'll never have. Ask those who've got someone they'll never love. Ask those with fibromyalgia or endometriosis or rheumatoid arthritis or symphysis pubis dysfunction or genital herpes or any of the hundreds of other painful conditions that in themselves are not fatal. Ask the homeless. Ask the sleepless. Ask the jobless. Ask them: *On a scale of one to ten, how much comfort do you take from the knowledge that at least what you're suffering from won't kill you?* Tot up the answers. Make a diagram. Write a report. And then try to look all these people in the eye as you tell them: *There's nothing to be afraid of.*

The jellyfish flashed like blue lights. The water was black, the sky big, the horizon distant. The darkness was compact and warm. The sand was as soft as baby skin in particulate form. She should go back to her hotel, but she didn't dare. She could have gone to sleep there, right on the beach, but she didn't dare. A man might come along. Or a woman. Or a catastrophe. A tsunami. Though it would probably be best to stay in that case. At least then she wouldn't be taken by surprise. Caught napping. Sometimes, when Clara wondered why she'd made the choices she'd made in her life, why she had, for example, become a journalist despite being so scared of other people she'd learned to dislike them, she decided she'd made many of the choices she had in order to avoid being surprised.

And yet, surprised she was, time and again. So much in life was unavoidable. You always had to have your back to something, making yourself vulnerable. With your pale, stunted wings turned towards the unknown.

Like now.

Someone came towards her from behind, over the damp slope that unfurled towards the beach, and there was no way she could have heard them. A pair of musk-scented hands landed over Clara's eyes. She screamed and turned around, ready to fight.

'Hey! Hey!' Elif giggled, parrying her flailing hands. 'It's only me. Elif. Don't tell me you don't remember me?'

Clara, who'd fallen backwards onto the sand, struggled for breath and got to her feet.

'What the fuck?!'

'I saw you from the hill. You looked lonely.'

'We're all lonely.'

'Oh, snap! A pessimist and a misanthrope. I knew it. I'm drawn to you guys like a junkie to smack. Can't stay away. All that negative energy is like sugar to me. Destructive, I know, but look at me, I'm a walking paradox: that which kills others makes me invincible.'

Elif made a sweeping gesture that invited Clara to inspect her skinny body. In her somewhat less rumpled state, Clara saw what she'd missed the night before, namely that Elif was without a doubt dangerously anorexic. Even though she was standing, her stomach — fully visible under the hem of her crop top — was as concave as a Tibetan prayer bowl. Her arms and legs crunched and rustled as she waved them in the air like a belly dancer.

'What do you even weigh? Forty-five kilos?' Clara asked, like the journalist she still was, wanting to have her facts all lined up before she could pass judgement.

'Forty-two,' Elif announced delightedly. 'Good guess though.'

'My brother's ex-girlfriend was anorexic.'

'What happened?'

'Her face got fuzzy. Then she died.'

'Why didn't she shave? That's what I do. Irritates your skin a bit, but it's easy to cover.'

'Maybe she thought it didn't matter that much.'

Elif and Clara looked at each other in silence for a few moments. Elif was still wearing her sunglasses and it struck Clara that she still hadn't seen her eyes. In some way it suddenly made her feel safe. Anonymous. As though she was the one who avoided exposing herself, though it was actually the other way around.

'I was watching the jellyfish. Have you seen them? They're luminescent,' said Clara.

'Shameless.'

'Not really. Jellyfish are taking over the world, did you know that? Or the oceans in any case. They thrive in eutrophicated seas. Soon everything will be just a big mat of jelly.'

'Extra shameless.'

Elif stuck her hand in the pocket of her denim shorts and pulled out a packet of cigarettes. With two cigarettes between her bright red lips, she sat down in the sand and patted the spot beside her.

'Sit down, baby. Or are you in a hurry?' Elif started laughing, as though she'd made a joke, which in some ways she had, of course. Because it was obvious Clara couldn't be in a hurry to go anywhere. You don't come to the loneliest place on earth if you're in a hurry. Clara sat down, but declined the already-lit cigarette Elif was holding out.

'Let me guess: your brother had another girlfriend who died of lung cancer.'

'No, that was my aunt,' said Clara — which was quite true, but Elif laughed again.

'Death is shitty,' she said then, turning her sunglasses towards Clara. 'But do you know what's even shittier? Life. That's why I'm on a hunger strike against life. My victory is inevitable, as long as I persevere and don't budge a mouthful. And as an added bonus, you don't shit as much if you don't eat. Nothing in, nothing out. Purity, huh?'

Elif stubbed the cigarettes out in the sand and started drumming on the taut skin of her stomach.

'*And*, I'm a firm believer in enemas.'

Then she detailed, one after another, her hitherto six encounters with death. It took a rather long time, but Clara was glad for any reason to avoid going back to her hotel room.

'Tell me now,' Elif said when she finished. 'What are you actually doing out here, on this island in the middle of nowhere?'

'I'm a journalist,' Clara replied. 'It's my job.'

'Well, blow me. A travel journalist?'

'Something like that. Or actually — no, not at all. I'm here to … meet some people.'

'Okay.'

'They're waiting, you could say.'

'What, now?'

'No, no, tomorrow. I'm going to meet them tomorrow. But that's why they're here. They're waiting for … I don't know. Like, the end of the world, I guess.'

It was impossible to say for sure, because of the sunglasses, but Clara got a definite sense that Elif's eyes widened. In any case, her thin eyebrows jerked momentarily.

'You mean a cult?'

'No …' said Clara, squirming a little. That had been the reaction from all the editors she'd pitched the story to so far, and it put her in a bad mood. She didn't doubt that in some ways Jordan could be considered crazy, but she couldn't imagine him as some kind of cult leader. Or perhaps she just didn't want to.

'They just … I don't really know. What they do. I think they're mostly grieving. I guess that's what I'm here to find out. Or something. Why are you here?' Clara concluded, boring her toes into the sand.

'Gonna record a music video. Sucky band, but what can you do when you're a washed-up former child star? You record music videos with bands who want a washed-up former child star, that's what you do. Or you become Macaulay Culkin. And who the fuck wants to be Macauley Culkin, amiright?'

'What films have you been in?'

Elif lit a cigarette and leaned back on her elbows.

'My first and biggest role was in *Racing for Rhonda*. I lived off the money for a decade. You've seen it, right? Don't tell me you haven't seen it. I'll end it, I swear.'

Racing for Rhonda — Clara remembered it vaguely from her childhood. It was about a family of cross-country skiers in Saskatchewan, Canada, who were competing to win the money to pay their St Bernard Rhonda's escalating vet's bills (she had diabetes, if Clara remembered rightly). It wasn't a great film, nothing like as good as *Babe*, at least that's what she recalled thinking. The other thing was that Sebastian had said it was for girls and that they should have rented *The Mighty Ducks 3* instead. Sebastian always lost when they got to rent a video: she and Matilda almost always wanted to see the same thing; except, of course, when Matilda allied herself with Sebastian, just to mess with Clara. That was how they ended up watching *Jumanji*, which scared Clara half witless. She hadn't slept properly for weeks. Robin Williams being captured inside a board game for decades. A metaphor for adult life, Clara thought.

'It was a good film,' Clara said, just to be kind. Elif shrugged.

'It was a film. It wasn't for real.'

Clara didn't know how to respond to such an obvious statement of fact. The conversation seemed to run aground, and Clara realised she desperately feared its ending. She didn't want this strange and frankly rather irritating person to leave, because when she did, she'd no longer be able to postpone returning to her own miserable hotel. She rooted around in her store of emergency questions.

'Are you here on your own too?' she asked in the end.

Elif was silent for a moment. Then she said:

'Depends on how you look at it, señorita. Depends on how you look at it.'

'Does it?' Clara asked, genuinely astonished. She'd always viewed being alone as a pretty absolute state.

'I'm waiting too, you could say.'

'For the film team?'

'Them too. I'm mostly waiting for my nemesis.'

'Your what?'

'Believe me, you're going to find out. If you stick around, that is. How much longer do you have?'

'Here on the island?'

'Yeah.'

'A while, I guess. I've booked a flight back to Santiago in three weeks' time.'

'You're going to infiltrate a cult in three weeks?'

'I'm not going to infiltrate it. Just do some interviews and so on. And it's not a cult.'

'Boring, boring.'

'And in any case, they already know I'm a journalist, so there's not much I can do.'

'You'll have to think outside the box a bit, won't you? Look at me. Just look at me. Do I not look like a wreck, ready for the apocalypse? Am I not the world's only three-time Emmy-winner to have taken home all their statuettes before the age of fourteen? Baby, I'll have them eating out of the palm of my hand in five. Then: they tell me all about their sick little secrets, their suicide pact, and their sex orgies and what have you, I report back to you, and you write.'

'I'm not interested in all that,' Clara said. 'Scandal-chasing. I just want to hear what they're thinking. About everything. Get them to open up a little.'

'Freaks don't open up to journalists,' Elif scoffed. 'Believe me. Freaks only open up to other freaks. It's exactly the same in Hollywood.'

'I don't think they're freaks. If they're freaks, I'm a freak.'

'You are a freak, I'm absolutely sure of it. But the wrong kind. The well-raised kind. Not gonna work with the doomsday-mongers. Just sayin'.'

'I reckon I'll be just fine, but thanks anyway. And I'm sure you've got enough to do. When do you start filming?'

'Any day now. The film guys were meant to come today, but they pushed it back, since the band aren't here yet anyway. Stuck in Kathmandu, apparently. Earthquake, they tell me. Fucking amateurs, I say. You always get stuck in Kathmandu, earthquake or no earthquake. Damn stupid to go there without room for manoeuvre. But people, I tell you. People. Not that fucking smart, for the most part. Nah, now it's time. Now it's damn well time to get down to hit the sack. You coming?'

Before Clara'd had time to blink, Elif had jumped up, shaken the sand from her jeans shorts, and started the climb up the rocks. Clara vacillated a few moments, cast the jellyfish a look, then followed. When they got up to the road, Elif headed away from the town centre. Clara, who was headed in the other direction, stood glued to the spot.

'What are you standing there for?' Elif shouted when, after two hundred metres or so, she turned around and realised Clara wasn't following her.

'I was going to say bye!' Clara shouted back, surprised at the strength in her own voice.

'Why?'

'Hotel's over there!'

'Shit, of course. Any good, your place?'

'No, there's a rat in my room.'

'You kidding?'

'Nah. And someone else's period blood in the bathroom.'

'Fuck, that's grim. FUCK, that's grim!'

'Yeah. But I've got to go now. See you!'

Clara started walking, but soon felt a bony hand on her shoulder.

'You can't share a room with a fucking rat. I know what it's like to live with rats, it's really not pleasant. Come and stay at my place tonight, I've got a suite. You can sleep on the sofa, it's real nice. And we can go and sort you out something tomorrow.'

Clara hesitated. Clara always hesitated. But in Clara's terms, the hesitation was short. Ten seconds, twenty max. Then she said:

'Are you sure? I already owe you, for yesterday.'

'Ah. No bother. But don't get ideas. I'm celibate right now.'

'Why do you keep saving me?'

Elif grinned.

'We've known each other since we were kids, don't you remember? Practically sisters.'

It was no exaggeration when Elif said she'd six times stood face to corpse-white face with death.

It was absolutely, completely true, absolutely completely, jeez ...

That's how it is, that's how it is when you start hanging out with film stars and coke-heads at a young age, so much drama, so many ambulances, red lights, blue lights, so much blood and vomit and noose-marks on pale throats, but what you gonna do.

So many black dahlias, so many white swans found floating dead in swimming pools ...

Elif decided early on that she'd never be one of them, that was why she'd always said no to hard drugs and pilates. Just look at Kasey, her best friend, she was blackmailed by her pilates instructor ...

It was Elif who'd found her, she'd shot herself in the mouth with an automatic, *bam*, couldn't take the stress anymore. So fucking unfeminine, blood's meant to come out from down there, not through your ears. Elif laughed when she said it, jeez, insensitive I know, but shit, Kasey, fucking fucked up and all over the place and totally fucking amazing ...

And Marisha, who got HIV off god knows who — okay, everyone knew who — and washed down seventy Vs with Mountain Dew — Diet, of course — she stayed true to her principles, right to the end, hats off to that! And tits off to Masja, Elif's Norwegian Forest cat, who was as loving as she was big and furry, she got breast cancer, so Elif had to take her to be put down by the celebrity vet in Malibu, that's what happens if you give your cat the pill, but Elif wasn't to know that! She just knew Masja should have the chance to live her life without unwanted consequences. And what the fuck, perhaps it was worth it anyway, for Masja. A short but happy life. That's more than most of Hollywood gets ...

Just look at Blanco! He crashed, high as a kite, in the Holland Tunnel, that was actually the worst one, such a fucking cliché of a death, but then he always was just one big cliché. A big cliché with a big ass, you could use it as a pillow ... Beautiful, beautiful Blanco ... Such a shame, such a beautiful person ... He was passionate about WWF, deeply passionate about the pandas ... Sadly less passionate about his career, but that's so often the way, when the drugs take over ...

Unless you're like Lucky! Lucky Lucky ... ! Born with a silver spoon between his legs! Yep, he was in porn, but he liked it ... Didn't want to be anywhere else, nope ... Incredibly well paid and after just a few years he was able to cast his penis in platinum and put it on the mantelpiece in his Alpine chalet in Chamonix, and he could take all the drugs he wanted, it never affected his potency or his competency, seriously, it didn't. Lucky Lucky, of course death was going to catch up with him, sooner or later ... That much luck has to be balanced out otherwise it's just ridiculously unfair, it's so fucking tragic, it is, that there's no such thing as pure happiness in this world, even for beautiful people. Really — what is there to aspire to ... Lucky's beauty was his downfall, he had a jealous boyfriend who beat him to death with that platinum penis, poetic justice, you could call it, but it was neither poetic nor just, so ...

Call it something else plz.

They were a bit of a gang ... Elif, Kasey, Marisha, Blanco, and Lucky, they were a gang, they met while shooting *Rhonda* ... so fucking tragic, really. Twenty years ago now, but Elif had still never had it better, as much Snapple as you wanted and people powdering you the whole time ... was that when she fell in love with powder? Maybe. So matte and pretty, turned you into a fucking doll ...

And Dakota was barely even born and Ava — beautiful, beautiful Ava, back home in Brawley, California — was still alive ... Actually, to be honest, she still could be, but ...

Let's talk about something else plz.

For the umpteenth time in much too short a period, Clara woke up in a new room and took a while to figure out where she was. Reality and its particulars came back to her slowly in the form of simple nouns. Island. Sea. Rat. Child star. Hotel. Clara sat bolt upright on what turned out to be a sofa, and looked around her, heart racing. It was a suite, an open door led to a bedroom, and she crept over and peeked in. In a huge bed wider than it was long, a four-poster with long white linen curtains half drawn, lay Elif. One shining leg hung over the edge. She was still wearing the shorts, crop top, and sunglasses, her long black hair covered her mouth, she was snoring. Clara calmly noted that she herself was also fully dressed, and the rest of the memories started flooding back without too much delay.

They'd arrived at the hotel. Elif had taken her by the arm and led her through the reception. At the front desk, Elif had stopped, tapped her hand on the bell to get the receptionist's attention, and in a deep vibrato announced: 'I'd like to note for the record that this woman is a journalist, not a prostitute. She's writing a story about me for *Esquire* and is going to spend the night in my room. Good night.' Then she'd led the rather embarrassed Clara out through the back to her bungalow. It had a well-oiled wooden veranda and they'd sat a while, drinking beer and talking about Greenland's calving glaciers. To be honest, it was mostly Clara who talked — Elif had gradually entered a kind of meditative state. At least, that's what Clara guessed she was doing, because she'd assumed the lotus position and started making a noise like an a/c unit. When Elif became totally unreachable, Clara had gone inside and lain down on the puffy white sofa. She'd fallen asleep almost before taking off her shoes.

Clara went back to the larger room and started looking for her rucksack. She found it under the coffee table and fished out her phone — it was twenty past eleven. It could have been worse. She could have totally overslept. She briefly considered waking Elif, who was still snoring loudly in the bedroom, but decided not to. Perhaps there would be a weird atmosphere. Clara didn't want a weird atmosphere, she wanted coffee, and if she was going to find some before she was due to meet Jordan at the settlement, or camp, or whatever they were calling it, she had to go now. She put her shoes on, wrote a quick note saying thanks for the hospitality and suggesting they should get dinner together that evening, put it beside a vase of extravagant cut flowers, and then crept out of the bungalow.

It was amazing, what a whole night's peaceful sleep could do. She could do this. Call it genealogical research or call it journalism, call it obsession or delusion. Whatever it was, she could do it.

Twenty minutes later, however, Clara wasn't feeling so cocky. She was sitting on a wall outside the campsite, squinting into the sun with a hibiscus flower between her toes. It had got caught there when she climbed up onto the wall, and she couldn't bring herself to remove it, because the crinkly pink petals moved so gracefully in time with her feet as they swung back and forth. She bit her nails and tried to bring her pulse down. She didn't know what Jordan looked like, but was betting on being able to recognise him when she saw him. Matilda had written of big hands, broad shoulders, a golden aura, brown eyes with flecks of turmeric and amber. This man might look totally different, of course, that was the most likely scenario, Clara told herself, and braided her hair, nervously unbraiding and braiding it again before twisting it into a knot on top of her head, fixing it in place with three hairgrips that flashed like fool's gold in the sun.

Leaning her head forward to gather a few loose strands at the base of her neck, she heard a little rustling noise and saw something shimmering between the stones in the wall, a little tail and two small moist eyes. A lizard. Clara loathed lizards. She leapt down from the wall, landed clumsily on the hibiscus foot, and tumbled to the ground.

Then along came Jordan. He popped up between two low wooden buildings she guessed were the campsite's reception and facilities. He was well over six feet tall and broad-shouldered; barefoot, with deeply tanned toes, and with laughter lines at the corners of his eyes, or maybe just the kind of wrinkles you get from a life lived in the sun. Clara was struck by the thought that for someone who had made climate angst his hobby and profession, he looked surprisingly happy.

She raised her hand in an awkward wave as she tried to get to her feet again. Jordan repaid it with a smile and started jogging. 'Clara!' he exclaimed warmly and pulled her up from the ground, putting one arm around her in a kind of half-hug. She briefly caught the scent of his hair and beard and plaid shirt: unwashed, but not unpleasant. A comforting scent, of sweat and bearskins and Life in the Woods. A manly scent, a fatherly scent, of wildness and warmth. It occurred to Clara that it wouldn't surprise her if all his followers were women. Like Charlie Manson's. Or Helge Fossmo's. Imagine if he really were a psychotic cult leader, imagine if he didn't care at all about animals and nature but had gathered his followers here just to avenge perceived injustices at the hands of women, possibly Matilda, because if she looked carefully, there were indeed flecks of amber and loss in his eyes, he did indeed look like a man who'd had the whole world in his hands but lost it in an instant. *Milk and honey, eja, eja, am I not its king today?* … Clara silenced the voice in her head, smiled her most professional smile, and said:

'So … is this where you shower?'

That wasn't how she'd intended to begin this so-called interview. It really wasn't. Irritated by her own puppy-dog gawkiness, a personality trait that reared its head only in professional settings, and which drove her round the bend, she set off briskly for the low wooden buildings, pointing with her whole hand.

'I mean in this building. Does it belong to the campsite? Or rather, how have you made a life for yourselves here? Could you tell me a bit about that? What are you actually doing here? Wait, I'll just grab my phone so I can record this. Can you hold this?' She stopped short in the gravel, thrust her rucksack into Jordan's arms, and started digging around for her iPhone. It kept slipping, fish-like, from her fingers, and Jordan asked:

'Do you need some help?'

'Got it!' Clara pulled out the phone triumphantly. She almost dropped it back in again but managed to catch it just in time, pulling the rucksack towards her with her other hand and hoisting it onto her shoulder.

'Is it necessary, that thing?' Jordan asked, nodding at the phone. 'I'm not a huge fan of technology. It stresses me out. You too, apparently.' He smiled calmly, Jesus-like.

'Of course I could just take notes … but it makes my hand ache so much. I've got a weak wrist. Tennis injury,' lied Clara and waved her right hand to illustrate.

'Yes, that would be a shame,' Jordan said. 'Oh, go on, record. But you have to ask my friends if they're okay with it before you speak to them. A lot of them have completely left the digital age.'

'But not you,' said Clara. 'We've been emailing.'

'Yeah.' Jordan said, with a shrug. 'I'm not a purist that way. But it's important not to become dependent on it, I think. So much so that it blinds you. We can live without almost all the things we have in the modern world, we just can't see it.'

Jordan and Clara walked into the campsite itself. A small number of tents were spread out across the short, stubbly lawn that sloped down towards the sea. As far as Clara could tell, they seemed to belong to regular tourists, and indeed, Jordan gestured as he said:

'We've set up further down towards the water. That group of tents there, can you see? But I thought we could talk alone a bit first. Get to know each other, what do you think? I've got my quarters over there.'

He waved to a copse of slender trees, barely more than saplings, which surrounded a home-made tent of wine-red canvas. Outside, two pairs of shorts were spread on a towel to dry in the sun. Three different models of Primus stove were arranged in a neat row.

'I planted the trees myself,' Jordan said. 'Witch hazel. It was a nightmare getting them through customs. Want to take a look?' He swept back the tent flap with a welcoming gesture. Clara bobbed an unplanned little curtsy, as at the entrance to a shrine, and bent down to enter. It was an enormous tent, perhaps three by three metres, high enough for the tall man to stand upright, and with two mosquito-netted windows on the back wall. Clara breathed heavily into the mic on her phone. The inside of the tent felt more like a fin-de-siècle boudoir than an outdoor residence. The ground was covered with woven oriental mats, and the wide airbed where Jordan evidently slept was covered with red and gold cushions. From the tent's ceiling hung several lanterns on brass chains, and an old birdcage that served as a bookshelf.

'I've spent a lot of time in South-East Asia,' said Jordan. 'It leaves its traces. And I don't think there's anything wrong with beauty per se.' He opened a leather chest and got out two small golden bowls, gave one to Clara, and nodded to her to follow him out again. They sat down on the ground, and Jordan lit one of the stoves, pouring tea leaves, water, and a cinnamon stick into a pan.

'Why do you have three?' Clara asked, pointing at the stoves.

'Didn't you know that preparing for the apocalypse is a materialistic sport?' Jordan said with a lopsided smile. 'No, but, joking aside, when you live like I have the last few years, you start to value different things. A good camping stove, for example. But it's not one-size-fits-all, you know, each model has advantages and disadvantages. Do you need to boil water quickly, or are you trying to fry a bit of fish nice and evenly? Things like that.'

'How long have you been here now?' Clara asked, though she already knew. It was a kind of warm-up question intended to get Jordan to open up and drop his guard. But it was ill-placed and unnecessary — he was already getting going, and the question just seemed to irritate him.

'Almost seven months. And you?'

'Me?'

'Yes, you. How long have you been on the island? A day? Two?'

'Yeah, about that.'

'And how does it feel?'

'Feel?' Clara realised, with growing panic, that she was in the process of losing Jordan before she'd even really hooked him. He sighed aloud and, she thought, demonstratively. He poured a great heap of brown sugar into the pan and sighed again before continuing.

'I assumed you had some kind of private motive for coming here. That you weren't coming just to write about a few freaks at the end of the world? Correct me if I'm wrong, but I get the impression the newspaper world isn't exactly overflowing with money for extravagant reporting trips like this nowadays, so I'm guessing you've invested a fair amount of your own money. And time. And all for a story that, quite honestly, even I'm not deluding myself, is going to win you any prizes. I mean, you obviously work with print, right? And print is dead. You should do a podcast. Weird guy with suspicious quantity of camping stoves attracts women to the loneliest island in the world. You can fill in the blanks.'

'But I don't want to make a podcast,' Clara bleated, defensive in spite of herself.

'So, what do you want?'

I want you to look me in the eye and tell me the world is lost but that it's okay. I want you to tell me about the sister I've already lost, and tell me that's okay too.

'Are you their guru? Please say no.'

Jordan laughed.

'Oh, Clara … I'm glad you asked that question straight off, so we can get it out of the way. No. I'm not anybody's guru. I'm not anyone's god. I'm not some cult leader. The people who've come here have come for their own reasons, not to be with me.'

'But you led them here.'

'With neither threats nor promises. I was here, minding my own business. I came in contact with these people on the internet, as you know. They were already in touch with each other, most of them. And they were intrigued by the place, I assume. As I was, before coming here. As you must have been. It's a symbolic action, of course. We could just as well have met somewhere else. But it just so happened that there was a place on earth where civilisation had already crumbled once, where you can still witness the ultimate consequences of human culture. I think that gives a sense of purpose. Good for creativity, too. Like working to a deadline, you know? This is our deadline; every day we see the evidence that it's growing closer.'

'And how … long is it? Until the deadline?'

'You want me to give you a date? A time? Down to the minute? God, you're predictable.'

'An estimate will do,' said Clara. Jordan burst out laughing again. He poured hot tea into the two bowls and passed one to Clara, who took it with both hands.

'Okay. An estimate — it's going to happen in our lifetimes, assuming we each live out our natural lifespans. First of all, we'll have peak oil, which will occur within ten to fifteen years. At that point the global economy will collapse. And that would be fine, if it weren't for the fact that global warming will be heading for two degrees by then. The party's over, the money's run out — what do you think will happen? A cosy hungover brunch, eating pizza and making out? Hardly. War. Climate refugees. Famine. People talk about the zombie apocalypse and laugh, as though it were a joke. But honestly speaking, have you seen starving people, dying of thirst? I have. And they behave just like zombies.'

'You mean you've seen people die?' said Clara, and tried to remember if Matilda had ever written about dead people. Of course she hadn't. Matilda had always seemed unmoved by death.

'Yeah, in Western Sahara. And I can never unsee it. Neither would I want to, it opened my eyes to something I think I'd always known, but hadn't wanted to acknowledge.'

'That we're all going down.'

'Yes.'

'You don't think you might just have PTSD?'

'What do you think?'

Clara said nothing and bit her cuticles.

'How long have you been biting your nails?' Jordan asked and gently pulled her hand away from her mouth.

'As long as I can remember,' Clara said, and allowed herself to rest for a moment in the warmth of Jordan's brown eyes with their flecks of turmeric and amber.

'I had a hunch,' he said. 'And you're asking me why I'm here.'

After the tea they took a walk, away from the campsite. Jordan wanted to talk more before he let her meet the rest of the group. At a respectful distance from the camping area, he pulled a pipe out of his tote bag, sat down on a carved bench looking out to the sea, and started smoking. His legs were so long he could twist them almost twice around each other. Clara wondered if he practised yoga. It seemed probable, for many reasons.

'Do you want to have sex with me?' Jordan asked suddenly, and released the smoke from his mouth in a little puff. Clara jumped.

'What? No. Really, no,' she said, hating herself for blushing even though it was completely true. Clara only slept with men she found inherently uninteresting. It was a kind of defence mechanism — that way she didn't need to be afraid they might find her conversation boring. And she only fell in love with men she didn't know — Justin Trudeau, for example, or the freckly Middle East expert who they sometimes invited onto *Agenda* as a talking head — that way she didn't need to be afraid of destroying a relationship because the relationship, strictly speaking, didn't exist. Some people might think this sad, of course, but she didn't think about it much at all. When she thought about love, she thought of her brother, the way love had hurt him more deeply than loneliness ever could. It was enough to make her keep her eyes to herself.

'Good. I suspect several of the girls in the group want to sleep with me, and it stresses me out, having to disappoint them. I don't sleep with any of them, you understand, on principle — I need clear boundaries. And I don't intend to sleep with you either.'

'No, as I said, that's fine,' said Clara, who hadn't sat down on the bench, but stood to one side and tried to find some relaxed way to arrange her arms.

'Now that's out of the way: can I come to your hotel? I want to use the internet.'

Jordan took one last puff on his pipe and then banged it on the bench to empty it. A few glowing embers fell onto the rocks.

'Watch out, you could start a forest fire,' said Clara.

'No forest, as you may have noticed. That's the main problem with this island, which I thought you knew.' Jordan leaned forward and hocked up a huge wad of phlegm onto the little heap of ash, mixing it into a moist paste. 'Happy now? Can I come or what?'

'Okay,' said Clara with a shrug. 'But it's a proper shithole.'

'As I said, I've been to Western Sahara. And Bangladesh. I think I can handle a lousy hotel. Which one is it?'

'Hare Miru Lodge, I think it's called.'

'Great. Let's go.'

They walked the twenty minutes to the hotel in silence. Once there, Jordan got all het up about the pool, and Clara offered him a towel so he could take a dip, out of sheer politeness, thinking he'd refuse when he saw the insects floating around on the surface. But he said yes, and they spent the rest of the day in the hotel garden, Jordan on his back in the pool, Clara curled up on the same sun lounger she'd slept on the first night, furiously writing down everything Jordan said in the pauses between backstroke and front crawl.

'I call it "Gesamt-world". The situation we're in now. Like a Gesamtkunstwerk, but, like, the whole world, you know. Man is a destructive creature, always has been. What's the first story in the Bible? The fall of man.'

'Are you a Christian?'

'That's not the point. The point is that several thousand years ago Christians —'

'Technically they weren't Christians then —'

'You know what I mean. The ones who wrote the Bible. They knew that man's most deeply felt instinct was to destroy all that's good and pure. And they were right. Look at history, we've done it again and again. Look at this island. Civilisations have come and gone, and man has been just as guilty for their fall as for their ascent. Human history is cyclical — you can predict our mistakes. But the difference, Clara, the difference this time is the extent of the catastrophe. I mean geographically, culturally, economically — the world today is woven into a web so intricate that if a few threads break, the whole world breaks. That's what I mean by "Gesamt-world". We're pulling each other down into the shit. If one falls, we all fall. And we're going to fall. Soon.'

Jordan pushed off against the edge of the pool, disappearing like a hairy torpedo under the water. Clara bit the end of her pen to quell the wave of nausea that Jordan's nonchalant confirmation of all her deepest anxieties had provoked. It was an ink pen, a regular plastic one, and the end was hard to chew. She longed for a yellow lead pencil, a little pale brown eraser, Crayola crayons in a box of the same shade of yellow, lined paper, a big desk-mounted pencil sharpener up by the teacher's desk. If you bit a pencil like that, you could put the tip of your tongue on the cool circle of lead; it always tasted cold, like snow. She'd give anything for a pencil like that. She'd give anything to still be eight years old, singing 'Last Night I Had the Strangest Dream' on UN Day, and writing, with large, serious letters, 'WAR & ENVIROMENTAL DESTRUCTION' after the words 'I hate …' in some friend's yearbook. War was a comfort blanket for children growing up in Lund during the nineties. Something that gave your own safety depth and contours. Did you even know where these abstract wars were happening? Clara couldn't remember them ever being discussed. As a child, she viewed the landscape of war as something mystical and strange, something not of this earth. And environmental destruction was tangible: abandoned plastic bottles in a beauty spot, an oil spill in the Baltic Sea, a clearly delineated hole in the ozone layer.

'What actually happened to the hole in the ozone layer? Has it closed up yet?' asked Clara when Jordan came up for air.

'No. Of course not. It's just been out-competed by climate change.'

'I suspected as much.'

'You seem sad.'

Clara tossed her notepad on the floor and drew her legs closer to her body. She realised she hadn't eaten anything all day, and hunger made her feel tired and irritated. How was it possible to be so calm in the face of the storm? Maybe Jordan wasn't psychotic, but he was definitely emotionally disturbed. Why did that surprise her? Great minds think alike.

Clara bent over her bag and got out her phone again. The only way to keep a cool head was to work. That's how it had always been for her. She pressed the record button.

'So you don't feel any sorrow, then? You wrote about it a lot. About sorrow. On your blog. Was it all lies? You wrote …' said Clara, noticing that her voice trembled, just a little. 'You wrote that you cried the first time you saw the blue patch under Greenland. Was that not true?'

Jordan placed his hands on the edge of the pool and hauled himself up. There was a droplet of water on each and every one of the hairs on his chest. Clara was struck by a sudden desire to reach forward and touch a drop. She loved water, she loved water so much and yet she was so very afraid of it, of the sea's depths, of death by drowning, of the seaman's grave, and she was so very afraid of the lack of water, or drought, cracked earth, thirst. She loved every drop and feared every sea.

But she kept her hand there in her lap.

'Of course it was true,' Jordan said, squeezing the water out of his hair and beard. It splattered onto the paving slabs and splashed Clara's legs. 'I'm an American, not a Buddhist; I've had a really hard time coming to terms with the fact that nothing can be done. You know, we're can-do people. Which is one of the reasons we've managed to fuck up so much of the world in such a short time. For a long while I was optimistic. Idealistic, even. But idealism is a drug, Clara, the modern world's opium for the people. You can't save the world with LED lights. You can't save the world with technology. You can't even save the world with radical directives. There's a chance it might work if we kill off half the population, impose strict birth controls, and move back into the caves. But that would be fascism, wouldn't it? Summa summarum, Clara, it's too late. We've taken a bite of the apple and we have to accept the consequences. When I realised that, I stopped fighting back. I'm actually not afraid any more, not since coming here. But I'm still sad. I'm sad I won't be able to pass this planet on to the children I'll never have.'

'Do you talk a lot about this kind of thing? In the group, I mean? Your feelings about … what's to come?'

'Yes, of course. But not only that. We talk a lot about what will come after.'

'After?'

'After the Anthropocene. It's not like the world is going to explode with a bang and disappear. There will still be life here on earth after we humans have destroyed one another. More adaptable, less stubborn, less arrogant life forms. Several of us know a lot about evolutionary theory, and there are several philosophers in the group — as well as a chump or two. Our evening discussions around the campfire get pretty interesting, you'll see.'

'When?'

'Tonight, if you want. We tend to eat together an hour before sunset. It's a kind of ritual, the only one we have, actually. As I said, we're not religious. We have different opinions on things, on causes and effects, the meaning of everything. But common to us all is an inability to carry on living in the hypocritical society that wants us to believe everything's going to be okay, when it quite obviously isn't. Hey, can you eat here? I'm absolutely famished.'

It wasn't until they were on their way back to the camp, or the 'fold', as Jordan called it in an ironic reference to himself as the shepherd, that Clara thought about Elif and her suggestion that they eat dinner together. Ah well, maybe Elif was the kind of person who ate a late dinner. Or whatever she did with her dinner, since she didn't appear to eat it. Sebastian's girlfriend used to sort of move her food around on her plate in elliptical patterns until it was spread out enough to look eaten, but Elif didn't exactly seem interested in hiding her disorder from anyone. Maybe she built towers. Yes, she would definitely build towers, and let them fall.

The sun hung low over the rocks and the grass, the close-clipped vegetation that made the whole island look like a knobbly scalp. Clara realised she'd been on the island for two days and still hadn't seen a moai. Maybe tomorrow. Maybe Jordan could show her. He hadn't mentioned the statues at all, but he must have some relationship with them.

The sound of a guitar came floating through the air as they approached the campsite down by the water. It sounded Spanish.

'Who's playing?' Clara asked.

'No idea. Bernie has a guitar, but he only plays Creedence.'

Seated in a ring around a host of camping stoves were around a dozen people of different genders, sizes, and skin colours. As if on a signal, they all lifted their heads as Jordan and Clara approached. That was when

Clara saw that the person playing Heitor Villa-Lobos's 'Prelude No. 1 in E Minor' was Elif.

'Clarita!' she called happily when she laid eyes on Clara. 'We've been invited to dinner!'

After the sun had set, most of the camp-dwellers retreated to their provisional homes — thin canvas, fragile branches. Clara couldn't help feeling a certain admiration for how unconcerned they seemed about the possibility of a storm.

A few stayed and lit a small fire. There was a red-haired girl from Ireland, barely out of short trousers it seemed to Clara, and probably one of the ones Jordan was convinced wanted to sleep with him. Clara wasn't so sure, perhaps because the girl had a kind of inward-looking gaze that made Clara suspect that what she actually wanted was inside her own skull. Her name was Siobhan, a name that, along with her otherworldly body language and flaming hair, made Clara think of Joan of Arc. There was a young Croatian woman, Vedrana, who appeared to like trees, postdramatic theatre, and Sufjan Stevens. Bernie, who wasn't Bernie Sanders but could have been. And an Australian woman with skin like a crocodile, and big, tobacco-stained teeth — Grace. At one point she pulled up her top to reveal four knives, each in a special holster on her belt. 'This is the one I keep sharpest,' she said, pointing at the one furthest to the right. Then she pointed at the one furthest left: 'And this one I keep the bluntest. I have a system, you see.'

None of the group's members seemed perturbed or even surprised that Elif had turned up, which, Clara found out later, had happened just after she and Jordan had set off for Clara's hotel. Elif had introduced herself as an angst-ridden former child star who'd come to face the end of the world with her equals, and she'd been welcomed into the fold like a stray lamb. Some of them, Grace among them, had even seen *Racing for Rhonda*, and had happily spent the day questioning Elif about all the details of Hollywood life. No one seemed bothered that none of them had had any previous contact with Elif. Despite the fact that many of them were young, younger than herself even, and obviously computer-literate, Clara soon noticed that their view of modern networked society most closely resembled that of a very elderly person. They seemed to believe the internet functioned as some kind of direct telepathic link to all the information in the whole world. Living a 'connected' life, as a young man from Bremen had informed her, meant absorbing a huge amount of information you weren't even aware of. The mind is like a sponge, he said, sucking everything up indiscriminately until it gets full and starts to leak. 'That's when you go crazy,' he whispered to Clara, and Elif, sitting alongside, nodded and said that yep, just look at Kanye West. Clara thought the young German seemed pretty crazy himself — he talked a fair bit, for instance, about how he could see things other people couldn't see.

Several of the camp-dwellers seemed to take it for granted that by this point their little colony was well known and being watched by the media all over the world, a delusion Clara didn't want to deprive them of, since that would mean having to admit that she herself had found out about their existence not via some kind of transmedia jungle drum, but because she, just like them, had actively sought contact with Jordan after he had abandoned his blog.

In other words, that she belonged with them, with their grieving tribe.

Jordan, in contrast to the rest, had seemed a little surprised by Elif's appearance, but hadn't made a big deal of it. Few things seemed to disturb his natural geniality. Even though many of them had already gone off to bed, he didn't hurry Clara and Elif away, instead encouraging them to stay, offering them tokes on his pipe, and sweet Madeira from a bottle he retrieved from his tent, cooking them rice at midnight which they ate with their bare hands right from the pan.

'Have you seen any of the statues yet?' he asked Clara, pointing the wooden spoon at her. She was forced to concede that she hadn't.

'I was thinking of maybe going on some bus tour,' she said.

'And line the palms of catastrophe tourism? Forget it. I'll take you. Tomorrow.'

'Ahem.' Elif coughed.

'Both of you,' Jordan said. 'Of course. Anyone else?'

But no one answered, because not one of the others — neither

Siobhan, Grace, Bernie, Vedrana, nor the young man from Bremen —
was awake. They'd just lain down around the fire and fallen asleep like
children when the light is turned off, with the sky as their blanket and
the stars as night lights, the distant roar of the sea a mother's voice,
slowly fading away.

She had a dream and in the dream she was a desert …

A force of nature …

It was a nightmare.

She had another …

She was a girl, a downy head on the knee of a blonde, chequered big sister-thing, they were smiling at the camera …

Ava! Elif!

It was a man shouting, broad-shouldered …

It was a dad! He was normal! With cherries in a basket!

'There's a pack of Ambien in there.'

Fuck, now he was gone …

Ava too …

But Dakota was there!

They were watching *Star Wars VIII: The Last Jedi*, NB: dream logic! A totally new film …

She was Rey, Elif was Kylo Ren, they could touch each other across time and space.

It was bigger than love …

Bigger than everything.

'Like, as in: cigarettes with butter on.'

Stop talking, you're destroying the dream …

Don't you ever have dreams like this …

That feel like cool clothes against your skin!

Who are you? What do you want from me? What do I want from you?

Only something eternal.
    You're not eternal ...
    You'll fall in love, that's all.

At around lunchtime the next day Jordan came and picked them up in a dirty old white Land Rover he'd borrowed from the couple who owned the campsite. Clara had once again been permitted to sleep on the heavenly white leather sofa, and Elif was still sleeping when there was a knock on the door of the suite. Clara let Jordan in with a hopeless gesture in Elif's direction.

'Still asleep,' she said. 'Impossible to wake.'

'Sleeping pills?' Jordan asked.

'Possibly.'

Jordan went over to the bed and methodically lifted Elif's eyelids one by one. Then he went into the bathroom, and Clara could hear him opening and closing cupboards. Presently, he came out again.

'There's a pack of Ambien in there. We can stuff her in the back of the car. You shouldn't wake someone who's taken it, you can never be sure they're actually awake. I was taking it for a while, it was weird as hell. I did things in my sleep that I never would have done otherwise. One morning my girlfriend told me she'd found me in the kitchen about to eat buttered cigarettes. Like, as in: cigarettes with butter on.'

Clara started.

'Girlfriend?' she said, before she could stop herself.

Jordan looked at her with one eyebrow raised.

'Yeah? I've had them. A few, even. Are you already jealous?'

Clara turned her back and crouched down beside Elif, holding up a hand in front of her mouth as if to check she was breathing. She was, of course: warm, moist breath in Clara's palm. Clara made a fist and tried to think of something to say, a suitably innocent question that would move her investigations forward. This was going too fast. She wasn't ready.

'What do all your girlfriends think about you moving to Easter Island with a harem, then?' was all she could come up with. It didn't sound the slightest bit innocent. It sounded like a chat-up line.

'Nothing in particular, I shouldn't think. Things ended with the last one a good while before I came here. Quite frankly, she broke my heart. And we weren't really right for each other, we were too similar in some ways and too different in others. She wanted to save the world but not herself; I was the other way around. And she was reckless, terribly reckless when it came to other people's feelings. I don't think it was intentional, that's just how she was. But seriously, that's not why I don't intend to sleep with you. It's totally about principles, you're actually very pretty. Remind me of her, actually. Same angularity.'

Clara snorted.

'You needn't worry,' she said. 'I like you less and less with every hour that passes.'

Together they stuffed Elif into the back seat of the car. To Clara's astonishment, she went on sleeping. Her snoring filled the car and made the silence a little less tense. They drove out of the hotel car park.

After a while, Clara asked Jordan about Bird Man. Jordan wasn't interested in Bird Man. He was more interested in talking about all the bees dying. Clara already knew everything about bee colony collapse, it's possible she even knew more than Jordan, but she let him talk — it seemed therapeutic for him in some way, his features sort of softened when he said words like 'death sentence' and 'tipping point'. They drove along a gravel track, over a rocky plateau and then another. Clara had seen on the map that the way to Ahu Akahanga passed over the island's highest point, 507 metres over sea level.

'What kind of creature is that, anyway?' said Jordan, nodding the back of his head towards Elif.

'No idea,' said Clara, which was only partly a lie. 'You've not been in contact before?'

'No, no …' Jordan said. 'She only turned up yesterday, you know. Never seen her before.'

He stroked his bearded chin.

'You know, I never thought it would be like this,' he said. 'That people would come here. It wasn't my plan. We were in touch a bit after I stopped doing the blog, it wasn't like I kept them in the dark about where I was. But I never intended for them to come here. And yet they came. One after the other. Like sirens from the sea. Not a single one of them reached out in advance. Apart from you.'

'Who came first?'

'Siobhan. Then Sytze. The last one to arrive was Horst. Well, not counting you.'

'Don't count me.'

Jordan cast her an amused look.

'You really think you're different, huh?'

Clara paused a moment. 'No. Not really. But I'm not staying. That's the difference.'

'Why not?'

She shrugged. 'You don't intend to sleep with me, so what's the point?'

At that point Elif woke up, maybe because the windows were shaking from Jordan's laughter. Like a porcelain doll she opened both eyes simultaneously, opened her mouth in an 'O' — and screamed. Jordan jumped out of his skin and almost skidded, but regained control just in time, and went on laughing. Clara, thrown against the door, was swearing hysterically she sounded like Matilda on a bad day. She wanted to slap Jordan round the head, but didn't dare, for fear he'd skid again. Elif, on the other hand, seemed amused. She leaned forward between the front seats and whistled.

'Jesus, it's you two. I thought I'd been kidnapped. I had such a crazy dream, you'll never guess.'

Elif fell back against the seat again.

'You were actually in it, the two of you. You fell in love and had thirteen children.'

'Yeah, that's sick,' said Clara. 'I'd be happy with twelve.'

Elif whinnied. 'You're funnier than you think, sister. Could be a comedian.'

'Don't call me that.'

'A comedian?'

'Sister.'

Twenty minutes later they swung onto a little gravel plateau that seemed to serve as a car park. There were a few scattered stalls where people were selling handicrafts and passion fruit juice and ice lollies from cold boxes with sun-bleached ice cream ads taped to their square bellies.

'This is my favourite place on the whole island,' said Jordan, cutting the engine. 'Or, I mean, not this very car park. But over there.' Clara looked out through the wound-down window in the direction Jordan was indicating. It looked like everywhere else on the island: green grass, worn down to hard stubble by the wind, which turned into rocky cliffs further down towards the sea. Small, small horses; big, big skies.

They clambered out and set off for the middle of nowhere.

'Where are they?' Elif asked when they'd been walking a while on a well-worn path and had almost reached the sheer face where land met sea.

Clara couldn't see them either, not even when Jordan pointed. The only thing she could see was a collection of boulders that lay higgledy-piggledy out on a peninsula.

'Are those the stones there?' Elif asked. 'Sorry, bit of a let-down, yeah?'

Clara shaded her eyes and squinted.

'I guess I was expecting them to be bigger,' she said.

'And stand up,' said Elif.

'That's what she said. But no, I mean, this is beautiful. Really. This is the real deal. Or did you think they'd been standing upright all this time? The truth is, most of them fell over — everything falls with time. It wasn't until the early 1900s that people started erecting them again. To turn the place into a tourist destination. Carving money from stone, literally. But not here. These ones were left as they were. And they're the only ones you're allowed to touch. I guess people think they're not as valuable. But if that's the case, they don't understand a thing.'

Jordan threw his rucksack over his shoulder and they set off towards the stones. As they got closer, Clara noticed there was a pattern in what, from a distance, looked like nothing more than a structure of stones sprung organically from the earth, spat out of the ground. In one large formation, a number of stones with vaguely human forms were laid out in a row. Jordan explained that this was called the King's Plateau. A few more figures lay scattered around, some framed by smaller stones, others alone, broken, disjointed. They all looked as though they'd stumbled, as though they'd stumbled on their way out of the shower. Clara averted her eyes: it felt so intimate somehow. Like looking at an elderly person shuffling along the pavement with a walking frame, or someone with a heavy cold on the metro whose nose won't stop running and who's desperately trying to hide it with their sleeve.

Just one of the stones had a face with human features. It lay on its back, staring straight up into the sky with eyes like bomb craters. It was round and chubby like a six-month-old baby, but instead of new life, it had ancient death in its eyes. Jordan sat down on the statue's belly.

'What are you doing?' Elif exclaimed. 'Show a little respect, please.'

Jordan just laughed.

'Respect,' he said, 'such an abstract fucking concept.'

Then he told them something Clara found simultaneously comforting, in that it was quite beautiful, symbolic, an example of an overarching order, and foreboding, in that it touched on death, and funerals, and buried people who would never meet. He told them that the king who'd given his name to this place, Hotu Matu'a, had had a sister. They lived on opposite sides of the island, and seldom did their paths cross. When Hotu Matu'a died, he was buried here. His sister, Ava Rei Pua, was buried in the place where she was born, on the opposite side. It turned out this was no accident. More recently, researchers had discovered that there was an astronomical, as well as a geographic, link between these locations. On the summer solstice, the sun rose where the sister was buried; on the winter solstice, it set over her brother's grave.

Jordan ran his finger across the sky, which was blue, blue, very blue.

'Sister, brother, summer, winter,' he said. 'Forever connected, forever apart.'

'Did you say her name was Ava?' Elif said.

★

Two days and two nights after the visit to the toppled statues, Clara set her alarm clock for three, three in the morning, because they were going to see the sun rise behind the backs of kings, and it would be, Jordan had said, the most beautiful thing she'd ever seen. Clara wasn't so sure. After all, she'd seen plenty of beautiful things in her life — most people have. And a sunrise? It felt cheap. Beauty, in Clara's experience, was a thing that didn't age well, a thing that had to be reinvented each time. It was, first and foremost, a thing that had very little to do with the picturesque, the rose-tinted, and gold-edged.

The most beautiful thing Clara herself had ever seen was probably a profoundly repulsive sight she'd once witnessed, in the corner of a window, when she was maybe fifteen or sixteen. It was a butterfly and a wasp. They were bound together, wrapped in a spider's web. Both were dead. It was beautiful because it was impossible to tell who'd tried to kill whom, and who, in the end, had succeeded. It was beautiful because no one would put it on a postcard. It was beautiful because it turned Clara's stomach.

She got up anyway, woke Elif, put on her best T-shirt, ochre yellow, bobbly, beautiful in its own way because it reminded her of Matilda, everything about it did: the colour, the bobbles, the fact that it had once — yes — it had once belonged to her.

It was painful, of course. And of course, that was why it was beautiful.

Elif and Clara went with Jordan, Horst, and Siobhan in the Defender. The others had packed themselves into a hired minibus. They drove through the dark like some segmented animal, the whole way to the other corner of the island. That was the location of Ahu Tongariki, the fanciest of the statue sites. In the car, Jordan told Clara something she hadn't known: that all the statues on the island had been stood facing inwards, not out towards the sea, as Clara might have assumed.

'But why?' Clara asked.

Jordan shrugged. 'The earth's navel,' he said. 'That's what Rapa Nui means. Maybe they're looking into the centre. To see if it's going to hold.'

Which, of course, it wouldn't, and never could.

It was still dark when they got there. It was just after five o'clock and only the merest streak of light, thin as a line drawn in pencil, could be seen above the ocean. They parked, then climbed over a wall and ran hand in hand over the short-cropped grass, in the dark.

Into the shadows, that extra-dark darkness which was part of the normal darkness and yet not, more like the darkness in a church, or an embrace. It was the statues that cast the shadows. There were fifteen of them; they were enormous. They were grotesque. They had hats of stone and each appeared to weigh millions of tonnes. It was exactly the kind of beauty that was the only kind of beauty Clara cared about. The brutal, imposing beauty and revulsion of apocalypse, the only sort of beauty that had anything to do with truth.

The statues had shadows because the sun was coming up. The sun was coming up because that was what the sun did, and would continue to do for many millions of years, regardless of the tall buildings people built to try to hide it.

They sat down on the grass. Then they lay down. They lay on the ground and watched the sun rise.

And Clara felt that this, because of the new-old sun, or perhaps because of the fear that always came like a dead Newfoundland dog on the heels of every genuinely beautiful experience, the fear that this beautiful thing would soon be irretrievably over, was a moment when everything that was said had to be the absolute truth. She picked up her phone, turned on the microphone, and held it out towards a woman she hadn't yet spoken to.

'Tell me.' Clara said. 'Tell me absolutely anything.'

Alicia, 53, Salamanca, Spain:

When I think of the end, I think of a fire. A great, crackling fire. You know how fire sounds? It's going to roar.

I know it's over the top, but I think the birds will fall from the sky. I don't want to be in a house when it happens. Imagine the sound of their beaks and claws grating against the windowpanes. Just imagine.

Vedrana, 29, Zagreb, Croatia:

I want to plant trees. You know, what can a single person do? Really? I'm going to plant trees. That's what I'm going to do with my life. I'm not naive enough to believe it'll make any difference. You can't save the world 'one tree at a time'; that's a slogan and, just like all the other slogans, it's a lie. My mother says I'm a cynic. My brother too. But honestly, I like trees. That has to mean I'm not completely screwed.

Siobhan, 24, County Galway, Ireland:

We shouldn't really be here. This isn't our place. Everyone has a place. It's the place where you were born. My place is Galway. Not the city, but everything around it. The trees. The cliffs. The stones. The wild plums. The salt spray. The kissing gates. Do you know the names of the trees in the place where you grew up? I do. Poplar. Ash. Yew. And the flowers. And the birds. Before I came here I'd never actually been anywhere other than the west of Ireland. And yet I recognised myself in this landscape when I came here. If I squint it looks like the cliffs of Connemara. I should have stayed in my place, I guess. But I'm not sure. I don't know anymore if I really belong anywhere.

Jordan, 35, Berlin, VT, USA:

There's an American thinker called Wendell Berry. He's a philosopher in some ways, an artist in others. He still tills the earth with horses.

He wrote a fantastic little text about a bucket. It's a bucket that hangs above a yard on his land. It hung there when he bought the land, and had probably been hanging there for decades before that. Over the passing years, organic matter has fallen into the bucket — leaves, the odd twig, a few dead insects. Rain, which drains away through three small holes in the bottom. In the bottom, as he's writing the text, there are three centimetres of perfect growing soil.

Three centimetres, in maybe one hundred years.

The littlest kid could figure we're screwed.

Rosa, 26, Viña del Mar, Chile:
I'm a marine biologist. At the University of Valparaíso's Faculty of Marine Sciences in Viña del Mar. Damn depressing job to have these days. Instead of discovering new species, we're surveying the dead ones. That's not what I dreamed of as a little girl. I wanted to swim with dolphins. I grew up in Valpo. We had sea lions, a lot of sea lions. Aside from the colourful houses marching down to the sea, the funiculars, and Pablo Neruda's house La Sebastiana, that's our biggest tourist attraction. You go out in these little chugging boats to look at them, as if they were prostitutes. It's undignified, but that's how it is. But we don't have any dolphins, I didn't see a wild dolphin until I was nineteen. That was in Mexico. The world's smallest species of dolphin lives in Mexico, right up in the Gulf of California. They're called vaquitas and they're smaller than a human. There are hardly any left. If you'd said to me when I was eleven that in fifteen years there'd only be thirty vaquitas left in the whole world, I would have chosen a different career. I swear, I would have.

Horst, 19, Bremen, Germany:
I hope I can avoid going blind. Or if I have to, that it will happen soon. That's what I hope. That the end will come and that'll be the end of it.

Clara, 26, Stockholm, Sweden:
That's what I hope too. *(Silence.)* And also not.

In the days after the excursion to Ahu Tongariki, Clara stayed away from the group in an effort to collect her thoughts and what she was trying to view as her 'material'.

She'd been on the island for seven days and was still uncertain what her story was going to be about, assuming it was actually going to get written. Elif had negotiated with the hotel reception and signed Clara in as a guest in her bungalow, so she'd left the rat hotel and was now spending her nights and days in the kind of luxury that simultaneously jarred with and underscored the story she was gradually coming closer to as she transcribed her conversations with the group's members. She worked on the terrace; Elif mostly left her in peace. Exactly what Elif did during the day was unclear, but Clara suspected that she spent quite a lot of time with Jordan and the others at the camp. She heard no mention of the alleged music video shoot, and neither did she ask.

Raised again on the third day, Elif seemed to have tired of Clara's new work ethic, and told her over a breakfast of papaya skewers, cigarettes, and coffee that she wanted to rent a boat, and that the boat was to be called Dakota.

'You can rent them down at the harbour. They're real nice, they look like little candies.'

'But can you sail? I can't sail,' said Clara, feeling like a baby hare.

'We can row, can't we?'

'Even if it's windy?' Clara looked out across the rocks and cliffs and the wind tearing at the tops of the palm trees.

'Come on,' Elif said, pinching the loose skin around her kneecap. 'Live a little.'

When they reached the boat rental, Elif took a while to choose a boat. The fleet consisted of colourful little skiffs, not totally dissimilar to candies in colour and shape, and it seemed you could choose freely. Elif walked from boat to boat before stopping at a turquoise one with a dirty little red-and-white sail and a pair of wooden oars worn smooth by many pairs of hands.

'Here she is! Dakota!' Elif squeaked delightedly, tossing her handbag into the stern. Clara didn't ask why she was so determined about the name; neither did she point out that actually, if the hand-painted letters on the stern were to be believed, the boat already had a name, and that name was Bernarda. Neither did she mention that she'd once had a dog with that very name, a dog who died suffering horrible stomach pains brought about by the 200-gram bar of Marabou Fruit and Nut that her sister, Matilda, had accidentally left out on the coffee table. She just said 'okay', a word that seemed to come easier to her the longer she spent in the sunshine, and climbed down into the turquoise hull. Elif raised her arm in a cheeky signal to the boat rental man, and before he'd even made it over to help them leave the jetty, she'd stuck an oar into the water, pushed off from the bottom, and got them out of the clump of boats, out into open waters. She made no attempt to touch the sail, but was an astonishingly strong and skilled rower. Soon they were far from land. Clara tried not to think about the fact that they had neither a motor nor any life jackets. They had a bailer, at least. She held the bailer on her lap like a kitten and thought of it as a metaphor for the fragility of life.

'Where did you learn to row?' she asked Elif.

'In Canada. You said you'd seen *Racing for Rhonda*? There's a rowing scene in it.'

'I thought it was about ice skating.'

'That too. Canadian kids are pretty sporty.'

'I can imagine.'

With the fingers of one hand, Clara touched the mast that stuck up between her and Elif, cutting Elif in two lengthwise.

'Who is this Ava person, anyway?' Clara said.

Elif stopped rowing.

'May I ask why you want to know?' she said.

'You say her name sometimes. In your sleep. You don't have to tell me if you don't want to. I just thought ... I don't know.'

Clara shrugged. She turned her face towards the sky. She couldn't see any birds. It frightened her that she couldn't see any birds. It frightened her that the sea was so quiet. It frightened her that she didn't know if there was land behind her, or if they were heading out, never to return. She thought about running in a milk-white space of shore, sea, sky, and floating horizon. Jordan had talked about it, what it was like to run here, on foggy days when the sand along the water's edge was thick and stiff, and the sky was so damp it seemed to stick in your hair. He said it was like running into nothing. Like inside a cloud. Like in a tunnel through your own head. He said it was an indescribable feeling. Clara thought it sounded horrendous.

'She was my first nemesis,' Elif said suddenly, lowering the blades of the oars into the water with two syncopated splashes that pulled Clara from her thoughts with a little shriek of alarm.

'Jesus! What did you say she was?'

'My nemesis.'

Elif began to row again, and Clara had a vague sense she'd changed direction but couldn't be completely sure. There was nothing on the horizon to orient herself by.

'You mean like an enemy?'

'No. A nemesis is more than an enemy. A nemesis is a part of you, something you can never escape or free yourself from. The dark side of yourself, the one you could have become but didn't.'

'I understand,' said Clara, automatically bringing the nails of one hand to her teeth, like she always did when she thought of Matilda. 'I think I have one. My sister. She's pretty evil. Although I love her, of course, in a way, so maybe it doesn't count.'

'Wrong!' Elif cried, agitated. 'That's the only way it counts! You have to both love and hate your nemesis. Otherwise it doesn't mean anything. Hate without love soon becomes indifference, just like hate that goes unacknowledged.' Elif tugged hard on the oars a few times and let out a theatrical little sigh. 'You don't know how lucky you are. I've searched my whole life for a new one since I lost Ava. I've had so many candidates, but all of them have disappointed me sooner or later. Even Lana.'

'Del Rey?'

'Hmm. She's not pure enough.'

'I thought you said a nemesis had to be evil.'

'Girl, think about it. You can't both be the evil twin. That wouldn't create a productive dynamic, just a race to the bottom. Since I obviously can't be the good twin, I have to find someone who's like me, but better. Someone purer. Someone like Ava. Someone like Dakota Fanning.'

'Who's that?'

'My nemesis.'

'I thought you didn't have one.'

'I have Dakota Fanning. I'll have her for the rest of my life,' Elif said, stroking the boat's sternpost with something Clara found reminiscent of longing. Elif lowered her voice to a conspiratorial whisper:

'You remember that evening we met on the beach? When I said I was waiting for my nemesis? I meant Dakota. She's on her way here. I promise, she is.'

Without Clara knowing quite how it had happened, they suddenly reached land again. Not at the same spot they'd left it, but at the beach by the campsite. Jordan stood in the shallows with his trousers rolled up to his knees, with a harpoon in one hand and a bucket hanging from his arm. Elif waved with both toothpick-thin arms, threw the end of the rope overboard, and jumped out into the knee-high water. She and Jordan kissed on the cheek. Clara stayed in the boat. She knew there were dead fish in Jordan's bucket; she didn't want to see them. Further up the beach, Horst sat with his toes burrowed into the sand, camera balanced on his pointy knees. She couldn't understand how it didn't fall off. Vedrana lay on her back alongside him, reading a book by Naomi Klein.

Elif shrieked. Jordan was chasing her with a still-writhing fish. Its eyes looked grotesque, like soap bubbles about to burst. Clara sank further into her jumper, lying down in the bottom of the boat. It was snug, but not claustrophobic. Almost cosy, in a slightly tragic way. She closed her eyes and wondered if the rope would be enough to moor the boat or if, when she opened them again, she'd be out on open water. You can't both be the evil twin, Elif had said. It was a thought that appealed to Clara, to her sense of order and balance. But if Matilda was the evil twin, that meant she was the good one — which was a little hard to swallow. She'd never thought of herself as either good or evil, she'd never striven to be anything at all. On the contrary, she'd always wanted to be nothing. Nothing but a ripple on the surface of the water; a little bud out on a tiny branch. And at the same time — she knew it was true — she'd also always wanted to be Matilda. The thing that she called evil was also a kind of natural force.

She sensed his presence the second before the fish landed on her stomach, but it was too late. When she opened her eyes, it was lying there staring at her. It was a kind of eel, long and slick and still alive. There was desperation in its eyes. Without thinking she grabbed the slippery body and hurled it into the water. It didn't take more than a second, but still, she thought she saw it bare its teeth before it lashed the water and disappeared.

'What are you doing?' Jordan said. 'That was our dinner.'

He stood with one hand on the boat and the other on his hip. He'd buttoned his shirt wrong. Right where his heart was he'd skipped a button and Clara thought she could see it beating in the gap in the fabric: the tanned skin moving. She put her hand there and pushed, hard. He lurched but didn't fall.

'You're fucking sick,' she hissed, and tried to clamber out of the boat. He offered her a hand but she batted it away. He laughed, and that laugh erased in Clara the last trace of doubt that this Jordan was the same man who'd had his heart crushed by her sister — even though he certainly seemed to have patched it up pretty well, she could still feel it in the palm of her hand. They were born of the same spirit, he and Matilda. No wonder they hadn't been able to make it work.

'Were you really scared? It was only a fish. And please don't kid yourself you saved it, it was already half dead.'

Clara didn't answer, just waded the last few metres to the shore. This seemed to irritate Jordan.

'Where are you going?'

'None of your fucking business.'

'Clara, stop being so childish. It was a joke, okay?'

Clara stopped at the water's edge. Vedrana was still lying there reading, unbothered by their little argument. Elif sat on a stone and looked like she was eating popcorn. Horst had his face in his hands like a very small child trying to hide by closing their eyes. Clara turned around.

'No. Not okay. Don't touch me again, you hear?'

Jordan's arms dropped to his sides. The sun burst out through a solitary cloud and fell like a golden cape over his shoulders. For a moment it seemed he was going to say something, then his jaw relaxed and instead he shrugged.

'Sorry.'

Clara wrapped her arms around her torso and walked away, hunched against a non-existent wind.

It wasn't an active decision that led her to the internet cafe. Later that night, as she lay awake on the white sofa and tried to convince herself she had no duty to reply, she thought it was just an accident that she'd ended up there, a quirk that had made her go in, order a stubby little glass bottle of Coca-Cola, open the web browser on the ancient Compaq computer, and log in to her email for the first time in ten days. She'd just wanted to check if anyone had offered her any freelance work, if there was a chance she was going to be able to support herself after leaving this island. Maybe, maybe, she pretended to admit to herself, she'd also wanted to see whether anyone she knew in Stockholm had noted her absence and got in touch. It wasn't so strange to want to be missed by someone, even by a stranger.

But no one had got in touch, except Matilda.

Of course. Why else had she sought out the anonymity of the internet cafe when she had first-class wifi in Elif's bungalow? So she could be in peace, in peace with her beloved, sorely missed sister's stories of life all the way over there.

There were four emails, sent at two-day intervals. Each had the same subject: *Sorry or whatever (AGAIN ... seriously, can you respond??).* Clara pressed the cold Coke bottle against her cheek as she pretended to herself that she was considering whether or not to open them. Suddenly she realised it was exhausting, being someone who made other people want to apologise the whole time. As if she were a helpless little animal, not a grown woman. She moved the cursor towards the first email, but jumped before opening it. A new email popped up before her very eyes, right above the others.

It wasn't from Matilda. It was from their mother.

Clara would come to wish, later, that she'd refrained from opening it. It was such a strange email, so wreathed in calming phrases, that Clara immediately felt very nervous. *My dear beloved daughter, I'm going to tell you something now that I'm sure you'll find odd … You needn't worry, but still, I thought you should know I've had a little difficulty locating your father lately.*

It was a while since Clara had given her father the slightest thought, and the fact that he seemed to have vanished wasn't what concerned her — he'd probably just met some new woman and gone off on some lovers' adventure, he was sure to come back as soon as he tired of it.

What really concerned Clara was the realisation that this was just the beginning. Something in her mother's attempt to simultaneously prompt anxiety and smooth it over told Clara that something was out of whack. Something small had happened to bring about something much bigger — that's how the butterfly effect works. Blow on a feather and you'll get a storm.

And right on time, a new email plopped in. It was from Matilda, and it was addressed to both her and Sebastian. *Has she gone totally crazy or what? I'm the mentally ill one in this family, for fuck's sake. But obviously I've always wondered where it came from — maybe this is the answer? Suddenly there are two possibilities. One: Mama's sick in the head. Two: WE HAD A DIFFERENT PAPA AND HE'S SICK IN THE HEAD!!! That must be what she means, right? What else could this be about?*

Clara went into the toilet and vomited Coca-Cola into the hand basin. Then she looked in the mirror. Then she went back to the computer.

She'd sat there for hours, watching the emails pinging in, from Sebastian, from Matilda, from Sebastian again.

From Matilda.

Clara, where the fuck are you?

And she'd started crying, loudly, right there, because she didn't know, literally, where she was. What was up and what was down in the world, what use there was in pointing at a map and saying: there, there I am, at this point on the globe; when every map was a lie, a fallible depiction of something that was too big for a human ever to understand.

'Who is this Ava person, anyway?'

Ah, she could tell her a thing or two.

Or not, there are some things that aren't so easy to talk about ... Though if she did, well, then she would have said: Ava was the world's most beautiful, the world's purest, loveliest little dove ... But she still got beatings, so many beatings from her dad that she could hardly leave the house. Blue as a smurf! On days like that, Elif would climb in through the window to be with Ava after the old creep had crashed out.

They mostly played games, y'know ... Apart from a Monopoly board with almost all the Chance cards missing — pretty frickin' symbolic, no? — Ava's family only had a drinking game with Simpsons glasses, but they found all kinds of ways to play with that, just call it intelligence, plz.

One time, Ava's dad bashed her about so hard he broke her pelvis. Elif found her on the floor of her room in a pool of piss and shit; it was Elif's first encounter with death. Okay, maybe death spared Ava that time, turned in the doorway and took off, probably to the bar, but Elif realised he'd been there ... his shadow was still swinging around, in the sun-bleached cotton curtains ... and Elif ran and found her mom. Ava wound up in hospital and her dad in the clink, always something, but —

after that, Ava's hips popped like castanets when she walked.

They were just eleven then, and then Elif got her part in *Racing for Rhonda* and sort of vanished, butterfly wings like: flap flap flap ... And Ava ended up with a foster family in Brawley.

Where was that beautiful fledgling now? No idea. But it was true Elif sometimes wrote Ava's name in the little Google box, even if she'd never once pressed Enter.

So Ava was like that damn Schrödinger's cat! Dead and alive at the same time ... as long as Elif didn't press Enter.

And maybe yeah, it was best that way, cos like —

call it self-preservation, plz.

'We want to show you something of incomprehensible significance.'

Below the veranda of Elif's bungalow stood Jordan, Vedrana, and the young man from Bremen, whose name Clara now knew was Horst Herbert Jacob.

Clara closed the computer and looked at the little group standing almost solemnly on the sun-parched grass. It was the middle of the day and the sun had arranged little pearls of sweat on Clara's top lip. She licked them away with the tip of her tongue, drank the last dregs from her maté gourd, and took the computer into the house.

'What shoes should I bring?'

She leaned her body halfway out of the door with a pair of espadrilles in one hand and a pair of hiking boots in the other.

'You've nothing in between?' said the young man from Bremen with unexpected agitation in his voice.

'No.'

'Take the boots,' Jordan said. 'We're heading up into the mountains.'

It was exaggerating to call it a mountain, of course: there were no actual mountains on Easter Island, just as there were no sledging slopes in Skåne — a fact Clara had become embarrassingly conscious of one time when they were visited by their cousins from Jämtland. She'd proudly shown them Himlabacken, the 'sky slope', as this mound outside the Malmö City Library was known — a mound which, every three years, got covered in a thin layer of dirty snow as suitable for sliding down on tea trays as on toboggans. Clara realised there and then that Skåne's flat landscape was something to be ashamed of. Personally, she found it comforting and beautiful that there was nowhere to hide or escape to. Easter Island had a largely similar landscape, with no forest, mountain ranges, or deep valleys. Okay, there were volcanic craters with their gently sloping sides, and there were cliffs that dropped off into the sea, sure, but the landscape could be read like an open book — no secrets. In the car on the way up to the island's highest peak, Cerro Terevaka, Clara tried to imagine how the island had looked when it was still covered with woodland. The thought sent a shiver through her, but also made her feel strangely elated, just like anything really fucking appalling did — jellyfish as big as three football pitches, men with elephantiasis, mirror neurons, things like that.

It was quiet in the car. Vedrana was looking out of the window; Horst sat beside Jordan in the front seat, writing something in a notebook he had propped against his raised knees, his feet against the dashboard. His head hung so low his fringe touched the paper and made a little swishing sound every time he moved his head. Clara imagined that they were a little family on a day trip. It was a terrifying thought.

One was definitely enough.

Several days had passed since her inbox had spontaneously combusted and started spewing messages from her mother, brother, and sister. She still hadn't replied, and didn't know if she ever would. If she was ever going to come back, or just disappear. Sink like an island into the water, a lost city. She allowed herself a moment to wonder whether they'd miss her if she never returned. If she were to stay on this island forever. In every family, thought Clara, there's someone indispensable, and someone you could take or leave.

'What are you writing?' she asked Horst and leaned between the seats. He jumped and hit the back of his head on the seat.

'Just a list,' he said, brushing his fringe out of his eyes. She saw them for the first time: they had a thin, milky grey colour, like rainwater. His eyelashes were transparent and he had freckles. All in all, his face reminded Clara of a seabed.

'Of what?' she asked, trying to stop herself stealing a glance.

'Just what I can see. You can't take photographs while moving.'

Horst patted the camera beside him on the seat. It was a good SLR, in a black leather case with a strap.

'Horst is our court photographer,' Jordan said. 'But I don't know if he's any good because he's never shown us any pictures.'

'Do you have a computer?' Clara asked. Horst nodded.

'But I only have it for uploading photos,' he said, almost apologetically.

'And I email my dad occasionally. My mum's dead. So.'

'I'm sorry.'

'She got glyphosate poisoning.'

'It still hasn't been proven, has it?' Vedrana said morosely. 'That glyphosate can kill you.'

Horst shrugged and went back to his list.

'Where are we going, anyway?' said Clara.

'Here,' said Jordan, turning sharp left onto a narrow track. He stopped the car at the edge of the track and threw the door open.

'Behold our little reconciliation project, our attempt at healing and improving, our symbolic restoration of the natural order. Behold our woodland.'

Clara looked out through the car window. She couldn't see any woodland. What she did see was a slope with around twenty peculiar stone formations. They looked like little campfires, circles of stone on circles of stone, each of them two or three feet tall.

'You have to go closer,' Vedrana said, nudging her in irritation. Clara opened the door and climbed out. Vedrana followed, taking her resolutely by the hand and pulling her over to the nearest stone circle.

'There. Tree!' she said, pointing down into the little crater. And there, inside the circular wall of stone, was a little tree, no taller than a forearm was long, spreading its few leaves with a wild joie de vivre.

'They're so fragile, you see,' Vedrana explained. 'Like children. A gust of wind and they're dead.'

'Really?'

'Have you looked around you?' Vedrana asked. Clara raised her eyes. There was no vegetation taller than a palm's breadth.

'The whole place used to be covered with trees. Palms, mostly.' Vedrana said.

'I know.'

'But that was four hundred years ago. A lot happens in the world in four hundred years. Erosion has impoverished the soil, and what little fertile earth there once was is long gone. It's extremely difficult to get trees to take root here, primarily because it's so windy. They have to stay perfectly still to stand a chance. Hence the walls. We dug hollows and filled them with compost from the mainland. We got the trees from Trees for Life.'

'What kind of tree are they?'

'They're called aito trees. They tolerate salt well. And they don't create a monoculture like the eucalyptus we have down by the coast.'

Clara looked at the car. Horst was gone. She saw him further up the slope, standing with the camera to his eye, the lens pointed at Vedrana and herself. She raised her hand in a tentative little wave. He turned away.

Jordan, who'd been doing a round of the plantation, came back to them.

'Looking good,' he said to Vedrana, who nodded severely. Clara hadn't once seen her smile. And yet, she didn't seem unhappy, not exactly.

'Come on, let's get watering.'

Clara looked around her, confused. There were no water sources anywhere on Easter Island. Jordan understood her confusion and nodded towards the car.

'We've got ten tanks in the back. You have to keep watering them until they've had a chance to establish themselves. But aito trees are good, they develop relatively deep root systems pretty quickly. We estimate that we'll have to carry on for another month or two, then the winter rains will come. And by next spring they'll probably be able to get by on their own.'

Jordan drove the Land Rover a bit further forward and Vedrana walked round and threw open the rear door. Sure enough, there were ten fifty-litre tanks full of water, along with three watering cans.

'Do you water by hand?'

'Yeah?' said Vedrana.

'I guess you could have a pump system, but to be honest, watering by hand is good for the soul. And that's the whole point, anyway,' said Jordan.

'I thought the point was to re-establish woodland,' Clara said.

'Have you counted the trees?' said Jordan. 'There are twenty-two of them. For this island, it would take two hundred thousand trees to stop erosion and recreate the natural ecosystem, if by that you mean the ecosystem that prevailed before the human deforestation-fest of the 1700s. Two hundred thousand. We can't plant two hundred thousand trees. The Chilean government could conceivably plant two hundred thousand trees, but they're not interested. People come to this island to see the statues — half of them are apocalypse tourists, half Indiana Jones. No one comes to look at trees. So why are we doing this?'

'Yeah, why?' asked Clara, rummaging in her rucksack for her phone while she followed Jordan, who was wandering around between the trees. It never failed to astonish her what a terrible journalist she was. She was even bad at *playing* the journalist, she thought, because by this point she'd begun to accept what the reportage had become and always been: nothing more than a pretext.

Vedrana had filled a watering can from the tap on one of the tanks and lugged it off to the furthest trees. She balanced the can on her knee, leaned it towards the stone wall, and let the water stream down onto the tree's narrow roots. Clara had at last got hold of her phone, opened the voice-notes function, and pressed record. As if on command, Jordan made off again, back towards the car. She followed him, holding the phone up while he grabbed another watering can and started to fill it.

'Why?' Clara repeated, silently worrying that the running water would drown out Jordan's voice on the recording. Perhaps she should make notes too. But where was her pad? In the tote bag she'd put down between the trees. Clara sighed. Jordan smiled.

'You said your brother's a brain scientist, right?'

'Yeah,' Clara said. Had she said that?

'So you know what neurons are. How it looks, inside a human brain.'

'Yeah.'

'But you've never seen it for yourself, of course, you can just imagine it.'

'I've seen pictures in *National Geographic*,' said Clara, immediately feeling like an idiot.

'Of course,' said Jordan. 'That's the kind of thing they write about, because that's the kind of thing that sells. We're so damn impressed with ourselves, so obsessed with ourselves, and nothing fascinates us as much as our brain, because in a way it's the highest proof of our complexity as a species, our superiority, and rightful dominance.'

'Yeah, yeah,' Clara muttered. Her arm was already aching from holding the phone up, *and* it was warm. A trickle of sweat ran between her breasts, which felt very uncomfortable — it felt like blood. 'Can we sit down?'

'Fuck no, gotta do the watering. Put that down and help out a bit.'

Jordan nodded at the phone, and Clara let it slip into the pocket of her shorts. She took the last watering can, filled it — though not to the brim because she was scared she wouldn't be able to lift it — and followed Jordan.

'When people think about trees, they think of their tops,' he said. 'Ancient trunks, bark, leaves. Bird nests. But, like, trees are like icebergs. There's more below the surface, as there is above. You reckon people would think differently about the natural world if we found it as easy to visualise a tree's root system as we do the electrical impulses in our minds? Trees are intelligent too. They communicate underground, their root systems stretch out towards each other like neurons, touching each other like the fingertips of two lovers, like God touched Adam. Most people today know nothing about this. That pulling a leaf from a tree at one end of a wood has the potential to affect a bush at the other, has the potential to affect everything — you too. You can't touch another person without becoming someone else, you know? But we think that we're in some way able to move through the natural world without the impressions we make on it making impressions at least as deep on us.'

Jordan fell silent and put down his empty watering can. He pulled off his shirt, a worn, washed-out red thing, and wiped his brow with it. Clara got the sense he viewed this action as a gift to her. She looked away.

You can't touch another person without becoming someone else.

So who were you, if no one had ever really touched you — touched your heart.

'Where did Horst go?' she said, to interrupt the thought.

'He's always running off,' Jordan said. 'He's a child.'

'Nineteen, no?'

'What were you like when you were nineteen? I was most certainly a child.'

'I was afraid of the dark.'

'See?'

They took another trip to the car for water, then another, then one more. During that time, Jordan went on talking about the tree as the ultimate symbol of humanity's lost contact with the natural world.

'You know, I'm from Vermont. It's challenging for me to live in a place like this, practically without trees. I think it's hard for all humans — in cities, in agricultural areas, all the places where there used to be woodland. We're primates, for Christ's sake. We were born in the trees. Think of all the religions that are rooted in trees — even Christianity. In the middle of Eden there was a tree, it bore fruit, Eve tasted the fruit, and turned her back on the tree. At that moment she stopped being an ape and became a human. But to what end? Sometimes I think we never should have come down from the trees. That was our Eden. Everything since is just one big long diminuendo.'

'So now you're trying to build a new Eden? Here? With twenty-two trees.'

'You haven't been listening, Clara. We're not trying to build an Eden, this isn't some fucking reality TV show. We're just trying to find a way to atone.'

'Like a kind of indulgence? Or whatever it's called, in the Catholic Church, you know?'

'I don't go to church.'

'But you are religious?'

'Depends what you mean. I think we need religion.'

'As in "believing in something greater"?' Clara made air quotes.

For the first time Jordan actually seemed genuinely upset.

'Yeah, that's exactly what I mean. Maybe you think it's uncool or whatever that ironic gesture was supposed to mean, but seriously, what's it about, believing in something greater? Greater than what?'

'Greater than ourselves, I assume.'

'Right. Greater than humanity. Look at it this way: we've believed in humanity as the highest, greatest form of life for several thousand years —'

'Okay,' Clara felt the need to interrupt, 'but the vast majority have believed in some kind of god for the best part of those years?'

'In theory, yeah. God as a heavenly entity, life after death, blah blah, but still, humanity has always been at the centre. At least in Judaism, Christianity, and Islam. And where has that led us? Here! To a world where in thirty years we risk spontaneous combustion if New York has an unusually warm summer, where there won't be enough soil left in sixty years to feed even half of us. And so on and so on: you can rattle off as many catastrophic scenarios as I can —'

'More, I reckon,' said Clara, and meant it.

'So yeah, and no: I believe we need to reconnect to something greater. But by that I mean something that's genuinely bigger. I mean the fucking planet, the oceans, the glaciers. I think we need to let them crash over us and crush us.'

With a grunt, Clara set her watering can down at the foot of one tree circle. She looked down at the tree. Even though it had no eyes, she had the sense it was closing them, like a newborn baby, nestling into the warmth of its mother's breast. The narrow leaves spread towards the sky and when Clara at last hauled the watering can up onto the edge of the wall and let the water run, she could have sworn the leaves flinched away from the stream in order to let the water reach the roots.

'Imagine if we actually could plant two hundred thousand trees here,' she said. 'It would be like healing a wound.'

'Ah,' Jordan said. 'You know as well as I do that no real change will come before the system collapses. We'll be wiped out as a species, maybe, but then the healing process will begin. This has happened before, it'll happen again. We just won't be here. But that's how it is. If you trash the party you can't expect to be invited next time.'

'I'm not so hot on parties,' said Clara.

Jordan was silent for a fraction of a second. Then, in a voice that sounded very far away, he said:

'I really am, unfortunately. That's the problem. I've loved this life far too much, and now I don't know what to do with myself.'

It took almost an hour to empty the many water tanks. When they were done, Clara was so sweaty her shorts had large wet patches, front and back, and her feet in the heavy boots had taken on a spongy texture. Her armpits were itchy and her lower back ached a little. But still, she agreed there was something satisfying about the thought of the water currently travelling down through the layers of soil. While Jordan and Vedrana went to fetch Horst, Clara obeyed an impulse and climbed over one of the walls around the trees to dig her hand into the now-wet ground. She clutched the thick clay soil, letting it ooze between her fingers. There wasn't much space between the tree and the little stone wall, and she had to wrap her legs around the fragile sapling in order to sit down. She leaned her forehead against the pale bark, breathed in the tree's salty scent, so different from the familiar sweet birch and sticky elm, but still comforting. Her heart beat heavy and hard, from effort and relief. Sitting in the cool of the stone wall, she felt as though she could sense every single one of her nerves — and the moisture was like dipping each and every frayed nerve into clear, warm water.

'Now we're done we were thinking of going for a swim. Here, drink.'

Clara looked up, confused and painfully embarrassed. On the other side of the wall stood Vedrana with a half-full plastic bottle of sun-warmed water in her hand. As always, she appeared to have the weight of the world on her shoulders. Clara tried to get to her feet but only managed when Vedrana offered her free hand. She glanced at Clara's muddy legs and damp shorts, took a gulp from the bottle, and said:

'When I was a child my best friend was a tree. I'd like to live in one.'

'Seriously?'

'Yeah. Have you read Calvino's *The Baron in the Trees*?'

'No.'

'Just as well. It's really a book about taming nature, which is vile.' She held out the bottle.

'Hmm,' Clara said. The water tasted of gravel and grass and satisfaction.

'Did you find Horst?' she asked when she was at last forced to relinquish the empty bottle.

'Yeah, he's in the car with Jordan. Come on.'

'Does he never help out with the watering? Or, I mean, does he just take photos?' said Clara as she climbed out over the wall.

'Horst is okay, but he's almost blind.'

'I thought that was just something he said.'

'It's true. Blind as a puppy, but in reverse. Soon everything will be black.'

Vedrana crumpled the bottle into a ball and stuffed it in her rucksack.

'And he has visions. He believes he has second sight.'

They drove to Anakena for a swim. After spending time with the empty mountain and the tiny little trees, it felt strange to be among people. Tourists with mirrored sunglasses and sporty backpacks and sunburn and shiny teeth and e-cigarettes. Tanned children in nothing but their underpants, coconut-sellers, and fishermen in their boats, on the way out to lay nets. The wind was blowing inland and the waves were high. Vedrana and Horst — *the serious children*, as Clara had begun to call them in her head, even though Vedrana was nearly thirty, older than herself — were carefully and methodically getting changed, but Jordan just threw off his shirt and rushed towards the water. His enthusiasm rubbed off on Clara, who yanked off her shorts and vest and followed him. She didn't like swimming alone, but with others there were few things she liked better than letting herself be knocked over by a giant wave, again and again and again.

The water was cool on her legs. As she ran out, she could see the mud and clay being washed away, dissolved in the foaming water. A wave built. The salt water would still be there, Clara thought. In spite of everything. The seas would become larger, not smaller, gradually they'd rise, swallowing islands like this one, like Manhattan, islands like Jersey and the Caymans, all the land humans had destroyed with gold and skyscrapers, all that glass, it would be smashed, washed out to sea, ground soft and smooth against the sand, and fall to the bottom like dark jewels.

And still the waves would wash, back and forth in their predestined patterns. That was what Jordan had meant by *what will come after*. Clara was filled with laughter, wild, uproarious — almost happy — laughter.

She let the wave drench her.

It washed past, and Clara got to her feet again, rubbed the water from her eyes, lifted her face to the sun.

Then she felt a grip around her ankles.

She screamed in wild panic, a scream that grew in strength as her eyes met Jordan's — he was standing several metres in towards the beach, so it wasn't him, and at the shoreline she could see Vedrana and Horst carefully skipping in. For a few panic-stricken moments, Clara felt a death by drowning clutch at her throat. This unknown person was going to pull her under the surface and not let go until her eyes were full of bristle worms and jellyfish. She cursed herself for once again falling for the soothing voice of that fright-delight. It was just like at that first hotel — under a picture-perfect surface, her own personal hell laid out a welcome for her. She gasped for air and reached her arms towards the beach, towards Jordan, who was looking at her, towards the serious children who looked uncomprehendingly at their own feet, like all serious children do.

Then a black curly head broke the surface.

'You fucker!' screamed Clara and beat the water after Elif. Elif laughed so hard she sprayed water from her sunken nostrils.

'Were you scared?'

Clara threw her arms around her body, her lower lip pouting.

'What are you doing here?' she said.

Elif raised her hands and backed away a few steps, offended. It was hard to hear what she said above the crash of the waves, but it sounded like *well, fuck you too*.

Another wave washed over Clara and when she got to her feet Elif had disappeared. She caught sight of her over on the beach. She'd come ashore a way away from the others. She looked as though she was heading in another direction, rather than towards them.

Clara felt something resembling guilty conscience. God knows why, but Elif had never been anything less than kind to her and she'd not done much to repay it. Maybe Elif was hurt? Clara made her way back to the beach with great strides and ran after her.

'Hey,' she said, laying her hand on Elif's shoulder.

Elif turned around slowly.

'Sorry,' she said. 'For grabbing your leg. It was childish of me. But you have to understand I didn't have much of a childhood. Corn?'

She nodded at a corn-on-the-cob vendor. Clara was caught off guard.

'Sure,' she said.

Elif bought two cobs, and they sat down on the sand. Elif picked yellow kernels from her cob and balanced them on her toes. Clara ate hers, because she was hungry.

'I mean, it's cool,' she said tentatively in between bites. 'I was just scared. I'm … easily scared.'

Elif chuckled.

'Tell me something I don't know. Sorry for saying this, but you seem a little tense, girl.'

Clara felt a bit offended. She wasn't the one who wore sunglasses twenty-four seven and had stalker-adjacent illusions about an American actress.

'I just have a lot on my mind,' she said, and put the well-gnawed cob down beside her. 'Family trouble, you could say.'

Elif nodded.

'I know all about those. Or knew, when I actually had one. A family, I mean.'

Elif flicked her big toe, sending a kernel flying into the air.

'We're pretty alike, you and I, you know that?' she said, turning the dark lenses she had instead of eyes towards Clara. 'I sensed it the first time I saw you. There you were, standing in the airport, looking like someone had died.'

Someone had died, but Clara didn't say that. Someone had died and taken her family with them. She didn't say that either. Instead she hummed in a way that was neither affirmative nor dismissive. In some ways it felt absurd that Elif, who resembled no one Clara had ever met, was laying claim to spiritual kinship. But in some ways, it also felt pretty nice.

'What happened to your family?' Clara asked cautiously.

'Well, they died. Each and every one. The ones who were my real family, I mean, I told you that already, weren't you listening? And the others. They're dead too. Mom, Dad. I never had any siblings. Partners, children, all that stuff — pfft!'

Elif made a little fluttering gesture with her fingers.

'I'm sure you can understand,' said Elif.

'Hmm,' said Clara.

'But you have siblings?' said Elif. 'Mom, dad, all that stuff?'

'Yeah,' said Clara, reluctantly.

'What's the problem, then?'

Clara hesitated a moment. Then she said:

'Communication difficulties. You could say. Differences, too.'

'And?'

'Things that can't be unsaid. Things that can't be undone.'

'Sister, get a grip,' said Elif, smacking Clara over the back of the head. 'As long as there's life, there's hope. Just say sorry. It's easy as anything.'

'Sorry,' said Clara, and Elif laughed, laughed and ran over the sand, towards the others.

When Clara undressed that evening, she realised she still had her phone in the pocket of her shorts, and that she'd forgotten to turn off the recording. It had stopped automatically when the phone ran out of space, but she still had several hours of sound recording, a distant roar from the sea, voices, laughter. She put in her earbuds and took the phone to bed with her. If she strained her ears, it sounded almost like tropical rainforests, erotic tempests.

And then three sentences, clearly discernible above the background noise:

You can't touch another person without becoming someone else, you know?

It would be like healing a wound.

As long as there's life, there's hope.

She opened the emails and wrote: *I'm here. Talk Tuesday?*

Death. Generally seen as the opposite of life. The gods: immortal. Humans: obviously mortal. Animals: also mortal. Pandas, tigers, killer whales. The cicadas on Easter Island, dying and dying, inexplicably. A dog died. A woman, just a girl really, died. They all died and died.

Except when they didn't.

Once there was an infant whose first cry caught in their throat.

But it came, it came later. It was just a little delayed.

Once there were three siblings, who'd never known which of them it was.

Who'd been, and perhaps still was, that child. Who'd dodged death by a hair's breadth, living but for the grace of God, so to speak.

The ocean: immortal.

But everything that lives in the ocean: mortal to the highest degree.

The evening before Clara was due to speak to her family she was so nervous she was literally climbing the walls of Elif's bungalow. She'd spotted a spider, possibly poisonous, in one of the whitewashed corners of the living room ceiling, and she wasn't going to rest before she'd driven it from the house. When Elif returned from a walk, with clinking bottles, Clara was doing her best to haul herself up onto a bookshelf. Her nails were shredded and white with paint.

'Girl, I don't know what you're up to, but you need to chill out,' Elif said and rang Jordan.

They took a taxi to Playa Ovahe on the north side, because Elif had read on TripAdvisor that it was the most beautiful beach on Easter Island. She'd been horrified when Jordan told her he'd never been there, even though he'd been on the island for several months. 'I can't handle any more earthly beauty,' was all the explanation Jordan had given.

Now he'd apparently moved the boundaries of what he could handle, because as soon as the taxi turned into the gravel area that served as a car park, his eyes lit up. The beach, which was surrounded by volcanic cliffs, was no more than a couple of hundred metres long and, what's more, it was completely empty. Not a person, not a parasol, not a discarded ice cream wrapper as far as the eye could see, which was far, because the sea took over where the sand left off: clear, vast, foaming with waves so perfect they made Clara think of the Fibonacci sequence and snail shells and a sunflower's heavy head just before the petals drop.

'This beach is no good,' the driver said as he counted the money Elif had given him. 'Falling rocks. Hit your head, you know? Not always, but sometimes. Go look fifteen minutes at sunset. Then I drive you back.'

Elif laughed and gave the driver another note.

'We'll be okay. You can go.'

'But it will get dark, and in dark you don't see rocks.'

'So we'll die unprepared,' said Elif, opening the car door. 'Come on, ladies.'

Jordan was barely out of the car when he tore off his shoes and ran down to the water's edge. Elif ran after him, leaving only Clara standing alone as the taxi driver started the engine and vanished into the distance. Clara wasn't all that concerned about the falling rocks, but more about how they'd get back. Phone signal was lousy, and she assumed it wasn't the kind of place you'd chance on a late-night taxi, or any other kind of car for that matter. But what could she do? Should have thought of that before. Before she left the comparative comfort of Hanga Roa. Or possibly even earlier, before she left Sweden, Europe, or why not even further back, before she left her childhood bedroom, her mother's tummy.

She gave herself a gentle slap on the face and started walking.

She caught up with them at the water's edge. The lowest part of the sun was just touching the soft line of the horizon; a mild pink light flowed out across the sea, like a glaze. They watched the sunset in relative quiet, letting the water wash over toes and flip-flops and ankles. Jordan had a bottle of bourbon in his rucksack which he pulled out and passed back and forth as tears ran down his cheeks. Clara had to look a second time to make sure, but yes, he was crying.

He looked like someone full of sorrow, and it was more than Clara could stand.

'Come on,' she said, nudging his shoulder gently. 'Let's swim.'

When they came up out of the water Elif was sitting with her legs crossed, blowing bubbles. She dug another bottle of bubbles out of her enormous bag and tossed it to Clara, who'd thrown herself shivering onto the sand, and pulled a towel over her shoulders.

'Open it,' Elif said.

Clara twisted the cap off the colourful tube and discovered, with an astonishment that was mostly a reaction at her own astonishment, that it contained not thick, glossy bubble mix, but fine white powder. Clara wasn't so stupid she didn't clock that it was cocaine, and she wasn't so innocent she hadn't tried said substance on one previous occasion, mainly because her fear of seeming stuffy had overcome her fear of dying a drug-related death.

'Now, now, don't be shy,' said Elif, nodding encouragingly at the tube.

'I don't know …' said Clara, turning half-entreatingly to Jordan for guidance. He didn't hesitate, boldly reaching for the tube, tipping a little sugar loaf of powder onto the back of his sun-bronzed hand, and hoovering it up without even making a line first. And it was obvious, thought Clara, that he would react that way — Jordan struck her as a man who loved the whole world, and as a rule, people who loved the whole world also loved narcotics.

'Shall I make a line for you?' Jordan asked, and Clara nodded silently. 'A little one,' she added. 'It's been a long time.'

Jordan smiled one of his easy, all-knowing smiles and poured out a small heap of powder on his hand, pulling a grip from Clara's hair which he used, with surprising efficiency, to draw out a helpful line before reaching his hand out to her, as though he wanted her to kiss it. Shyly, Clara tucked the hair that had come loose behind her ear and leaned forward. Halfway down she realised something was wrong.

'No banknote?' she asked.

'You don't need a banknote.'

Clara felt stupid, but also absolutely certain.

'I need a banknote. I can't otherwise.'

'Sure you can. It's not hard. You don't need to do it hard. Just close your eyes and inhale and the powder will come to you.'

'Okay, but I don't want to.'

'Why not?'

'Control issues,' Clara said. There was a moment's silence, then Elif's laughter rang out. She began to dig around in her apparently bottomless handbag and fished out a baby-blue calfskin wallet. 'I've got banknotes, baby. What do you want? 10,000 pesos? 20,000?'

Jordan waved his free hand in irritation towards Elif.

'Fuck the notes, Elif. She can do it without.'

Clara was still hesitating. Then she felt a weight and a warmth on the back of her head, fingers closing around her neck. Jordan was pushing her head towards the back of his hand. She pictured her face as the face of the sunflower, all her thoughts and fears were like petals falling to the ground, her mind a perfect shell painted with mother-of-pearl shimmer; she heard the waves, they rolled through her body and became an involuntary moist patch in her bikini shorts.

'It's okay,' Jordan whispered. 'I've got you. Just close your eyes and inhale. That's all a person ever has to do. Close your eyes and inhale.'

And so, Clara closed her eyes and inhaled, and when she opened them again the world's contours were a little clearer, Jordan was holding her by one hand and Elif by the other, and together they ran over the sand, out into the water again. It closed around her body like a mouth with a tongue and teeth and she wasn't afraid. She thought: you float better if you give yourself fully to the water after all.

And they floated. There was nothing to worry about, never had been. Of course they found a taxi. Of course they got back to Elif's bungalow in one piece, of course they put the jacuzzi on in the bathroom, sank light-headed beneath the surface.

Clara drank more than usual, more than she should have, but not as much as Elif. Elif drank till she couldn't stand up. Then Clara took her bony arm and led her into the bedroom. Laid her in the foetal position on the taut bedspread, blinding white in the moonlight.

She sat beside Elif a short while and listened to her rattling breath. She wondered if this was what it felt like to watch over a child. If this was what it had been like for Sebastian to watch over Violetta. She wondered why people thought watching over someone would make any difference.

Elif stirred and said, barely audibly:

'Dakota, is that you? Have you come at last?'

'Hush,' said Clara and gently moved a sticky lock of Elif's black hair. 'Sleep now.'

When she came out of the bedroom Jordan was looking out of the window. The sky outside was like a curtain, thought Clara. Pull it aside and the whole universe would fall down onto them. Even though she knew it wasn't the case, she couldn't escape her childhood sense that the earth was like a scene in a snow globe, not round like a ball but flat as a pancake and protected by the dome of the heavens.

A radio alarm clock glowed red in the darkness: 2:17. Less than six hours to go. She suddenly felt much more sober, much more tired.

'Hey,' she said, putting a hand on Jordan's shoulder. 'She's asleep now. I put her in the recovery position.'

Jordan raised his hand and took Clara's. They stood a while like that, looking out into the darkness like an old married couple before the gravestone of their prematurely deceased child. Jordan's hand was large and warm and Clara was sleepy. Full of crawling insects, but still, in some way, calm, prepared. She went into the bathroom to brush her teeth and wash away the last remains of her mascara, which had settled like a thin membrane under her lower lashes. When she looked up from the basin, she caught sight of Jordan's face, just behind her own in the mirror.

He was getting undressed, again.

'What are you doing?' said Clara, letting go of the hair she'd been holding in one hand as she washed her face, trying to laugh as lightly as a bird.

'Come on, let's get back in.'

Jordan nodded at the jacuzzi, which was still bubbling away.

'Not me,' said Clara, reaching for the controls to turn it off. 'I need to sleep.'

But Jordan would not be dissuaded. Before Clara could defend herself, he'd scooped her up against his bare chest and plopped her down into the jacuzzi, still wearing her dress. And Clara actually began to laugh, but automatically, like girls do when boys tease them, that acquired reflex that makes you say 'heehee' instead of 'ow' when they pull your hair.

But it wasn't particularly funny. The water, which had been bubbling away in its very own closed system for at least an hour, was now lukewarm, closer to cold than hot, and suddenly Jordan had no pants on. His penis, which, when accompanied by Elif and a half-gram of cocaine, had been neutral, was now acutely present, almost threatening, especially as it slowly rose like a wonky drawbridge before Clara's sleepy eyes.

'You can lower that,' she mumbled, waving at his crotch. 'I thought we'd decided this.' She put her hands on the edge of the bath, intending to get to her feet and out of the tub, but stopped when Jordan, without warning, placed his cock right onto the back of her hand. Rested it there, just like that. The smooth weight was absurd. Not unpleasant, to be sure, but what did that matter? This wasn't what was meant to be happening.

She didn't say anything. Nor did Jordan. The situation, Clara felt, was unsustainable. She was angry, not necessarily because Jordan had made advances, but because he'd done it in such a clumsy way it was impossible to accept or rebuff with their mutual honour intact. The seconds passed. She could hear Jordan breathing heavily, whether from arousal, tension, or general intoxication she couldn't tell. Maybe his legs were just tired. He was tall and had been forced to bend them a little to get in the right position for this peculiar manoeuvre.

The back of Clara's hand started to get sweaty and she'd begun to find the situation unpleasant. It was weird, thought Clara, as Jordan almost imperceptibly began to rub his cock back and forth over her hand like a sausage in a bun, that she hadn't anticipated this. What had she been thinking? That she could come here, like a bystander to her sister's life, without being drawn into her world and its weirdness. It had never worked before. Wasn't that why she'd withdrawn in the first place? Wasn't all this — the trip, the hunt — just a study in pride? Wasn't this the logical punishment? Was that why she was incapable of pulling her hand away, getting out of the bath, and resolutely leaving the bathroom?

She shouldn't have come here.

Embarrassing situations, confusion, chaos, and mess, you can avoid it all if you just close your eyes.

And she didn't want to see this. It was unworthy. Unworthy of her, unworthy of Matilda. Unworthy of him.

And yet she couldn't tear her eyes away: the way it was sliding, back and forth, the way everything was sliding and moving, even the tectonic plates. She wished he'd put his shirt back on, stand on a cliff, and look outdoorsy. She wished he wasn't a person with a person's desires, that he hadn't humiliated himself in this way, that he hadn't forced her to take responsibility for restoring their dignity.

Then suddenly there he was, standing in front of her in the tub. He took her by the wrists and pulled her to her feet. She wobbled, about to fall over, but he grabbed her. Instinct made her grasp his upper arms. He seemed to take it as a sign of enthusiasm and pushed his mouth immediately onto hers, pulling down her wet dress in one smooth motion so it floated like a water lily around her knees. Lips, earlobes, throat, collarbones, breasts, he pressed her body against his face and licked it like an ungainly, grunting dog, dropping to his knees in the water. Belly, groin. The image of a dog en route to her crotch disgusted Clara so much she finally managed to push his head away. What she saw was a look so pitiful she wanted to cry.

'What? Don't you want to?' he said, half disappointed, half incredulous, and stroked the fingers of one hand along the inside of her thigh. 'I thought you wanted to.'

'No.'

'Are you sure?'

His face was still level with her genitals, his warm breath laced her dark, rough curls with moisture. For a moment she felt tempted to give in. Hadn't she made a rule only to sleep with stupid people? Well, here was someone kneeling before her who was obviously stupid enough to think she wanted him, that that would make things better, for either of them. In which case, she *should* want him. In which case, maybe she *did* want him? Was that logical? In her dazed state, Clara couldn't tell. She thought it better to be safe than sorry, pushed his face away with her hand, and took a big step out of the bathtub. With trembling fingers, she reached out and grabbed the soft fabric of a towel. The encounter with reality was electric, like a whole fucking life in a single second: all her pent-up rage flowed out in a coursing river of adrenaline.

'What the hell?' she shouted, throwing a ridiculous little shampoo bottle at Jordan, who was sitting, confused, in the tub, with water dripping from his beard and the wet rag of her dress in his hands. 'What the fuck are you doing?'

Jordan dropped the dress, parried the bottle with his hand, and started laughing.

'Calm down. Okay, you don't want to. I get it.'

Jovially he jumped out of the bath, reached for a towel, and began, slowly and carefully, to dry himself.

'You get it? Now you get it?' said Clara, holding her towel tight against her body.

'Yeah? You just threw something at me. I read that as a pretty clear no.'

'And when I said no? That wasn't a clear no, you don't think? "Are you sure?"' said Clara, this last in some kind of clumsy imitation of Jordan's resonant voice. She snorted. For a moment, Jordan actually looked a little ashamed.

'Like, it all happened kind of suddenly. That you didn't want to.'

'Suddenly? You know what happened suddenly? YOUR COCK ON MY HAND!'

Now he looked really ashamed.

'Okay, maybe that wasn't a great move. But it just happened, okay? Things happen. Unexpected things.' He started to look for his trousers, found them, fastened the buttons one by one over his hairy stomach. 'I misunderstood and I apologise. Are we good?'

'You're sick in the head,' said Clara, opening the bathroom door with a little kick.

'Yeah, you said it,' Jordan sighed, pulling his shirt over his head. 'But at least I admit it. And I swear, I thought you were into it. Now I know, so —'

'Get out.'

Jordan sighed, threw the towel in the bamboo basket provided for the purpose, and headed obediently for the door.

'Clara, sorry. Okay? I'm going to go and lie down on the sofa now.

I'll leave you alone, I promise. God, I'm not a monster.'

'Get out. I mean it. Back to one of all the other girls you think want to sleep with you. See if it's true. You're not staying here, in any case.'

'But Clara,' he groaned, 'it's still dark! YOU can go, if you don't want to be in the same room as me. You're not actually staying at this place either, strictly speaking.'

'And leave you with Elif? Forget it.'

'Come on, Clara, what do you think? That I'm some kind of sex psycho?'

'YES!'

Jordan threw up his arms and returned to the suite without a word. He sat down on the sofa demonstratively. Clara swept past without looking at him, grabbed her bag, and walked towards the door.

'I'm not her, okay?' she said, before throwing the door open to the night.

He jumped to his feet and rushed after her.

'Clara!' he shouted as she vanished down the stairs onto the decking on a path of moonlight. 'What the hell are you talking about? Come back! You're only wearing a towel, for fuck's sake.'

Clara realised that he was right and stopped short. Defeated, she turned back towards the bungalow, which, with its oil lamps lit and the shadows playing over the deck, looked like a beacon in the compact darkness. Jordan stood there, and she realised he was the only person she'd ever met who seemed as afraid of the dark as herself. Standing with the starry sky as his crown of thorns, his flannel shirt dirty and incorrectly buttoned, and his arms outstretched in theatrical humility, he made Clara think of Jesus on the cross. It wasn't until she went, still trembling, into Elif's room to check she hadn't choked on her own vomit, that Clara realised it was an image that, if you thought about it, made her God.

In the end they fell asleep. They never talked about Matilda.

The sun still hadn't risen when Clara crawled out of bed. She had to climb over Elif, who lay with her arms up over her head like a baby. On the sofa in the living room lay Jordan. They were both sleeping deeply after the night's excesses, but Clara hadn't got more than a couple of hours' broken sleep. She'd dreamed of peacocks and didn't know why.

Her skin was clammy with sweat; she couldn't tell whether the scent on it was her own. The uncertainty put her in a bad mood and she went to the bathroom to wash it off. When she turned on the tap, no water came out. She twisted and twisted but nothing came out. The thirst set in almost automatically. She went to the minibar and pulled it open, but the only thing left apart from chocolate was a bottle of some juice Clara didn't recognise, maybe guava. She downed it but immediately regretted it. The walls began to sway. She had to go out onto the veranda.

The sunrise was brilliant red. Two weeks she'd been here, but she still hadn't accustomed herself to the apocalyptic light that set the sea on fire every morning. Fulmars shrieked as the red rays bored through their feathered coats. They moved in flocks; she counted fourteen of them rising and sinking, rising and sinking on thermals over the sea.

In contrast to practically every other human being, Clara had never dreamed of being a bird. Floating free on the air, unprotected, vulnerable … Thanks, but no thanks.

At precisely eight o'clock, the phone she was holding in her hand began to bubble. She sat cross-legged on the wooden duckboards and looked at the flashing screen. It was so long since she'd spoken to anyone in her family, and now she was going to speak to all of them at the same time.

Who was she doing this for? She had thought it was for her own sake, but now she wasn't so sure. For her mother's? Maybe. Whatever was weighing on their mother's mind, in a way it was their responsibility, as her children, to take the burden from her. Clara knew that in every family an exchange happens, sometime after the children have left home, a redistribution of the roles of protector and protected. The parents' responsibility for their children turns into the children's responsibility for their parents. She hadn't expected it to happen so soon, but maybe this was where it would begin.

So, let it begin.

She pressed the green receiver. They popped up, each in their own corner — Mama, Sebastian, Matilda. The screen was so small that their faces were no larger than a thumbnail. And still the sight of those three familiar faces, their meagre, pixelated representations, made her pulse rise.

'Clara?' Mama said. 'Are you there?'

'I'm here. Can you see me?'

'Barely,' said Sebastian. 'But it's still crazy. To see you at all.'

'Yeah, crazy,' said Clara, not feeling the slightest bit seen.

Matilda said nothing. She seemed distracted. Somewhere in the distance, Clara could hear a child hollering. Matilda vanished from her square, a door slammed. Then she was back.

'Apparently Siri's sick, so she's off school. Wouldn't fucking know it from her energy levels. How the hell did you manage three at once?'

'You were quite good,' their mother replied.

'Tsk, Bastian and Clara maybe. Bet I was bloody hard work.'

'Still are,' Sebastian laughed. Clara, on the other hand, was having difficulty breathing.

'So, tell us,' Matilda said. 'Who's our real papa?'

'Tilda!' Clara said through clenched teeth, never failing to be astonished by her sister's brutal frankness. Or her own. After all, this was the first thing she'd said to her sister in more than a year.

'Well?' Matilda sighed. 'We can get to the point, can't we? I've got yoga in an hour.'

Now their mother interrupted.

'I promise this has nothing to do with your father. Well, of course, it does in a way, but —'

'Where is he?' said Matilda.

'What's that?'

'Papa? Sebastian tells me he's here in Berlin.'

'No, I'm not sure he is. But I believe so.'

'Who's this woman he's met?'

'I don't know much about her, I really don't. I know that she's younger, quite a lot younger, and that —'

'What, like twenty-two?'

'No, no, nothing like that. Maybe thirty-five? I'm not sure.'

'Has he been seeing her long? And why's he never got in touch with me if he's in town?'

'I don't know, Tilda my dear, I don't know. We've not had all that much contact since the divorce. He lives his own life and I think that's a good thing. But —'

'You still want to get hold of him?' Matilda pressed on. 'Is it about our inheritance?'

'Inheritance?'

'A dead aunt we never knew about? That's what Bastian thinks. Right?'

'It was just a theory,' protested Sebastian.

'Aha, no, no.'

'So what is it, then? Mama, tell us. We're listening.' Clara heard herself say. Matilda's frankness had been passed down from their mother, and their mother's present inability to get to the point was making Clara nervous. There was a silence on the line. No one said anything. Then their mother cleared her throat.

'Yes, children … I have something to tell you that your father and I have known for a long time but which we, for various reasons, haven't wanted to share with you. I'm sure you'll understand why. We love you so very, very much, I want you to know that. The same amount. We love you. All three. You must never doubt that, you have to promise me. My decision to tell you this now was not some mere impulse, no. I've thought about this a long time, a long time, and I finally feel the time is right. You're adults now and you have your own lives, you seem to have found your paths in spite of everything … well, you understand. When you were going through what you were going through, Tilda, before you went to Bangladesh … it would have been impossible. And then everything with Violetta, Sebastian, that was a sad chapter in itself … But now I think you've all figured things out quite well, wouldn't you say?'

Clara looked around her and thought: *I'm sitting hungover in the loneliest place on earth, waiting for the apocalypse with a superannuated child star and a feeble-minded young Thoreau with an uncontrollable libido. Peak life.*

The phone was quiet again. Clara avoided looking at her siblings. Instead she looked at her mother, counted her grey hairs. Waited.

'Mama?' Sebastian said at last.

And she burst out crying. Their mother, who'd never cried over anything but the story of Moses in the rushes, was crying like a screeching ambulance.

'Oh, children! I have to say it. I just have to say it, now I'll say it,' she sobbed, but said nothing.

'So?' Matilda hissed. 'Say it, then!'

'Please don't push me, Tilda,' their mother asked.

'Mama,' said Clara, who felt like she couldn't take it much longer. 'Don't worry about Tilda. It's okay. Whatever it is you can say it. Is it … Is it what Tilda thinks? That Papa isn't our biological father?'

The words felt absurd in Clara's mouth, not at all like words, more like something strange and thorny, sea cucumbers, perhaps, or chestnuts with thick green shells. When they were out, though, they didn't feel that threatening.

They felt logical. Feasible, in their unfeasibility. In every family there was someone indispensable, and someone you could take or leave, wasn't that what she'd been thinking?

'No, no, I said,' their mother sighed, pulling herself together with a sniff. 'Or, he's the biological father of … of two of you. Oh Jesus, there, I said it. Heavens, it feels so much better already. There. Phew.'

There was another silence, but a different kind of silence. Clara felt the phone grow slippery between her fingers. She didn't understand, and yet she did. She understood everything.

Someone you could take or leave, yeah.

Except it wasn't their father.

Of course, Matilda was the first to regain her powers of speech.

'What the fuck do you mean? Mama, you can't get pregnant by two different men simultaneously, it's impossible. I think? Or is it? God, I thought I knew all about this stuff ... Sebastian, you're the scientist. If you sleep with two men in a short space of time and — god, Mama!'

'Tilda, I haven't slept with anyone but your papa, that's not what I'm saying.'

'Never? Wow.'

'Tilda, just shut your mouth!'

It was Clara, Clara was the one screaming. Same way she'd screamed back then, after the funeral. Same way she hadn't screamed when she was born.

A third kind of silence fell. Clara looked away from the screen.

'Mama, explain.' She heard Sebastian's distant voice, a voice that sounded very, very tired.

'You know, it was all very dramatic when you were born. One of you wasn't breathing, as you know, and then the other two of you came horribly quickly and it was all an ungodly mess, blood and tears and we were so terribly worried, of course, because of course the midwife, one of them, ran off with one of you to intensive care, right away, well, and then she came back and the baby was fine, you all were, and then we could finally breathe again ... and you were so lovely, how lovely you were! The most beautiful things we'd ever seen ...'

'I still can't understand how you could not know which one of us wasn't breathing,' said Matilda, who'd always struggled with this obvious nonchalance towards the three of them as individuals.

'Giving birth to three children at once is a very special experience, Tilda my dear. Bearing children is always animalistic, it's our Lord's way of reminding us of how fleeting life on earth is, but multiple births are even more so — at that moment you don't think of the babies as individual babies any more than a bitch or a sow would. You think of the brood. Of everyone's survival. That was the only thing we were thinking about, your papa and I.'

Their mother paused a moment, inhaled.

'Or,' she went on, 'it was the only thing I was thinking about, at least. Your father ... well, I wish he could have been here so he could tell you in his own words, because quite honestly, I don't know how it happened, I've never understood it, though the Lord knows I've tried to get him to tell me about it. In any case, he thinks ... well, yes, he thinks ... that, well, when the nurse came back with the one of you who wasn't breathing, it was a ... a different baby.'

'What the —' said Matilda.

'A *different* baby?' said Sebastian.

Clara said nothing.

'But why —' continued Matilda.

'I know it sounds strange, but that was what he said. A little later. That the baby who came back wasn't the same one they'd taken away. In all the chaos he hadn't said anything, he wasn't certain and thought that maybe he was just in shock, what with everything else, but later he told me he was sure, quite sure.'

'But who —' said Matilda.

'We don't know. Oh, my darling children, we don't know!'

'But that's totally impossible. Of course you know!' said Matilda.

'No, we don't. I've already told you how everything was, it was complete and utter chaos. All the blood, and one of you not breathing, and then the other two of you who needed weighing and measuring and feeding and, well, there was quite simply a lot going on.'

'A lot going on? That's all you have to say? Good god, didn't we get those little ... those little bracelets?' Matilda went on.

'Yes, yes, eventually ... but, you see, hospitals weren't so careful with that kind of thing in those days; there wasn't the same fastidious culture as there is now, you see. And there was another thing, too ...'

'What?' said Matilda. 'Out with it.'

'You could say that your father hasn't always been the best at preserving the sanctity of marriage. If you see what I mean. I was very distressed, even before, because of something he said to me. So. I guess you could say it was a case of it never rains but it pours.'

Clara's head was buzzing. It was pouring, in Clara's head. The water was streaming from her eyes. Three hours. It would take three hours, three weeks, three lifetimes for them to hear her if she screamed.

'Clara?'

It was Matilda. Or was it? Who even was she? Where even was she?

'Yeah?'

'Why aren't you saying anything?'

'I ...'

'Clara?'

It had slipped from her hands. This. Everything. But mainly her phone. Like a sliver of soap, it had disappeared down between the boards of the decking, their voices on speakerphone continuing to stream up through the floor. *Clara? Why aren't you saying anything? Clara?*

What could she say. She'd left it there, the phone, and gone her way. The palms had swayed so calmly. The tipanier flowers had nodded their humble heads in the pale dawn. For a brief moment she'd felt drunk, uplifted, ecstatic. After the first shock — the rush. *Just close your eyes and inhale. That's all a person ever has to do.*

And none of it had been her imagination, it was all true! It was all logical, clear, obvious. They were like something out of Happy Families: she was the Ugly Duckling; Cinderella with soot on her nose. They walked on cobblestones; she preferred the cliffs, the meadows. They loved each other; she loved no one. They belonged together, and she was a heavenly body, solitary but sparkling. She could do anything she wanted now. She could stay here forever, or go somewhere else entirely. She could disappear without leaving a hole, quite the opposite: maybe the hole would finally heal over. Or at least be forgotten, replaced by something more urgent.

The euphoria lasted until she got down to the beach. Then came the anxiety, it washed in with the unceasing waves. She lay down on the beach and looked up at the cloudless sky, the one people liked to convince themselves was different to the sky you saw from the other side of the globe. It was possible to leave the sky behind you and get used to a new one, it was just very, very painful. She knew, because she'd tried and failed. But what now? The sky back home wasn't the same any more either.

She burrowed into the sand with her fingers until she reached the cold and damp. She thought she could feel the earth tremble. She turned her face towards the ground and wept.

When she got back, she'd reached a decision. She couldn't stay here. She'd come to the loneliest place on earth, but never before had she had so many interpersonal problems weighing down on her at once.

She thought about her father, or whatever he was to her now; she thought of how absent he'd been in this conversation, not just in the sense that he didn't take part — they'd spoken about him as though his disappearance was nothing out of the ordinary, nothing to get upset about. Clara thought it was sad. But maybe that's exactly what he'd wanted? He'd disappeared, and no one seemed to be making any particular efforts to find him. If she disappeared, hid herself in broad daylight, would they look for her?

Clara stopped on the track that led to Elif's bungalow. It struck her that she didn't know who she was imagining would look for her. Her family — who weren't even her family, when it came down to it — or this motley gathering of desperate people who'd become her friends over the last few weeks?

To Clara's relief, Elif appeared to be alone in the bungalow. She was on the decking, sitting with her legs dangling over the side of a wooden chair, the same chair Clara had sat in a few hours previously. She was drinking coconut water straight from the nut through a striped paper straw. Clara immediately honed in on that detail. She used to find solace in the existence of paper straws, bamboo toothbrushes, tampons made of natural sponge. Now it seemed to make no difference that people were trying. All these pathetic little changes people made in an attempt to regain control, when everything, big and small, was so obviously falling apart.

'Has Jordan gone?' Clara asked, climbing up onto the deck.

'Yeah, yeah. Left as soon as he woke up. Looked like a beast of a hangover. How are you feeling?'

Clara looked down at her hands. They were shaking.

'Like shit,' she said.

'It shows. Here, have a coconut.'

Clara sat on the wooden deck and took the coconut. It was lukewarm and tasted disgusting. Coconut water was disgusting. That was a fact too few people dared to acknowledge.

'Why do people drink this shit?' Elif asked. 'Tastes like cat's piss, for fuck's sake. I'd shoot a cop for a Coke.'

'Elif, I have to go home.'

Fast as lightning, Elif threw the coconut into a bush of flowering oleander and pushed her sunglasses up onto her head. It was the first time Clara had seen her eyes. They were the bluest she'd ever seen, possibly excepting Violetta's. Clara was so taken she at first didn't notice Elif was genuinely upset.

'What the fuck are you saying?' she roared.

'I have to go home. Things have happened. With my family.'

'Did someone die?'

'No. Or, I don't think so? My dad's disappeared.'

'And you want to look for him? That's good. You should look for your dad when he disappears.'

'I guess?' said Clara. 'I don't know. There's other stuff too. Other shit. I can't explain, it's really messy.'

'Go ahead, please, I love mess.'

'I don't.'

Elif had got up from the chair and was now striding back and forth across the deck. A cockatoo leapt from a bush with a squawk. A solitary cicada wandered along the smooth wooden boards, golden in the sunlight. It dragged its legs behind it, its wings hanging.

'You see,' said Elif. 'That's where your problem lies. And mine, I guess.' She pulled out a cigarette and a lighter. 'To a certain extent I love mess. To a certain extent. But when that extent is reached, *bam*, then I'll do anything to get a little order into my life. Which generally means I stop eating.'

'You have admirable insight into your illness,' Clara said wearily.

'All anorexics do. Or do you think we're stupid? Do you think we seriously believe we're worthless fatfaces when our total bodyweight amounts to less than what the average American eats for breakfast? We know it's all about control. But I'll tell you this for free,' said Elif, leaning into her cupped hands to light her cigarette, 'that's more than you can say about most people. You, for example, with all your phobias and your longing for the apocalypse, have a crazy damn control complex. Which you can no longer handle. Which is the reason you're here, and why you hope, deep down, that your cult buddies are right. You want fire and brimstone. Anything less and you'll never escape this, this … SYSTEM of interlinking phobias you've created for yourself so you can avoid living like an independent fucking human being.'

'And why would I have done that, if I may ask? I mean, to start with. Maybe you can illuminate me on that front, since you seem to know so much about people.'

'Fuck do I know? Insecure childhood? These things leave their mark, believe me.'

Elif immediately grew animated, waving the half-smoked cigarette in a motion that made Clara think of a Möbius strip.

'Think of it this way, Clarita: what is a family?'

'People who are connected … by blood?'

'Wrong! The nuclear family is a safety net, a kind of system set up and institutionalised to ensure care and security and support and all that shit before the state existed and —'

'You sound like Jordan.'

'You wanna hear what I have to say or what? And nowadays, I mean, broadly speaking, about civilised countries like the one you come from, not my own shithole of a motherland, nowadays that system's not needed because you've got, like, universal income and state brothels and —'

'We have neither universal income nor state brothels.'

' — and people don't actually need to form small nuclear families to survive. But it doesn't matter, because the family has also replaced *another* support system, namely religion, and instead of forming families for practical reasons, people form families for spiritual ones. What I'm trying to say here is that the family is, and always will be, the world's foremost support system. And when there's a blip in the system at a young age, this little human has to find support in something else. Me with my hunger strike against life, Clarita, an obvious reflection of the emotional starvation my pop subjected me to, and you, well, you've tried to replace a suffocating and tyrannical system, i.e. the happy middle-class family, with another, i.e. your — forgive me for being blunt — sick phobias.'

Elif concluded and rested her hands on her hips in satisfaction. Clara didn't know what she should say. Elif started laughing so hard she had to dry the corners of her eyes with her cerise shawl.

'Ohmigod, ohmigod. You should see your face! Such fucking bullshit, so much fucking bullshit … That was a little variation on a thing I rehearsed for an audition one time, this indulgent frickin' film by fucking Almodóvar. Ohmigod. Pop psychology, I mean … *love* that shit. But seriously: life's just one big mess. Gotta learn to live with it. You, Clarita, gotta learn to live with it. Otherwise you might as well die.'

'Is that Almodóvar too?'

'Elif original. So you're staying, right?'

'What? No.'

Elif put her head in her hands and sighed.

'Clara! You can't go! I need you.'

'No, you don't. I'm not your nemesis, if that's what you're thinking.'

'No, that's not what I'm thinking. It's Dakota and no one else. But you'll do for the time being.'

'Thanks. Moved to tears, really I am.' Clara stood up. 'I'm sorry it's all such a rush, it's been lovely … getting to know you? And thanks for everything you've done. That you let me stop here and so on. I owe you one. But I really can't stay. It's all too much.'

'So, okay, if I've got this straight: you ran away from your family because it was "messy", and now you're planning to head back because it's got even messier? Makes no sense, señorita.'

'It's messy here too, so I'm thinking it's going to even out.'

'What do you mean, messy? This is paradise. Did something go weird between us? Do I snore? I can pay for a separate room for you if you want.'

Suddenly Elif looked small and alone. Clara felt herself soften, as though she were the chocolate cake and Elif the fat, lonely child clutching it much too tightly in their hand. She sat down again and looked at Elif.

'It's not you … So, okay. It's Jordan.'

'What about Jordan?'

'He tried to sleep with me. Last night.'

'And?'

'Yeah, but, I didn't want to.'

'Okay.'

'It felt unpleasant.'

'What do you mean? Was he threatening?'

'No.'

'But what do you mean, then?'

'He put his cock on my hand.'

Elif snorted with laughter.

'It's not funny!' Clara cried. 'I was totally unprepared. And then it was suddenly there. On my hand. How did he think I was going to react?'

'With enthusiasm?'

Clara sighed.

'I thought you liked him,' said Elif.

'I do. In some ways.'

'I mean, that you were into him.'

'Maybe I do. But what does that matter now? He destroyed everything! Do you know what the biggest problem with men is?'

'There are so many problems with men I can't even count them, baby.'

'The biggest problem with men is that they look so fucking *stupid* when they're turned on.'

'So you rejected Jordan because he looked stupid?'

'No, idiot, because he put his cock on my hand.'

'What, how long was it there for?'

'Several seconds!'

'But then he took it away?'

'Yeah, in the end. And he was really embarrassed.'

Elif was laughing so hard she was shaking, clutching her ribs like a character in some old farce.

'Oh god, oh god ...'

'So, anyway,' Clara said, getting up again, determined this time. 'I get that you might not think this is a big deal, but I came here to do a job and I can't do that job anymore, because of ... everything, actually, everyone. You ... Jordan ... I've got too tangled up in this, whatever it is, in this group. It will be a bad story.'

'But a great podcast.'

'I don't want to do a fucking podcast! I want to get out of here. So I'm going. Now.'

'Now? What, *now* now?'

'Yeah, I rebooked. I'm flying back to the mainland in four hours.'

'But you were going to stay! You said you'd stay! There on the beach, you said it. I never would have let you stay in my suite if I'd known you were the kind to just take off. I'm not that kind of girl.'

Elif howled the last words after Clara, who'd vanished into the bungalow to gather her few possessions. With her rucksack on, and her laptop under her arm, she looked around the little luxury bunker, which was beginning, more and more, to look like a lived-in, permanent home. Which perhaps it was. Perhaps Elif, just like herself, had nowhere else to go.

So which of them was the stronger? Elif, who'd stopped pretending, or Clara, who was at least trying? She didn't know.

Elif sat out on the wooden deck, crying theatrically. Clara nudged her with her foot to communicate her departure. Elif looked up. She was wearing her sunglasses again.

'What should I tell Jordan? That his manhood was too much for you? You were so shocked by his horse-sized member you had to do a runner?'

Clara tittered.

'You really don't take anything seriously. I really take everything much too seriously. It's a terrible dynamic, I've come to realise. Bye, Elif.'

'Bye, sourpuss. Vaya con dios.'

Clara decided not to go via the camp. She would have liked to say bye to the others, in spite of everything, but the thought of meeting Jordan in broad daylight made her stomach quiver in a scary way. It was bad enough, she generally thought, having to look a man in the eye the morning after the boundary-dissolving state that was the only — but, in Clara's otherwise (one point to Elif/Almodóvar) very controlled existence, oh so meaningful — benefit of casual sexual encounters. Looking into the eyes of a man with whom she'd simultaneously *had* and *not had* a sexual exchange, a man who both *was* and *wasn't* her sister's ex, was more than someone of Clara's categorical nature could handle. She didn't dare trust him to pretend nothing had happened. She didn't trust him to apologise. She didn't trust him not to try again. Quite simply, she didn't trust him, just like she didn't trust anyone, least of all herself. Instead she went straight from Elif's bungalow to the hotel reception and asked them to call a taxi.

Twenty-five minutes later she walked into departures, which was the same hall as arrivals. This time the floor was free of insects, polished to a high shine, like ice. The hall was almost completely empty, because the only outbound flight, the one she was travelling on, didn't depart for several hours. In fact, apart from Clara's old friend the security guard, a few flight personnel, and a cleaner in a rustling pink coat, there was only one other person there. He was sitting on a bench between the two baggage carousels, resting the heavy, shiny camera on his knee. Clara raised her hand in an awkward wave, but soon realised she'd have to go and say something. Goodbye, for example.

'You're leaving,' Horst said when she'd taken the ten steps over to the bench. She didn't sit down.

'Yeah. It happened a little fast, but. Yeah. You too?'

'No. I have no such intentions.'

'But why … ?'

Clara turned to look at the arrivals board, but it was empty. She tried anyway.

'Are you waiting for someone?'

'I was waiting for you, of course.'

Clara felt like something was spreading along her spine, what people called a cold chill, maybe, or just the memory of a cicada's thousands of feet.

'I spoke to Elif,' Horst said. Clara heard herself exhale. Of course.

'I'm sorry I didn't come and say goodbye,' she said. 'But you know, it ...'

'Sometimes that's the best way. It can be hard to say goodbye.'

'Yeah.'

'It doesn't matter,' said Horst. 'You'll be back.'

Clara laughed.

'No, I don't think so. I really don't think so. This is the kind of journey you only make once.'

'You'll come back. It's already happened, because I've seen it happen. And when you do, everything will end, everything will continue, and everything will begin again. May I take a picture of you?'

Clara looked down at Horst's hands. They were so unnaturally still, there on either side of the camera, like two dead birds on his lap. Then they suddenly came to life, moved, opening their gaping mouths towards the world.

He raised the camera, and she looked straight into it.

III
CICADA

Kathleen always said: Imagine you have a colour balancing on your nose. That's the colour of life. It's like a butterfly. You can't touch it without killing it. All you can do is open yourself up to the colour touching you. Imagine you can smell the colour, that it's floating in through your nostrils and spreading through your face like warmth. Outwards from your nose, over your cheeks, across your forehead, down your jawline and throat. Give in to it. Feel your ears, feel how the colour warms your ears, your scalp, how your face moves backwards towards the inside of your skull and your spine is extended upwards. Imagine the colour is an insect buzzing in your brain.

At the beginning of June, Jennifer Travis went crazy.

To Sebastian, the tipping point wasn't quite clear, perhaps because he had his hands full trying to curb the spiralling madness they call sexual obsession. As if that wasn't onerous enough for someone with latent, low-intensity depression, a fair bit of Sebastian's energies went on thinking about how on earth he was going to save his own crisis-ridden family — of course, the crisis had been going on for a long time, but their mother's little revelation had undeniably taken it to a new level.

Or, not quite new.

One thing was as old as the sun, and that was that Sebastian was the one expected to solve the problems. But how could he do that? He wasn't even quite sure what the problems were.

In any case, when Travis dived into his office one sunny morning with eyes like saucers and arms covered with secret codes scribbled in what appeared to be kohl pencil, it was clear to Sebastian that the mysterious phenomenon known as *the puzzle* had begun, and that this was what it was doing to Jennifer Travis. Her flourishing madness was underlined by the fact that the first thing she said — no, *hissed* — was: 'I'm not crazy, Sebastian!'

Sebastian — who'd been busy trying to realign the neurological pathways that associated Laura Kadinsky with fantasies about oral sex and cherry blossom, with the help of affirmative phrases pronounced with gravity and precision, according to the theory that language is a reversible tool which not only expresses the workings of the brain's impulses but can also change them — welcomed the interruption.

Travis seeking him out in his own office was remarkably out of character — an anomaly in an otherwise structured whirlwind of organised insanity. Ordinarily, she fluttered through the institution's corridors like a butterfly, apparently aimlessly, but never without purpose, with the inherent, inalienable purpose of all beautiful things, shining with a light brighter than fireflies on a warm, muggy night.

Travis was a rarity: a person who genuinely seemed to be self-sufficient, an unreachable, unshakeable presence through absence, as elastic as a rubber band, as light as a feather, as elusive as a shadow sculpted from a block of light. She was a soap bubble that seemed impossible to burst, a paradox of flesh and ether whose otherworldly dimensions could only be matched by the brutal presence of her hands, constantly in motion.

And now here she was, sitting in front of Sebastian and insisting that she wasn't crazy. As if he didn't already know it, as if he couldn't recognise genuine insanity after years in the field.

'No, Travis, in fact I think I'm the crazy one. Pathetic, inadequate, and crazy all at once. Confused,' said Sebastian, running his hand through his hair.

'Enough!' said Travis, holding up her hand. 'I'm sorry, Sebastian, but we don't have time to talk about you now. Later, maybe, when I've got past the first gatekeeper, but right now things are on the line, if you see what I mean. Do you see what I mean?'

'No,' said Sebastian, with a sigh of relief. Because where would he have even begun, if Travis actually had wanted to listen? It was a blessing in some ways, to have a chance to devote his attention to something outside himself.

'You don't know about the puzzle?'

'Actually, no. Sounds like some kind of hacker competition?' said Sebastian.

'NO!' shouted Travis, and pushed off in the office chair with such force she almost flew backwards into the door on the other side of the room. 'Er, sorry. Sorry, Sebastian, really. I'll calm down now. It always gets like this here, every year, to begin with anyway; it tends to settle down once it's been going a while. Just ask Jensen, I really cuffed him one last year.'

Travis began to spin slowly in the chair, and raised the index finger of one hand critically.

'The first iteration of the Cicada Puzzle was created four years ago. It was my last year at Cambridge. Suddenly a puzzle turned up online, with the stated purpose of recruiting *exceptionally intelligent individuals* for … what? No one knew. Correction: no one knows! Still! Maybe the NSA do.

Maybe the FBI or the CIA or even MI5. There was a big hubbub among mathematicians, that's for sure. Yeah, I was reading abstract mathematics back then. I'd never seen anything like it. So refined! A bunch of us had a go … Childs, among others. We were up at Cambridge at the same time, did you know that? That's why he hates me. We never got any further than the third puzzle. Got stuck. It wasn't that difficult, really, a simple zigzag code, but there was this thing with the correlates we hadn't thought about. That the puzzle also existed *in the physical world*. Which made it impossible. What did we know about William Blake? Nothing. Childs blamed me for the defeat, which he was quite right about, of course. I've never met anyone more intelligent than myself, and still I failed. Sometimes it scares me. Really scares me. To think what's out there. But of course, that's ridiculous.'

'I don't think so,' said Sebastian, like the well-brought-up boy he was. 'And I'm sure you'll manage it this time.'

'You know what,' said Travis, and her eyes and cheeks lit up, 'I think so too! Every year I get further and further. Last year I was near the finish, I'm sure of it.'

'What happens if you manage it?'

'NO ONE KNOWS!' Now sparks were flying from her eyes and her chest was heaving in agitated jerks under the lab coat. 'No one has ever officially solved it. Maybe the ones who did were forced to sign NDAs. Maybe right now they're in a hideout somewhere, in the process of solving … *everything*. The whole shebang.'

'Or maybe it's all a big bluff,' wondered Sebastian aloud. 'Maybe there is no solution.'

'There's a solution.'

'How do you know that?'

'There's always a solution, Sebastian. It's just a case of raising your sights high enough. Have you ever seen the world from above?'

'You mean like from an aeroplane?'

'Exactly.'

'I'm not sure I understand.'

'Doesn't matter. Not many people do.'

Travis stood up and straightened her lab coat, as if she was ready to go. She glanced indifferently at the very moral monkey and walked towards the door.

'Wait!'

Sebastian got up from the table, scared of being left alone again with his idling brain. 'What was it you wanted? Why did you tell me all this?' he asked Travis's white back as it headed into the corridor.

She turned and looked at him in surprise.

'It's obvious, no? I need your help.'

'Mine?'

'Yes, yours.'

'Mine, why?' said Sebastian. 'We hardly know each other.'

Travis shrugged and blew away a few strands of hair.

'Because I trust you. And I need someone less ambitious at my side.'

He didn't know how to respond.

'To be ambitious is to create a rod for your own back, Sebastian. Be thankful you lack any hint of it,' said Travis, fluttering out of the room.

The same afternoon, Corrigan called Sebastian to his office for the second time ever. After concluding a session with one of his less interesting subjects — an older lady with a violent excess of euphoria — Sebastian took the lift up to the Institute's top floor and knocked discreetly on the door.

'Come in!' roared Corrigan, and Sebastian obeyed.

Corrigan sat at his desk with a telephone receiver jammed between his ear and shoulder, and signalled with one hand for Sebastian to take a seat. While he went on humming into the receiver, he pushed a plate of Jaffa cakes across to Sebastian, who took one, letting it melt on his tongue.

'Of course, of course. He's here now. I'll let him know. Absolutely. Pleasure was all mine, do call again! I mean it. So delightful. Mmm. Anyway, goodbye now. Goodbye.'

Corrigan slammed the receiver into its cradle — it was an old Bakelite telephone — and looked thoughtfully at Sebastian. He said nothing, and Sebastian felt the mouthful of Jaffa cake swell against his palate. *He's here now*? Who'd called? The possibilities fluttered through Sebastian's head.

The first thing that came to mind — the first thing that always came to mind these days — was Laura Kadinsky. Had she made a complaint? But nothing had actually happened! Nothing at all! Sebastian was sweating. Though Corrigan didn't look angry? But … jolly?

'So,' said Corrigan at last. 'It seems you have some family problems?'

Sebastian nearly choked on the Jaffa cake.

'Sorry?'

Corrigan nodded absent-mindedly at the phone.

'That was your mother. Terrific woman. Why've you never mentioned you're a triplet, Isaksson? We could do such fantastic observations. Though to be frank, in light of what your mother was saying, well —'

'Sorry, but. My mother? Has something happened? Is someone —'

Sebastian fumbled for his own telephone, which he'd turned off precisely to avoid his mother's calls for a while. Corrigan waved dismissively.

'Calm down, calm down. No one's died. She just wanted to ensure I was up to date on your situation. Considerate woman. Whatever, Isaksson, it would be interesting, eh? To know who's out. Triplets give more bang for your buck, of course, but even twin studies are interesting, and harder to arrange than you might think … Reckon it's you? Or one of your sisters?'

Sebastian sat with his phone in his hand, trying to get a handle on what Corrigan was saying.

'Your mom says she doesn't know? Undeniably rather unlikely, wouldn't you say, but I mean, women … A mystery.'

'A mystery,' Sebastian repeated, confused. 'My mother … told *you* … all this?'

'Don't look so surprised, your mom is terribly chatty, you must know that at least. And she really is very worried about you, Sebastian, you should call her more often. I know what I'm talking about when I say that few things hurt a parent more than a child distancing themselves from them.'

Corrigan leaned down behind the desk and slid out the thermos, setting it on the table with a decisive crash and twisting off the lid.

'Do you have children?' asked Sebastian, who couldn't conceive of anything more in conflict with the natural order.

'Not within ten metres of me, no,' said Corrigan, pouring coffee into both cups. 'Cheers.'

Sebastian raised his cup awkwardly.

'Well. As exciting as this little story about your family is, Sebastian, — and honestly, I think you ought to option it for TV, it's better than *Coronation Street* — it wasn't what I wanted to talk to you about.'

Sebastian automatically sat up straighter in his chair. Perhaps it was about Laura Kadinsky after all?

'Travis,' said Corrigan, locking eyes with Sebastian. 'She seems to have lost her grip a little. I'd like you to keep an eye on her for me.'

'Travis?' said Sebastian.

'Yes. This puzzle she's so obsessed with. It's a dead end. Goes nowhere.'

'I don't really know what I can —'

'Tsk. I'm not asking much. Just keep an eye on her. That's all I want. Tell me if she gets too crazy. Paranoid. You understand what I'm saying?'

'No.'

'That's good. Excellent.'

Sebastian felt worried.

'You mean I should spy on her?' he ventured.

'No, no, no! Of course not. Nothing so … sinister. Just be a friend. That's all. A friend with a duty to report. Travis is talented, Isaksson, but that's also her curse. I don't want to see her make herself impossible, that's all.'

'Impossible?'

Corrigan sighed deeply. Then he said, with exaggerated clarity:

'A certain degree of discretion. A certain degree of ignorance. The occasional blind eye. It can be good sometimes, Isaksson. Otherwise it's easy to go crazy. With your new family situation, I imagine you're inclined to agree. So. Understood?'

Sebastian nodded slowly, and Corrigan gestured to the door to signal the conversation was over. However, just as Sebastian was standing up, Corrigan appeared to remember something.

'Your sister,' he said. 'Matilda, is that her name? Your mother said she's both a synaesthete and bipolar? You should bring her here. I'd be lying if I said I wouldn't like to take a look.'

Kathleen always said: 'The body is a metaphor.'

Matilda missed Kathleen. Or, not actually Kathleen as a person — she didn't really know Kathleen any better than anyone knows anybody else, that is, on a spiritual level, or however Kathleen herself would have expressed it. She missed Kathleen's voice — American, slightly shrill, but melodic and bubbling with good humour. Of course, Kathleen wasn't American but Canadian, but what European can hear the difference anyway?

And she missed Kathleen's hands. It sounded erotic, Matilda thought, to miss someone's hands. And maybe it was. Sensuality had no definite colour and no definite goal. Kathleen would have agreed. She would have said it's a Western convention to draw a comparison between sex and sensuality. No, she wouldn't have said that. Not during a class. But maybe outside of the studio, if they'd been friends, if they'd been sitting facing each other on her sofa on Sonnenallee or wherever she lived, drinking nettle tea. Then Kathleen would have said that real sensuality wasn't about sexual lust but lust for life. *All bodily desire*, she would have said, *is sensual — and there's no desire that is only bodily, because the body and the consciousness are one. When you lift your heart to the sky in* chakrasana, *the pleasure you feel is the same as when your lover brushes the tips of their fingers across your eyelids.* And Matilda would have said: *My lover never brushes my eyelids with his fingertips.* And Kathleen would have leaned forward across the sofa and gently stroked her thumbs across Matilda's closed eyes. It wouldn't have been a big deal. It just would have been life, its movement back and forth, like the waves.

Matilda pressed the soles of her feet against the wooden deck, drew up her thighs, drew in her navel, lifting her hips towards the clear blue sky and closing her eyes so she wouldn't have to see it. Arms close to her head, hands behind her ears. Shoulders lifting up from this support, and a feeling, for a moment, that she was a tree springing up out of the earth. *Chakrasana.* Her arms were still as strong as tree trunks, as supple as lengths of willow. She closed her eyes and breathed into her diaphragm, as she'd learned to a long time ago, from someone who no longer wanted to know who she was.

It wasn't Kathleen.

Matilda Isaksson — twenty-six years old, dark hair, blue eyes, dog-killer, probably swapped at birth, and resembling nothing so much as an evil doll — was normally resident in Berlin, but found herself, at that moment, in the Västerbotten archipelago. A fucking annoying place to be, with this body and this reborn anxiety she knew so well, the newborn colour that really was new, but she did what she could to keep herself in check. *Halasana*. Backside in the air, toes behind her head, touching the warm wooden decking. The thing to remember in difficult positions is that they don't last forever. One summer, just one summer, then they'd go back home. No more arguments, no more migraines, no more jumping in the car and hurtling off to the Coop in Robertsfors because Billy forgot his snuff when they did the main shop. It was ironic in many ways, thought Matilda, breathing from the heart, that she was the one with the driving licence — when he was the one who'd grown up in Northern Sweden, when he was the man, and what a bloody man too. A man who carried heavy things, as in, for a living. Amplifiers: heavy, heavier, heaviest. Instruments. Mixing desks. Drunk teenagers, sometimes, if they were getting into trouble. But he said he'd never had to drive a car. There were always friends around. And if you couldn't drive, there was no need to stay sober. He'd say that with a grin whenever anyone asked. The joke had barely been funny the first time, and she'd heard it so many times since. She'd got her driving licence before going to Bangladesh. It wasn't required, but it was desirable, and Matilda wanted to do everything she could, she always did. What was the point, otherwise; of living, being human.

Her arms began to shake a little as the lactic acid flowed. She breathed: in, out, in, out. Then she slowly raised her legs and came down, bone by bone, until her whole back was on the warm wood. She stretched out her legs and arms, spreading like a broken egg. *Shavasana*. 'There's one sun in the sky, and one behind the pubic bone.' Kathleen actually had said that once. Probably the reason Matilda thought of her as a sexual person. Admittedly, Kathleen had been talking about *mula bandha*, the 'root lock', how it's like a sun rising from deep in the pelvis and moving through the body with its life-giving power. But still. Accurate, sexually speaking. Matilda felt a breeze like a hand caressing her nipples, so sensitive, another through her hair, the sun warming her inner thighs. There was only one good thing about being here, in this practically deserted inlet, and that was naked yoga. Not when Siri was in the vicinity, of course, Billy had expressly forbidden that, but he and Siri were often out on the boat, or on hikes in the woods, and then she was fine just to throw off her clothes. Matilda didn't like clothes, never had done. They chafed against her skin.

Maybe that was why she was drawn to warm climates. Bangladesh was fantastic in that way. Naked nights under the thinnest of sheets. By day, dresses that were little more than a piece of cloth with a few stitches at each shoulder. She often went without underwear. She'd told Billy one time, which was a mistake. Now he always wanted her to talk about it when they were having sex — but it wasn't a sexual thing! Or at least, not in that way, not fuck-sexual, even though some things about Bangladesh had been. It was just liberating. Everything about Bangladesh had been liberating. There was something about the colour palette, beige-yellow-gold-brown, those colours were good for her. The colour of sun-browned skin. The colour of dry earth. Turmeric, cumin, good deeds. Deeds, too, had colours, not just feelings — good ones were all golden-brown-tinged. As though you could hold them in your hands, like warm, pulsating, earthy orbs.

Evil deeds, on the other hand, were blue.

That was why she was so horrible here, it must be. The sea, the sea, she knew she couldn't live by the sea and yet still she'd agreed to come. 'Just for the summer,' Billy'd said. 'For Siri's sake,' Billy'd said. And she hadn't been able to say anything, because Siri wasn't her daughter and she refused to play the role of self-absorbed stepmother. If Billy thought Siri needed to go to Sweden every summer to pick blueberries and look for bear dung and celebrate midsummer in the pouring rain and everything else that was part of their culture, *fine*. She came too. All of a sudden, she had a lot to think about, a lot to process. Perhaps a change of scene would do her good. Perspective. That's what she'd thought.

But — she'd probably been mistaken, she thought now. There was a reason she'd decided to live in Berlin, after all; well, of course there were many, but one of them had been the lack of sea. There was only the River Spree with its grey-brown water. Not entirely unlike the Ganges, if you squinted a little.

'Tilda, for god's …'

Suddenly Billy was in the doorway. Matilda opened her eyes, back to reality and the decking, so brutal. Far from the optimal way to finish a session. But that was life with Billy, passionate and impulsive, and in some ways, she liked it. Always had done. Being taken on the bed, before she'd had a chance to say no. That was how they'd met, after all, an encounter that had more in common with a bloody traffic accident than the prelude to a — thus far — eleven-month-long love affair. Matilda had been out running along the Landwehr Canal when her knees had buckled and she'd fallen onto the pavement.

Though the fall had been fairly minor, the aftershock was anything but.

She'd been knocked over by a five-year-old on a scooter, and of course the five-year-old had fallen off and grazed her knees too, and Matilda had barely got to her feet before a bearded hipster with a — Matilda could hardly believe her eyes — studded wristband, like this was Sweden Rock in Sölvesborg or something, was bearing down on her, screaming in dodgy German that she should watch where the fuck she was going, fucking jogger bitch, running over little kids, and who the hell did she think she was, did she think she owned Neukölln or what, was she some kind of child-hater? In that case, he was here to let her know that children were unsullied souls and maybe that was why she hated them so much, because she was such an egotistical cunt she thought her own, to be fair, pretty sexy calf muscles had more right to take up space on this planet, this canal-side, than his angelic daughter's, alright? And Matilda had screamed back in equally dodgy German that it was actually his daughter who'd scooted into *her* and that perhaps he should pay more attention to her upbringing and that it was hardly surprising she had such an aggressive scooting style, given her father's obvious issues with aggression. And Billy, because of course it was Billy, had been so riled up he'd been unable to say anything, and instead breathed so hard some saliva escaped, and it was just as a fleck of spit mixed with snuff landed on Matilda's cheek that Matilda had realised that a) they were both Swedish, and b) she would end up in bed with Billy that very evening.

The latter turned out not to be true, because Matilda, in her childless way, had forgotten to account for Siri — in fact they hadn't gone to bed together until three days later, when Siri was at her mother's place in Reinickendorf. Two weeks later, Matilda had given notice on her flat and moved in with Billy and Siri on Weichselplatz. That was in September, and she liked to stand at the French windows at night and smoke grass in secret, watching the smoke do the same thing as the mist that had lain down to sleep over the play park below.

A dress landed on Matilda's face.

'Put this on. Siri incoming.'

'See any bears?'

'Just Johansson. He's bought a new chainsaw.'

'What shall we have for lunch?'

'Dunno. Siri wants pancakes.'

'I don't know how to make pancakes,' said Matilda, jerking the dress out of her face.

'How can you not know how to make pancakes?'

'I can splint a leg, build a house, and run a marathon. I don't intend to apologise for not being able to make pancake batter, I really don't.'

'One one two.'

'Okay?'

'One egg, one flour, two milk.'

'Okay?'

'It's also the emergency number. Kind of thing you have to know if you're a parent.'

'Which?'

'I'll go make pancakes now. Put some underwear on, too. I think Siri wants some cartwheel training.'

'Get me some?'

'No.'

Contrary to what Billy might have believed, Matilda loved Siri. At least, she did a little. At least, she did when she came up, like she did now, and pulled on Matilda's dress, and wanted Matilda to teach her everything she could about the art of circus and survival. Matilda's arms were all floppy from the yoga, but she couldn't resist Siri's eager prodding. She jumped down from the decking and did three cartwheels across the yellowing lawn that ran down to the sandy beach.

It undeniably helped that Matilda felt sorry for Siri. Her mother was an alcoholic and a workaholic, a strange combination normally only seen among men in the finance world. In some ways it was unfortunate that she was so high-functioning. Went to work, earned money, cleaned the apartment every Friday before she started drinking. Käthe — that was her name — was a make-up artist, and for that you needed steady hands, so she never drank in the week. She worked at ZDF, had done for several years, and had done make-up for almost every famous German, even Angela Merkel, who wanted a lot of eyeliner, at which point Käthe had to put her foot down. ('You have to be able to do that if you really take your work seriously,' Käthe had said when she was telling Matilda about it. 'You can't be afraid of anyone. Not even the Chancellor.') Working in TV was good if you were an alcoholic — most programmes were recorded during the week, Käthe only had to work occasional weekends, and she would know about them several weeks in advance and could switch both the drink and Siri to more convenient weekdays. It would be different if she worked for herself. 'A lot of weddings and so on. And who gets married on a Tuesday?' Not many people, Matilda had to agree, as she'd stood there holding Siri's hand the first time she'd dropped Siri off at Käthe's.

Of course, Käthe hadn't actually said that thing about switching the drink. It was Billy who'd said that, later that evening when Matilda had related the conversation and wept a little. 'She doesn't drink when Siri's there, does she?' Matilda had asked, blue patches floating before her eyes. 'When else would she do it?' Billy laughed scornfully. 'She's an efficient woman, my ex; she never does just one thing at a time. But Siri's okay. She's grown up with it and knows when it's time to go to bed and leave Käthe in peace. And if anything happens she can call me.' Matilda had protested that Siri was only five, she couldn't use a phone, but Billy had just laughed again and said Matilda obviously knew nothing about five-year-olds' telephone habits. And Matilda couldn't contradict him.

In any case, she felt sorry for Siri for having a lush for a mother, though not enough of a lush that Billy could take her away once and for all. Siri lived with Käthe two weeks in four, and of those two weeks, Käthe was drunk for at least four days, which Matilda thought was four days too many. Matilda felt ashamed that she couldn't do anything for Siri, but that was just how it was, only Billy could decide these things, and all Matilda could do was try to be a strong female role model for Siri. One who could do cartwheels and didn't care too much about her appearance, who drank Bionade instead of wine and tried to be a good person in spite of everything. It was easy to be good when Siri needed it. But that made it even harder with Billy — after all, she didn't feel sorry for him.

'Tilda, hey, Daddy says you can walk tightrope but I told him I didn't believe him. Can you?' said Siri, pretending to walk along the rope attached to the motorboat pulled up onto the sand.

'I can, Siri.'

'Did you go to circus school or something?'

'Yes, I did, actually. I wanted to be an acrobat when I was little. I used to try doing tricks with my brother and sister, human pyramids and stuff like that, but they were so bad at it I used to get angry.'

'Was that why you never became an acrobat?'

'No,' said Matilda. 'I changed my mind.'

'Why did you change your mind?'

'I just did. People do.'

'Hmm,' Siri said, hopping down into the boat. She climbed up onto the edge and started balancing her way along the rim of the plastic hull instead. She stopped short, as though something had just occurred to her.

'How come I've never met your brother and sister?' asked Siri. 'Are they dead?'

Matilda stiffened from head to toe. Billy. That fucker. Always nagging. As if it were that simple. But using a child as a go-between, that was ugly. Ugly and elegant all at once.

'They don't live in Berlin,' Matilda said quickly. 'You know that. Sebastian lives in London; it's a long way away. You have to fly. And Clara's on the other side of the world right now. I think.'

'What do you mean? We flew here, flying is REALLY EASY!' Siri shrieked, jumping down from the boat with flapping arms. Matilda caught her and whirled her one, two, three times through the air before dropping her in a giggling little heap in the sand. Matilda fell to her knees alongside and started to tickle her. It was by far the easiest and best way to end a discussion, forcibly and with laughter.

Then: OW. What the fuck.

A stabbing pain in her groin, a jerk somewhere in the monstrosity that was her muscle memory. The straining sensation of ligaments stretching. Automatically, she brought her hand to the top of her pubic bone before realising what she'd done — it couldn't be … No. Could it? God, no. Mouth suddenly dry. She forgot what she was doing, turned her eyes to the sea, felt a flash of blue split her skull. Siri pulling at her dress.

'Tilda! Tilda! What's wrong?'

'Nothing, buddy, I just pulled a muscle. I think it's okay.'

Tentatively, Matilda pushed her hips forward in camel pose, *ustrasana*. Let her head drop, hands on her ankles. Felt her stomach stretch like the skin of a drum.

It wasn't possible. And yet, of course, that was precisely what it was. Possible, and so familiar.

Oh lord fucking god.

As if she didn't already have enough to think about.

It was a few days after Sebastian's meeting with Corrigan, a Thursday of heavy clouds and unnatural warmth. TV and the front pages of tabloids flashed with the words EXTREME WEATHER. The Institute's employees sweated under lab coats and huddled around water coolers. In Kensington Gardens and Victoria Park, outside the Olympic Stadium and Somerset House, the fountains had been turned on for children to play in, even though the summer holidays were still weeks away. In Russell Square, too: Sebastian was standing at his office window watching scantily clad nannies with sunglasses on their heads trying desperately to stop two-year-olds in heavy nappies taking off their sun hats, when he suddenly realised his hair was wet too. He looked at the ceiling in confusion. The sprinkler system had started spitting out water, and the next second, he heard the lonely sound of the fire alarm's call to action, but Sebastian couldn't move — there was something almost magical about the sudden cool, an unexpected blessing. He caught the water on his eyelids.

The stillness lasted only moments, before he heard footsteps rushing along the corridors, the sirens of one, two, three, four fire engines, a recorded message saying: PLEASE EVACUATE IMMEDIATELY PLEASE EVACUATE IMMEDIATELY PLEASE EVACUATE IMMEDIATELY, and suddenly Sebastian realised that he had to save what could be saved. He threw a fire blanket over his work computer, more as protection from the water than from fire, since nothing can stop a fire, lifted the very moral monkey's cage in his arms — the monkey was whining louder than the alarm — and rushed out into the corridor, as Childs came along on a scooter.

'Is it a real fire?' Sebastian shouted.

'God knows,' said Childs, stopping short. 'Good times, anyway. We were thinking about going to the pub, coming?'

Sebastian shook his head. 'Have you seen Travis?'

'Down with the creepy-crawlies, last time I saw. But fuck her, she's a cat. Nine lives and counting.'

Childs scooted off towards the emergency exit and Sebastian followed him, as fast as he could with the monkey in his arms. Down on the ground floor he left by one of the emergency exits at the rear of the building, where large numbers of the staff, finding themselves suddenly without work, had formed clusters of excited bodies — cigarettes, bare skin, and the odd water pistol could also be seen.

It wasn't until he'd put the monkey down beside a wheelie bin and swept his fringe out of his eyes that Sebastian realised there actually was a fire — thick black smoke was belching from one of the windows in the basement. Three fire engines were ranged along a side street, with yellow hoses running along the ground from the first two. He couldn't see the firefighters holding the hoses; they'd been consumed by the smoke. In panic, Sebastian counted the windows — the fire was in Travis's lab, he was almost sure of it, and when he caught sight of a flash of gold, a flash of silver, and two transparent wings pierced with flame in the cloud of smoke, his last doubts evaporated.

'Travis!'

Sebastian threw himself into the cloud of smoke and started tugging at a fireman's arm.

'There's a person in there, a person!' he shouted. '*A human being!*'

Irritated, the fireman pushed Sebastian away.

'Stay back, sir!'

'But you have to send someone in, she'll die!' Sebastian screamed. It was all he could say before two strong hands took him by the shoulders and pulled him out of the smoke. At the same moment as Sebastian managed to free himself from the other firefighter's grip, he saw a window open on the ground floor.

Out of the window climbed Jennifer Travis, soot-faced and tousled, but otherwise apparently unharmed.

She stood on the pavement, coughed a little into her sleeve, and then caught sight of Sebastian. She looked thoughtful, rather than particularly shaken.

'Travis, Christ!' Sebastian shouted, trying to reach her, before being stopped once again by a fireman. Just then, an ambulance rounded the corner and two paramedics jumped out and got hold of Travis.

Sebastian stood rooted to the spot, unsure what he was expected to do. Demand to go with Travis to the hospital? He had difficulty believing she'd want him there. Try to help put out the fire? He'd probably just be in the way.

With something resembling excitement, Sebastian realised there was nothing he could do there. So he took his monkey and left.

But where should he go? The thought of going back to Tulse Hill and his dingy attic room, which would probably be boiling hot, the air stifling, greasy and hazy with dust, was not exactly appealing. The fact that he was toting the very moral monkey narrowed his options, too. What he would have most liked to do was go into the British Museum and lay his cheek against the cool surface of the Parthenon Marbles, but of course that was impossible, and the possibility of them letting him leave the monkey in the cloakroom at the British Library, his second choice, wasn't particularly likely either. What's more, he stank of smoke from the fire. But just as he was standing around equivocating on the pavement with the monkey's cage balanced on his hip, a bus came up the road. It was a bus to Camden.

It's hot, thought Sebastian. There are things to drink in Camden.

He got off at Mornington Crescent. A Dalmatian peed on a lamppost, the tiles on the Tube station opposite shone blood-red in the sunshine. The air smelled of exhaust fumes and caramelised almonds and expensive perfume evaporating from the sweaty skin of women; it smelled of marijuana. Sebastian was, by nature, a very honest person, he rarely lied to anyone, not even to himself — naturally, he knew why he'd come here. He wanted to see her house, her door, her windows, he wanted to see the magnolia in her garden that she'd spoken about with a kind of tenderness in her vocal cords. He wanted to see her child, perhaps. Her husband, her shopping bags, her pot plants, if she had any. He tried to convince himself that this wasn't pathological behaviour, but he wasn't sure. Was it really so strange, to want to know everything about another person? Wasn't that the very essence of love?

And yet he didn't love Laura Kadinsky, he was quite sure of that. He just wanted to know what she ate for breakfast, how her hallway smelled, whether she had carpets or parquet, and how many pillows she laid her head on at night. Just wanted to know something about her that no one else knew. Wanted to leave a trace, any trace, an indelible little mark on her cerebellum.

There was one thing he did know: her precise address, 42 Mornington Terrace. He knew the front door was the colour of lime blossom, because he'd seen it on Google Street View. He also knew that the risk of Laura herself coming across him was very small, since she was most likely at work. Which was lucky, considering he was still carting the monkey around. That would be very difficult to explain away. The monkey was restless — she'd been sitting in the cage much too long and was scrabbling at the bars with growing irritation. He'd have to let her out somewhere soon to feed and water her. He went from Mornington Crescent up the side street down which Laura had disappeared that evening they'd eaten hot dogs in Regent's Park. The street led up to what looked like a promenade along some kind of canal, but was actually just a wall that separated Mornington Terrace from the railway line that ran through London's northern suburbs in to King's Cross. Sebastian set down the monkey's cage on the wall and unbuttoned his lab coat, only now realising he'd forgotten to take it off. He looked out across the train lines towards central London, which opened out on the other side of them. In the foreground, the British Telecom tower poked a hole in the sky, an older but spindlier sibling to Berlin's Fernsehturm.

He thought of Matilda.

She'd called him the previous day; apparently she was in Sweden for the summer with Billy and his kid, whatever her name was. Siri? Like the girl in the telephone, the one who calls people for you if you ask her to. Intelligent, but not human — Sebastian didn't know whether he found the singularity of it fascinating or just tragic. In any case, he hadn't told Matilda that their mother had been so irrational as to ring his boss — *his boss!* — and expound upon their peculiar set of family problems. It was all so messy and weird. First he'd planned to talk to their mother, ask her what she'd actually said to Corrigan, and maybe also make the gentle suggestion that she in future refrain from so liberally imparting information about Sebastian's personal circumstances to those it didn't concern. But he still hadn't been able to bring himself to. She'd ask about Clara, for sure, and then he'd be forced to tell her that neither he nor Matilda had been able to get hold of Clara since the conversation either, and that would undoubtedly make their mother anxious. She'd long lived under the impression that the siblings were in constant contact with one another, that they were a hermetic trinity, when the truth was they never had been, not even as very young children. As adults they seemed, without ever having talked about it, to have agreed to keep up the charade, since it minimised the individual pressure on them from their mother. 'You look after each other, that's good,' their mother would say with confidence in her voice, though the reality was that not one of them even appeared to be capable of looking after themselves.

With his lab coat bundled under one arm and the monkey's cage under the other, Sebastian began to walk along the road. He walked slowly, so he wouldn't miss the door. Matilda hadn't seemed all that worried about Clara's silence. She'd mostly seemed angry. She'd said that Clara had always been much too sensitive, even cowardly, and that it was just like her to withdraw when things got tricky. Couldn't Sebastian try to get hold of her, *find* her, wherever she was hiding? No, he couldn't, he'd tried to explain that to Matilda, that Clara didn't seem to want to talk to him either and that actually, he didn't have some kind of mysterious supernatural ability to *force* Clara to answer the phone. But, Matilda had said, sounding genuinely dumbfounded, you're *you*.

Whatever that was supposed to mean.

In any case, they hadn't talked about the real issue, that is, who was the impostor, the fraudster, the lost child's shadow. Maybe Matilda thought it was her. Maybe Sebastian thought it was him; he didn't know. They'd probably never find out what their mother thought, or knew. As long as she didn't talk about it to Corrigan, Sebastian reflected, with all the cheerfulness of despair. Good god, the sun really was too much, how he longed to massage his thumping temples, but with both arms full of absurd paraphernalia, there was just no way. He stopped.

There it was — Laura Kadinsky's front door. There was the famed magnolia, which had lost all its blossoms by this point — the little square of grass under the tree was a bed of pale pink decay, steaming in the heat. Against the fence was leant a little bicycle with one of those rods on the back for a parent to hold on to. There were pots of lavender and poorly looking herbs on the stone steps leading up to the door. On the street, outside the gate, was a bright blue BMW; he wondered if it belonged to Laura and her husband, he wondered if he'd be able to live without ever knowing.

The monkey started fretting in her cage again, and he bent down to comfort her. It was as he stood up again that he caught sight of Laura. She was walking along the other side of the road, slowly, as though walking a tightrope. She was alone.

He bowed his head and pretended to be busy with the monkey. Perhaps if he walked quickly and discreetly past. Perhaps she wouldn't see him, perhaps she wouldn't look across the road, and even if she did, perhaps she wouldn't recognise him, or the monkey, perhaps she'd think: there's an ordinary young man taking his chinchilla to the vet's. He set off again and when he came to the end of the street, he saw — as he'd expected because he'd seen it on Google Street View — a pub with a gaudy outdoor seating area. He opened the door to the pub and slipped inside, certain he'd evaded discovery.

The bartender who was behind the bar when he entered the empty pub was not happy about the monkey.

'It says dogs are welcome.'

'Dogs are man's best friend,' the bartender said, without batting an eyelid.

'But apes are man's closest relation,' said Sebastian, and when that didn't help: 'Please?'

'What do you want?' she asked.

Sebastian sat in a corner of the outdoor area looking out across the street. When the bartender brought his beer, she was carrying a dog's drinking bowl full of water. She nodded at the monkey.

'Thought it looked thirsty.'

Sebastian thanked her and decided to ask if he could let the monkey out of her cage for a while. The bartender just shrugged, which he took as a yes. He opened the cage and let her climb up the fence that separated the seating area from the street. She hung and swung from a climbing rose, happy in spite of the thorns. Then her fuzzy face took on an expression of deepest dissatisfaction and, turning her back on Sebastian demonstratively, she climbed away along the fence, jumped down, and started sulking between two pots of sage.

'That monkey doesn't like me.'

Quick as a flash, Sebastian turned his head. With the sun behind her and Sebastian at her feet stood Laura Kadinsky. She was wearing sunglasses, which she pushed up onto her head before sitting down opposite Sebastian with a rather ungainly plop.

'Mrs Kadinsky —'

'I saw you,' said Laura. 'Did you see me?'

'Yes,' said Sebastian truthfully.

'Did you come here to spy on me?' said Laura.

'Yes,' said Sebastian, though he'd intended to say no.

'I suspected as much,' said Laura. 'Can you buy me a beer? As you know, I'm not so good with glass.'

Sebastian nodded and got up. He went to the bar, only realising when he got there that he had no idea what kind of beer Laura wanted, he couldn't even imagine it, so he went back.

'I wasn't sure what you wanted.'

'Anything except lager.'

Sebastian carried this piece of information back to the bar as though it was his most treasured possession. From now on he would always know this — admittedly quite unmentionably private — fact about Laura Kadinsky: that she drank anything except lager.

When he came back, Laura was crying. It was the most tragic thing he'd ever seen.

'You don't need to ask why I'm crying,' said Laura, drying her eyes with the sleeve of her blouse. 'I intend to talk about it quite voluntarily, because I've no one else to talk to about it. I'm crying because I've just got the sack.'

'The sack?'

'In principle.'

Sebastian didn't know what it meant to get the sack in principle — how it differed, if at all, from getting the sack in practice, and what you were supposed to say in such circumstances. So he did what he did best: he said nothing.

Laura picked up the glass with both hands and took three thirsty gulps. His legs were crossed under the table and he could feel the sharp point of her shoe hitting his leg as she kicked her foot, which she was doing frenetically.

'I got taken off von Horváth. Those were her exact words: "Laura, I'm sorry, but I have to take you off von Horváth, it's not going to work." Which she was quite right about, of course. It wouldn't have worked. Nothing works anymore. I can't even butter toast properly. And Philip doesn't notice. He has no idea. He thinks I'm still shaving my legs. The truth is, Sebastian, I haven't shaved my legs in three weeks. I'm scared I'll slip. Why else do you think I'm wearing tights in this heatwave? I used to have lovely legs.'

'I'm sure you still do have lovely legs.'

'Thank you.' Laura brushed a strand of hair from her face. 'But do I have a career? Apparently not. "Gardening leave." That's not a career. It's getting the sack. In principle.'

Astonished, Sebastian observed the way Laura leaned back in her chair and absently undid the top button of her blouse.

'Why were you spying on me?' she asked.

'I wanted to know more about your life,' said Sebastian, though he'd been intending to change the subject.

Laura opened her mouth, and for a moment it looked as though she'd forgotten how to close it. Her eyes, too, were wide open, dazzlingly blue. Then her face closed again around the hard kernel Sebastian had always found both heart-rending and irresistible.

After all, it took strength of a certain kind, to deny yourself something, year in and year out, whether that thing was food or happiness.

'You know,' said Laura, laughing her hard laugh, 'I think you already know more about my life than any other living person. Pretty tragic, isn't it?'

'Yes,' he said. 'It is pretty tragic.'

He reached across the table, touching her cheek for the first time, and she let his hand rest there for exactly four seconds before carefully lifting it away and laying it back on the table.

'Thank you,' she said, and the words sounded unfamiliar and clumsy in her mouth.

When Laura came home to Mornington Terrace later that afternoon, it was to a daughter on her way to drowning in a sea of tears, a little Alice who was no longer so little — when and how had Chloe grown so tall and slender-legged? And where was Laura during that time?

For a while, Laura stood in the doorway, a silent witness to her daughter's despondent sobbing in the hallway. Chloe was leaning against the wall with her head on her knees and her long butter-yellow hair swaying like a curtain of seaweed above the floor. Her wrists were so slim, without even the slightest trace of baby fat, and in a flash, Laura saw not a seven-year-old before her, but a seventeen-year-old, rejected, despairing, her child's spirit stunted and withered. Of all the horrors Laura had seen in her future since the day she was born, rosy, red, and raging like a little fury, which was it that had finally got to her, broken her? Had she been abandoned, rebuffed, jilted? Abused, raped, assaulted? Had she failed the test? Had she discovered she wasn't unbeatable? That she wasn't the best at everything? Had she lost her most treasured possession? Had she realised that her body would one day inexorably betray her? Her mind? That she too would one day be a puzzle where the pieces fell one by one between the floorboards, never to be recovered?

'Chloe ...' said Laura, more quietly than she'd meant to, but her daughter heard her, and Laura felt relief sweep like rain through her body when she saw her face, still without doubt a child's face, with a child's unblemished cheeks, clear eyes, button nose.

'Mummy! Mummy!' cried Chloe and threw herself into Laura's arms, so trusting that Laura would have felt tempted to start crying herself — again — if she hadn't been fully occupied with trying to arrange her arms around the child's body, finding her contours. 'Essie's missing! She's escaped!'

Relieved, Laura stroked Chloe's hair and let her rub her snotty nose on her blouse, even though it had just come back from the dry-cleaner's.

'Essie escapes all the time, sweetheart. She must be in the cellar. Or have you looked behind the cage? Sometimes she goes to sleep there instead.'

'You know I'm scared of the cellar, but Giselle has looked and she says Essie must be dead because she's been missing since yesterday and the Robertsons have got a cat and cats eat guinea pigs!'

'Has she been missing since yesterday? Why didn't you say anything?'

'Yeah, but Giselle said she was sure to turn up like she always does but now she hasn't she's saying that she must be dead and Mummy and Daddy will have to buy a new guinea pig but I won't get a new guinea pig, will I? Because Daddy HATES guinea pigs!'

'Chloe, Essie's a hamster, you know that ...' Laura mumbled, getting up to look for Giselle. With Chloe at her heels she went into the kitchen, where Giselle was clattering the dishes.

'Giselle, Chloe says Essie's missing and has been since yesterday?'

'Right.'

'But that's really strange.'

'Not really.'

'Why didn't you say anything?'

'Told Philip yesterday.'

'And?'

'And what?'

'Have you really looked everywhere?'

'Pretty much. I'm going home now.'

Giselle turned on the dishwasher, hung up her apron, kissed Chloe on the head, and said her customary 'Bye bye, Liebchen!' before making for the hall. When Giselle was halfway out of the door, Laura called:

'Giselle? Do you want tomorrow off?'

'Off? Course.'

'I'll be working from home, so I can pick Chloe up. Can you come again on Monday?'

'Course. Have a good weekend, then.'

'You too.'

Laura and Chloe stood there in the kitchen, holding hands. One finger at a time, Laura released herself from her daughter's grip, lifted the still-upset child onto the counter and, with lots of meaningless chatter and considerable spatial effort, began to make a nourishing moussaka.

When Philip came home at half nine, Chloe had finally fallen asleep, after repeated promises from Laura that Essie would turn up, and if she didn't, well, then perhaps they could consider getting a cat instead and if they did, yes of course Chloe could call it Marmelade. Pronounced the French way, of course, if that was what Chloe wanted. And Chloe — who was in a deeply Francophile phase — practised those guttural 'r's (*Marrrrrrrmelade, Marrrrrrrmelade*) until the moment the 'rrrrrr's turned into snores.

Philip was whistling in the hallway as he kicked off his shoes, as he always did when he was in a good mood, and bounced — yes, literally bounced — into the living room where Laura was sitting on the sofa taking great gulps of amaretto. Philip brought the summer in with him, the scent of barbecued chicken and gladioli and spilled beer evaporating off sun-warmed skin and tarmac, of perfectly ripe peaches and shisha and Pimm's and women's half-heartedly manicured feet in open-toed sandals. It was only the middle of June, but summer had well and truly arrived in Camden, where it always seemed to come earlier than in other parts of town — this was a well-established fact and possibly one of the reasons for the sky-rocketing house prices whose trajectory hadn't slowed since Frank Auerbach had first begun to paint Mornington Crescent in various shades of yellow.

'Good news!' hollered Philip as he went into the kitchen to get a glass.

'Do you ever have anything else,' Laura muttered and went to the bar to get the bottle of amaretto. It was Philip's favourite drink, rather than hers; she preferred a good, honest G&T, but since she'd lost control of the third dimension she'd been more and more inclined towards simplicity. A G&T involved too many bottles, knives, ice cubes, and lemons. She took the bottle back over to the sofa, managed to set it down on the teak coffee table and had just bent her knees to sit down when she realised she'd misjudged the distance between her bottom and the sofa cushion. Just as Philip came back into the living room, now topless and with a lit cigarette in the corner of his mouth, Laura thudded down, arse first, onto the ground, like a baby who'd just learned to walk. Philip grinned and held out a hand.

'Drunk on a Thursday, love?'

She batted his hand away and got to her feet again.

'No,' she snarled, throwing herself onto the sofa, this time with a more successful outcome. 'I'm angry.'

'You're always angry these days,' Philip sighed without actually seeming either worried or bitter. 'What have I done now?'

'Essie.'

'Yes?'

'She's escaped.'

'All's well that ends well.'

'It's not funny! Giselle told me she told you about it yesterday. Why didn't you mention it when I got home? Maybe we could have found her. Now it's probably too late.'

'Giselle told me? Yesterday? Yes, I suppose that's possible. You know, I often have difficulty hearing what she's saying. It's that lisp, you know?'

'Giselle doesn't have a lisp.'

'Are you sure? She has got some kind of speech impediment.'

'It's her bloody accent! An accent isn't a speech impediment, for Christ's sake.'

'An accent? Where's she from, then?'

'Brazil, you know that.'

'Thought she was from Newcastle.'

'Oh Christ.'

Philip shrugged and filled his glass with amaretto. Laura sat in silence and looked at her husband's chest hair as he stood there in front of her, drinking with the poise of a warrior. He was beautiful, that was certain, the dark hair was so wonderfully symmetrical on his broad chest, but he drove her mad. She picked up a sofa cushion and threw it at his stomach. He threw it back.

'Want to have sex?' he asked and crashed his glass onto the table with a force so perfectly judged it made both glass and table resound dramatically but not break.

'Sex?'

'Yes, you seem so tense.'

'What, so you thought you'd make the sacrifice?'

'Yes, I am your husband, after all.' Philip grinned widely and started unbuttoning his fly without further ado. 'And,' he went on, pulling off first one trouser leg, then the other, 'I'm in a good mood because of my good news, which you appear to have forgotten to ask about. So for that reason I'm going to tell you about it quite unbidden: I've been given an OBE. And if there was ever a time to pleasure one's wife, I should think it would be after one's been given a title.'

'Are you serious? You're on the honours list?'

'Why do you sound so surprised? If there's a Sir Paul McCartney, it was just a matter of time. But before forty-five, that really packs a punch, I must say.'

Philip pulled off his boxers and climbed triumphantly onto the sofa where he methodically started to remove Laura's jeans, socks, and the blouse covered in Chloe's snot. Laura noted that he at least had a semi and even though the thought of being sympathy-fucked by an Officer of the Most Excellent Order of the British Empire was fundamentally distasteful to her, she couldn't get it together to stand up and leave. She wanted so dearly to be given both sympathy and a good seeing-to, so who cared about honour and dignity. Not Laura Kadinsky, who, as she closed her eyes and raised her hips so her husband could pull down her underwear, couldn't stop herself imagining another pair of hands, another mouth and tongue, a body as golden as sponge cake and as hairless as a mannequin. Philip placed his hands under her back and she closed her legs on him like a snare.

The next morning, Laura took her daughter to school, then went home to look for the hamster. It was a desperate task in every sense. Deep down she knew she wouldn't find Essie — because Essie didn't want to be found. Only those who are in a cage can understand the joy of being released. Yet still Laura searched: fumbling, jumbling, stumbling, under stairs and behind the bookshelves' rows of books, under, inside, and above cupboards, out in the garden, in the spare room, among cables and washing, between tubs, bowls, and Pillivuyt crème brûlée pots, under rags and rugs and lilies and roses and under the grate of each of the three open fires. She didn't stop until she slipped on the cellar stairs and found herself on all fours with sore palms and kneecaps in front of Essie's empty cage, cheeks streaming with tears.

The hamster wheel was still, as was the air, and time. She was a wreck of a human being, and she knew it.

There was no reason, no reason at all, to pretend any different. So she got to her feet, brushed the hamster dust from her hands, painted her lips red with a steady hand, spritzed the scent of her own anxiety behind her ears, opened the door, and stepped out into her last summer. And through the park, that great green space, with its neatly gravelled paths and its golden insects, its powder-pink sweet peas and its murmuring waters, she walked with brisk steps towards her shabby, magnificent downfall.

See the dream.

You're dreaming of him and in the dream he's a beautiful criminal, high up in a paper tower. He pulls his hair, and he rubs his cheekbones, and it's you he loves though he is not permitted to say so. Perhaps that is his only crime. That he loves without permission and bites his tongue until it bleeds to keep the words away.

And the walls make him thinner and thinner until he is nothing but air, and when you wake, nothing but dust.

You dream of him and in the dream he is a beautiful marine biologist. He swims with the fish and the fish swim with him. He swims in the belly of the whale and the whale's belly is his. He climbs down the whale's gullet and points, saying: Have you ever seen such complex intestines. I don't believe you have.

You dream of him and in the dream he is a beautiful panda. You stroke his fur and whisper: Soon it will be over. Soon you will cease to exist and then you won't have to bear the weight of soon ceasing to exist.

You dream of him and in the dream he is yours, but also a house where someone has put a hand grenade on the mantelpiece.

At the Institute, the air was still behind closed doors. It was the day after the fire, but work had already begun anew — during the evening a very rare thing had happened: an email had arrived from Corrigan ('Keep calm and carry on!') in which he encouraged the entire staff to present themselves for work the very next day. The fire, he went on to explain, had been contained to a very small area, and had started in a cleaning cupboard, probably as a result of a damaged cable — the large volume of smoke had been caused by a hamster food store catching fire. Thanks to the fast work of the fire service, and the excellent sprinkler system in the building, all the animals had survived, aside from a number of Jennifer Travis's cicadas, which had been in the laboratory closest to where the fire broke out. Thanks were due to Travis and her audacious rescue attempt that not more had been lost in the flames — risking her own life, she had moved a whole three hundred cicadas out of the danger zone. For this rash action she'd been sentenced to a week-long working ban, a punishment Corrigan was convinced would sting the young workaholic in earnest. The fire service had inspected the rest of the building and the cable-chewer had been identified (it was one of Childs' rats) — in other words, there was no reason at all not to immediately begin work again.

Sebastian had taken the news with relief, because it meant he wouldn't have to keep the very trying monkey in his home for more than one night. Now he was sitting, as usual, at his desk, diligently collating data on the very moral monkey's reaction to all the speeches made by Winston Churchill, Clement Attlee, Margaret Thatcher, and Tony Blair during their prime ministerial tenures. Sebastian had concluded at an early stage that the monkey was a Labour sympathiser — the point of this specific experiment was to deduce exactly what it was in these ideologically coloured litanies that provoked a response in the monkey's moral compass, and whether there could be other factors — such as gender, age, tone of voice, and so on — that played a role and must be controlled for before any final conclusions could be drawn regarding the connection between politics and morality.

It was nice, Sebastian felt, to have something concrete to work on: graphs and statistics, the mechanical notation of figures in columns. It felt orderly, it felt like control. He found himself wondering if that was how his father felt about his work at the tax office — Papa had always said there was a certain beauty to the study of corporate reports that a layman would never understand. And sure enough, Sebastian hadn't understood it, not until now. He shuddered to think what that might mean — after all, it wasn't only his father's predilection for numerical figures he'd inherited.

Sebastian made it no further with this thought about the connection between statistics and sexual morality, because at that point a draught blew through the room, a strong gust that lifted all the papers from the desk and plastered them like sweaty handprints onto every wall and surface in the room.

Sebastian looked up. In the doorway stood Laura Kadinsky, her eyes burning with fever.

You dream about him, and for half a second, the dream is real.

The sea flashed blue, a wash of static in blues and gold glitter. And in the dark green undergrowth were blue, fluid-filled berries, unexpectedly heavy when they filled cupped hands. And the sky: blue, and the bicycle on the road: blue, and the memory of the poisonous frogs at Berlin Zoo: so mercilessly nail polish–blue, and the rings under those eyes in the mirror, and the gables on the house, and the knots on the hammock ropes, and the beads in Siri's hair: all of it so fucking blue! The headache was blue, too; it was always blue, just like period pains were brown and heartbreak was green and the mindful breath was golden, and Matilda wondered what had come first: did she get headaches because everything was so blue or was it all so blue because she had a headache?

'Out here, are you?' said Billy, spitting a wad of snuff over her shoulder. It flew past her in an arc, down into the blueberry bushes. He wiped his cheek with his hand and sat down beside her on the terrace. How had she never noticed how blue his eyes were? How was it that his gaze hadn't always given her a migraine?

'This place is too blue for me,' she said, turning her face away.

'You're sick in the head,' said Billy, half amused, half tender.

'My brother says it's normal. It's a neurological condition. Ask him, it's called synaesthesia and it's actually pretty common.'

'Ask him? When? I've never met the bugger. For all I know he might not even exist,' said Billy.

'Shut it,' said Matilda.

Siri ran across the sand with an inflatable dolphin under her arm, a fucking dolphin, blue of course, and her thin lips were blue like all children's lips are blue in the summer, because they're stupid and then swim in June.

'Did you know that dolphins engage in ritual gang rape?' said Matilda. 'As soon as a female comes of age all the males swim out to sea with her and rape her one after the other just to celebrate.'

'No, I didn't know that.'

'I hate dolphins.'

'But, I mean, they're animals? What can they do? It's programmed into their DNA or whatever,' said Billy.

'Humans are animals too. We're also programmed. No one wants to admit it, but it's the truth. What the fuck? Now she's KISSING the dolphin. You have to do something. I really don't think it's okay that your daughter is kissing a serial sex offender,' said Matilda and wrinkled her nose in disgust.

'Hey, what's going on with you?' said Billy, looking at her. 'You're so bloody angry these days.'

'I told you, it's too blue for me here. My head is about to explode.'

'So go in and have a lie-down. The bedroom isn't blue.'

'The bedclothes are blue, though, or had you forgotten?'

'That depends on how you see it. The main colour is white,' said Billy.

'I don't give a shit about the main colour! For Christ's sake, there are millions of blue dots in between the flowers. Dots, they're the fucking worst, they flash like little lightbulbs in my head.'

'I can change the sheets if you want. Though then we'll have to have Siri's Barbie sheets because there aren't any others.'

'Are you mad? We can't fuck between Barbie sheets.'

'Okay, I give up,' said Billy, holding up his hands in resignation. When had he stopped taking the bait? Matilda wanted to fight.

'I'm going to go and get some rest,' she said angrily. 'Maybe you can persuade Siri to stop Jack the Dripper down there, it's fucking perverse.'

'You're perverse,' said Billy with a grin, lifting his hand to touch her.

She didn't want to swat his hand away, but she swatted his hand away. There was something in her that just couldn't stop, a desire for violence, a desire to harm. He had so much goodwill, knew so little of the world's evil. It was enough to make her storm off into the bedroom, even though it was all her own fault.

She buried her face in the pillow with her hands tucked in under her stomach. Touched the sore spot between her pubic bones gingerly. Just a few days. Could still be a mistake. No point mentioning it.

Not like with the phone call. The one that had taken place a week or so before they left Berlin. The phone call that simultaneously explained everything and made everything very unclear.

The natural thing to do when you'd just found out you probably weren't your parents' child and your siblings' sibling would be to tell your partner. Especially if your partner is kind-hearted and insightful and extremely good at taking things, and life in general, as it comes.

But Matilda wasn't natural. As Matilda had always known, she was highly unnatural — half human, half monster, capable of cruelty but also fully capable of being ashamed of her cruelty. All these good men she loved and had loved. Everything she'd kept from them, for fear of hurting them. All the ones she'd hurt without meaning to. It was no surprise that her sister and nemesis had turned her back on her, refused to reply to her emails, vanished to the other side of the planet, and then, if their mother and Sebastian were to be believed, vanished altogether. They too had tried to get in touch with her, also without success.

Matilda sighed into her pillow. She couldn't tell Billy any of this. He'd make the problems seem smaller than they really were. She normally liked this aspect of his personality, but when it was about her whole existence, who she was, who she — deep down in her rotten soul — *was*? No. Fuck that. Maybe, thought Matilda, Billy's ability to tone down problems was a consequence of parenthood. You couldn't let a child know that some problems can't be solved. Not even alcoholic mothers, fake sisters, not even fucking *death*.

Not colours that didn't exist, and yet were there. That had floated above a coffin, taken root in your soul. Maybe even in your uterus. Ghost colours. Unnatural colours.

Leaving one hand under her abdomen, she pulled out the other and rested it on the back of her head. Pushed her face so deep into the pillow that all the colours in the world, natural and unnatural, faded to black.

Chestnuts and churches, sirens and *Syringa vulgaris*. He never got used to the sirens. The violence of their howls, the way they attested to the fact that misfortune never ends, it just moves on, from one broken bone to the next, from one burgled shopkeeper to the next, from a beaten woman to a beaten child to a beaten pensioner to a beaten heart, one bleating blue light to the next, and the next, and the next, like a torch. Now, don't lurch! Not into that lilac with its bewitching scent. Can't help himself. Stumbled onto a bus, stumbled off it, stumbled into a churchyard where the chestnuts formed vault after vault of aerated serenity. The sound of the sirens found its way in even here, though only just. He lurched along a gravel path that soon vanished under his feet, was soon no more than toppled gravestones covered in ivy; he tripped over one and fell flat on his face, cutting a gash in his forehead.

He felt his forehead with his fingertips and there was real blood. But it didn't hurt. He drew a shaky conclusion: *Endorphins have a pain-relieving effect. I feel no pain. It is likely that my body is filled with endorphins. Therefore, it is likely that I am happy, at least temporarily. This theory is supported by the fact that I have just slept with a beautiful and very eager woman who …*

Sebastian couldn't think about it without blushing. He lay recumbent over a crumbling gravestone and tried to staunch his bleeding brow with a fern leaf, tried to still his galloping pulse with thoughts of the most obvious thing, given his surroundings, that is, *death*; he was normally good at it.

A church spire cast its shadow over his stomach, the white coat he'd forgotten to take off. It was crumpled and stained, the collar full of brick-red lipstick marks, a button torn off, the cloth scented with sun and sin. Against his will, Sebastian closed his eyes and instead of a hideous corpse with violet lips, he saw a living body before him, Laura's body, over, above, floating like an airship, though with less rounded contours. He replayed the details over and over in his memory, compulsively — it didn't help when he tried to listen to the worms in the corpses under him, the images still welled up, mangled, bloody, as though torn from the flesh of time. With bare nails. The way her nails had pressed into his torso, had they drawn blood? In his mouth, certainly. Oh, her mouth. Her mouth! And her eyes, when he'd opened the door, their clear whites and dark pupils, tattooed with the devil's ink. The power of her arms, thighs, the power of her longing, and of his.

But for what? Presumably the same thing sex between strangers was always about, the desire to form a connection where no connection had previously existed, to draw a new line on the map, the desire to cleave to something beyond the familiar, the habitual, the mortal.

Of course, Sebastian knew nothing about this, because he wasn't accustomed to sleeping with strangers, and like everyone who makes a discovery, he believed the discovery was new and must be added to the record with a question mark after it. So he wrote her name on his arm with a fern dipped in old rainwater. After a few seconds, the letters sank into his skin and disappeared, but he knew the damage was permanent.

What had he actually done? Laura Kadinsky was a married woman, a woman with a child, a woman with a family. The fact that Sebastian didn't have one of his own, that the one he'd happened to be born into — (or at least, if he allowed himself to think the thought, quite frankly an unexpectedly liberating thought) happened by dramatic coincidence to have *ended up in* — didn't give him the right to just wade on into hers. But was that what he'd done? Or were there other forces in operation? And wasn't it her — Laura Kadinsky! — who had come to him, in his office, just now? Had it even happened?

From the undergrowth came the sound of someone clearing their throat and a whirring noise. Sebastian sat bolt upright on the gravestone.

'Travis? What the —'

A head popped up between the bushes and trees. It was a blonde head with pink cheeks and it belonged, sure enough, to Jennifer Travis. She too was still wearing her white coat, despite the regulations prohibiting staff from wearing them beyond a five-hundred-metre radius of the Institute. A few twigs of faded bird cherry blossoms had caught in her hair and some of the buttons on her lab coat had come undone to reveal a purple *My Little Pony: Friendship Is Magic* T-shirt bearing the text 'Daddy, I want a pony'. One of her lab coat pockets bulged. That was where the whirring was coming from. Jennifer Travis emerged from the thicket and brushed the hair from her eyes.

She looked low-level crazy.

'Sebastian, are you alone?'

'Yes,' said Sebastian, looking around him in confusion. 'At least I thought so ... How long have you been here? Why —'

'Not long. As long as you. I had to wait in the bushes in case you'd arranged to meet someone. Have you?'

'No. To be honest, I don't even know where we are.'

Jennifer Travis laughed her purring laugh.

'Don't know where we are! You're funny, Sebastian. Abney Park, of course. But this is no time for jokes.'

As if he didn't know. He put his head in his hands and groaned.

'Travis, I've done something very, very stupid. Something I could get the sack for. Potentially, or rather, definitely. And immoral to boot.'

'Talk to someone else, I know nothing about morals. But hey, look at this ...'

Travis pulled a jar out of her bulging pocket. A cicada sat hunched inside the jar; it was copper-coloured and of medium size. She tapped her finger on the jar and the cicada unfurled its wings.

'Want to see?'

She held out the jar to Sebastian, who didn't understand what he was supposed to be looking at.

'See that patterning on the left wing? If you put two left wings together, they form an "M". It's the first letter in the entry code. I've found four more: little "x", little "q", little "n", capital "A". Three more and I'm on to the first cipher itself. It's insanely frustrating, that first step, so banal, I think it's just there to wear you out, it's like they're trying to take the piss ... But enough of that. I followed you because I'm barred from the building for the rest of the week. That's why I want to talk to you. I've got some bananas with me. The world's most potent produce.'

Travis put the insect jar back in her pocket, sat down, and pulled a bunch of bananas from the tote bag she had on her shoulder. She broke off one for herself and one for Sebastian, placed the rest of the bunch neatly between them on the gravestone, and then ate hers in three large bites. Sebastian ate his, too. It tasted like a sunrise, like the first fruit in the first garden.

In other words, like sin.

Sebastian blinked the thought away. So drunk was he on the drama of his love life he'd almost forgotten that just the day before Travis had been close to being burned alive.

'What actually happened? Yesterday?' he said.

Travis bit her bottom lip nervously. She turned to look over first her left, then her right shoulder. A slight rustling in the leaves a few metres away made her prick her pretty little ears up. But it was just a bird. It seemed to have hurt one of its wings, was dragging it like a shackle.

'Did you know they clip the wings of the ravens at the Tower?' Travis said instead of replying to his question. 'So they don't fly away. You know what they say, that if the ravens leave the Tower it's the end of the monarchy and all of elite British culture.'

'They only do that for the tourists, you know. But hey —'

'That's what they want you to believe! Maybe they even believe it themselves. That it's only about tradition. But you know what. I actually think they're scared. The royals and all their henchmen. I think they're genuinely scared of their own downfall. Their own decline. Clipping the wings of a few ravens is a low price to pay for sleeping soundly at night,' said Travis, now almost whispering. 'If they only knew ...'

The June sun didn't quite make it down into the graveyard and Sebastian's behind was starting to get cold.

'Maybe we should go somewhere else?' he asked.

'Soon, soon. We're going to go to a pub and drink ourselves into oblivion, Sebastian; I just have to say this first. Okay. Now I'm ready.'

She took a deep breath, then crept closer to Sebastian and whispered in his ear:

'I've discovered certain things. Irregularities. At the Institute. Things that chill me to the core of my soul, and that's really saying something, since according to unequivocal testing methods, I don't even have one. Recently I've come to realise that we are no more than pawns in a gruesome game, Sebastian. You and I and all the others, we don't know what we're doing. It's only them up there who know, and the question is whether even *they* fully understand the consequences. Please, don't think I'm crazy, because I'm not. Corrigan and I have a special relationship —'

Sebastian involuntarily flinched at the thought of Corrigan and Travis's 'special relationship', a thought that became doubly repulsive when crossed with scenes from his own 'special relationship' with Laura Kadinsky. Travis tittered and boxed Sebastian on the arm before whispering:

'Not like that, dimwit! There's an intellectual understanding between Corrigan and me, like between father and daughter, it's just … Or …' Travis's voice caught slightly. 'That was what I thought. Until he tried to set my cicadas on fire.'

'Corrigan? No, Travis. Just, no. It was an accident.'

Travis rolled her eyes.

'A very convenient accident, in that case. In a very convenient spot.'

'But why would he want to —'

'The puzzle, Sebastian. The puzzle.'

'I don't understand …'

'No matter,' Travis said. 'Maybe that's for the best. Safer, for the time being. The important thing here, and the reason I need your help, Sebastian, is that Corrigan has started to shut me out. He doesn't confide in me in the same way anymore, and he's started expressing dissatisfaction with me. If he finds me in places he doesn't think I should be in, he yells: "Travis, back to the cellar!" It hurts — I mean, theoretically — but it's mostly worrying, from a human perspective. Something's happening and I no longer have the opportunity to stop it.'

'But what do you want me to do?' said Sebastian, who was beginning to suspect he was heading for a life as a double agent.

'Don't be silly! Corrigan likes you, that's obvious. The way you've advanced so quickly. You could become the new me —'

'But I'm not a Multi-talent.'

'No need. You're a man.'

'And —'

'Has he given you coffee and biscuits?'

'Yes.'

'That's how he operates. But it's fine, Sebastian, it's really fine. Now it's you and me against them. The best thing would be for me to create a code we can use to communicate. You'll have to remember the key, but it's not that hard; I can teach you a few techniques. You'll make your notes in the code, then send them via the regular postal system, I mean the Royal Mail, to one of my PO boxes —'

'But what am I supposed to —'

'Everything, Sebastian. *Everything*.'

It was late. Sebastian and Jennifer Travis sat outside the Jolly Butchers drinking Kriek. The drink was the same colour as Travis's alcohol-inflicted blush and Sebastian's bubbling blood. They'd been drinking for several hours, nothing but Kriek, and the sweet-sour cherry flavour had begun to fill Sebastian with a slight nausea. Maybe it was just the sense of loss of control that was making everything spin.

But it felt good! To lose control, lose his judgement, shoot his mouth off, not need to be responsible for anything at all, not even Travis. All this stuff she was talking about was a game, right? A seductive game — she didn't really believe it, did she? Impossible. Conspiracy theories. Arson. Ha ha! Sebastian was drunk. He couldn't remember the last time he'd been really drunk. Being drunk was fun.

'I've done something so fucking irresponsible, Travis, just wait until I tell you ... so fucking *irresponsible*!' he said, laughing loudly and throwing his arms out, nearly walloping Travis with the back of his hand. She lurched back and giggled, before slamming her head into the table.

'Well, that was irresponsible for sure!' she laughed. 'But you know what, I'm not interested!'

'In me?' slurred Sebastian, almost a little put out.

'No, not that either. But I meant, I'm not interested in what you've done.'

'Even if it's something so bad I would get the sack straight away if anyone found out? Even if it's something *obscene*, as my mother, I mean, maybe-mother, would say? Look! The sky!'

Travis turned to look at the sky, where the sun was just beginning to set behind the buildings on Stoke Newington High Street. The bricks glowed, the chimes of St Mary's struck ten, the horse chestnuts threw down their blossoms like confetti in a gust of wind, and the sky itself had a colour even Matilda couldn't have described with words. It was so beautiful Sebastian was having difficulty breathing, but Travis just shrugged.

'Can't you see?' Sebastian almost screamed. 'THE BEAUTY! It's bloody irresponsible for the world to be so beautiful when all you have to do is scratch the surface to see it's full of shit and anguish. Don't you think? Don't you feel the *pain* inside when you look at all this and know it's going to end? Love, life. Everyone lying and betraying and hurting. The fact we're all going to die … and so on.'

Travis just shrugged again and drank some more.

'I stopped thinking about that stuff a long time ago, Sebastian. All that fluff.'

'Fluff? How can you say that? Have you never been in love, never —'

'No,' said Travis, matter-of-factly, as if it was nothing to get agitated about, love, death, *and so on*. 'Not all people are like you. Not all people are even people.'

'Hello, hold on a second! Okay, you're a little weird, Travis, but you —'

'That's exactly what I'm not. Weird. *Ec-cen-tric*. Simply not true.'

'Sorry, sorry, I didn't mean …'

'It's fine. I know, I'm not really like other people, but it's just because I'm *not really a person*. Biologically, maybe, yes. I am of woman born. But there's something up here,' said Travis, rapping her skull, 'something up here that's *deeply inhuman*. Wanna know how I know? I've done the test and failed.'

'The test? Which test?'

Sebastian had lost her.

'The Turing test, of course,' said Travis.

'But that's what they use to judge —'

'Artificial intelligence, yes. But why shouldn't it work the other way too? You know, when we use the term "artificial intelligence", we really mean the *opposite* of intelligence. We mean the emotional stuff, the irrational stuff — the human. I must have been about fourteen; you know how it is when you're fourteen, you think about this fluff a lot. Existence, identity, the soul, all of that. Who am I. I had this feeling I couldn't shake off, that there was something about me that wasn't like other people —'

'Doesn't everyone feel like that at that age?'

'That doesn't mean it's not true. For some people. I've always been odd, but it became more tangible then, in my teens, I mean. I saw patterns where others saw life. I saw causal relationships where others saw movement. When a guy was interested in me I didn't know whether to be happy or angry, because I didn't know what had caused it, I mean, what he wanted, and without a logical basis I can't feel any emotion. I became more and more nervous that maybe, in spite of everything, I wasn't human. Because what is a human really? The sum of certain parts, certain neurological patterns, and I was convinced I was missing several of these parts. At that point it no longer makes any difference that my body is flesh and blood and that I have the same physical needs as other people. It's not our bodies that make us human.'

'But ...' Sebastian was upset from the depths of his Christian-humanist soul. 'That's a fascist mindset. The idea that the value of human beings is conditional.'

'Yes and no. But I'm not saying I have less right to live because I'm like this. Non-human. That I'm worth less. There are many people who aren't humans in the true sense of the word. Coma patients. Some people with other brain injuries. Newborns. I'm not saying we don't have a right to exist. If that was the case, I would have killed myself. I'm just saying there's a line between you and me and that's what the test showed: that I'm not human. I'm a *machine*.'

Sebastian looked at Travis. She looked back, smiled a little. He tried laughing. He got no laugh in return.

'You see?' said Travis, calmly. 'A *human* would have been hurt that you just laughed. But not me. I'll buy you a beer instead. Another Kriek?'

Three days after Laura and Sebastian's carnal union, the magnolia's buds burst.

Again.

It was nothing short of a miracle, because the magnolia had already blossomed, its time was long past. Laura was sitting on the front step with a cup of tea balanced on her knee, despairingly fascinated by how easy it suddenly was to tell the ceramic from the sunbeams stroking it, to slip her hand between light and material and lift the cup to the mouth that had just torn a hole in another person's skin.

Her nostrils were full of world. Her world was devoid of people. Chloe was at school, Giselle had a day off to go to the doctor's, Philip was somewhere where men with three-day shadows slapped each other on the back and bought and sold chunks of Marylebone. Everything was summer and warmth. For the first time since the problems had started at the theatre and Laura got the sack — the sack! — she didn't feel threatened by the fact she had nothing to do.

Perhaps it was possible to live like this — from moment to moment, without plans or objectives or a bigger focus than what was in your hands, whether that was a cup or a very beautiful man's genitalia. What did it matter that the rest of it was flat if the potential existed for a bottomless source of satisfaction and meaning in the moment? This was roughly what Laura Kadinsky was thinking as she sat there on her step and suddenly heard a juicy 'pop', followed by another, and then another, and yet another. She looked up and there in front of her, like blotches of colour on a sky-blue canvas, bud after bud turned into a little pink cloud, an abstract postcard scene, a Jackson Pollock in a girly colour scheme.

At first Laura was astonished. Then close to tears, from equal parts sorrow and some kind of reverence. For five springs she'd watched the magnolia blossom, but never like this. This was magic, a new spring just as the old one ended. Maybe it was some kind of compensation, thought

Laura, for the spring she'd missed. The lack of depth suddenly seemed less of a handicap, more of a gift. Experiencing the world anew! Like a child or a fool! Like an artist! Wasn't that something to be thankful for? Overwhelmed with awe at the world's mysteries, Laura jumped up from the step — the cup fell from her lap and smashed to bits against the stone, but it was only an ugly stoneware one Chloe had painted in her first year at Montessori school — and stretched her arms towards the tree, before fumbling forward and finally falling against its rough trunk. She hugged the tree. Breathed its sour scent. Wept and scratched her cheek against the bark.

'Mrs Kadinsky? Laura?' She opened her eyes. On the other side of the fence sat Mr Robertson, her neighbour of cat and catheter, in his wheelchair, looking at Laura enquiringly. 'Everything as it should be?'

'Mr Robertson! Yes, everything's fine. Or, well, not everything. I'm looking for Chloe's hamster, you see,' Laura lied. 'Essie. She's escaped.'

'I don't think hamsters can climb trees,' said Mr Robertson.

Laura fought back the tears and stuck her hip out a little, something she knew old people thought looked jaunty. 'Well, that's just what I said to Chloe. But she insisted. She's crazy about that hamster, and even crazier now it's gone. Have you seen this, by the way? Our magnolia. Isn't it strange?'

Laura nodded at her tree, but didn't get the response she was expecting from Mr Robertson. She looked up and the blossoms were gone. Every single one, as if they'd fallen to the ground the moment they opened. It was the shortest blossoming in the world.

'Are you sure everything's fine, Laura? You look a little pale,' Mr Robertson said.

'It's just rehearsal week at the theatre,' Laura said slowly. 'I must be going.'

The former may have been a lie, but the latter was true. Laura had an appointment booked with Sebastian at the Institute.

She thought of his hands, how they opened for her like petals.

When she arrived at the Institute about an hour later, there were still crumbs of tarmac on her forehead. She'd tried to make a rapid exit from

Mornington Terrace in order to avoid further detention and enquiry from Mr Robertson, and had swept the fragments of the cup behind a plant pot before locking the front door and jogging down the path and through the gate. She'd turned and waved to Mr Robertson, who was on his way up the ramp to his front door. This was an overconfident step too far — when she turned her head back, the world slammed like a door in her face and she fell face first onto the pavement. On her way down, she thought she spotted something brown and fuzzy from the corner of her eye. She stretched out her hand, but it was too late. Essie, if indeed it was Essie, had already disappeared into a bush.

But the faux pas was forgotten the same moment she locked eyes with Sebastian in the corridor outside his office, as he rushed from one direction and she made her way tentatively, heart stumbling, from the other. Without a word, he opened the door to his office and showed her inside. She slipped through the tense silence and sank into the chair in front of his desk. When her knee accidentally touched the desk, all her blood flowed immediately down into her groin. Sebastian came and sat on the other side of the desk. Without saying anything, he leaned forward, and with a gentle hand removed a few black specks from her forehead. Stroked his finger over her cheek where the magnolia's bark had left a cobweb of scratches and cuts. Laura squinted. Over the room hung an erotic smog so thick it was impossible to see through. Everything was blurry, as if they were both drunk, but the filth of life had a golden sheen, small grains of something eternal, immortal, and pure.

Let it bloom, thought Laura.

Then, all of a sudden, Sebastian turned away, tapped at his keyboard a few times and cleared his throat.

'Any new observations since we last met, Mrs Kadinsky?'

'Sebastian, stop.'

'Laura,' he said, curtly.

'Yes?'

'What happened between us shouldn't have happened.'

'Yes,' Laura said, decisively. 'Yes it should.'

'I have certain responsibilities as an employee of this institution, and one of them is to not have sexual intercourse with my subjects. It's explicitly stated in my contract. It applies both to human and animal research subjects. I think it's primarily a rule to protect the latter, but the fact remains: you're in a position of dependency on me and it would be wrong of me to exploit it. Also, you're married.'

'Seb—'

'Stop.' Sebastian raised his hand. From one corner Laura could hear a shrill, agitated gurgling. She looked towards it and caught sight of that damn monkey.

'Can you shut that thing up?' said Laura.

'No,' said Sebastian. 'That's exactly what I can't do. That's the problem. Laura —'

'Stop saying my name if you don't intend to fuck me again. I can't stand it.'

'This is not easy for me, either. I'd be very happy to —'

'Yes?' said Laura, fixing him with her gaze. 'What?'

The monkey howled. Sebastian put his hands over his ears. Then he stood up, without a word, and went over to the cage. Lifted it up and carried it out. A few minutes later he came back, empty-handed. No, not empty-handed; he came back with his hands full of her, she could see it. She got up, went over to him, pushed the door shut behind him.

He took her hands, kissing her fingers. 'Don't you feel guilty?' he mumbled.

Guilty? Maybe a little. But what was a little guilt? Just dirt under your fingernails, a sorrowful lining to an existence that would otherwise lack all contours.

Slowly she pushed her fingers deep into his mouth.

The window of the Dalston cafe where Jennifer Travis had asked Sebastian to meet her hadn't been cleaned in a long time — when he stood outside and looked in at her she appeared stripy behind the streaked pane, as though someone had torn off strips of her, like old bleached wallpaper.

He could only see one half of her face. She closed her one eye, her head resting against a red velvet chair, one knee up against her chest, her grandmother-pink blouse dishevelled, on her finger the concentrated glitter of a sunbeam reflected from a ring. She told him later that she'd been given it by the guy in the cafe. It had been hanging with a bunch of other geegaws from a chain by the bar and he'd just reached out his hand, pulled it off, and given it to her. Said it was an antique, though anyone could see it was made of plastic. Then he put it on her finger. 'Why did he do that, do you think?' she asked Sebastian, seeming genuinely perplexed. Because you're beautiful, of course, thought Sebastian, because that's what anaemic young men who work in ironically decorated bohemian cafes do when faced with the beautiful and the oblique. Try to charm, in any clumsy way they can. Try to touch. But Sebastian didn't say anything, because the last thing Travis needed was yet another filter to view the world through.

The cafe door tinkled when Sebastian opened it, and Travis immediately lifted her head from the wing of the chair and waved her beringed hand. Her fingers left a trail, rents in the dust that hung heavy and dense in the thick air. It smelled strange, too. As though someone had tried to conceal the smell of rotting corpses with large quantities of potpourri. One of Travis's pumps had fallen off her foot, and when she bent to pick it up Sebastian noticed a large marmalade cat under her armchair, staring out indifferently. Sebastian couldn't decide whether this place was trying to be cosy or terrifying. He sat down in the armchair opposite Travis and asked, without irony:

'Come here often?'

Travis looked at him, uncomprehending.

'Here? Of course not.' She looked around the cluttered room as though realising for the first time that she was in a physical place, a place that, through its try-hard decor of small occult objects, stuffed animals, cushions with cross-stitched cats, cracked cups, and pornographic watercolours of indeterminate date, was screeching for attention.

'Take a look at this ...' Travis rummaged around in her handbag and simultaneously summoned the pallid waiter with her eyebrows. When he arrived she ordered, without asking Sebastian, cream tea for two, and then shooed the waiter away like a cat. She'd finally found what she was looking for in her handbag and triumphantly hauled out a paperback so thick Sebastian wondered how on earth she'd managed not to locate it immediately. She threw it over to Sebastian and he caught it the moment before it hit the shelf of medicinal glassware thickly coated with grease and dust that was on the wall above his seat. The volume — *The Complete Poems: Philip Larkin*, edited by Archie Burnett (Farrar, Straus and Giroux) — was a modern edition, but was starting to fall apart at the spine as a result of what must have been very thorough study.

'Larkin ...' Sebastian muttered, trying to remember something about that elusive name. Hadn't Violetta ... ? No. Maybe not.

'Larkin is currently irrelevant. Passé, so to speak. I just wanted you to understand. Look —'

Travis bent forward and quickly flicked to page 84. The margins were full of long scrawled strings of numbers and letters. Sebastian's eyes scanned the poem, which was annotated with these strings of code via arrows, underlining, and little hearts. It was called 'The Building' and was very clearly about a hospital, though when Sebastian starting reading it, it felt like the poem was about his immediate surroundings:

Higher than the handsomest hotel
The lucent comb shows up for miles, but see,
All round it close-ribbed streets rise and fall
Like a great sigh out of the last century.

'Sebastian. Focus! Have you seen this?' Travis tapped her finger on the bottom of the page where someone — she herself? — had written under the page number (84) and the title of the collection (HIGH WINDOWS), scrawled in capitals: 48 BALL SPONDRD. 48 Balls Pond Road was the address of the cafe, and for a very short while — before he realised he actually only had Travis's word as evidence someone was trying to communicate with her via a book, since he couldn't decipher the mathematical patterns Travis apparently detected where he only saw poetry — Sebastian felt a slight tickling sensation in his brain's thrill centre.

'It took several days but I cracked it, Sebastian. I've made progress. Here in London! There have never been any correlates here before, so what does it mean? Maybe nothing, maybe everything. Remains to be seen, of course. Here are our scones. Thanks, love.'

Again, Travis sent the young anaemic packing with a wave of her hand. She pushed a plate of fat-laden fruit scones towards Sebastian. He was about to take a reluctant bite when Travis said: 'What do you know about Francesca Woodman?'

Sebastian jumped when he heard the name, his wrists and legs jerking so hard he dropped his scone in his lap. He left it there, bewildered, left it there to spread its greasy shadow across his trouser leg, like the body painted on a wooden floor in a picture he'd seen once but could no longer remember clearly, overshadowed as it and all the other images Violetta showed him had been by the last one, the one that came through the mail in a little envelope the day after *what happened happened*, and the one who hung, hung, just hung there, toes pointing to the underworld.

'I think this place is unpleasant,' said Sebastian. 'It feels like a burial chamber. Or the underworld. This floral scent, it reminds me of Hades and Persephone and everything rotting and breaking down.'

'You should see the basement,' Travis said. 'You can really feel the moisture running down behind the wallpaper. But you know, artists, they love that stuff. Apparently they have exhibitions and stuff down there. And an aquarium with no fish. I think it's weird. But that was where I found the picture.'

'The picture?'

'The Woodman picture. You never answered. Do you know who she is? Francesca Woodman?'

'Yes,' Sebastian said. 'Better than I'd like to.'

'I had to google,' said Travis, double-tapping her index finger on her phone on the table between them. The screen lit up and Sebastian felt all his muscles stiffen, as though anticipating pain. But the screen showed only a wallpaper of a sleeping baby with cheeks like plump currant buns. Sebastian didn't ask whose baby it was. Travis provided the information anyway, as she picked up the phone and started tapping away.

'She's cute, right? She's the first result you get if you google "cute sleeping baby". I don't know her name but I call her Beanie. I think babies should trigger certain emotions, you know? So I thought I'd try for a bit and see what happens. If I look at her a few times a day. So far it doesn't seem to be doing much, thanks for asking, but I haven't given up.'

'What does this have to do with Woodman?' Sebastian asked impatiently.

'Nothing. Woodman is the important thing. That was just a tangent. Woodman is the next step. Not on her own, of course, but together with this code.'

She held up the phone for Sebastian. Against a dark background he saw a large number of symbols, mostly the kind found on the outer rows of buttons on a complicated calculator. Together they formed a slightly lopsided 'y' shape, the lower part of which curved to the left in an organic arc which made the shape look more alive than dead, more like art than mathematics.

'Get it?' said Travis. 'This is step three, but it's been completely impossible to even try to figure it out before I found the correlate. You always have to find the correlate. And the correlate here is Woodman. Maybe the image down there, maybe a different one. Probably a different one. Possibly something to do with death, angels, or birches. It's open to interpretation, and yet not. This bit is hard for me, absolutely the hardest bit, actually. Emotional intelligence, as they call it, but I don't know if I'd even call it intelligence. Sebastian,' and here Travis leaned forward and took hold of Sebastian's knees with both hands as though her life depended on it, as though he were a lifeboat and not just an ordinary fragile husk of a human, 'is there logic in art? Please, say yes! Otherwise I'm lost.'

Sebastian pushed away Travis's hands, almost aggressively, because now he understood exactly which picture she was talking about. Without a word he stood and walked through the sleepy cafe, followed a sign pointing towards DOWNSTAIRS SEATING AND GALLERY SPACE down a narrow flight of stairs and into a room where the ceiling pressed against his head and the sound of an aquarium bubbled out of time with the hiss of an Air Wick plug-in that rhythmically squirted out a plume of synthetic lily scent. Everywhere he looked there was something missing. Fish in the aquarium. A lightbulb in the cracked Tiffany lamp on a pedestal in the corner. People in the perversely plump velvet three-piece suite in the same shade of grandmother-pink as Travis's blouse: if she'd sat on it, her head and throat would no longer seem continuous with her lower body. But no one was sitting on it, and to judge by the layer of dust on the coffee table, with its yellowing copies of *National Geographic* and old Penguin paperbacks, no one had in a long time. Along one wall, opposite a bookshelf full of porcelain dolls in crêpe de Chine dresses and a plastic palm in an used beer keg, there were stacks of old records piled in what Sebastian took a while to accept was a white coffin, child-size, with rips in the pale pink satin lining.

And there, above it, hung the picture.

Just as small as the first time he'd seen it, maybe twelve centimetres by twelve. Stuck there between dozens of gaudy photos, posters, and illustrations, it glowed in black-and-white clarity. Everything was as he remembered. The dark hexagons on the floor, whose marble chill you could feel against your feet just by looking at the picture. The shiny wood of the chair, its heavy, dark carvings, as though made for a confessional. The light switch, the cord, the table, the picture, the scrap of paper on the door that said: nothing.

And the body, hanging in the doorway that wasn't a doorway because the door was shut — a lopsided 'y', the lower part of which curved to the left.

The toes pointing to the underworld.

'Tilda?'

'Yeah?'

Matilda looked up from the bowl of pick'n'mix. Billy was standing in the bedroom doorway, drying his shoulder-length black hair with a towel. He was wearing nothing but shorts, shorts and tattoos.

'Siri wants to go to my dad's; apparently he's bought a trampoline. I told him he'll regret it when all the neighbours' kids get word, but, hey. He wanted to do it for Siri. Coming?'

Matilda felt confused.

'Coming?'

'To my dad's? For Tosca cake? You love Tosca cake.'

'Oh right, no thanks.'

Billy furrowed his brow.

'What is it? Seems like you're somewhere else somehow.'

Matilda pushed the sweets away and leaned back on the sofa. It took all her energy to smile like a normal person.

'Just a migraine,' she said. 'Say hi to Greger.'

As soon as she heard Billy's and Siri's bikes turn onto the forest track, she pulled the bowl back towards her. It was still there. The colour. Or whatever it was. It was a boiled sweet, tucked between an old-skool liquorice boat and one of those white cubes they call sugar cubes even though they're, like, five times bigger than a normal sugar cube. Matilda dug her fingers into the bowl and wiggled out the enigmatic candy. It felt like a totally normal boiled sweet, with even, smooth edges, a glossy surface, slightly sticky to the touch. Smelled of lemon. So it would be logical to assume it would be yellow. It wasn't. Neither was it green, white, or orange, which would also conceivably have been citrus colours. Neither was it red, pink, purple, blue, brown, or black, all of which would at least have been colours, conceivable in that they *actually existed*. Neither was it transparent. It wasn't a soap bubble, a rainbow; it wasn't a black hole.

It was the colour of life. Or maybe death. Fuck knew.

The first time Matilda had seen the colour was in the churchyard, when the coffin containing a girl's body — a girl who, ironically, was named after a colour — was lowered into the cold earth. The colour had hovered there, like a little cloud.

She realised immediately that it wanted to tell her something. Unclear what. Afterwards there'd been arguments and tears and Matilda had almost forgotten it.

That was the first time. The second was several months later, after she'd moved to Berlin and met Billy. They'd been to the cinema and seen a film she couldn't remember the name of, and she probably wouldn't have remembered it at all if it hadn't been for the fact that the film's leading actress — Dakota Fanning — had come striding into the bar on Weserstrasse, where she and Billy had stopped for a beer after. She was wearing a dress, a polka-dot dress, and the dress was that same colour. 'Look,' Matilda had said, pointing at Dakota Fanning, and Billy said, 'Fuck, that's crazy,' and Matilda could hear clearly from his voice that the crazy thing, according to Billy, was Dakota Fanning herself, not her otherworldly dress — he didn't sound quite jittery enough.

The third time was one night in late spring, when she and Billy had sex on the sofa in their apartment. The windows had been open to the chestnuts outside and the colour had snuck in, like a fog around the big terracotta pot with the monstera in it. Was it then, maybe? Was that when it happened?

It had just been those three times, though she could see now that her relationship with all the other colours in the world had gradually grown more strained in the months leading up to the conversation, their mother's big reveal. Then they came up here to the cabin, and now this weird colour was popping up everywhere!

Every time Mama called, and that was often, almost every day.

Every time she sent an email to Clara without getting a reply.

Every time she threw up, every time she tried seriously to think about what she should do, with the maybe-baby in her belly and the baby who was herself. The swapped-at-birth baby, that is. Their mother was still straight-up denying it. Oh Tilda, I really have no *idea*.

Not to mention the baby who was Clara, the little spoilt brat.

Matilda sat on the sofa with the sweet in her hand. Tosca cake. Course she bloody liked Tosca cake, smooth and syrup-coloured. This boiled sweet, on the other hand. A goddamn taunt. What the fuck did it want? Huh? She stared at the sweet, as though she could will it to change colour. She couldn't, of course. She found herself longing, really longing, for Sebastian. Billy would never understand — if she told him she was seeing a colour that didn't exist he'd drive her straight to the nearest nuthouse. Matilda had never felt it was a mistake to tell Billy about her illness, her history of epic mental breakdowns, but it would hardly make her more credible.

Sebastian, on the other hand — he'd understand, maybe even know. Why her brain did this to her, tormented her like this when she had quite enough torment already. Sebastian, she thought, lifting the hand holding the sweet to her lips, could solve everything if he only wanted to.

But he wasn't here. Only she was here. Tentatively, she opened her mouth, and though there was some resistance, she popped the sweet in, bit down, and crunched and crunched and crunched.

On Saturday, shortly after their meeting in the peculiar cafe in Dalston, a letter arrived from Travis. It was completely incomprehensible. Sebastian stood by the mailboxes in his stairwell and twisted and turned the letter in an attempt to get the message, neatly inscribed in a rounded schoolgirl style, to mean something. After a few minutes he gave up, stuffed the letter back into its envelope, and was just about to go up to his flat when there was a knock at the door. Travis stood outside, dressed in a shalwar kameez, something Sebastian could only interpret as an attempt at disguise.

'Did you get my letter? Let me in, quick.'

Travis forced her way past Sebastian into the stairwell, removed a pair of film star–sized sunglasses, and let the shawl she'd wrapped around her head fall.

'You think I'm being ridiculous,' Travis said, eyeing Sebastian sulkily.

'I didn't say a thing.'

'There was a man at Peckham Rye. He looked at me. Like, for a long time. I couldn't stop thinking there was something going on. He had a red beard.'

'A red beard?'

'Like Corrigan.' Travis started up the stairs to Sebastian's flat, simultaneously wriggling out of the embroidered shift of the shalwar kameez. Inside, she stepped out of the loose trousers and folded everything into a neat pile beside the two pairs of shoes Sebastian owned.

'Got any tea?'

Sebastian filled the kettle while Travis dropped onto the divan. It was a warm day, another one, and she was wearing only shorts and a semi-transparent folk blouse — Sebastian caught a flash of palm-print bikini under the blouse. He wondered, as he did every time he saw Travis in civvies, what principles guided her apparently haphazard wardrobe. He dropped two teabags into discoloured mugs and said:

'Are you saying this red-bearded man was a spy sent out by Corrigan, on the basis that he had the same hair colour? Or that he's somehow related to him? Have you thought about the fact,' said Sebastian, irritated, 'that it sounds completely fucking crazy? That the guy was probably just staring at you because you've got palm trees on your tits?'

'Can you see them?' Travis asked in surprise.

Sebastian banged the cups down onto his only table, making the tea splash rainbows in the dusty June sun, and said:

'Travis, why are you here? Why did you send a completely incomprehensible letter and then come and knock just as it was delivered? Why did you dash out of Peckham Rye station and buy a shalwar kameez to avoid being shadowed by a man with a red beard?'

Travis got up from the divan and came to sit at the table. She sighed heavily.

'I sent the letter yesterday. Then, just after I'd posted it, I realised we'd never gone over the code. So then I thought, I might as well track you down and take you through it. The code, that is. And then, later yesterday evening I had a breakthrough on the Woodman front. I found the real correlate! The right picture. And then —'

'Is it the one from the colony? *Untitled*? The one with the arms and the birch bark?'

He couldn't stop himself. Travis clapped a hand over her mouth.

'Sebastian!'

'Yeah?'

'That's the one! How did you know?'

'It was what you were saying ... Birches, death, angels, I don't know, I went through all the images I could find online and felt like it had to be that one. Somehow. I thought it was emotional, because it made me think of ... of someone. But you're telling me it *is* that one?'

'Yeah. The pattern ... So beautiful. Genius, actually. But you understand why I got a bit paranoid? I'm going to tell you something now, something I didn't say before. I have a suspicion.'

Sebastian sighed. 'Let me guess: there's a conspiracy of red-headed men trying to establish a fascist world order based on mathematical principles?'

'Ha ha, very funny. But really, that's not far off. I think … Don't look at me like that. I think Corrigan's the actual *mind* behind the puzzle.'

'Corrigan?'

'Not just him, of course, but the Institute. Management. The ones on the top floor. They want something, that's obvious, from all the work we're doing. I'd bet every penny it's something extremely shady. An exceptional brain is a powerful tool, Sebastian. The things the eugenicists tried to do in Nazi Germany would *pale* in comparison to what neuroscience could achieve in human engineering. And I personally think it sounds very, very unpleasant —'

'Travis, stop. Just stop.'

'Think about it seriously. No one knows what we're doing at the Institute. No one knows what the actual point of the puzzle is —'

'That is not even anywhere near being a connection.'

'He tried to kill my cicadas!'

'Well, you think so. Do you have any evidence?'

'Not yet, but soon. You and I are going to crack this together, believe me. By the way, did you know Corrigan sometimes has tea with the Queen?'

'So now the Queen's a fascist too? Travis, please stop.'

Sebastian got up and went over to his provisional desk — four empty wooden boxes he'd got from a skip behind Borough Market, which had once upon a time contained salami and still smelled a little rancid, and an old wooden door of indeterminate origin that had been in the room when he moved in — and began to distractedly fiddle with pens and Post-it notes. Pink, yellow, pink, yellow, he laid out the squares in a row across the desk, trying to decide if he should show them to Travis or not. They didn't really mean anything, they were just words, names, doodles, a little pencil sketch of Laura Kadinsky's eyebrows — random thoughts that had flowed from his hand like rain while he was doing other things — talking on the phone to his mother or Matilda, frying eggs in the kitchenette, bashing his head against the wall at four in the morning when sleep refused to come even though he'd maxed out the sleeping pills.

But he knew Travis wouldn't see it like that.

She'd look at the notes, at the pencil-smudged birch trunks and the rearranged letters of his sisters' names, at the toes towards the underworld and *that time Papa said: well, they've all got blue eyes at least*, at the question marks and the four dashes that marked the number of times he'd rung Clara's phone and got her voicemail — and she'd see something he couldn't.

Maybe it didn't matter, he thought, that it would be an illusion. Travis was clearly mad, but it was a madness he envied. It seemed nice, in some way, to be able to fit anything that didn't conform into an ever-expanding narrative in which nothing was an accident. Travis would undoubtedly cast her eyes over his collection of Post-its and give him an answer to whatever question he asked. *Who's out, me or one of my sisters? It's obvious, isn't it? Look at this. Why's Corrigan so interested in my family problems? Because he's your biological father, clearly. So who's my mother? The Queen, duh. Why did Violetta take her own life? Because a lightbulb exploded in her brain, because you couldn't stop her, because she had no more subcutaneous fat that she could pinch to see if she was real. Will Laura sleep with me again? Yes. Will she leave her husband for me? No. Will Clara come back? If you find her. Will I find her? Will everything fall into place, like pieces in a puzzle?*

'Sebastian?'

Travis was standing beside him.

'What's that?'

He nudged an old copy of the *Metro* so it covered at least a few of the most cryptic notes and shrugged.

'Nothing. I was just thinking.'

'Think about this instead: you know I said Corrigan had started shutting me out?'

'Yeah,' said Sebastian, wondering — with a certain degree of guilt — whether he should tell Travis that Corrigan had asked him to spy on her, before concern for what Travis would do with that information stopped him.

'Can you guess when it began?'

'When the puzzle started?'

Travis nodded earnestly.

'Exactly.'

Sebastian scratched his head. He was undeniably accustomed to women on the edge of breakdown, but Travis really was in a league of her own. He couldn't decide whether the best thing would be to suggest discreetly that maybe it was just puzzle-related nerves putting her on edge, or if he should play along with her conspiratorial delusions. The first option was possibly the right one, but the latter was surprisingly tempting. When it came to it, it felt easier to take care of Travis's madness than of his family's. He could feel how he wanted to sink into it, to disappear into it, to sit up all night in Travis's lab and write equations on the walls with the scrapings from the bottom of a baked-beans tin.

Will my family ever heal if I tune out too? Will they get their shit together themselves? Monkey says no.

Sebastian realised he'd been holding his breath. He exhaled with a sigh and chose, as always, a middle way — the coaxing, conciliatory, slightly indulgent attitude he'd learned was the way to cause minimum damage, at least in the short term.

'Honestly, I don't think Corrigan has anything to do with the puzzle or with any kind of neuro-revolution, but I'll keep an eye on him, okay? I agree he's weird. All of it is weird.'

'All of it is very, very weird,' Travis said, almost critically. 'I read somewhere that that's the very foundation of human life.'

'How ... Is it going well? With the puzzle, I mean? Are you ... we, winning?'

Travis laughed.

'Winning! It's hardly a matter of winning. But ask, and I'll answer. It's in the letter here. The key is here. Learn it and burn it.' Travis pressed a folded piece of paper into his hand, reached for the shalwar kameez, and pulled the shift over her head. 'Meet you *you know where* same time Tuesday. Lie low and don't mention anything to Corrigan.'

'About what?'

Travis's head popped up through the kameez.

'Nothing about anything,' she said, wrinkling her nose. Then she took her bag, blew Sebastian a kiss, and disappeared out the door.

He stood there in the minimal hallway, leaned his head against the doorpost, and let out yet another long sigh. It was only half eleven in the morning, it was a Saturday, it was almost two days till he could let himself be swallowed up in the Institute, drown in the drone of the MRI scanner, not needing to think of anything but beautiful, ugly, shimmering brains. He wondered how he'd make the time pass. He should try to call Clara again. He should talk to his mother and promise her, once again, that nothing had changed and that everything would go back to normal as soon as his sisters had a chance to calm down a bit. He should wash up his only mugs, wash his face in ice-cold water.

But he did none of this (apart from the last bit — he also changed his underwear), because his phone began to blare from the windowsill, and when he lifted the glossy screen towards his face he saw a number he didn't recognise.

'Hello?'

'Sebastian?'

Another madness to take care of, to sink and disappear into.

'Laura?'

'I'm stupid for ringing. Am I stupid for ringing?'

'No.'

'Philip — that is, my husband — he's taken off rather quickly. He's taken Chloe with him. To Warwickshire. He knows someone with an estate and four tennis courts. He wanted to practise his backhand.'

'Aha, hmm.'

'Not that it's needed, if you ask me; he's already a tennis ace.'

There was a silence on the line. Sebastian looked at his bare feet against the floorboards. He shouldn't say anything. If he just held his tongue, nothing would be his fault.

'Sebastian? Let me come to you.'

Like in a fever, and yet not. She had to lay her palm against the condensation-covered, single-glazed pane of the bedroom window to judge her own body temperature. Was he really lying beside her, were those really his hands, whose hand was it, against the window, was it really hers? Yes. This strange room, so like another room she remembered, her first studio flat in Dalston, on Balls Pond Road; it was cheap there back then, run-down, the lack of organic dairy products was acute, there were mice in the kitchen, and her gas hob shared her temperament: sometimes off, sometimes on, *incredibly capricious*. And now: the same hand against the same kind of window, it was just a little drier, more sinewy, the hand, with a gold accent — more specifically, a gold ring that clinked against the glass. What if he woke up? She didn't want him to wake up. The glass was cold, despite the summer heat outside; the condensation ran across her fingers. She didn't want him to wake up, she wanted him to reach for her in his sleep, to make love to her without opening his eyes, to be *celestial*, nothing but a ray, a ray of pulsating heat. She wanted him to be simultaneously real and unreal, just like everything else in this world — not so much to ask, surely? That love, lust, desperation, whatever this was, should follow the same rules as the rest of the shit that constitutes human life.

He didn't wake up. But neither did he show any signs of wanting to embrace in the grey area of dawn. In the end, Laura was forced to sit up in bed, meditate on his choice of bedclothes, see herself reflected in his bare walls. They were white and slightly dirty, with scratch marks visible in one corner, doubtless a sign of mouse infestation. Here was the narrow bed, in which they sailed as if in a drifting ship. She didn't want to think how long and for how many rotting bodies this mattress had served as a place of rest and a place to fuck, but she did anyway, settling on somewhere between fifteen and twenty years and roughly as many bodies. You don't live longer than you have to in a place like this. He too will disappear; sooner or later he too will take out a mortgage and get a wife and a springer spaniel. Someone else will move in and throw their trousers on the dusty couch. Someone else will put their milk cartons in the yellowing fridge.

The fridge. She looked at the fridge.

There it was. The fridge, alongside the tiny kitchen unit, under a yellowed square of wallpaper where a portrait of the Queen had probably hung for the best part of the twentieth century. She had to blink, turn her gaze towards Sebastian's sleeping body and then back again, to the fridge which stuck out, hulk-like, from the wall, to the couch's moss-green mounds and levels, to the radiator's rusty curlicues, the curves of the pot that held a dead plant, the bay window's protuberance, its *protuberance*!

'Sebastian!'

Laura shook his shoulder, suddenly desperately longing for him to wake and witness the miracle that was her and him and the apparent power of their bodies in union.

He opened his eyes — and screamed. Laura jumped back towards the end of the bed and Sebastian sat bolt upright, his chest heaving like an accordion. For a second, which became two and then several, his eyes were elsewhere, and Laura couldn't help feeling offended.

'Am I really that ugly in the morning?' she heard herself mutter while Sebastian slowly seemed to come back to the room, to the moment, to her half-naked body.

'I thought … Sorry … Laura. It's you. Who's here. We've … hmm.'

'Yep,' said Laura, absent-mindedly slipping her hand into her handbag. 'Again. But I'm not sure it's going to happen many more times if you don't stop acting so strangely.'

In the bottom of her bag, Laura had found a handful of fluffy gummy bears, the remains of a Chloe bribe, and now she impatiently popped them into her mouth, one by one.

'Did you think I was someone else or something?'

'No, of course not. Or, it depends what you mean by *think*, but —'

'You were talking about her in your sleep. Viola or whatever.'

'Violetta. Her name was Violetta,' Sebastian said.

Laura didn't like the way his voice sounded when he said her name.

'Was? Is she dead? Do you want a gummy bear? They're Chloe's. But I'm eating them. That's the kind of mother I am.'

'No thanks.'

Sebastian leapt out of bed. Had she hurt him by talking that way about that woman? But it's not totally out of the ordinary, is it, thought Laura angrily, to want to know who your lover is dreaming about at night.

'We shouldn't do this again, Laura,' he said. 'It's not right. Do you want some coffee? I'm going to make some coffee.'

Laura laughed abruptly.

'What?' said Sebastian, pulling on his boxers and T-shirt. 'I'm a brain scientist, you don't think I can make coffee?'

'It wasn't that. You make your coffee. But listen. I almost forgot, because you screamed like that when you woke up, but now it's coming back to me: do you know why I woke you? I wanted to show you something. Or not show, tell.'

'Is it about your daughter?' said Sebastian. 'Tell me more about her, please. About your husband. Tell me about them.'

That was precisely what Laura didn't want to do. And why did he want to hear it? Was he trying to give her a bad conscience? So incredibly enervating if that was the case. So incredibly *not* what this was about. Didn't he get it? He didn't get it.

'We shouldn't do this again,' he repeated.

'Can't you just keep quiet for a moment?' said Laura. 'This is exactly what we should be doing, it's what we have to do. Listen: you know I told you about how I can see you? Like I can't see anyone else?'

'Apart from the hamster.'

'Apart from the hamster. But you know what? When I woke up I could see everything. I mean *everything*, here, in this room; I could see the fridge, the radiator, everything! It was like I was *well* again.'

Sebastian poured coffee into a limescale-flecked percolator and held it under the tap.

'Well?' he said. 'I don't understand …' And it was true, he felt insanely lost. The abrupt switches in roles and subjects of conversation — lover, researcher, homewrecker — was more than his just-woken brain could take, all he was capable of thinking about with any clarity was that he was in deep water and about to drown, and the water was running into the percolator and he wasn't paying attention, and then it overflowed and the coffee grounds ran over his hand as the condensation had run over Laura's hand earlier, but he didn't know that, of course, because at that point he'd been asleep and dreaming of Violetta's lopsided body, hanging from the door frame, only half the way he knew she'd wanted it to be.

And yet, there was a symmetry between him and Laura that had been lacking between him and Violetta, a symmetry reminiscent of a pattern so magnificent it made you want to cry.

'I don't understand either,' Laura whispered, suddenly behind him, wiping the coffee grounds from his hands with a filthy towel. 'I don't understand why, or how. But I think you make me *well*, that what we do together is making me whole again.'

And then everything was red and black and she licked the sweat from his throat with her unexpectedly broad tongue.

They had flatbread wraps with vegan hot dogs and mashed potato for dinner. Like most single dads, Billy took a very simple approach to cooking. He always said that messing about with cast-iron pans and Vietnamese summer rolls was a privilege reserved for men with partners. 'Single dads have got to be best friends with the ready meal.' And when Matilda calmly — or, okay, rather acidly — pointed out that he actually had a partner now and that anyway the food he made on the days when Siri was with her mother was equally bad, he tended to snort something unintelligible and playfully pat her on the head. And to be honest, Matilda had nothing against his junk food. It would have been infinitely worse if Billy had been the other way around, the kind who brought their child up to think of spinach smoothies as sweets and called goji berries 'jokey-berries', as she'd once heard a mother do in the food hall in Lund while her child was sceptically eyeing a raw food ball. But hey, why did she care, anyway? Billy could bring Siri up however he wanted, couldn't he? She wasn't her child.

Matilda took a sausage, put it on her flatbread, and scooped out some potato, which she formed into two neat balls at the bottom. Then she took the ketchup bottle, drew a few jaunty arcs spurting from the top of the sausage and wrote 'YUM!' across the bread with ketchup. She looked up and caught Billy's eye.

'Mature,' he said.

Matilda reached for the tub of fried onions, took a fistful, and sprinkled the dry flakes over the two mashed-potato balls.

'Now it's more like yours.'

'Daddy's what? I want to do some drawing too. Give me the ketchup!'

'No, Siri, that's enough. You've got loads of ketchup,' said Billy, glaring at Matilda.

'But it's not a picture!'

'It doesn't need to be a picture! It's food. Tilda was just joking. She's going to eat it all up now.'

'Of course,' said Matilda, spreading the potato over the flatbread before rolling it up. 'It's a yumwrap! It's going straight in my mouth. Slurp!'

Billy grinned as Matilda bit off half the wrap in one go.

'Yummy?'

Matilda nodded eagerly, chewed and swallowed. She rapidly gobbled down the other half and reached for another flatbread, ravenous. But when she rolled the second wrap and brought it to her mouth, nausea rose in her throat. She had no choice but to drop it on the plate and rush to the toilet. She didn't even manage to kneel down, just vomited in the hand basin — the convulsions came quick and violent but relented as soon as the hot dog had come up. She raised her face from the basin and caught sight of herself in the mirror. Big staring eyes, pale cheeks, clammy forehead. Her breasts two throbbing lumps. Pattering feet outside the half-open bathroom door.

'Tilda? Are you sick?"

'No, Siri.'

'But why are you being sick, then?'

Billy shouted through the house.

'Siri, come back here! Leave Tilda in peace. She's got a migraine!'

She had a migraine. Too fucking blue here.

'Should I get you a glass of water?' asked Siri in a considerate voice, the one she put on when she wanted to be praised for her kindness. She was a little actress, just like Matilda. Strange, actually, that she wasn't Matilda's child, they were so alike that way. Matilda had observed her in playgrounds — saw how she would sometimes jump nobly off a swing and offer it to another child. Saw her offended expression when the other child didn't say thanks. The sharp stone she'd sneak into the child's shoe in the sandpit. Though maybe all kids were like that? Maybe the value inherent in being considerate towards others was something it took a long time to learn, to come naturally. But how long? Twenty-six felt a little too long. Matilda brushed her hair off her forehead and smiled at Siri.

'No, it's okay. Go back to Papa. It's bedtime, no?' Matilda pulled her phone out of her back pocket. It was just after nine.

'But it's still light,' Siri muttered.

'Just like it has been every night since we got here. It's called the midnight sun. It was always like this for your dad when he was little.'

'But it's weird. I want the world to be dark when I go to sleep.'

'Siri —' said Matilda, hesitating, before letting it out with the irrepressible pleasure of cruelty: 'The world is always dark, day and night. Tell Billy I'm heading out.'

She walked along the forest track down to Jönsviken — Joker's Bay — that really was what it was called, and in comparison to many other Norrland place names it was pretty lenient on the few cabin owners around. The sun hung over the tops of the firs like a polished gold coin, spreading a syrupy light through the trees, which made the blueberries in their ankle-high bushes take on a more forgiving, purplish hue. Matilda hadn't grown up with the forest, but wasn't it crazy early to have blueberries ripening at the end of June? Unnatural. Monstrous, almost. Apocalyptic.

As always when she was out alone in the forest, Matilda started fantasising about bears. Billy always laughed at her and said only southerners are afraid of bears. You're as likely to see a bear as you are to see a fucking forest nymph. And it was true. Unfortunately. What Billy had assumed was that Matilda was *scared* of bears. Not at all. On the contrary, she cherished the thought of a bear encounter as a kind of erotic fantasy, one she summoned whenever she needed to feel life coursing along her spine. Kathleen always said that all humans have a *spirit animal*. Actually, no, she didn't. Kathleen would never say anything so banal. But Matilda still liked the thought. Hers would be a bear. No, who was she kidding. Female bears are known for one thing and one thing only, their explosive protective instinct towards their young. Matilda's only similarity to a bear was her scruffy brown hair. But imagine seeing one. Just being in the presence of such enormous physical force. Standing naked before it, awaiting the blow. She quickened her steps on Owl Bend — Siri had seen an owl there once — and swerved around the great boulder that looked like a gorilla, turned off the path, over the stretch of clear-felled ground down towards the sea on the other side of the peninsula. There was a bench there but no cabins, one of the few places around the bays where you were guaranteed not to be spotted by someone before you'd seen them, whether they came from the water or the open ground. She'd come here sometimes with Siri and swim naked, in secret because Billy was so funny about nakedness — they called the place the Secret Shore.

The water was as thick as spilled oil and as still as snow in the strange light that was neither day nor night. Matilda had been walking quickly and was sweaty and surrounded by midges when she reached the bench and sank down onto it. She squashed a few that had settled on her bare inner thigh, smearing their blood with her palm like a trickle from her genitals.

That was going to fool no one, least of all herself.

There'd been nothing for she knew not how many weeks, only that it was many more than four.

Which wasn't so unusual in itself. She'd almost managed to convince herself that it was because she'd got so skinny since the colour showed up. Though that's what she'd thought the last time, too. The female reproductive system was so fragile: more fastidious than an orchid for some women, and she'd never been really regular. A little here, a little there, it didn't matter much until suddenly three, four months had passed and all that came was clear, transparent mucous. Tight ligaments, tight jaws, oh god. She dug her hand into the inside pocket of the Fjällräven jacket she'd had since she was thirteen and pulled out the pack of three ready-rolled joints she'd brought along from Berlin, just in case. She hadn't smoked in a month at least, but now she was fucking well going to get high as a rustling pine, a glimmering nymph, a whistling wave.

She lit a joint and moved to the most secret spot on the Secret Shore, two old flaking boat huts that stood at an angle to each other, offering shelter and secrecy. She sat cross-legged in *sukhasana*, inhaled through her mouth, held it for one, two, three, exhaled through her nose. Kathleen always said: find a crack in time and enlarge it with your breath. Would Kathleen think the grass was an unnecessary shortcut? Certainly. But the effect was the same, so who could care less. Time opened like a fan, the moment became a gif — a simple movement that bounced back and forth for eternity, delaying the point when she'd have to tell Billy everything.

Everything? Yes, everything. If they were going to keep it, in any case. They should probably ask a midwife. *Die Hebamme*, with her big warm hands and homeopathic tinctures, at least that was how she imagined things were in Germany. She took another breath, held one, two, three, released. They'd never talked about kids. Not about having one, together. One who wasn't Siri. Or, well, Billy had mentioned it once in passing, one day in spring when they'd taken Siri out to fly a kite at Tempelhof and caught sight of a mother who was really taking the idea of 'attachment parenting' to a new level. She'd had one baby on her front, one on her back (it was conceivable they were twins), and a slightly older child clutching each fist. When she, or rather, they, had sat down on a picnic blanket, Billy and Matilda had noticed that she was actually breastfeeding the child on the front in its carrier. After a little while, the baby on the front had fed enough, and the woman just swapped the two carriers in some magic manoeuvre and started feeding baby number two. It was at this point that Billy had pinched her and whispered: 'Must've been like that for your parents, no? With three, what a fuckin' carousel. No wonder you're so dizzy.' Matilda had jokingly pulled his hair. 'Is it hereditary, the triplets thing?' he said then. 'I mean, just so I know what I'm getting myself into.' She couldn't remember now what she had answered. Maybe nothing, maybe she'd been saved by the bell — otherwise known as Siri — and avoided answering. In any case, it was the only time the matter had come up, even in passing. But that wasn't really so weird. Only eleven months, and there was no rush, she wasn't even thirty. She hadn't even given it a thought, not really, and had taken it as read that Billy hadn't either. He already had Siri, after all.

But god! Matilda suddenly realised what a bloody error that had been: subconsciously she'd always thought Billy wouldn't be interested in having any more kids because he already had Siri. But actually, it was just the opposite! The thing most likely to guarantee that a man *won't* want to have children is that he doesn't have any. But men who already *have* children have clearly demonstrated their interest. People with children always want to have more, just think about that mother-of-four at Tempelhof. Of course Billy wanted more kids too. Probably triplets, ideally. Was that one of the things that had drawn him to her? Hadn't she told him early on that she was one of triplets? She usually did. Christ on a bike, now she was getting paranoid. She'd been smoking too quickly. Should have taken it easier when she'd had such a long break. Of course, she shouldn't have been smoking at all, if what was undoubtedly true really turned out to be true. Had to be. But it only mattered if she was going to keep it. Would they? Probably. Seems he'd want it and she couldn't, not again. And she couldn't lose Billy, not when she'd lost so much else — not ever.

Kathleen always said the body was a metaphor. Any changes emanating from the body will change the rest of your life as well. She meant it in a good way. She meant that if you treated your body with love and forgiveness you'd be a better person: more forgiving of yourself and others. She always said that every physical movement makes rings on the water, like when you use your hand to throw a stone at a glassy surface.

Matilda used her hand to throw a stone at a glassy surface. The sound was heart-rending, the ridiculous plop a taunt to the moist silence of the Swedish summer evening. Matilda started laughing, she laughed out loud. Triplets! As if they could have triplets! Matilda wasn't a triplet, not really!

What she was, was a question mark. That was another thing Billy didn't know, another thing she'd have to tell him. She stubbed the joint out and walked home, waiting for the bear that never showed its face.

June turned into July, and Laura Kadinsky took a turn for the better. Not a huge one, but still noticeable. Sebastian kept diligent case notes, like he'd learned from Barázza, and like he'd taught himself while Violetta still needed him. It was double bookkeeping, with dual purposes: one scientific, the other extramarital; one scientific, the other sexual and hi, please. Help. Me. Someone. He picked up the tape measure he'd once been given by Violetta and regularly measured the circumference of Laura's heart, mouth, hands, skin.

In her case notes, he jotted down all his observations. A selection:

One evening she danced naked to a jazzy cover of 'Ashes to Ashes', then tripped over her own feet and took a curtain along with her. But when she got up her cheeks were glowing and her eyes were shining.

One morning her hands found his face even though her eyes were closed.

Another morning she asked if she could iron all his shirts (she laughed when he admitted he only owned three) and succeeded in getting the creases right on every one!

After a while she even stopped talking about her daughter's hamster, stopped talking about Philip, stopped talking about her lost job. Instead she talked about Lorca (sometimes) and Frank Auerbach (now and then) and Goya (often). Of Goya she said: 'What I appreciate about Goya is that he wasn't afraid to paint it black.'

When they fucked she stopped boring her teeth into his neck like a bloodthirsty animal and started throwing her head back instead, eyes on the ceiling — or more precisely, towards the cracked, dripping ceiling which was the roof of their love, the star banner of their hotel room, the damp skies of his flat.

She swung her feet less when she sat on bar stools. On the seventh of July she ate a pastry. On the thirteenth she told a funny story that had no point. On the twenty-second she let him stroke her hair as she rested her head on his stomach. The next day she smoked a cigarette without speculating on the possibility she would die of cancer, at least not verbally — though it's possible she did in her head; Sebastian knew better than anyone that the human cranium is an impenetrable barrier, a Great Wall of China as high as it is long, and every time he looked Laura in the eye he was reminded of this simple yet tragic fact: that one person can never really know what another is thinking.

The fact that Sebastian still didn't know what was wrong with Laura was a speck of dust on the surface of a goblet that otherwise seemed full to the brim with milk and honey. No one could say he hadn't put the work in — he devoted himself to Laura, not only as the object of his desire, but as his subject of study, with an intensity that was even noticed by his colleagues.

On the twenty-second of July — a Friday — Team Bletchley had one of their formal gatherings. These gatherings were always lively, and generally took place at a somewhat less than hygienic pub — 'for obvious reasons', according to Travis, though what these might be, Sebastian had never understood — close to the RNIB on Judd Street. To a certain extent, the gaiety derived from the copious amounts of alcohol consumed at the meetings, but it arose too from the joy Travis took in using one of her high heels as a gavel, which in turn encouraged, or yes, even incited, discussions that would require its enthusiastic use. Perhaps that was why she let Childs insinuate that Sebastian might be engaged in an illicit relationship with one of his patients? Of course that was why. The possibility that it might be true, and therefore worthy of discussion, never occurred to Travis, who, with her lack of insight into the nature of love, would have thought a man in the grip of a wild passion would have behaved more like Madame Bovary and less like Sebastian Isaksson.

In any case, it was Childs who, after an initial, fruitless discussion on the possible relationship between certain decimals of the number π (specifically decimals thirty-seven to two hundred and four) and the previous year's relocation schedule, turned to Sebastian and asked nonchalantly:

'Who's that woman you're constantly seeing?'

Sebastian coughed and tucked the minute-keeping pen behind his ear in an unsuccessful diversionary manoeuvre.

'Who do you mean?' he said.

'Slim. Brunette. Rich. Comes to your office at all hours. Leaves with her clothes all wonky.'

'Aha, yeah, that sounds like one of my studies. Kadinsky. Very complex case.'

'I can imagine,' said Childs, taking a sip of ale and smacking his lips. 'The rich ones tend to be. Just look at Travis.'

'I'm not rich,' said Travis and wiggled the toes of her unshod foot. 'Just comfortably off.'

'Rich, posh, whatever. But I mean, Sebastian, is she into you? See an awful lot of her in the hallways.'

'That's confidential, isn't it?' Sebastian tried to joke.

Travis banged her heel on the table encouragingly.

'You're not writing. Everything has to be in the minutes.'

'But, Travis … This has nothing to do with anything.'

'That's what you think. But who knows?'

'Did you say Kadinsky?' Childs said suddenly, looking at Sebastian in a way that couldn't be described as anything but *thoughtful*.

'Yeah?'

'I wanted her. The one with the vision problems, right? Issues with depth perception?'

'I think it's more complex than that, but yeah,' said Sebastian.

'I think so too. That's why I wanted her. Benedict showed me her interview; you know how he is, can't button his lip about anything. That's why he is where he is, on the bottom rung, actually, he's not a bad diagnostician. But, anyway. So, I went to Corrigan and asked to have her in my group. Seemed interesting, and to be honest, exactly the kind of case you want to crack, if you catch my drift? The ones I'm working on now aren't exactly going to be stepping stones for my career. But he said no.'

'Shame.'

'He said no, because he wanted *you* to have her, Sebastian. Not Harvey. Not Travis, which would be logical if he was going on merit. You. What do you think of that?'

'It's weird,' Sebastian said, and meant it. He'd never considered that anything other than pure chance could have been behind Laura's presence in his life. That Corrigan should have chosen him for a case which, if Childs were to be believed, was something special compared to most of the degenerate brains he shared out among them, was both improbable and unpleasant.

'You're in his good books, it's obvious,' said the normally taciturn Charles Harvey, looking at Sebastian in a way that couldn't be described as anything but *begrudging* and *somewhat threatening*. Charles Harvey looked quite a lot like his namesake, surname Manson, and was said to have more lab animals with 'cause of death: unknown' than anyone else at the Institute, whatever that implied.

'Or maybe the opposite,' Sebastian ventured. 'Maybe he wants me to fail, ha ha!'

'If that's how it feels, maybe you should ask to have the subject reassigned,' Childs said matter-of-factly. 'As I said, I can take her.'

'Me too,' said Harvey.

'No!' Sebastian shouted in panic, managing, in his inability to channel his fear of yet another loss, to knock over his beer. 'She's *mine*.'

'Yeah, yeah, calm down. We were just kidding. She's yours.'

'She's mine,' repeated Sebastian, mumbling, while he vainly tried to wipe up splashes no one else could see. Travis bashed her shoe on the table, interrupting him.

'Next on the agenda: arrangement of twenty-four-hour surveillance of bug lab. Sebastian, are you keeping the minutes, or am I going to have to ask Harvey? You know he's missing his right index finger.'

Afterwards he went to meet Laura at a hotel among the rubble and dust of the building sites around King's Cross station. Sebastian didn't like meeting in hotels, it felt dirty, tainted, not to mention banal — but it was hard to avoid: Tulse Hill was simply too far for Laura to get to in the few hours they had between him clocking off early and her needing to get home to keep up the charade of still being employed and a responsible mother. But the fact that Laura hadn't admitted to Philip that she'd got the sack meant that sometimes, like today, she could delay her homecoming a few hours under the pretence that she had to work late — not that Philip noticed anything, but it was important for the nanny, Sebastian understood.

That too was too banal for his sensitive stomach.

He lay on the bed, watching her dress. Knickers, bra, thin socks. A skirt with a zip that she fastened in front before twisting the skirt so it ended up at the back. Her spine like a mountain range. Dark birthmarks, neck like the crest of a wave, and a comb nestling in her hair. Little gold shells through her earlobes, little shell-likes shimmering like gold: earwax and powder. She turned to pick up her camisole from the floor. Their eyes met and she smiled. Took the camisole and turned to the mirror again.

'Have I got fatter since you first saw me naked?'

No, thought Sebastian. *The first time I saw you naked you were already thin and crinkly, almost transparent, like the paper on a Chinese lantern. Yet you still wanted to be thinner, and I let you, because I didn't know how to stop you. I couldn't stop you.*

'You're perfect,' he said.

'That wasn't what I asked. I mean, it's fine if I have, I don't care, but you know, I can't tell, because I can't see my own contours. Isn't that crazy?'

'You don't need to have your problems to not be able to see your own weight.'

'Philip said yesterday that my face has grown rounder. I don't know what that's supposed to mean. Then he said I should get more exercise, if for no other reason than for — and I quote — "your coronary arteries and your own enjoyment." I don't know what that means either. He only exercises when he wants to get out of the house. And, of course, he runs up and down the steps to the Tube at Covent Garden when he's been in the studio. It's two hundred and twenty-three steps. He notes down all the steps in a book and when he gets to ten thousand he'll donate that many pounds to Oxfam.'

'That's a lot of money.'

'He's not a man to do things by halves. Apart from maybe loving me.'

Neither of them said anything for a while. Laura pulled the camisole over her head, picked up the pillow chocolate from the floor where it had landed after she'd pulled back the covers, plucked the dry rectangle from its shiny wrapper, and popped it in her mouth. She was a bird and a pearl, doubly beautiful because she would soon be ugly. She was funny and nasty and apparently intelligent, even if she was too absorbed in projecting a version of herself to show or make the most of it. In many ways she was the antithesis of everything Sebastian had learned to love in the world. That was probably why he felt, at that moment, that he loved her more than he'd loved anything, ever, more than his sisters, more than his childhood dog, Bernarda, even more than Violetta.

'Does it hurt you when I talk about Philip?'

'A little.'

'Good.'

She walked over to him as he lay, still naked, on the bed, sat down on the edge, and ran her hands along his hip bones, first one, then the other. Leaned forward and whispered into his stomach, her voice feeble and hoarse: 'I wish I had two lives so I could live one with you.'

'That's exactly what you do have. It's exactly what you're doing,' said Sebastian. 'It's called a double life for a reason.'

'This is no life. It's a state of emergency.'

'But you're a different person when you're with me. That's what you're always saying. And if that's not another life, I don't know what is.'

'Touché,' she said, sounding so inconceivably sorrowful that Sebastian immediately regretted what he'd said.

She lifted her face from his torso, looking towards the window even though nothing could be seen through the curtains.

'Have you thought what would happen if you died for some reason?' she said. 'I wouldn't be able to come to your funeral. Right? People would think it weird. And if I cried I wouldn't be able to explain to anyone why. Maybe I wouldn't even find out that you were dead, ever. Who would inform me?'

'The Institute, I imagine. They'd have to reschedule your appointments. The others would fight over you.'

'Am I that abnormal? Ugh, don't answer that. But I mean, in the future. When none of this exists anymore. When you're just someone I loved once. Months could pass, years, you know. Maybe I'd never find out.'

'Do you think that's what will happen?'

'No. I'll die before you. It won't be an issue.'

'Don't say that.'

'But it's true. There's no way out for me. If not today, tomorrow, right? Something's slowly eating my brain with a spoon. When there's nothing left, I'll die.'

'Not if you recover first.'

She got up, started fiddling with her powder, lipstick, and phone.

'But I'm not going to recover, Sebastian.'

'I'm helping you recover. You said that yourself. And you've been a lot better the last few weeks, haven't you?'

'I can't build my life around your presence.'

'Why not? That, if anything, is what lives should be built around. You could leave Philip and be with me.'

It was the first time he'd said it out loud.

'That's not what you want. Nor me. I love you, but I wouldn't be able to live with you. It's so strange.'

'Not particularly,' Sebastian said, feeling let down, thinking how very ordinary it sounded, all of it, but also how very true.

Laura snapped her powder compact shut decisively, put it in her handbag, and slid her feet into her shoes.

'We can't take care of each other's sorrow, Sebastian. We're not self-sacrificing enough for that, you and I.'

She left without kissing him goodbye, and the void she left behind had a familiar form. Sebastian dressed slowly in the semi-darkness. When he came out onto the street, the sunlight hit him so strongly all the people seemed to have lost their faces.

July came to Västerbotten too, a month of shimmering heat; the blueberry brush smelled of smoke, and the berries withered from lack of water. Matilda woke sweaty and breathless every morning, nauseous, angst-ridden.

It was one of those mornings. She'd got straight out of bed, gone through the bedroom door, lain down on the veranda with her legs against the wall. *Viparita karani*. Maybe she shouldn't be doing inverted poses now but that was the only bloody thing that helped, that made the nausea subside enough for her to be able to eat breakfast and pretend everything was normal. It helped with the anger, too. Kathleen always said the blood in your veins could be either fire, water, or earth. Matilda's was almost always fire.

Clara's was water.

Sebastian's earth.

When they still believed their blood had one and the same source, Matilda had found it a satisfying thought, that the universe had divided these three elemental forces between three little babies and stuffed them inside the same uterus. A kind of cosmic joke. It had made her feel that their family was meaningful, in some way. But ha ha — the joke turned out to be a different one entirely and the fire that ran in her blood came from an unknown source.

When she felt sufficiently calm she brought her legs down from the wall, rolled over onto her side, got up slowly. She followed the deck around the house to the front side where Billy and Siri had laid the table for breakfast.

There was something extra enervating about Siri today. Her energy levels were always high, but now she was literally bouncing out of her chair. She was about to fall over when she caught sight of Matilda.

'Tilda! Tilda! Tilda, y'know what?' she roared.

'Hush, love. Put a lid on it a little,' said Billy and pulled out a chair for Matilda. When had he started pulling chairs out for her? He'd never been a man who pulled out chairs. Softy. Matilda reached for a piece of rye flatbread, folded it in half, and bit into it without butter. She could see that Siri was trying to wait for Matilda to finish chewing, but she couldn't manage it:

'Tilda, I'm getting a DOG!'

Matilda nearly choked. She spat out the bread onto the lurid pink plastic plate — quite an irritating colour — and turned to Billy.

'Billy? What did your child just say?'

'A dog, Tilda! A really big one, maybe a Rottweiler! A Labrador! A Schäfer! A ... a ...' Siri furrowed her brow and tried to think of other big dogs. Matilda went on staring at Billy.

He shrugged apologetically.

'You don't want to give her a dwarf rabbit, but now you've promised her a DOG?' said Matilda.

'Yeah?' was all Billy said. 'I thought this family could do with a dog.'

'You thought?' Matilda repeated. 'That this family. Could do with a dog.'

'Don't you like dogs?' Siri squeaked, completely astonished.

Matilda gripped the seat of her chair hard.

'Siri, petal,' she said. 'Go and play, please.'

'Are you going to have an argument?'

'Yes, Siri,' Matilda sighed. 'We're going to have an argument.'

Siri jumped from her chair, unconcerned, and darted off into the house. As soon as she was gone, Billy raised his hands in a conciliatory gesture.

'Okay,' he admitted. 'Perhaps that was rash. But come on. A dog. You like dogs. Didn't you have one when you were little?'

Oh yes, indeed she had. Bernarda, Bernarda. That was the problem. Or, one of the problems.

'For fuck's sake, it's not about that,' Matilda snarled. 'It's about the fact that you damn well should have checked with me first! Where were you planning to fit a dog in our apartment? Who's going to walk it? Wash it? Brush its teeth? Feed it? Make sure it doesn't get hurt? Huh? Are you going to? Or Siri?'

'Yeah?' said Billy, wounded. 'I've raised a child; don't you think I can take care of a bloody dog?'

'A *bloody dog*?' Matilda said. 'Is that the way to talk about our new family member? Because if that's the way you feel, I can tell you right now this family's not going to be growing any time soon.'

Billy got up so quickly his chair fell backwards, hitting the veranda with a smack. His brown eyes, always so soft, mild even when he was angry, were almost black.

'What the fuck is up with you at the moment? Tilda? Huh?'

'With me? What's up with me? I'm not the one treating this family like a game. Of course, let's get a dog! Let's have a baby! Why not another? A lover! Whoops, one of the kids killed the dog! Whoops, divorce! Who cares, it was fun while it lasted!'

Now Matilda had got up too. There was a flash, somewhere behind Billy's head. It was *the colour*. She couldn't see him clearly. But she heard him, heard him when he said:

'Who said anything about children, Tilda? Who said anything about all that? It's just a dog. A dog.'

'That's how it begins,' Matilda said coldly. 'That's always how it begins. With a *bloody dog*.'

Billy pushed the table to one side. Not violently, but there was resolve in his movements. He took a step forward in the space left by the table and said again, almost as an afterthought, his voice tentative, soft: 'Who said anything about children, Tilda?'

He reached over to touch her shoulder with his hand. She raised her arm to bat his away, but he saw it coming. Caught her wrist and held it there, in mid-air. She could feel his pulse thumping through his palm, into her blood.

She was fire. Billy too.

They stood like that until the colour disappeared and Billy's eyes were brown again.

August came and Laura got worse. He fed her with his body, but the effect grew weaker each time. Now, in Laura's notes, instead of progress, he entered only defeats.

A selection:

She stopped taking the Tube. She said the Tube was too warm in the summer, but one evening when she'd drunk more than usual she admitted she was afraid of accidentally stepping between the train and the platform and having her leg cut off at the thigh.

She started replying: 'Was that sarcasm?' every time he gave her a compliment.

And every time she saw a withered rose — tears.

The clinical tests still produced no results. If Sebastian hadn't had successes with his other subjects, Toilet Baby among them, he'd have been seriously doubting his own prospects. Now he doubted Laura's instead. She liked to say over and over that she was condemned to death, and Sebastian liked to deny it, but in his heart, he knew she was right. There was, as far as he could deduce, no clinical explanation for her perception problems. With his other cases it had been easy to locate the cause of the problem; their brains had unravelled themselves like maps under Sebastian's fingers. Laura's, on the other hand, was a labyrinth.

Deep down, Sebastian knew he should go to Corrigan and admit that he was getting nowhere with Subject 3A16:2: Kadinsky, L. But that would mean Corrigan would take her away from him! It would also mean he'd once again failed to do the only thing a person really needed to do to earn their place on this earth: do good for another.

So he went on doing the only thing he could for her: loving her, raw and hot, with half his heart and the whole of his body. He administered himself like medicine, in ever-larger doses, according to her needs and wishes.

He never said no.

When she rang from the hotel room in the middle of the working day and wanted him to come, he dropped everything and rushed off with his trousers around his ankles. When she sent cryptic texts in the middle of the night, he replied as if he'd been awake the whole time, which he admittedly often was — his insomnia had escalated apace with his relationship with Laura. He stretched himself like a cobweb over her days, ignoring everything else: his sisters, his mother, even Travis. In some ways it was a blessing, to forsake and sacrifice, to finally have a way to make amends for crimes he'd once committed without even realising it.

One, for example:

One day Laura rang and told him that Philip and Chloe were going to Iceland and would be gone for almost a week. 'Come and be with me,' she said. 'Come and really be with me.'

And then she laughed, shrilly, like a hyena with its teeth sunk deep into dead flesh.

Bygdsiljum is home to what might be Sweden's least charming mini-golf course. A worn, dirty green carpet of fake grass between two low-slung yellow youth hostel barracks, a felted moonscape whose topographical highlight is a selection of cracked concrete lanes completely without ornament.

Billy thought it was cute.

'Serious Soviet aesthetic,' he said, delightedly twirling his golf club like a majorette. 'Imposing! Grubby! Crumbling at the edges!'

'Swedish aesthetic, you mean,' said Matilda. 'This is what Sweden looks like, Billy. This is Siri's inheritance.'

'Yeah, isn't it brilliant?' said Billy, poking Siri in the tummy. 'Last one to the first hole goes last!'

Matilda limped after Billy and Siri, who dashed over to the starting lane on the other side of the green battlefield. Thank god for the dirt taking the edge off all that green. Green is half blue, and was therefore the second-most difficult colour for her to deal with. When she woke up that morning, she'd thought for a moment that it was a good day, a day for silence and contemplation. The sky had finally been a hazy grey, the bed floating and warm, her body surprisingly soft and relaxed. But then the bedroom door had burst open and Siri had come hurtling in like a triple jumper, landing right across Matilda's middle. Instinctively, Matilda had thrown her off, to protect the baby perhaps — in a generous interpretation — or just to protect herself and the fragile little bubble of calm that had for a moment danced before her eyes.

'We're going to play mini-golf! We're going to play mini-golf! MINI-GOLF!'

'Have you ever played mini-golf, Siri?' Matilda had said, unfurling herself from within the bed, the constant nausea a lump in her throat and a ghost in her soul.

'No, but it's super fun!'

'It isn't, believe me. It's as boring as Yahtzee.'

'But Yahtzee's fun. Hello!? You told me you liked Yahtzee!'

Hurt, Siri had grabbed a pillow and thrown it at Matilda. Good lord, she'd been exposed: she'd lied to the truth- and security-starved child of an alcoholic, and it wasn't even nine o'clock.

'Okay, you're right. Mini-golf is really fun. And Yahtzee. I was only joking.'

'Papa says mini-golf is the best thing ever.'

'Well, well.'

Matilda did indeed know that Billy liked mini-golf: not really, but in that ironic way Matilda found so irritating, particularly since she'd got to know Kathleen and decided to become a better, more open, less cynical person. He liked bingo, too — surprise, surprise — was always going to what was probably Berlin's only bingo hall, by Rathaus Schöneberg, to flirt with the desperate old ladies with chipped blue nail varnish stamping away their pensions as though it was 1979 in some post-industrial British city. Once, when they'd just met, Billy had taken her along and Matilda had made a scene and accused him of being a condescending hipster tourist. When Billy tried to point out that he, in contrast to her, actually was working class and had spent many a childhood Saturday with his mother, a moderate player, at the bingo hall in Sollefteå, and had very fond memories from that time, it didn't fly with Matilda. The fight had been short and stormy, and afterwards they'd gone to Dunkin' Donuts and then rolled around a few times on the lawn where Kennedy gave his 'Ich bin ein Berliner' speech, kissing so fiercely Matilda ended up with a split lip. Today there would be neither fights nor kisses.

The thirty-kilometre drive from the cabin to Bygdsiljum had, as always with Billy and Siri, been noisy. They'd played Bröderna Lindgren at full volume on the car stereo, and Matilda had felt the migraine creeping up on her by the second time Siri's favourite song came around. She'd looked out of the window and resolved not to argue. Today wasn't about her.

But it was hard. Hard not to fight with Billy, whose snuff-infused attempts to kiss her made her flinch in nausea and distaste. Hard to accept that the grey sky had broken up and was now just as blindingly blue as on all the other days. Hard not to get annoyed at Siri, who planned every shot with a precision bestowed on few astrophysicists, but missed every time and had to be consoled and encouraged and cheered on as if she were a fucking CHILD. Which, Matilda realised, she actually was, making her annoyance even more disproportionately large and black and insurmountable. When they'd finally finished playing (Siri won, of course), Siri wanted to go to the neighbouring playground. Billy said okay without asking Matilda and sat on a bench with his phone, looking on Instagram or something similarly removed from the world.

Matilda normally found playgrounds pretty fun — the acrobat within her appreciated the challenge of scrambling around on climbing frames designed for bodies that were half the size of her own, and so it had become the norm for her, not Billy, to play with Siri when they were there. Today it annoyed Matilda inordinately that Billy seemed to have grown accustomed to that routine, not making the least bit of effort to join in the game. What's more, Siri insisted on climbing into a tube, which not even a hyper-nimble wisp of a woman like Matilda could get into, and demanding that Matilda run from end to end of the tube trying to catch her.

The game was so boring the clocks stopped and a violent craving for lunch tore Matilda's fortitude to shreds. The shreds formed a curtain and when it was raised Matilda saw her future like a distant circle at the end of an eternal climbing-frame tunnel.

A tableau: herself, six years later, with a contrary little five-year-old monkey on reins and another woman's teenage daughter like a pendant growing ever heavier around her neck.

A husband who no longer wanted to sleep with her sober — because that's how it always ended up, wasn't it? And a Berlin apartment with ever-rising rent, thanks to all the chic twenty-somethings breathing down the necks of honest slackers like Billy and Matilda, with their wads of Daddy's cash.

A brain turned to mush by grass and colours.

And in time — everything falling apart. A separation, fights with her siblings, the discovery that even the strongest ties can be cut, simple as that.

People with kids, Matilda thought as Siri threw herself once more into the tube, always tended to say their children had made them better people. Matilda didn't doubt that it was true of most people. Billy had almost certainly become a better person through having Siri, Matilda had confirmed that for herself via archaeological digs in his internet persona: under layers and layers of quasi-political status updates and photos of Siri in Hertha Berlin shirts, Matilda had finally found the time before her birth. The post about 'How to open a door with your dick' had been enough to make Matilda shrink from that particular abyss, determined to never again look back.

It was different with Siri's mother — having a child seemed, according to Billy's accounts and Matilda's own experience, not to have affected her one way or the other.

But finally, there were also people like Matilda, whose lot in life seemed to be like that of Judas: to play the scapegoat for the evil, treacherous sides of human nature. People who are unmoved by YouTube videos of baby sloths, and get a spontaneous desire to kick dogs out of their way on the pavement. People who can't tell a nose from a femur on an ultrasound because they just don't try hard enough. Who can't resist exploiting a person's weakness once they've glimpsed it. Who never lie out of kindness, but only for their own gain, who don't care about other people's allergies (who, to be quite honest, doubt other people's allergies), who plead PMS three weeks a month, to whom it would never even occur to fake an orgasm, who would never give anyone else the last biscuit or the biggest apple, who smoke beside prams, stub out cigarettes in public flowerbeds, who push their own sisters away without even trying.

People like that shouldn't have children.

Quite honestly, they should redeem their sins by other means. It was like dieting or whatever: some methods simply didn't fit some people. Matilda was a macro person. She could only do good in big ways, not little ones. Billy, on the other hand, was a man of minor miracles.

And that's why he'd want to keep this child.

Oh god.

While she vainly tried to get hold of Siri's feet, Matilda saw, as clearly as if she'd never thought anything else, that there wasn't a chance. There wasn't a chance in hell she could let this child be born.

Afterwards they went to Westmans so Siri could get a cake shaped like a frog. Westmans drew visitors from all over the region, because they had two peacocks called Göran and Anitra in their garden.

According to Billy.

But when they got there, it turned out only Göran was left. Anitra just lay down and died one day the previous autumn, the teenage waitress behind the cake display said guardedly. Traumatic withdrawal syndrome, the vet had said, which the waitress not-so-subtly implied was code for Anitra not getting enough. 'But, like, peahens aren't exactly much to look at so most tourists are happy anyway,' the waitress added, pouring burnt filter coffee into two white mugs. 'Apart from the ones from Sundsvall. But you're not from Sundsvall, right?' Matilda, who'd been left to pay, confirmed that indeed they had not come from Sundsvall, then she took the tray and went out into the garden where Billy and Siri had already chosen a table under some birch trees by the edge of the lake. The relentless sun made the water flash and flicker in shimmering cerulean layers. Matilda squinted her way over to the table, plonked down the tray, and nudged Siri who was sitting in the only chair that faced away from the water.

'Jump down, petal. I'd like to sit on that chair.'

Billy frowned.

'But Siri's already sitting there. Take a different one.'

'Please, don't argue,' Matilda begged. '*She* can take a different one, can't she? It's not like she's going to sit down for more than five seconds anyway.'

'Okay, but what difference does that make, you can move when she's done.'

'Hello!' Siri shouted. 'Don't talk about me like I'm not here! That's

KINDER ZU REDUZIEREN, you know? You said that yourself, Tilda.'

'Huh?'

'To Mama. But that time you did the same thing because you said to Mama that I was highly intelligent and that she's a BETRUNKENE FRAU OHNE BESCHÜTZERINSTINKT, just like I wasn't there.'

Billy started to laugh, though it sounded forced, it sounded like someone trying to smooth over a subject that's a little too awkward to discuss. Matilda knew exactly what that laugh meant — 'We'll talk about this later, Süße, don't think you're getting away with it.' There was an unspoken agreement between Matilda and Billy that Matilda couldn't criticise Käthe with Siri in earshot. It was a totally reasonable agreement, thought Matilda, but even reasonable boundaries sometimes needed to be overstepped.

The pastries were sweating in the sun. A Swedish flag flew from the stern of a boat on the water. Wasps crawled all over an empty soda bottle that had been dropped on the grass beside the empty table next to them. Siri pushed a fork into the mouth of her frog and smiled sweetly, as though she hadn't just made Matilda look bad in front of Billy. Demon child, thought Matilda, she knows exactly what she's doing. How long had she been sucking on that little caramel; how long had she been saving up that affected little misstep of Matilda's? And why had she chosen today of all days to betray her? 'Judas,' muttered Matilda, casting herself into the empty chair. Billy said nothing. Siri asked if she could play Toca Town on his phone. Billy said no. Siri whined for five seconds, then she lit up:

'There he is! There's Göran!'

Matilda turned her head and gazed up the slope towards the cafe. As she did, a peacock rounded the corner of the building, slow and stately with his tail feathers trailing like a bride's veil. Matilda's first thought was that he looked desperate. Her second was that he looked idiotic.

He was also, like all peacocks, very, very blue. Shiningly, radiantly blue. Words were not sufficient to describe how blue the glossy body was. Matilda turned her head quickly, but the damage was already done, the scissors already driven between the two halves of her brain. She wanted to shriek in pain and anguish. Instead she muttered something about having to go to the toilet and got up from the chair in a daze. She shouldn't have. Siri took it as a sign Matilda wanted to go and look at Göran with her, and grabbed hold of her wrist.

'Come on!'

'No, petal, I'm just going to the toilet.'

'Ah, you can hold it in! Adults can hold on as long as they like! Come on!'

'I said no, Siri. Billy?'

'What?' Billy looked up from his phone.

'You child isn't letting me go to the toilet.'

'So hold on. You're an adult.'

Siri tugged and pulled. Nausea spread like a fever through her arms and legs. Matilda tried to fix her eyes in the opposite direction to Göran but then they snagged on the rectangular shape of the Swedish flag, the glistening water, the bright blue dome of the sky. She looked down at her feet, they seemed to her swollen and enormous, looked within, saw only a void.

'He's putting up his tail! Come on, Tilda, COME!'

Siri was tugging so hard her arm was almost coming off. Matilda lost her footing and was forced to stumble after the little imp.

'He's coming this way! Look, Tilda, look!'

And suddenly she could resist no longer. Maybe she didn't even want to. Maybe she wanted to finally push herself over the edge. To let all the revulsion and fire spill forth.

She looked up. Stared right at the glowing blue bird-body, a gemstone of flesh and feathers, blue and sparkling like the lid of the mermaid Polly Pocket she'd once stolen from Clara and buried under Mama's most beautiful camellia.

'Ohmigod, he's so lovely. Don't you think?'

Matilda turned to face Siri, who'd fixed her big round eyes on Matilda's face. There was something strange about them. They weren't the colour they should've been. They were no longer their usual brown, but neither were they green, or blue.

They were that colour. The one that didn't exist.

'Tilda, what is it? Are you sick? Is it because you've got a baby in your tummy? Papa says he thinks so, but that I'm NOT allowed to ask … OH NO, I just did!'

The fucker. The little fucker.

She wasn't sure if she meant Siri, or Billy, or both.

Hand.

Child.

Ear.

A thousand peacock eyes staring.

There was a Tube strike the evening Philip and Chloe came back from Iceland. It had been planned for a while, but Philip, with characteristic optimism, had been convinced it would be called off. It wasn't, of course, and when they arrived at Paddington it was impossible, even for Philip, to get a cab, and all his friends with cars resolutely refused to answer the phone (they weren't stupid). Consequently, Philip had forced Chloe to walk the whole way home from Paddington. For a mere mortal, this walk would have taken an hour, though Philip could have done it in half that time. For Philip plus a seven-year-old and two suitcases (valises, to be precise), however, it turned out to take two hours and thirteen minutes, excluding toilet stops, swearing, sweetie bribes, and — if Philip's breath were to be believed — at least two double whiskies *sans* ice.

So when father and daughter finally came up the steps to 42 Mornington Terrace, Philip was annoyed. Laura saw it at once — his left eyebrow twitched now and then, the only visible sign of annoyance Laura had ever detected in this man, who she'd never seen angry in thirteen years. Even the unruly eyebrow was a rare sight — the last time Laura had seen it was five years previously, when her childhood friend Denise had come to visit and made a passing comment doubting the Duchess of Cambridge's ability to bear children. Laura knew Philip had a soft spot for Kate Middleton.

Sebastian had left her at dawn, but Laura still hadn't got dressed. Neither had she made much headway with the cleaning. She had tried, yes, but just an hour after Sebastian had slunk out the back door, the effect on her motor skills of his breath on her neck had faded, leaving an absence much worse than the one it had originally filled. Laura had little experience with drugs — really just a few joints in college and, of course, that time she'd tried cocaine but found, to her disappointment, that the dominant sensation was of having swallowed three Nurofens without water: a bitterness in her throat and a runny nose, and only a modicum of happiness — but she assumed this was how it felt to fall into addiction.

She had resisted the impulse to call Sebastian and ask him to come back, if only to help with the cleaning. People often turned up unexpectedly at Laura and Philip's place — only Philip's friends, of course; they paid visits in the classic manner, without calling first, without bringing a bottle, generally during the day. They had crisp handkerchiefs and fans and hats and Rimbaud in the original in their pockets and not infrequently a violin under their arm. If refused entry, they got offended and took revenge. Not by breaking contact, but by getting in touch twice as often. Laura tended to avoid them by staying out of the house with Chloe on Sundays, the visitors' favourite day, but today she couldn't even pull on a camisole in less than fifteen minutes, much less imagine how she might manage to prevent one of these acquaintances of Philip's from entering the house. In other words, calling Sebastian back had been impossible.

She did succeed in changing the sheets and washing between her legs, though not without considerable effort. After this strain to her hand–eye coordination she was so wobbly she had to have a lie-down on the sofa. She fell asleep and slept until dusk began to fall. A short while thereafter, she'd heard Philip and Chloe on the steps outside, and now here she was, standing in the doorway in her camisole and knickers and tousled hair, watching the syncopated twitching of her husband's eyebrows.

'Are you unwell?' Philip asked, throwing the valises in through the door while Chloe, exhausted, sank onto the steps and rested her head against Laura's leg. Laura let one hand drop, exhaled when she felt Chloe's hair under her fingers, and began to gently stroke her smooth scalp.

'A migraine. Thank god none of your henchmen came by today.'

'Charles was here, but no one answered. He messaged and was very upset. Were you out?'

'No, I was asleep. I must have missed it.'

'Asleep?'

'Yes.'

'During the day?'

'Yes.'

'Daytime is a time for being awake.'

'Not necessarily. Not if you have a migraine.'

'But you never have migraines.'

'All women have migraines. Where is this going?'

Philip didn't answer, just lifted Chloe over his shoulder and carried her into the house. Laura closed the door and followed them in, but tripped over one of the valises and went flying across the hallway.

'What's going on?' came Philip's voice from within the kitchen.

'That was Mummy going flying again, I think.'

'Let her stay there. Right, let's make toasties.'

An hour later, Philip had given Chloe dinner, brushed her teeth, dug a clean nightgown out of the wardrobe, and tucked her up in bed, where she'd fallen asleep in a hot minute as soon as he started sing 'Der Erlkönig'. It had always pleased Laura — she saw it as a mother's triumph — that not even Chloe could bear a bit of bedside Goethe and would fall asleep out of pure self-preservation, but this evening she'd have liked it if Philip could have gone on a little longer. A curious feeling came over her when she heard her husband's muted voice through the wall, smelled the late summer evening from the street, the soft-worn sheets against her skin. It was a feeling so unaccustomed she had to search her memory for its name. It was *security*.

But then she heard the floorboards creak, and soon Philip was in the doorway with the extra memory foam pillow he sat on when singing to Chloe dangling from one hand, his shirt unbuttoned at the throat — it was pale blue, an Eton; Laura used to love ironing it when she could still iron, and love.

'Laura, it feels extremely strange to have to ask this after thirteen years together, but —'

'No!'

Philip stiffened in the doorway.

'No, what? This generic denial makes you appear very, very guilty.'

'No to whatever you were about to ask!'

'I was going to ask if you'd been taking drugs, and if so, which, and what plans you have for rehabilitation, assuming you have any, which I doubt.'

'Oh, good god.'

Laura, who'd lifted her head in order to finally look her own treachery in the eye, let it drop to the pillow again in frustration. If she'd hoped Philip would have her up against the wall for presumed infidelity — and Laura wasn't sure whether that was what she'd been hoping for or not — it was not what was happening. Philip had, as so many times in their marriage, buried his head not in the sand but in his own arse, and found there an explanation for Laura Kadinsky's occasionally irrational behaviour, which glimmered like fool's gold, as seductive as it was worthless. It made Laura want to laugh and cry in equal measure, and indeed that's what she did.

'Chloe says you're constantly dropping things. You're out at odd times without anyone knowing where you are. Giselle rings me time and again wondering when you'll be home so she can go home to her own children. And you're totally fixated on that hamster. I bumped into Robertson in Paddington this evening; he said you'd gone round to ask about the hamster, and then he'd seen you trying to look in through their cellar window a day or two later. This behaviour is all very strange, Laura.'

'Doesn't it mean anything to you that all of this is hearsay?'

'Are you telling me it isn't true?'

'No. I'm saying that it says a lot about you as a husband that you have to base your accusations of addiction on other people's observations, since you're never here to observe your addict wife in person.'

'I'm aware of that, Laura. But, quite frankly, I've been an absentee husband since the day we married, so I'm having difficulty believing it's that that's driven you to drugs.'

'For Christ's sake, I'm not on drugs! I'm just unhappy!'

'Because I'm away a lot?'

Laura sighed.

'As you said yourself — you've always been away a lot. One of the pillars of our marriage is that you're away a lot. I really don't think we'd still be married if you hadn't been away so much. So no. That's not why.'

'So, what is it, then? If it has nothing to do with me.'

Laura took a deep breath.

'I'm unhappy because I got the sack.'

There. It was said — this unhappy, shameful failure, which a man like Philip would never be able to understand since he'd never failed at anything his entire life.

'The sack?'

'Yes.'

'When? Why?'

Laura pulled the duvet over her head to signal that the conversation was over. Through the darkness she could hear that Philip was still in the doorway.

He doesn't know what to say, thought Laura. He who always has something to say. It felt like a triumph of sorts, but a tragic one.

In the end she heard Philip clear his throat.

'I've booked a trip to Madrid. There's a man there who's built an atonal piano. He wants me to come and play it. I said yes, because I know you like the Prado Museum and drinking wine from square glasses.'

'I do,' Laura mumbled under the cover.

'And I like *you*.'

A tear broke loose and Laura pressed her head against the mattress, whispering into it so he wouldn't hear:

'I really believe you love me, Philip. But for the life of me I can't understand why.'

The same day as the very moral monkey went missing without a trace, to Sebastian's sorrow and everyone's confusion, the balance was shifted by the fact that someone who had in a sense been missing — Clara, that is — finally turned up. She did so in the form of a real, handwritten letter which Sebastian found in his mailbox when he came home after a long day's hunt for the monkey in every nook and cranny of the Institute.

Yes, the monkey had vanished, from one moment to the next. Sebastian couldn't understand how. One second, she'd been there with him in the office, the next she was gone. And not only the monkey, the whole cage was gone. Okay, maybe not in a second, maybe a few minutes — Sebastian had briefly left his office to talk to Laura on the phone — but still, in principle: the work of a moment.

Sebastian had immediately sought out Travis. Together they'd searched everywhere, even though they both knew it was futile. The monkey could hardly have taken the cage under her arm and walked off on her own — her arms weren't that long.

Someone had obviously stolen her.

But who? And why? Of course, Travis had her answer at the ready: it was obviously Corrigan, who else?

Yes, who else. Maybe Childs or Harvey, Sebastian thought, maybe they wanted to damage his standing with Corrigan so they could take over Laura's case. Or maybe it was just a practical joke, and the monkey would turn up again the next day, as if nothing had happened.

But deep down he knew it wasn't true.

There was a logic to the monkey's disappearance, even if he couldn't see it. Everything disappeared, after all. Sooner or later. Everything and everyone he'd ever cared about had always been taken from him. It was a pattern just waiting to repeat itself, over and over, for all time. Why the monkey had disappeared wasn't important.

The important thing was that she was gone and she wouldn't come back.

Sebastian,

I'm writing to you mostly so you can tell Mama I'm not dead or anything. And so that you can know it yourself, maybe, if you care — I don't know. Or, well, I guess you do. You've always cared about others, too much, I sometimes think.

Did you know there's plastic in the clouds, Sebastian? In the clouds. Tiny little particles. You know, people always say we're made of stardust. In the future we'll have to tell our children we're made of microplastics. Instead of stars in the sky we'll point out constellations of plastics and say: 'Look, see that? You're made of the same shitty shit!'

Sorry. That was depressing. I'm not depressed, I promise, don't worry. In some ways I'm happy, even though everything's going to shit. When all's said and done there's a pattern bigger than me, than you, than all of us; I'm in a place where everything fits together, even though everyone thinks I'm falling apart, and the cicadas are all dying.

But they're not afraid, I mean, one of them's almost blind but it doesn't seem to scare him much, not really. Not even the peacock feathers that were hanging there, just hanging there, seemed to scare them. Me neither. I don't think I'll ever come back. I just wanted you to know that.

I love you,
Clara

Sebastian stood outside Corrigan's office. He wasn't doing well. It was with some hesitation that he knocked on the door, because he understood why he'd been summoned, at least superficially: the monkey, who by now had been missing a whole week.

'Isaksson? Come in!' came the roar from the other side of the closed door. Corrigan sat with his feet up on the desk, as usual. His moustache twitched.

'You wanted to see me?' said Sebastian.

Corrigan flung his feet down from the desk and drew himself up to full height.

'Are you aware your monkey has disappeared?'

'Yes,' said Sebastian.

'And you didn't feel the need to tell me?'

'I assumed the information would reach you anyway.'

'A good assumption. All information is by nature mobile, and reaches its destination sooner or later. But in this case, I wish the information had reached me sooner rather than later, if you see what I mean.'

'My apologies. There's been a lot going on lately. With the extra assignments, I mean.'

'Yes, yes, Travis, yes. I must say I'm disappointed. You've not been very good at submitting reports. I assume she's the one who's taken the monkey?'

'That's — that's hard to imagine, sir.'

'So how did it happen?'

'Unclear.'

'Okay, so let's start here: when did she disappear?'

'Travis?'

'The monkey.'

'Last week.'

'Wait a moment, has Travis disappeared too?'

'No. Though my father has. And my sister Clara ... She wrote to

321

me but I don't know where she is. I mean, physically speaking. Do you?'

'There's no logic to what you're saying, Isaksson. Are you quite well?'

'Not at all, actually.'

'No, I can tell. A woman?'

Sebastian saw no point in trying to lie to Corrigan.

'Partly. And all this stuff with my sisters …'

'Yes, of course, you have two. Matilda as well … How's she getting along these days? She's the synaesthete, right? Interesting phenomenon, though not all that unusual.' Corrigan drummed his fingers on the table. 'It's a real hash, this situation.'

'Yeah.'

Sebastian swayed back and forth. The floor was completely silent. He wished it would creak, just a little. He would have liked to get out of there.

'I understand you're worried, Isaksson, I do. I mean about Clara. But I think she's in calm waters, in spite of everything. This talk of cicadas and microplastics and blind boys and so on … peacocks. It's nothing to concern yourself over. I understand your feeling it; it's enough to have one sister gone cuckoo, I get that, it's more than most people can handle. But two? And a slightly batty mother and a vanished father to top it all off? Kiddo, I understand why you've been sleeping poorly.'

Sebastian swallowed, but there was nothing to swallow. Somewhere there was a plausible explanation. If Clara'd written the same thing to their mother and their mother had … or if the monkey … but the monkey had disappeared. Why did everything he touched, everything that touched him, disappear? Why —

'Chin up, Isaksson!' Corrigan said. 'I promise you there's nothing wrong with Clara. She's just having a minor crisis; after all, it can't be so easy for her, suddenly realising she was swapped at birth. But it'll pass. She has friends, they're taking care of her, you —'

Sebastian jumped. 'What did you say? Why should it be Clara?'

Corrigan raised his eyebrows. 'Is that what I said?'

'Yes,' said Sebastian. 'You said Clara was swapped at birth.'

Corrigan didn't reply. Instead he opened a drawer in his desk and tossed something onto the table.

'This arrived for you. As you know, we operate a strict censorship policy here, so I've read it, of course. Not that I could have avoided doing so. It's a postcard, as you see. So, here, take it.'

Sebastian stretched out a trembling hand to what was indeed a postcard. Was it from Clara? No. The postcard depicted Mornington Crescent in the light of dawn. From Laura! It must be from Laura. He felt at once giddy, uplifted, almost euphoric. So, it was all in the open, his career was over, he'd have to leave his post, but what difference did it make? Laura was a lot of things, but stupid wasn't one of them; she wouldn't have sent this postcard to him like this unless she'd wanted to tell him something special, if she hadn't wanted it to be discovered, and why would she want that? Naturally, to put a stop to this charade so they, she and he, could be together for the rest of their lives …

Sebastian stroked the front of the card. All the strange things Corrigan had said melted away like snow on bare skin; it meant nothing, nothing meant anything — he and Laura were going to run away and live happily ever after. His sisters, his mother, Travis, Corrigan, they could look after themselves. They weren't his responsibility.

He turned the card over.

Lieber Sebastian;
Es gibt ein System, das so großartig ist, dass es blendend ist.
Deine Schwester wird bald zurückkommen.

Einmal, am Rande des Hains,
stehn wir einsam beisammen
und sind festlich, wie Flammen —
fühlen: Alles ist eins.

Horst Herbert Jacob

The phone rang at the same moment that Sebastian, with the mysterious postcard in his hand and a head full of unformulated questions, staggered out of Corrigan's office.

It was Laura.

He hadn't realised she was home.

Five days ago, she'd backed out of a hotel room behind Paddington station with an apologetic expression and almost in passing mentioned that she was off to Madrid with her family, where it was probably awfully sweaty this time of year, as August became September, but what did it matter as long as there were fountains and oranges and the shadows of the plane trees in the park in front of the Prado. She'd stumbled on the doorstep on the way out and he'd had to help her up.

'Laura,' he said into the phone now, 'is something wrong? I thought you'd gone?'

'Tomorrow. We leave tomorrow. But I have to see you first; I won't be able to cope if I can't see you first. Chloe and Philip are going to the puppet theatre. They won't be home until nine.'

It was as though she could hear the doubt in his voice, even though he couldn't hear it himself and wouldn't realise for a long time that it had been there in his voice, the whole time, every second since that first time he'd said her name.

So she begged and pleaded.

She said she wanted to go to Hampstead Heath. She wanted to go all the way up to the highest point, put her arm through his, and look out over Parliament Hill. She wanted to see if it worked, to bring out the trees' spiny contours one last time. Then she wanted to eat bubble and squeak at the Spaniards Inn, then take a taxi to a hotel, any hotel, and make love until she lost consciousness. She said:

'Please.'

And he said yes.

★

They decided to meet by Camden Lock and walk together through Camden and Belsize Park. Sebastian steered his heavy legs towards the Underground. He bought two almond croissants at the bakery chain Paul and took the greasy bag down into the earth. He thought of them as an offering. The thought of feeding Laura with fat and sugar, of putting his buttery fingers into her soft mouth and feeling her suck, made him momentarily regain his strength, and he ran and jumped into the carriage just before the doors closed.

It was still at least two hours before rush hour, so the train was half empty, and he sank into a seat. Something was chafing against his heart. He put his hand into his breast pocket and pulled it out — his heart, that is. And the postcard — the thing that was chafing. Actually, he didn't need to look at it to look at it, he knew every brushstroke of the image — Laura had a diary with the same picture on the front; he'd seen it what felt like thousands of times, though in fact it was precisely seventeen. Every time they parted after a liaison, she took it out of her handbag, leafed carefully through to the following week and searched, her finger hovering over the page, for a suitable gap in her schedule for possible future meetings. It was a charade, of course, given that Laura had very little to do since getting fired, and most of their encounters came about just like today's: with Laura suddenly calling and demanding he be somewhere half an hour later. But still. He liked the ritual, and she seemed to need it. She never wrote anything in the diary, not even an S or a cross or a code word. She was careful like that, *too* careful, thought Sebastian. Hadn't he heard a thousand times that unfaithful people — at least those with passionate, long-lasting affairs — wanted, deep down, to be found out, and therefore made small yet decisive mistakes that sooner or later led to them being found out? The hotel bill in the jacket pocket; the lipstick on the collar; a phone left on the counter, plinging out the sound of sex. Laura didn't do any of that; she left behind none of the incriminating remains of love. No body, no crime; no body, no sweat, no kisses, no lust. Just a scientist and his subject, strip lights, pathology.

He ran his finger over the front of the postcard. Mornington Crescent in flaming yellow. Laura's hand, digging around in her bag.

When they were together she probably spent half the time she wasn't on her back looking for things in her handbag. Lipstick. Sweets. Cigarettes, sometimes, but only when Philip was away. New nylons in sealed packages. Her phone. Small bottles of perfume. Hand cream, also in small shiny tubes.

And the diary, with its yellow cover.

He'd asked Laura about the picture, the first time he saw it, and she told him it was painted by a man named Frank Auerbach. He was born in Germany in 1931, but lived virtually all his life in Camden, after coming to London with the Kindertransport in 1939. He spent half a century painting the same motifs: Mornington Crescent in different lights, the trees on Primrose Hill, portraits of a few friends and acquaintances.

Sebastian let his fingers run over the image, the dark yellow shadows, the inverted sky — lemon-yellow where it should have been blue, blue in the corner where a child would have put a half-lemon for the sun. The buildings reaching for the sky, apart from one that seemed to lean, about to topple to the ground. Two red dots and a line made windows, but also a face — once you'd seen the picture that way you couldn't unsee it. And it became comical, almost ridiculous, even though a whole city appeared to be floating somewhere among the clouds: the sublime and the childish all at once. It struck Sebastian that this was a description that also fitted Laura quite well.

But the postcard wasn't from Laura. He'd been mistaken. Laura hadn't tried to communicate with him via that card. It was someone named Horst Herbert Jacob and he wrote in German. He or they? Was it one person or three? Was it someone he'd met at the Institute, a research subject, perhaps, or was it some kind of weird joke? And what was that text that had shimmered before his eyes there in Corrigan's office? Sebastian's German was dodgy, but he understood *Schwester*. It meant sister. *Zurück* meant back.

Was the card from Matilda? She lived in Germany. She was his sister. But Matilda didn't need to communicate via cryptic cards, she made ordinary phone calls.

He turned the card over carefully and studied the text more closely. *Es gibt ein System.* There is a system. Was the card from Travis? It would be typical of her, after all. His eyes drifted up to the corner, to the postmark. *Isla de Pascua.*

It had been posted from Easter Island. Clara. But it wasn't Clara's handwriting. He went on studying the card for clues. He read the small print, the printed information about the postcard image in the bottom left-hand corner. *Francesca Woodman: Untitled, Rome, 1977–78.* © *George & Betty Woodman.*

He blinked, blinked, blinked again. That couldn't be. That couldn't possibly be. He turned the card back over; it was Mornington Crescent. The walls of the Tube crowded in on him. Sebastian's thoughts were racing, running through his sweaty fingers like sand. This was too much. He couldn't handle any more now. And still he began to claw — compulsively, driven by an animal impulse to tear apart that which didn't fit — the postcard's edge. And sure enough, Mornington Crescent fell like a yellowing leaf to the floor and underneath, tacky from the glue that had held the cards together, he saw the same scene he'd seen in every dream, every night since that first one,

the one when she'd been hanging there,

just *hanging* there,

with a tape measure like a snare around her neck.

Sebastian looked up, catching sight of his clammy face in the dark glass. And suddenly everything lit up, they squeaked into King's Cross, people moved in the aisle, trying to push their way out with large suitcases. Outside the window, billboards floated past — one featuring a naked woman's body behind a wall of paper, the paper torn and rolled up over her stomach so the stomach was the only thing visible, muscular and hard. It was an advert for some kind of protein powder, but Sebastian didn't know what protein powder was; he knew nothing about strength but everything about Francesca Woodman's video installations and there was one that looked just like this: the artist naked behind paper, tearing away strip after strip until the whole image of her emerged clearly, much more clearly than if the viewer had seen her naked body all at once.

Like a puzzle.

Over the tannoy came the generic British female voice: *The next stop is King's Cross St Pancras. Change here for the Victoria, Northern, Hammersmith and City, Metropolitan, and Circle Lines, and for national and international rail services. Alight here for the Royal National Institute of Blind People.* He stood and forced his way out of the carriage, everything seemed dark and blurry, *Alight here for the Royal National Institute of Blind People, Blind People, Blind People* —

He ran up the escalator and towards the exit, but fell into the ticket gates; managed with slippery fingers to get out his travelcard and beep himself through; crawled up the steps, out into the sun; tried to find something, anything, to fix his eyes on.

Travis. He needed to talk to Travis, straight away. He rang her with fumbling fingers.

'Sebastian! This is NOT a secure line.'

'I have to talk to you.'

'Meeting place 17B in forty-five minutes.'

Jennifer Travis stood in a circle of blue light, in front of a display case of glass and white-rendered concrete. Her face was reflected in the glass, and therefore in the object behind it, so that he could see, over and over, the back of her blonde head, her serious face, and the machine's. It was impossible to separate the three images. Across her face were the words LOGICAL COMPUTER in block capitals. The machine looked at him with rosy cheeks and big, innocent eyes. It smiled.

'Sebastian!'

'Travis.'

He went and stood beside her and read the sign.

'Isn't it beautiful?' Travis said, touching the glass gently. 'It's the most beautiful machine I know of. So pure. Rudimentary, of course, but that's what I find so appealing. I like to come here and look at it when I'm wound up. Right now, I'm awfully wound up.'

Sebastian had been thinking Travis seemed unexpectedly calm and harmonious, composed, in fact, but now he could see there was something new in her face, something strained and hopeless that put shadows in the corners of her eyes, and made her tongue glide over her teeth time and time again, as if it couldn't find peace enough to lie still in her mouth.

'You wanted to see me?' Travis said and started to walk through the gallery. They were alone in the Science Museum's permanent mathematics collection, because it was the middle of the week and the museum would soon be closing.

'Yes …'

Sebastian ran his hands through his hair. He didn't know where to begin. Talking to Travis had felt like the only right thing to do, the only conceivable thing. Now he didn't know which of all the frayed nerves he should tug on first.

'So … it's about Corrigan. I know I haven't always believed you about Corrigan … I mean, the idea that he has something to do with all this. The puzzle and so on. It seems crazy somehow.'

Sebastian, upset by the day's events and revelations, had initially taken a wrong turn, ending up in the poorly air-conditioned earthquakes and volcanoes gallery, and was finding the cool, deserted hall full of circuit boards and sextants very soothing. They'd stopped in front of an enormous construction that looked not so much like a mathematical wonder as one of those plastic toys children have at the beach: a system of cogs and paddles, and a funnel at the top into which you pour water, which theoretically — if rarely in practice — should trickle down and make the cogs turn. This machine, which Sebastian learned was called the 'MONIAC' and was constructed in 1949 by researchers at the London School of Economics to illustrate the United Kingdom's national economic processes — 'a way of teaching economics in thirty fascinating minutes' — was constructed from hundreds of components.

'Pareidolia,' said Travis, letting her eyes wander from paddle wheel to paddle wheel.

'What?'

'The craziness you're talking about. There's a clinical name for it. He always tells me I have it — Corrigan, that is. A mutated form, even, pareidolia multiplied by a thousand wingbeats.'

'I don't know what it is.'

'Rorschach tests. Computers that learn to recognise faces. They're based on the same thing. The tendency to detect a familiar form, even where it doesn't exist. The desire to see patterns is so strong in the human brain that once we've seen them we can't stop seeing them.'

For a moment, Sebastian thought Travis had been afflicted with some form of self-awareness; that Travis, according to some rule about cosmic symmetry, about debit and credit in the balance sheet of madness, had taken on the common sense he no longer had. But no. She went on with a snigger.

'He's wrong, of course. The world doesn't take the brain's shape; it's the brain that's taken the world's shape. It's because patterns exist that we're eager to see them. Which mathematics acknowledges, but not always the humanities.'

Sebastian was growing impatient.

'Travis, listen: I don't know what's going on, what weird role he has in this — I mean, in my life, my family — I just know it has to end because I can't take it anymore, do you hear what I'm saying?'

A museum attendant who was standing by the exit looked at his watch and hummed, a hum that echoed around the empty gallery. Travis didn't even seem to notice it.

'I don't know if we'll ever even get to the end, Sebastian. Of the puzzle, or anything. That's what depresses me. Look at this machine. Fantastic, in many ways. But still far too simple. Anyway: I'm not crazy. It's just that the world is too big.'

'I know you're not, Travis! I know that now. I think. Listen, I got a letter. From Clara. A real letter, on paper —'

'But I've given up, really given up. I actually think I must have gone wrong somewhere this time. I think you're right.'

'She wrote that it's all over.'

'It doesn't have anything to do with Corrigan. The puzzle, nothing.'

Irritated, Sebastian prodded Travis, whose gaze was lost somewhere between the import and export of colonial goods.

'Hey, I was trying to tell you something. About Clara!'

'I'm sorry, Sebastian, but unfortunately I feel nothing for your sister. Because I don't feel anything for anyone, as you know. And so, I'm struggling a little to summon any real interest for her. What did you say was over?'

Travis tore herself away from the mathematical toys and started walking towards a few machines that looked like fuse boxes without their casing.

'Everything. But more specifically, Corrigan, he —'

'Everything?'

'That's what she wrote. But I don't know what she means.'

'She probably means what she says. Everything.'

Sebastian took hold of Travis's arm and made her stop.

'Listen, Travis, for god's sake! She wrote that she doesn't think she'll ever come back. She wrote about someone who was blind and about a pattern that was bigger than herself. She wrote about constellations, peacocks and cicadas. *Cicadas!*

'And?'

Sebastian noticed that Travis reacted to that information in spite of herself. He leaned closer, taking her face in his hands so she couldn't pull away.

'I was talking to Corrigan, later. About the monkey. And he KNEW. Everything in that letter, he already knew about it! I mean in detail, I don't know how. Like he was the one who'd orchestrated it all. And he gave me a postcard, and —'

Travis bit her lip.

'Go on,' she said doubtfully.

'It was in German. The postcard. I don't know who speaks German, maybe Corrigan, but it was posted from Easter Island. But that wasn't the weird thing. The weird thing was that there were two, I mean two postcards, they were stuck together … Have I told you about Violetta? I haven't, right? And another thing: my sisters, one of them has to, like, go, and Corrigan says it's Clara, but how could he know that without having known my family a long time, like, since it happened? I think maybe he's her dad, though that seems really, really weird, because he's American, but he's very interested in Lund, don't you think? Why was he even looking there? Why did they hire me? Huh?'

He was still holding Travis's cheeks in his hands, and he suddenly realised he was holding so tight he was about to lift her off the ground. The attendant by the door kept casting suspicious glances in their direction and looked to be on the verge of an intervention. He let go.

'Sebastian!' said Travis, putting a finger on his lips. 'Cool it. Breathe. What you're saying is very interesting, but I don't understand any of it. Go back to the beginning. Why in heaven's name do you think Corrigan is your sister's dad? I don't know much about that aspect of human biology, but I would have thought that also meant he was … yours.'

Sebastian was having palpitations. He saw his face reflected in a glass display and for a second, he could see that the whole thing was madness, pareidolia multiplied by a thousand wingbeats, but it couldn't be helped, it felt so good to let go, and Travis was interested now, he saw that in the corners of her mouth, she wanted to hear it! So he told her: about his father disappearing, his mother wanting to get something off her chest, about the mix-up on the maternity ward, and Clara, who hadn't taken it well, not well at all, and Matilda, who was on his back about 'finding' her, like it was that easy, about Corrigan knowing everything, and that postcard … He stopped there. Of Violetta and toes pointing to the underworld he said nothing, nor of Laura and Mornington Crescent in the golden morning light; he saw that Travis had already taken in more information than even she could process in the short time available before he had to go, because Laura, Laura was waiting! How long had she been waiting? He looked at the clock but couldn't get the numbers to make sense —

'Hmm,' Travis said, and no more.

'What do you think?' Sebastian asked, and could hear how eager he sounded. 'I think Clara knows it's her, and now she's not planning to come back. This card … I don't know what it means, but I don't think it's true, what it says; I know Clara, she's so easily hurt, and —'

Something clicked in Travis's eyes, like when a counter stops on the right number. She was silent a moment, then she said slowly:

'But it's not Clara.'

Sebastian had begun to wander back and forth between the old computers — that was what they were, the fuse boxes, he read on the information panels: RECOGNISING PATTERNS: *In 1950 Alan Turing, now famed for codebreaking during the Second World War, asked the question: Can machines think? Three decades later, the machine to your left debuted on national television. It seemed the answer might soon be yes.*

Sebastian turned left abruptly.

'What did you say?'

A critical sign of intelligence is recognising patterns. The machine had first been trained with pictures of its creators' faces. Then, one after another, the scientists sat in front of a live camera linked to the machine. It had to decide whether any of the faces it saw matched the face patterns stored in its memory.

'Of course, I don't know what your sister is thinking, but the fact that it's not Clara changes things. But that doesn't mean she has nothing to do with this, of course she does, the question is just how … And the puzzle? What does he want? Sebastian, I think all this, I mean, your whole, shall we say, "family situation"' — Travis waved a little dismissively, as though she'd already moved on to something else, which she had, which she always had — 'is going to resolve itself as soon as we've cracked the puzzle once and for all. Don't you think?'

'Ma'am, sir, we're closing now.'

The restless attendant popped up between two glass cases and tapped his watch to underline the point. 'Please make your way to the exit.'

Travis waved him away, but he was unrelenting. Reluctantly, Sebastian took Travis by the arm and pulled her with him towards the stairwell. The despondency that had appeared to be weighing on Travis when he'd first seen her in the museum's cold neon light, and which, now he thought about it, had appeared to be weighing on her for days, even weeks, the despondency that he somewhere in his effervescent heart understood had to do with self-doubt — it was as if it had been blown away: she practically danced down the stairs and through the space galleries — the heavenly bodies on the ceiling lit up her hair and it was all he could do to prevent himself stopping and shaking her, forcing her to answer.

'Travis,' he hissed as they collected their bags from the cloakroom, 'what do you mean, it's not Clara?'

The swing doors spat them out onto the street. Before them, along the wide museum promenade, a flood of people coursed down towards South Kensington station. Young families with arms full of stuffed toy dinosaurs and magnifying glasses, men with strange hats selling ice creams and balloon animals, middle-aged couples with bags from the V&A and their sights set on Italian delicacies. Autumn was around the corner, but it was still warm, it had been warm all summer long — so warm there were no leaves left on the trees. They lay scorched on the paving stones, unmoving in the still air. Sebastian pulled Travis onto the pavement and into a narrow alley guarded by a mime artist.

'Why are you so sure it's not Clara? Please, can you just answer me?'

Travis blew away a strand of hair and rolled her eyes.

'Do I really have to explain everything to you?' she said.

'Sadly.'

'Okay, assuming your mother isn't lying about what happened when you were born ...' Travis clicked her fingers. 'Simple. Lowest common denominator, and all that. You said yourself your dad's not the sharpest knife in the block. But hey, we have to focus on what's important here. Corrigan —'

But Sebastian could no longer hear what she was saying.

She was right.

It really was very simple.

Lowest common denominator, and all that.

So many people everywhere.

He put his hands in his pockets and started walking.

Travis rushed after him, laying a hand on his arm, but he shook it off.

'Where are you going, Sebastian? We have work to do, don't you get it? We're so close, so incredibly close. We'll solve this, find your sister, and then —'

'I'm going to call my mother.'

He left her standing there on the pavement, pushed his way into the stream of people, and was gone.

It recognised them all, calling out each scientist's name. Then a scientist new to the machine walked in. 'INTRUDER! INTRUDER!' it shouted. 'The computer immediately spots the odd man out,' the television presenter said. 'The security implications are obvious.'

Stand on the bridge and wait.

See the soap bubble drifting towards its downfall. See the beauty in an indeterminate colour. See the early September sun in your lover's hair, though he's not there, though he's not coming this time. See the scent of henna over Camden Lock, the way you can cut open the syrup of it like a skull and find the cranium empty. See the beauty in the emptiness, in the soft, hash-scented clothing. See the oily convexity that you can't touch without soiling your hands. See those seven seconds in which perfection exists outside your body. See the fact that you've stolen this moment from your own child, see her sitting there on the sofa with her nanny, watching TV with a Cheerio on the end of each finger, completely unaware that her bubble wand is not in its place on the hat shelf, and that her mother's footsteps are not clicking their way along the street on their way home to her, but have rerouted themselves here, to the bridge by Camden Lock under a late-summer sky made for children. See that you yourself are a simple imitator, a traitor of the worst kind, a kidnapper, a criminal, and a charlatan, a plagiarist, a doer of violent deeds. See that you've stolen all your attributes from a child you never were and have no right to be, not now it's too late. See your lover's sister Clara, whose existence you're only vaguely aware of, get up from a sofa in an anonymous hotel room on Easter Island, Chile, and coldly say: 'We're borrowing this earth from our children, señor, don't you understand that?' to an immeasurably intoxicated travelling napkin salesman. See your lover's other sister crying over the memory of a dead bird she once saw in Volkspark Hasenheide. See the short-lived happiness of the innermost space of an orgasm. Look into the eyes of the woman who stops in front of you on the bridge with an open cigarette packet in her hand from which she takes two cigarettes, lighting both with one flame and handing you one before silently walking on, a woman whose name you don't know and who you will never see again and whose age you can't determine. Smoke the cigarette, chew some chewing gum, don't ask where my right to give you all these orders comes from, or my voice, because I don't know. Look at me as you look at evolution: look away. Look at yourself instead, see yourself as your lover sees you, a lament in the form of a woman. See the next soap bubble, and the next, the way you're blowing them carefully so that each is larger than the last, see how that could be seen as a metaphor for consumer society, if you were the kind of person who thought about that kind of thing. See a dad stop beside you with a baby in a pushchair. See the child grip the father's phone while the father talks to a hippie who may be selling drugs, the child's wide-eyed fascination that so much can be contained in such a tiny thing, can flicker past on the screen any time the father bends down and presses a button or two.

See what the child sees.

See a cat playing the piano on YouTube.

See all the thousands of cats playing the piano on YouTube and see that not a single one of them has asked for the attention.

See that he's not coming, not this time. That he has more important things to do than see you; see that you're not the centre of the world.

See the bubble again, see it as a crystal ball, bursting into a million pixels, each and every one of them a meaningless little rainbow.

'Mama, it's me, isn't it?'

'Sebastian …'

She sounded tired, but not surprised. Tender, indulgent. Like when he was a child and asked questions that were really much too big for his little blond head. *How many birds aren't there?*

'I told you I don't know,' she went on. 'There's no need to keep brooding on it.'

'Stop it! I know it was me, and I know you know it was me. You just have to think about it logically.'

He could hear her walking about at the other end of the line. Distant birdsong. Worms tunnelling through the earth, leaves letting go of branches with little pops as sharp as lightning flashes. She was at Fright-Delight, he was just as sure as if he'd been there himself. In his new, enlightened state he could feel it, as though all his senses had been sharpened to supernatural strength: he could hear everything, see everything.

'If it was Papa,' he said, 'if it was Papa who figured it out, the difference between the baby they took away and the one who came back must have been blindingly obvious; he wouldn't have been so sure otherwise. And —'

'I think you're underestimating your father, Sebastian.'

'We're talking about a man who can't tell a crow from a hen! Don't you remember, that time we were in Öland —'

'Yes, yes, I know, he's always struggled with worldly things —'

'And the only difference I can think of that not even Papa would mistake is sex, Mama. Sex! That was it, right? They walked off with a girl and came back with a boy? Okay, it would have been the other way around too, but if you think about it carefully, the lowest common denominator and all that … I'm blond, for fuck's sake!'

'Sebastian …'

'It's true, isn't it?'

338

His mother sighed on the other end of the invisible telephone line.

'You've always been intelligent, Sebastian. Too intelligent for our family, that's the only thing I know for sure. I mean, there's nothing wrong with your sisters' understanding, but …'

'So it's true?'

His mother sighed again, even more deeply. He heard her sit down, the seat of her jeans on the damp earth, her eyes looking towards the maternity ward at Lund General Hospital.

'You have to realise that by the time he told me it was too late. A week had passed, Sebastian. A week. Do you know how much love a parent can summon forth in the first week of a child's life? An infinite amount. I mean it when I say that, *infinite*. To tell the truth, Sebastian, it wasn't something your father told me of his own accord. I got the notes back, you see, from the hospital. I honestly don't understand how no one at the hospital reacted to it at the time, given that the notes stated it in black and white.'

'That there were three girls?'

'No, no, it said two girls and a boy. But if you read the small print — and you know I always read the small print — it also said that the first born, girl 1, wasn't breathing at birth. There was some uncertainty over who was born next, girl 2 or the boy, because everything happened very quickly and both the midwives' attention was on girl 1.'

'Hmm.'

'I said so too. Because whatever the order was afterwards I was pretty sure the baby who came back from intensive care three hours later was a boy, just as I was sure the two babies I had at my breasts were girls. I assumed there'd just been a mistake in the notes, you see. As they pointed out, everything was an unholy mess and they were quite right that Clara and Matilda came close together, very close together; I'm not even sure myself which of them came first, even though I think it was Clara, because the last baby was the only one who cried, and Matilda was much more of a crybaby when she was tiny — well, even as an adult, I'm sure you'll agree. But then I read it out to your father. "Claes," I said, "it says here that it was a girl they ran out to intensive care with." "Yeah," he said, "that's right." "Okay, but they came back with Sebastian," I said then. "Yeah," he said, "that's right too.""

Sebastian said nothing.

"'So how do you explain it?" I said then. "I can't," he said. Now pay attention, Sebastian, he didn't say anything about it being wrong. Nothing about an exchange or a mix-up. For him there was no question of a mistake. I think it was as simple as this: he saw you, and he saw his son. There was nothing else to it. He's governed by his feelings, you know. I myself am more of a brooder, but he's a drifter, he is. Lord knows that has its drawbacks, but in this case, I think it was a blessing in disguise. Because we got you, didn't we? Our son. I'm sure we would have felt the same about a daughter if it had turned out that way, but it didn't. And I still trust in our Lord enough to believe that there's a meaning to it. I have to, anything else would be a disavowal of our love for you. And that, I can tell you now, was so intense after seven days that not for a moment would we have considered trying to swap you. You were, you *are*, our son.'

'Mama, this is crazy. What you've just told me is crazy, you must be aware of that?'

'Yes, yes. It's somewhat preposterous, I can't help but agree. But you know what they say about the ways of the Lord, Sebastian.'

'Inscrutable,' he muttered.

'Yes, that too. But they're also meandering. He's long-winded, God, just like all men. Why make something simple when you can make it complicated? The theologists need something to get their teeth into, after all.'

'But stealing someone else's child … it's not a theological problem, it's breaking the law.'

'We didn't steal a child, Sebastian. We just took what God gave us. Moses was swapped at birth too, you know.'

Sebastian closed his eyes.

'But the others … the other parents. My parents — my biological ones, I mean. They must have noticed the same thing. That they got back a girl and not a boy.'

'They probably did. Or, I know they did. But I guess they thought the same thing we did. That that was just how it was. I don't know, nobody at the hospital said anything, of course, it would have been chaos if they had. And later, well … It was what it was. Biology really isn't everything, Sebastian. Joseph loved Jesus as though he were his own flesh and blood.'

'He was the son of God. I think it's a slightly different matter.'

'You too are the son of God, Sebastian. We all are.'

'I don't know what to do with this information, Mama.'

'You'll learn to make sense of it. I'm sure of it. Just let a little time pass and it'll start to feel less strange, you'll see.'

'But I mean practically, Mama. Should I tell Clara and Matilda? Should I tell the authorities? Should I try and find my biological parents? Will Clara and Matilda want to meet their sister? Are there going to be four of us? It's complicated enough with three! Oh, god.'

Suddenly he remembered something.

'What did you mean, you know they noticed? My … biological parents?'

'Huh?'

'You said: "I know they did." How do you know that? Were you in contact with them?'

'Aha, that. Yes. Yes, we were.'

'You told the three of us that you weren't. When we last talked about this. Was that a lie?'

'Yes. So, it wasn't until later. Much later. You were already grown by that time.'

'So you know who they are?'

'Yes, yes.'

'And?'

'And what?'

'What are they? Where do they live? Is it anyone I know?'

'I don't think we should talk about it quite yet, Sebastian. You have a lot to process, you know. I mean, are you even sure you want to know? It's a lot to take in at once, it is. And it doesn't mat—'

'Of course it matters! I'm not a child, I know you and Papa are my parents and not them, it's not that. But I have to know. Christ.'

'It's just that it's quite complicated ...'

'What do you mean, complicated? Have they told you they don't want me to know? Exactly how much have you talked about this? Are you in regular contact?'

'No, I wouldn't say that, no. But ... I don't know what to say, Sebastian. I can't lie to you anymore, I've promised myself that, but at the same time I know this information won't be good for you. I would really like us to do this under slightly more orderly circumstances, for you to come home, for us to do it together, perhaps get help from a priest, or even a psychologist if that would feel better ... It really wasn't my intention for it to go so far. I just wanted you to know about ... each other. But not her, necessarily. Oh, Jesus. Sebastian ...'

'Which her? My sister? Or, I mean, their sister. My sisters' sister.'

He gave a laugh, short and hollow.

'I can't get my head around the fact we're having this conversation. And that I'm sitting here on a bench by William Hill while we have it.'

'Who's William Hill?'

'It's not a person, it's a chain. Of betting shops.'

'Have you been gambling? You know I don't like gambling.'

'Stop playing your cards so close to your chest. Have you met her?'

'Who?'

'Your third daughter!'

'Well, yes, I have.'

'Many times?'

'Yes, I suppose you could say that. But darling, I think —'

'Many times?'

'Yes, but I didn't know ... How could I have known? There was no resemblance. I don't think. Or at least, now I can see it, maybe, but then ... Not like Clara and Matilda are alike. But there was something familiar, of course; you know I didn't like it from the very beginning but I never understood why, I didn't. Oh, Sebastian, you don't hate me, do you?'

'No, of course not. But ...'

'Because I swear we didn't know anything. And later, when her parents got in touch, it was already too late ... Or, I mean, we talked about it and they also thought it was ...'

Something in Sebastian's nerves began to jerk, a creeping sensation under his skin, ants. Antennae waving in the air.

'Thought what? Who?'

'But you know what, I thought the whole time there was something a bit unpleasant about how alike you were, as people, I mean ... And yet so different. I thought it before I even knew, that you fit together in some way, like dark and light. Shadow siblings. That's what I thought. And I think you sensed it too, and that's why you were so drawn to each other. Because it's not normal to have as strong a connection as you did, not at that age, it just isn't.'

'Mama,' said Sebastian in a cold voice. 'Mama, tell me straight out who you're talking about.'

His phone beeped three times. The battery was dead.

He woke with creases on his cheeks, sand in the corners of his eyes. For the first seven seconds he had just one thought, and strangely enough it wasn't that he'd found out the previous day that he wasn't his sisters' brother and his parents' child, neither was it the ice-cold insight that his soulmate had been the dark shadow of his life in more than one way. No, it was that he'd let down Laura Kadinsky's sorrowful eyes.

She'd waited for him, and he hadn't come. Instead of throwing himself onto a train and going to her he'd stayed there on the bench by William Hill, stayed there until it grew dark and the streets gradually emptied of people. Then he'd walked, the whole way to Russell Square, snuck in the back door, and found his way to his office in the dark. He'd sat on his swivel chair, put his forehead on the table, and fallen asleep.

He hadn't thought a single thought, except that he missed the monkey.

The monkey would have known what to do with this information. The monkey wouldn't have left any room for doubt. But she was gone.

And now Laura was gone too. Had he really sat there and let her wait in vain for him? And where was she now? Was she sitting in Heathrow with Chloe on her knee, two well-used cabin bags at her feet, a double mocha frappuccino in one hand that Philip had queued and jostled among thousands of tired morning tourists to buy her? No, he corrected his imagination, Laura didn't like that kind of over-sweetened gunk, he knew that now, he knew she liked her coffee the same way she liked her sex — without twiddles. But did Philip know that? What if he came back with a caramel latte topped with chocolate powder, what if she was right now thinking: *No one, no one in the whole world cares about me anymore, not even Sebastian.* What if Philip hadn't even bought her any coffee, what if she'd been forced to get it herself, had knocked over the cup and scalded her beautiful hands? Or, the most probable option, what if Philip had come back with exactly the right coffee, kissed her on the brow, and said: 'I'm so glad we're going away today, I know I've been a bad husband lately, but that's going to change, I'm going to take care of you now, take care of you the way you deserve.' And what if Laura had lifted the cup to her mouth without difficulty, smiled, and said: 'I've been a bad wife, too, but that's over now. From now on it's you and me again.'

Sebastian devoted himself to this familiar emotional paradox for a while, to the battling forces within him that on one hand wanted nothing but for Laura to be so unhappy in her family life that she found herself a new one (ideally with Sebastian), and on the other couldn't bear the thought of destroying what was obviously a rickety but beautiful family structure, a life that Laura had chosen and would continue to choose, if only her hands would stop missing their target. Could it be the case, Sebastian wondered with the new clarity he seemed to have acquired at some point between the conversation with Corrigan, Travis's eye-roll, and his mother's nonchalant admission, that Laura was constantly reaching out for Philip and that it was the fault of her vision problems that her hands landed on Sebastian instead?

The thought gave him the same rough feeling in his throat he got after vomiting. He looked at the clock. It was quarter past eleven. He needed to talk to Travis, if for no other reason than to pluck the idea that Corrigan was his father out of her skull, the thought he unintentionally — it seemed to him now — had happened to place there. It was a relief, at least, that this wasn't the case.

He went out to the toilet in the corridor, hastily washed his face and armpits, misting the mirror with his breath until his face disappeared. Then he went back into the office, pulled on the lab coat that had been hanging on the back of his chair, and was about to leave when he saw the light on the intercom flashing blue. It was odd: the intercom normally flashed red for an incoming external call, green for a voicemail message, and yellow for a call via the switchboard or other internal connection. Even stranger was the fact that the flashing didn't stay blue, but started hopping back and forth between the different colours until the light seemed to have no discernible colour at all, to flash white, or nothing. And still it flashed, clearly, concerningly. Sebastian sank sweatily down into his chair and pressed the button to stop the flashing.

'Sebastian? Benedict here. Are you busy? There's a woman here in my room who wants to see you. She is, I should say, very determined, but in all honesty, she also appears rather mad, so I'm not sure what to do. Shall I send her up?'

It would be an exaggeration to say that Sebastian's heart stopped, but his heart stopped (love is an exaggeration, after all). So she hadn't gone! She was here, she was still here, still the saddest woman in the world, whose mouth only he could feed!

'Laura Kadinsky?' Sebastian asked the speakerphone. 'Send her up.'

'Er, she says she's your sister,' Benedict replied.

Sebastian's shoulders sank.

'Kadinsky? She's my patient.'

'Wait a moment ... No, it's definitely not Mrs Kadinsky. She says her name is Matilda and she's your sister and that, wait ...'

Sebastian fell back into his chair.

'Matilda?'

'Yes.'

'My sister Matilda?'

'Yes, by her own account, in any case.'

'Here?'

'As I said.'

'Well, send her up, then!'

'She looks completely crazy, Sebastian, it's something in her eyes. I think it would actually be best if you came down.'

It was when the siblings were fourteen, while they were preparing for their confirmation, that Matilda's illness reared its devilish head for the first time. Unusually early, the doctors said, onset rarely occurs before the late teens, but of course, there are exceptions.

What happened was that Matilda became obsessed with her own moral shortcomings and those of others. Their mother had blamed the priest — he'd spent far too much time talking about sin, shame, and penitence, she thought, and far too little about the message of Christian love. He was a member of Yes to Life! and one evening after the reading, Matilda had come home with a postcard bearing a picture of an aborted foetus's little clenched fist, and, half crying, half shrieking, asked their mother to tell her how God, if indeed he existed, could have allowed such a thing as abortion to have been invented. Their mother had answered with something vague about theodicy and women's rights and Elise Ottesen-Jensen and moral grey areas, on the personhood debate and personal responsibility and the humanness of making mistakes, even if a child was never really a mistake but at what point did it actually become a child, it was both a scientific and a philosophical question, and why was Matilda suddenly thinking about this so much, was there something she needed to get off her chest? It hadn't helped.

Instead, everything had escalated. First, Matilda got involved with the church's youth organisation, but when a similarly militant humanist classmate convinced her one day that religion was the cause of much of the world's misery, including war and the circumcision of little boys, she'd made an abrupt break with her childhood beliefs, refused to go to her confirmation, and instead joined Amnesty, Greenpeace, and — not quite aware of the organisation's Christian foundations — the Red Cross Youth.

All of a sudden, she gave up her various fun pastimes, circus school included, instead ploughing all her waking hours outside school into her voluntary activities. She took part in a study group on the Balkan War with the Red Cross, and travelled to Bosnia and the white gravestones in Srebrenica. 'It was like a forest, a forest of death,' she told Sebastian, and he thought she'd disappeared there, in some ways, got lost. Matilda told him a lot during that time, still did — she lacked the boundaries to tell what was private and what wasn't, and it wasn't just her illness that made her that way, Sebastian was sure of that, it was just the way she was. Immoderate. Unreserved. A babbler. He liked that side of her, always had done, even if it had sometimes scared him.

He still remembered how big and dark her eyes had been when she told him about her trip to the Balkans, two blue-black holes intense enough to swallow up the comforting glow cast by his bedside light where they half lay, top and tail, he and his crazy sister. She told him how they'd met a mothers' group and the mothers had cried. They'd sat in a room with strip lights and watched a film where Ratko Mladić waved a branch around, and in the town there were no children, only cigarettes that cost less than bread and old women with washed-out scarves. On the way back to Sarajevo an exhausted Matilda had fallen asleep with her head against the coach window and when she woke up the windowpane had seemed to her to be covered in blood, though it was no more than the steam from her breath. Not even losing her virginity that very same evening in a Sarajevo backyard to a Friend of Palestine ten years her senior who was so drunk he tried to light the wrong end of his Serbian cigarette seemed to have given her a healthier level of teenage self-absorption.

On the contrary, Sebastian recalled, her rapidly escalating feelings for the Friend of Palestine had led to an equally rapid involvement in the Palestinian struggle. The Balkan War was over, after all, but there was still work to be done in the Middle East. So, back at home, she'd also joined the Palestine group, as well as the asylum group and the Western Sahara project, because the Friend of Palestine had a finger in those pies too.

During this period Sebastian hadn't seen that much of Matilda; she was rarely home, and neither was he — he spent whole afternoons and evenings in Cafe Ariman, playing chess with a young Liberal by the name of Max Friberg, listening to the Radio Dept. and waiting to fall in love.

Two years would pass before he did, and by that point Matilda had already had several stays at the psych unit. She'd got her diagnosis, got her medicine, and got a more nuanced view of the world.

And now here she was. Sitting in one of Benedict's chairs, thinner than Sebastian remembered her, wearing a pale-yellow knitted top that made her face look like she'd powdered it with ash. He tried to remember when he'd last seen her, properly, when he'd last seen her in all three dimensions. At Violetta's funeral? Yes. A little over a year ago. Just before she'd met Billy and moved in with him and his kid. Billy, whom Sebastian had never met, had never been interested in meeting, something that actually had nothing to do with Billy or with Matilda. He hadn't wanted to meet anyone before he'd come to London and been so painfully forced to. He didn't want to meet anyone now either, least of all Matilda, who didn't know what he knew.

Who didn't know that the last time they'd seen each other was at her own sister's funeral.

If it hadn't been so grotesque, it would have been almost funny. How much he suddenly knew and how little Matilda did, when in all honesty she was the only one of the siblings who seemed eager to investigate the peculiar family situation they unexpectedly found themselves in. Or at least eager for *him* to investigate it. She'd been in Bangladesh for two years and barely sent a postcard, but she'd been ringing him several times a week since the big conversation — he'd thought it was her dramatic side somehow getting oxygen from the whole sad business, as though she were enjoying it, couldn't get enough of talking about it because it was the sort of thing the manic side of her brain — robbed by her drugs of its natural tendency to spin out over the smallest thing — went for. As though the death of the nuclear family, which she'd always promoted politically and was now experiencing in reality, made her feel alive in some way.

But, thought Sebastian as he stood in the doorway observing his strongest, most fragile sister, maybe that was unfair. Maybe she'd been genuinely worried the whole time, and he hadn't been capable of helping her, and now here she was, a guardian angel in need of a saviour.

The question was whether he could save her. The only thing that could save this family, thought Sebastian, was everyone finally knowing the truth. But Matilda had never been good with the truth, and this, Sebastian suspected, would break her.

How thin she was. So unpleasantly alike the dark shadow that hung there behind her head, the dark shadow only he could see.

'Matilda,' he said. 'You don't look well.'

She raised her hands, swathed in the misshapen sleeves, from her face.

'Do you remember Bernarda, Sebastian?' she said. 'Do you remember the time Papa had to take her to the animal hospital because I left a chocolate bar out in the living room and she ate the whole thing? I didn't leave it there by accident. I did it on purpose, because I wanted her to suffer. And then she died. And *now* I've gone and hit a child.'

IV
EASTER ISLAND

Only 0.01 per cent of the earth's total biomass is people; people's hands, heads, hearts, feet. And yet these hands, heads, hearts, and feet have driven more than four-fifths of all other mammal species to extinction: trampling, tearing, biting, and stamping them to death one by one. Pulling the wings off birds and stuffing cushions with them. Picking buttercup petals and painting canines with precious metals. Making the world's biggest spettekaka, Christmas stollen, cheese slice (Sjöbo, Dubai, Ånäset). Putting a man on the moon (the moon), and pulling up herbs by the handful (everywhere). Sifting plankton through their teeth, slicing tusks from gracious beasts, pushing camels through a needle's eye, growing acre upon acre of lush green lawns and Eternit barns.

There was once a child who thought honeysuckle only bloomed on odd-numbered dates. At that time, she still harboured an unshakeable belief in the Gregorian calendar's power over nature. She had a book of prehistoric animals. They'd been given such beautiful names — the dawn horse, the terror bird — that she almost thought it was lucky they no longer existed. They wouldn't have lived up to the myths about them.

Just look at humanity.

Thirteen per cent of all life on earth is buried in the earth's crust in the form of bacteria. We let them stay there, maybe like a kind of insurance. In every bed warm from body heat, there are a billion tiny, tiny organisms living off a person's body. We lay our babies there, right in the middle of that soup — an unconscious sacrifice. We look at a dandelion clock and decide to blow, just this once.

There was once a child who always slept with the window open, even though she was afraid of everything that lived in the night. She lay in bed and whispered nonsense verse so she could cope. *Dusty night, musty night, bats in flight, cats in flight.*

Water fright.

There was once a child who hated brushing her teeth because the water was full of microscopic little living things she didn't want to have in her body. She had a sister who told her that the bacteria already on her teeth were worse, because they bit.

So she swapped one unpleasant life form for another. It was a kind of zero-sum game.

Eighty-three per cent of life on earth is plants. That figure isn't getting any lower, it's just that the trees are becoming fewer and the cornfields are getting bigger. Dead wood doesn't have time to rot in the woods, but we still have smooth-sanded planks, winter tomatoes, orchids in glass pots arranged on white windowsills. That's also a kind of zero-sum game, one where the defining factor *is* the figure zero. Nothing is lost but everything is lost.

There was once a child who was a baby who was guilty before she'd even drawn her first breath. You could say as much of any child, because the destructive force of every newborn is as great as that of a very old uranium atom. There was once a specific baby who was mixed up with another in the maternity ward. However she looked at it, she couldn't make it seem like an insignificant exchange of equally significant entities. She wanted to think of herself as an ant or a worker bee, an inconsequential little cog in a machine that would one day rust or rot or end up as ruins, and if that was the case, it didn't matter anyway. Who belonged with whom. Who belonged with no one at all. Whose eyes had the same colour as the patch under Greenland.

There might not be any dodos left, but there are pigeons and there are poems, which is almost the same thing (both the pigeons and the poems). There will always be pigeons, and possibly poems, too. And maybe music, though not in the form of whale song. There's still a practically infinite source of living bacteria frozen solid in the polar glaciers, and there are blackberries. All across the northern hemisphere, when everything has been burned and bulldozed, there will still be blackberries, rats, pandemics.

There was once a child who was afraid of everything. She became a woman who tried to learn to think things were fine that way, things were okay that way. There were over eight hundred kinds of wild blackberry, after all. There are species of grass so resistant to humanity's intervention that if you try to pull them up with your hands, you cut yourself. In the summer they grow ears with great plumes, and in the autumn the ears come loose, and if the wind blows hard enough (hurricanes will exist, if not forever, then for a long while yet), the ears fall off. If any humans are still standing, they'll be able to harvest the ears and cut the hollow tubes into pieces. With a little will they'll be able to make something from them resembling pan pipes.

He was there when she landed. On the same bench in the terminal building he'd been sitting on when she left, two months earlier. As though he hadn't moved a muscle. She hadn't told him which flight she was going to be on, so maybe he really had — sat there the whole time. Waiting. Or maybe it was true what he said, that the future was a mirror he could hold in his hand. Nothing felt improbable any more, not after what she'd seen in Berlin.

He didn't seem to see her at first. Not until she dropped her rucksack at his feet did he look up from his clasped hands.

'You're here now,' he stated without moving any part of his body apart from his mouth.

'Yes. It happened,' said Clara.

'You've been in Berlin,' said Horst.

'Yep, like I said in my email.'

'But you didn't find your sister.'

'No.'

Clara's correspondence with Horst had been brief. He'd written about madness and apocalypse and the loss of his own sight, which, according to his email, was imminent. He'd written that the day he lost his sight completely *everything would end*. Just like a roller blind, a process less like dying than being un-born. A girl would arrive, with translucent skin and all that, and then it would all go black. He'd written that Clara had to come back. *Du mußt zurückkommen. Alles kommt zu einem Ende und ich habe keine Kamera.* Clara had stared at the email for a long time. The last bit was a lie, in any case. Horst did have a camera. It was one of the few things she clearly remembered about him, aside from the soft blond locks that looked like a child's, his long fringe, and timid manner: that he had a camera, a beautiful, expensive thing, and that he used it all the time and with a reckless disregard for personal space.

He'd once read a short story, he wrote in his email, about a blind girl in New York who took photos constantly, even though she didn't know what she was photographing. The story ended with the protagonist, who was possibly in love with her, finding her dead, hanging from the ceiling, *wie beim Schlafen. As though she was asleep, but she wasn't sleeping*, was the last thing he'd written in the letter.

That same evening, Clara found her sister, but it was the wrong sister. And moreover.

Sie war tot.

So she wrote back, wrote that she'd come as soon as she possibly could. She wrote that she hadn't found what she was searching for and that there was no longer anything tying her to any specific geographic location.

She wrote that she might as well be on an island in the middle of the sea, since she was an island in the middle of the sea.

Clara automatically made for the row of taxis when they came out of the terminal. To her surprise, Horst took her arm and waved at the familiar white Defender that was parked a short distance away.

'Is Jordan here?' Clara asked, confused. She wasn't ready to meet Jordan, not yet.

'He let me borrow it,' said Horst. 'Maybe he felt guilty for misplacing my camera.'

'But you're practically blind!' Clara protested. 'And what do you mean? Did Jordan lose your camera?'

'By accident. *Vielleicht.*' Horst shrugged almost imperceptibly — he made Clara think of a little bird, ruffling its feathers, a little sparrow or wren. 'Or maybe it was someone else, *weiß nicht*. Strange things have been happening here. Creeping things.'

'Creeping things?'

'People creeping about. Taking things. Making things appear. I'll show you.'

Clara glanced quickly at the car.

'Don't be afraid,' Horst said. 'Many blind people can drive. It's just that they've never tried.'

'I'm not afraid,' Clara said, and immediately felt it was more or less true. 'I'm afraid of almost nothing these days.'

He took her to the tree plantation on the slope of Cerro Terevaka. Through the car window Clara counted the tiny horses biting and tearing at the grass. She kept losing count, because they looked so similar — shiny brown and only a hand high. Had they grown so small to better stand the winds? They were all related, an extended family of weathervanes.

'They say it's beautiful,' Horst said when they stopped at the usual place. 'I want you to tell me if it's true. I want you to tell me what you see.'

He made no attempt to move, so Clara got out of the car and started walking towards the trees. From a distance she could see something had changed. The thin stalks stuck up out of the ground in the same apparently random pattern as before. She didn't know what she'd been expecting, actually. Maybe a minor catastrophe, a little forest fire, the remains left by a violent wind.

But instead: a new sea, twinkling bluely. Something hanging, dangling, shimmering among the branches. Spinning in the wind like dreamcatchers. Who'd hung them there? Whose were the dreams?

She stood there a while, at a distance. It was true that it was beautiful, but it was also frightening in some way. It made the trees look like birds and the birds look like feathers. It made all the boundaries dissolve, again. Clara closed her eyes. Though she could no longer see it, she thought she could smell the blue colour, spreading through her nose, skull, spine. It was a cold colour, but a warm colour. It was the colour of water, as a child would draw it. It was the colour of the sky, as the eye saw it. It was the colour that made humans human, thought Clara, opening her eyes.

It was also the colour of peacocks, because what was hanging there were peacock feathers, peacock eyes staring, shining, blue. Several in each tree, she saw that when she finally walked in among them.

Close up it looked less magnificent, more comical. Someone had tied several dozen peacock feathers onto the narrow trees' even narrower branches. Someone from the camp, she assumed. Maybe Vedrana, who seemed to have a rather spiritual relationship to trees. Maybe Siobhan, who was a hippie. Maybe Horst himself, who was possibly a medium. What struck Clara as odd was that there were no peacocks on Easter Island. Whoever had tied them there had come to the island with a suitcase full of peacock feathers. It was, undoubtedly, very strange.

A gust of wind blew through the branches and the grass. The blue eyes spun. Clara felt like she was being watched, not just by the feathers.

When she turned around, Horst was behind her. He looked extremely naked. Clara realised it was because he didn't have his camera. For the first time, he looked like a blind man, a blind man whose dog has run away.

'What do you see?' he said.

'Feathers,' said Clara. 'Who —'

'Only feathers?'

Clara turned back to the trees. One, two, one, two, eyes of such unnatural blue. Had she had them from birth, or did they develop with time? Like a shield, a blinding detail to prevent her being recognised.

None of them had such blue eyes; not Sebastian, not Matilda, definitely not her.

'Eyes,' Clara said. 'I see eyes.'

'Whose eyes?'

'Just eyes,' Clara lied.

Horst smiled blithely.

'That's what I see, too, though I can barely see them. They tell me they're feathers, but nothing is ever just one thing, is it?'

'I'm cold. Can we go now?'

'If you want. There's just one thing I wonder: whether you know whose eyes they are.'

This time Clara replied truthfully.

'Yes.'

'She's the one who hung them there.'

Clara snorted.

'She's dead.'

'In a way. In another way, she's only just begun to exist.'

It takes no more than a few minutes for a brain to erase the whole world. Up to twenty, if the world is your own face, seen in one or several mirrors. First you become a monster. Then you disappear completely, melting like wax.

In other words: first everything goes to hell. Then it ends.

If the world consists instead of pastel-hued dots, thirty seconds' full focus on a visual centre-point might be enough for everything to turn white. It's called the Troxler effect, but Clara didn't know that. Neither did her world turn white. It turned violet, with patches of the purest blue.

This happened in Berlin, which was where Clara'd gone after leaving Easter Island two months previously. Her new, distorted face came with her when she returned. It surprised her that no one could see it, aside from maybe Horst, who could see nothing.

That she was no longer the same.

That she was no longer only herself.

It was in a gallery on Kottbusser Tor. She hadn't gone there on purpose. She'd rung a doorbell, in another part of town, but no one had answered. It was her sister's door. She'd rung her sister's doorbell so many times a neighbour had stuck his head out of the next-door flat and informed her that der Herr and die Frau were on holiday. On holiday where? 'Schweden,' the neighbour had said, clutching an orange in his hand. He'd been wearing a knitted tank top and reminded Clara of a mole as he backed into his hallway and closed the door. She'd gone back down the stairs, and the dusty carpet that was fixed to the steps with tacks that glinted like gold was a winding path she felt sure would lead nowhere.

It had been a dumb idea in the first place, going to see Matilda. She didn't want to see Matilda, or her father, or anyone else in this city. She didn't want to be in Berlin, and yet she'd already been in Berlin for several weeks, all through this boiling summer and the nights between days that were as soft and wet as naked swims in dark lakes. It was Clara's first visit to Berlin and she was sure it would be her last. She didn't like the way the rain here fell wetter and heavier than in other places she'd been. She didn't like the empty spaces that sometimes opened up between city districts like burial sites, unexpected and deserted. She didn't like the way it felt like she was imitating a life that wasn't hers, but Matilda's.

Clara belonged among nettles and soon-to-be extinct animals, not under striped marquees on squares with fountains and playing children. She definitely didn't belong in poorly lit galleries with video installations of cats playing pianos, and yet it was in just such a place she'd ended up, after walking as far as she could — in an attempt to shake off the anticlimactic moment she'd spent outside the mute front door of Matilda's house, with its handwritten sign bearing the names M. ISAKSSON, B. KARLSSON, S. KARLSSON-NOLDE arranged around a stylised diamond — along identical streets of run-down art nouveau houses and noodle restaurants. She'd stopped only once, in front of a building where climbing roses stretched all the way up to the sky. It wasn't until she'd stretched out her fingers to touch them that she'd realised it was a mural. She got crumbs of stucco under her fingernails, and later, in the gallery, she'd tried in vain to get rid of them with a cocktail stick.

She'd walked into a man wearing a green silk jacket. That was how she'd ended up in the darkest corner of the gallery. He'd turned around and grabbed her arm to stop her falling onto the pavement. He'd laughed and pulled her up the steps and shoved a glass of white wine into her hand. She'd seen a butterfly on a little clip in his hair and a great number of people who appeared not to eat enough. He'd said he was the Artist. He'd said it in English, but she could hear he was Scandinavian. She hadn't let him know she'd heard it.

He'd told her about all the things that could happen if you looked at yourself too closely in the mirror. He'd said that his work was a reflection of modern humanity's obsession with its own reflection, both in a concrete and a metaphysical sense. She hadn't understood whether his repetition of the word 'reflection' was conscious irony or just a mistake that confirmed his own theory.

He'd told her to go into a room and sit down and not come out for twenty minutes. He'd stand outside and keep guard so she couldn't cheat. Then she'd sat down on a chair and a curtain had been drawn behind her. A single red lightbulb had turned on above her head. In front of her, three mirrors had been arranged in a triptych. She could see her face from all sides except the back, but still her gaze had constantly been drawn to a point on the central mirror. When she could no longer resist, she'd allowed her gaze to rest there. It was just over her nose. She'd looked at her eyes, a vague blue, her eyebrows, two dark lines where each hair grew clearer the more she looked at it.

It was the first time she'd really looked in the mirror since she'd been informed that her face had been shaped by a different set of genes than she'd previously thought. She'd felt out of sorts, but been unable to get up from the chair or close her eyes. She'd become angry with herself when she realised she was searching for traces of Matilda in her own face, traces of Sebastian, their mother, father. There'd been a constant hubbub from the gallery behind her; someone had screamed *I love you* in German without sounding like he meant it.

Then something had happened to the space between her eyebrows. It had begun to run and drip, like ice cream melting over her mouth and chin. Her nose had swelled and disappeared. It was the strangest thing Clara had ever experienced. She hadn't been able to stop watching. After a while her whole face had turned into a hole with ragged edges, she'd started to feel nauseous and closed her eyes to make it stop.

When she'd opened her eyes again, the face in the mirror was still distorted. She'd tried to touch it, but discovered her arms had been tied to the chair. Then she'd let out a silent scream, because now her face was her own again, but also someone else's — the two faces, one living, one dead, had aligned themselves and intertwined their fingers. They'd had an umbilical cord around their necks and their necks had been one and the same.

Then everything had been torn apart and her knuckles had begun to bleed.

There had been a huge commotion. Someone had pulled aside the drapes and someone else had wound a thin scarf with a peacock print around her hand and someone had filmed the whole thing and whispered that this was excellent material, excellent. Someone had thought they should call for a doctor and someone thought they should wait and see and someone had asked her name.

In response, they'd got a strange, broad smile.

In a vase on a long, narrow bench, a lily had dropped its last, dry petal. On the wall there'd been an angry yellow Post-it note, and the note had said: nothing.

Clara had resolved to get her first meeting with Jordan out of the way as quickly as possible, so when Horst finally dropped her off at the crossroads between the camp and the hotel, she went straight to his tent. He didn't look particularly surprised when she tore open the flap and stuck in her head. He'd been reclining on his elbow, reading a book, the same book by Wendell Berry that he'd been reading two months earlier, and now he calmly closed the book, threw it into a corner of the tent with the other hand, sat up, and crossed his legs.

'Clara,' he said, patting the spot beside him on the sleeping bag.

'I'd rather stand,' Clara said, half inside the tent and half outside.

'Then let's go outside.'

Clara backed out, and Jordan soon followed her. There was something about his manner that seemed different to Clara, kind of milder. Even his stubble looked softer, and the thick lumberjack shirt was worn thin. It had a button missing, Clara noticed, as he stretched out like a cat, and he was barefoot.

'You should put some shoes on,' Clara said, looking down towards the water. 'We're going down to the cliffs.'

'It's fine, I'm used to it by now.' He smiled at her and she had to look away. In her mind she struggled to connect this gentle, honourable hermit with the yapping man-dog who'd tried to mount her in a jacuzzi, but she knew they were one and the same — people didn't change that quickly, the fact was that people didn't change at all, at least not to any significant extent. When people think they see changes in other people, it's more often the case that they've discovered something that was previously hidden.

When they got down to the cliffs, Clara climbed up to the highest point she could find and patted the ground beside her just as Jordan had done. He sat down obediently. For a while they sat in silence, eye fixed on the horizon. She thought of all the horizons beyond it, line after line, endlessly. The thought that there was an infinite number of horizons but no future to experience them in brought her to the brink of tears, and before she'd had time to register that she was about to say something, she heard her own voice cutting through the air like the shrill cry of a seabird.

'Jordan, I'm in so much shit right now. My life is a ridiculous joke. I don't even know who I really am. Isn't that pathetic?'

'Yes, of course.'

She glared at him. He raised his hands.

'Was that the wrong answer? I thought the question was rhetorical.'

'It was, I was talking about you.'

He grinned. 'Hey, I'm sorry I came on to you like that. It was unfortunate. I misunderstood. But honestly, I have to say — there was no need for you to just up and leave. A little melodramatic.'

Clara snorted.

'Well, I can relieve your guilty conscience. I didn't leave because of you. I had some personal problems, as I said. Family problems.'

'Oh fuck. And now you've solved them, have you?'

'No,' snapped Clara. 'I realised they couldn't be solved.'

'Then you've come to the right place. Has Horst told you about doomsday? It's coming, you know. Which is old news, of course. But now it's close, if you ask our young medium.'

'Oh.'

'It's crazy, Clara,' Jordan said, shaking his head. 'I think most people actually believe he's a prophet.'

'But what if he is? What if doomsday really is just around the corner?'

He looked at her curiously, for a long time.

'Don't say that,' he said at last.

'Why not? I thought it would make you happy. To be right.'

'I've never believed in any kind of sudden, punishing apocalyptic catastrophe, you know that. You don't either. Which makes you and me devil's advocates on this island right now. The voice of common sense. The defenders of reason.'

'I think you overestimate my belief in rationality,' said Clara, fingering a dry, lilac flower sticking up between the rocks. It looked like sea thrift, but it could hardly be that. There were other plants here, too, in the cliff's crevices; she counted four different types. She knew it was irresponsible to pick them, but couldn't help herself; suddenly there was nothing she wanted to do more than pull up the flowers by the roots and braid them into a crown. She picked a great pile and put them in her lap, started plaiting them with clumsy fingers.

'What exactly does Horst think is going to happen? It's not like we've had extensive contact.'

'And yet you came back here?'

'It was an impulsive decision, you could say. I was in Berlin. It was vile. Without going into detail, certain things broke that I'll never be able to repair. Then Horst emailed and said I should come. And I thought, what the hell. It cost me all the money I had left, so I guess now I'm here for good.'

It was hard for Clara to determine how Jordan felt about this last statement because she didn't dare look at him when she made it. In any case, he didn't comment, and Clara found herself unexpectedly disappointed.

'Honestly, nobody knows,' was all he said. 'I mean, what Horst thinks. If he thinks anything at all. I mean, he's not religious. You're left with meteorites, a massive earthquake, or nuclear war. And as far as I know, he's neither a seismologist nor a spy. You know. No one knows. But everyone *believes*. He's been talking about some woman coming. Is it you? Are you here to destroy us? Or just me?'

'You don't seem so worried about the world anymore,' said Clara.

'Of course I'm fucking worried, Clara. I've been worried since the first time I saw a Brazilian soy field. I was in a plane, one of those little ones, you know, heading from São Paulo to Cuiabá. I was seventeen, on the way to an international ping-pong tournament. Seventeen years young and so goddamn hyped about the rainforest. I thought I was going to get to see it. Was sitting there with my nose pressed against the window like a child. But did I see any rainforest? Hardly. A tiny bit of the Amazon out of the corner of my eye, then the soy fields. Field after field in symmetrical blocks, kilometre after kilometre after kilometre.

Got travel-sick in the end, felt like being on the open sea, nothing to fix your eyes on. It was harvest season, and I don't know if you know what ripe soy looks like, but it looks like death. Just dry twigs sticking up out of the ground. One of the most vibrantly alive places on earth, turned into desert.'

'Touching story,' said Clara.

She looked out to sea. There was a line, maybe a hundred metres from the shore, separating dark and light.

'For me it was the Gulf.'

Jordan raised his eyebrows.

'The golf? I wouldn't have had you pegged as a golfer. You don't look like one.'

'The Gulf Stream, idiot. The blue patch.'

'Under Greenland.'

'Yeah.'

Jordan didn't say anything. Clara kept on braiding. Without noticing, she'd begun to sing in her head an old Swedish rhyme about a midsummer's crown of viburnum, a long-dance, a jumping dance, on fires a-burning, Ull-stina, Kull-lina, and so on. The crown she held in her hand looked nothing like a midsummer's crown. It looked like a crown of thorns, spidery and dry, with flecks of colour that didn't belong in her version of nature — the soft green, pale white, cow parsley in the ditches, birch and bird cherry and lilac. Golden rain in the city's parks, goldenrod under the park benches, *Sorrow fills the world with ache, glitt'ring gold is mostly fake*, where were all these verses coming from, *Honey and milk in that land overflowed, golden the harvests I reaped in it, eja, precious the gems in its rich mother lode*, didn't Mama use to trill those lines, with her on one knee and Matilda on the other? Clara tried not to dwell, but she couldn't help wondering: if her mother had ever mourned the child who was lost, the one she'd never known, if it had affected her feelings for the intruder, the impostor, the false child whose greatest misfortune was not even knowing it was an impostor. What did viburnum actually look like? She wasn't sure. Maybe like bird cherry, or like elderflower? Maybe viburnum was what some people called false elder. Impostor elder.

'What are you thinking about?' said Jordan.

'Things that aren't what they appear to be.'

'That wasn't particularly specific.'

'Time for another sweeping statement on how the world works? Let me guess: nothing is what it appears to be.'

'You know me so well,' said Jordan, pretending to be shocked.

'You're pretty shallow, from a personality perspective.' Clara held up the crown against the sun. The sun fit perfectly into the hole. It looked like she'd made a crown for the sun.

Jordan sighed.

'You're probably right. Maybe that's why I don't have any authority here anymore. Which is perfectly fine, I've never sought it. I know you think I set out to be some kind of cult leader, but it's simply not true. I just wanted to have a little company through my grieving process, a few singers to join me in the earth's long swansong, that's all. But now I've lost every single person to a half-blind German teenager with delusions of grandeur. No one listens to me anymore. Not even Elif.'

Clara dropped the crown in her lap in astonishment.

'Elif?'

'Yeah?'

'Is she still here?'

'Fuck yeah. Or, I think so. Don't see her that often. I don't know what she's up to; she certainly doesn't help out around the camp. Honestly though, Clara, you should talk to her.'

'About what?'

'Search me. But it really threw her when you left. You don't want to know what she called you.'

Jordan leaned back and lay flat on the cliff with his arms out to the sides. Clara put the crown on his head. It hung to one side, and when she tried to right it, a thorn scratched a little gash in his forehead. A tiny drop of blood welled up and she wiped it away carefully with her thumb.

She knew she should still be angry. He'd crossed a line, and she should despise him for it. But the only thing she felt was a strange gratitude that he was still there.

'Clara, Clara, Clara ...' said Jordan, catching her wrist. 'Why did you abandon us? Everything spiralled when you left.'

'I had my own life to take care of. Or I thought I did, anyway. But it turned out my life had belonged to someone else the whole time.'

'That just doesn't make sense. The life you have is the life you have. It's always yours. Your own responsibility, too.'

'Why haven't you left too, then? If everything's so crazy here.'

Jordan started to laugh, he laughed so hard his eyes disappeared into their creases.

'What's so funny?' Clara muttered.

'You want to know why I stayed?'

'Yes, please.'

'Because Horst kept saying you were going to come back.'

'And you believed him?'

'Yeah. Isn't that funny.'

She left Jordan by the water and went to pitch her tent by the others at the camp. She wasn't a journalist this time, she was herself — one of them, so of course she would live among them. After briefly welcoming her, the others retreated to their own tents. None of them made any effort to help her, which felt like a relief, but also a little sad.

While she battled the tent posts — Clara had never camped before — she noticed that certain things in the camp had changed. Ironically, seeing as they were apparently preparing for their own extinction, the encampment had lost its makeshift festival vibe and now felt like a significantly more permanent settlement. Lines had been strung between the palms, and clothes were hanging out to dry, what looked like a compost heap had been built, as well as a permanent food preparation area with a firepit, and primitive yet sturdy tables and benches for the cooking, all protected by a one-and-a-half-metre-high windbreak. Most people had built small rain-sheltered spaces with sticks and tarpaulins attached to their tents. A few had even created small gardens with flowers and herbs.

On the way from the airport, Horst had told her they'd been given permission to farm a small patch of land on the edge of the campsite, in return for quite a hefty rent payment. In general, Horst had said, the campsite owners were very understanding, and completely supported their project — whether that was due to genuine sympathy for the cause, whatever the *cause* was, or due to the money they got, he didn't say, though Clara had the sense it was the latter. The place hadn't exactly been crawling with other campers when she'd last been here, and now there didn't seem to be a single one. Either the movement had bought out the whole place, or it was low season in August — the bitterest month, by the Chilean winter's standards. Regardless of the reason, the owners were pleased with their new settlers. Clara hadn't seen any of the owners — when she'd arrived the reception had been empty and dark, and so the worry over how she was going to pay for two months' camping was delayed until sometime in the future.

That is to say, if there was any future.

Clara had been back on the island for two weeks when the foreshocks of the apocalypse made the ground shake almost imperceptibly. September had come, the beginning of an autumn without leaves, an autumn that wasn't autumn but spring, a fact Clara had to remind herself of every morning when she woke up in her tent and thought for a fraction of a second that she could smell apples rotting on a lawn, butter and cinnamon, and the dusty scent of a radiator warming up for the first time in many months. This, Clara thought several times a day, wasn't only a different place, but a different time. A different life, in mirror image. *I'm not really here. But I wasn't really in my old life, either. It was a life I'd been borrowing, and the one whose life it was got death instead.*

In its quiet way, the group had accepted Clara's return as inevitable. Perhaps they'd believed Horst when he'd assured them her abdication from the family was only temporary, just as Jordan had. Clara had begun to think of them that way — like a family. They had their roles and positions, their routines and rituals. Theirs was a cautious love, a fragile vessel they passed around the fire each evening. Jordan was the easy-going father, no, grandfather — he'd created the family but was no longer the head of it. Strange as it might seem, it was Horst, with his unobtrusive yet penetrating presence, who had taken on the role of father. Bernie and Rosa shared the role of mother, Siobhan was the baby, Vedrana the blasé big sister, an allocation of roles that became a little tricky for Clara when she realised Horst and Vedrana were now sharing a tent. Incestuous relationships were something Clara didn't care to think about too much, and so she immediately up/downgraded Vedrana to the role of mistress — the gods knew many families seemed to be able to make space for them too.

Who Clara was in this family constellation, she hadn't yet managed to figure out. Maybe she was the dog. There but not quite, appreciated but not irreplaceable. She liked it that way. It was an easier place to be than at the centre of things. When things collapse, it's easier to escape if you're on the edge — that policy had always worked brilliantly for her father, after all.

The days were long and thick as treacle, tinged with a leisurely calm-before-the-storm feel, but every evening still came as a shock. The open sea, the light — and then the sun slipped below the horizon as though into a sleeping bag, and the sky went black.

This particular evening, Clara didn't feel like sitting around the fire with the others. She'd been up at the tree plantation with Vedrana, watering all afternoon, and every muscle in her body was humming with exhaustion. She crawled wearily into her tent and got her phone out of the waterproof compartment of her rucksack. She'd almost given up using it, never read emails, and certainly never anything that was tweeted or streamed or had to be scrolled. Just the news, sometimes, and the weather forecast. This was a fixation more than a necessity — most days here were the same whether it rained or the sun shone, and the fluctuations in things like temperature or humidity were so small as to be irrelevant. But Clara had been obsessed with weather forecasts ever since she'd heard the term 'extreme weather'. Extreme weather was actually a misnomer, Clara thought, because it encompassed so much more than just unrelenting drought and fist-sized hailstones. All the tiny changes, the average temperatures increasing a decimal at a time — that was extreme weather too.

But here it was: extreme weather in its most extreme form.

A hurricane.

She crawled out of her tent, no longer the slightest bit tired because her body was fizzing with adrenaline, and went over to the cooking area where Jordan, Horst, and Bernie were sitting around the fire, grilling fish and courgette.

'Where are all the others?' Clara asked.

Jordan shrugged.

'We have to find them,' said Clara, waving to Siobhan who was sitting in the branches of one of the campsite's few trees, reading a book in the light of an oil lamp balanced precariously on a branch. 'There's going to be a massive storm tonight. It could be less than three hours away.'

'How do you know that?' Bernie asked, holding a finger in the air. 'The wind's barely blowing.'

Clara waved her phone. Bernie chuckled.

'I forgot you're still addicted to your daily fix of unnecessary information.'

'I'd think it's pretty much essential to know that we'll be blown away in a few hours unless we evacuate.'

'Evacuate?' Bernie said. 'Where to?'

'I guess we'll have to go to a hotel or something? They'll have to let us in if our lives are in danger.'

'Our lives aren't in danger,' said Horst. 'Not tonight. But of course.' Clara looked at Jordan, whose silence was palpable. He was chewing his bottom lip with one hand around his neck. Just like on that first day when he'd swum in the pool at the hotel from hell, Clara was struck with a virtually insurmountable desire to reach out her hand and touch him, to pull that lip out of his mouth and lay her hand on his cheek as you would — she imagined — with a child who can't sleep. The last traces of disgust ran off her like water. He was afraid, so afraid of thunder.

'There's the house, of course,' she said. 'Jordan? What do you think?'

'It's very small,' said Bernie, sceptically.

'Yes, the house is best,' said Jordan and spat out his bottom lip, getting up with a determined jerk. 'It's stable. And there'll probably be space for us. After all, there are 124 million people living in Java. Just to put things in perspective a little.'

There was an immediate problem with the plan to spend the night in the abandoned campsite reception building. It turned out that the whimsical Siobhan had, for some unfathomable reason, been entrusted with the key, and when they finally managed to get her to come down from her tree and put her hand in her pocket, it was empty. She'd lost the key, it was unclear where, but plausibly in the vegetable plot, where she and Rosa had been preparing the ground for the quinoa earlier that day. Clara retained command. She and Jordan would look for the key, while the others gathered the rest of the group, took down the tents and storm-proofed the storage areas as well as possible. To her surprise, no one protested. They seemed to be gradually realising that this threat, in contrast to the vague atmosphere of doom that was the camp's constant undertone, was something they could get hold of, prepare for, control. Listlessness was swapped for febrile activity. Even Siobhan left her own head for a while, and went with Bernie into town to gather home the group's stray lambs.

The only one who didn't seem at all energised was Jordan. He walked to his tent in silence and came out with two head lamps. Then they began to make their way across the pitch-black campsite, two pale patches of light bouncing about on the ground in front of their feet. Further off they could see the light from the hotels across the road, but just like every night, they seemed to Clara so infinitely far away, as if on the other side of a dark mirror. She thought she heard a laugh, but it vanished so quickly it could have been the rising wind, the bells along the high street, the moribund hummingbirds in the souvenir shop windows.

Just before they reached the clump of trees that protected the plot from the hard westerly winds, Jordan stopped short and put his hand on Clara's arm to stop her. His face looked long in the light of the head lamp.

'There's something I want to tell you, Clara.'

'What makes you think I want to hear it?' The words sounded sharper than she'd intended as they fell out of her mouth. But she had a feeling she knew what Jordan wanted to talk about and she didn't know if she was ready for that discussion right now. It was hard enough not to think about Matilda as it was.

'You're human, right? Which means you're curious, because everyone is.'

'Come on.'

Clara walked on, but stumbled on a root. Jordan caught her. For a moment she hung in the air, in the dark, unable to tell up from down. It was a feeling of space and infinity so sudden and terrifying she screamed. Three hours, she thought. Three hours until Santiago hears me scream.

'Shhh,' Jordan said, setting her on her feet. He took her face in his hands; they were as big and warm as oven gloves. Then he checked himself and immediately let go. The absence of his hands felt like an ache inside her.

She swallowed a mouthful of tears and snot, turned her back on him, and ploughed on through the trees.

'Come on now, we have to find the key.'

They searched for at least twenty minutes. They went over the areas where Siobhan said she'd been working, then the rest of the plot, with a fine-toothed comb. It was a thankless endeavour, and Clara found herself wishing Jordan would talk.

'What was it you wanted to tell me?' she asked at last.

Mercifully, Jordan made no mention of her about-turn.

'I got a girl pregnant once,' was all he said, and hid his face in the darkness.

Clara stood still. She'd pictured this conversation so many times, more than she even wanted to admit to herself, but never with this detail, never — because she hadn't known about it. Of all the words Matilda had written on paper aeroplanes and sent flying across the sea, the ones she'd read and filed deep in her mental archive, not a single one had prepared her for this.

Clara swallowed in the dark, she swallowed the dark, she swallowed the brewing storm that was playing a violent game with the stick-like trees all around them.

'Okay,' she said. 'Thanks for the info.'

'I was ready to be a father, if she wanted,' Jordan went on. She couldn't see his face, only the harsh light of the lamp blazing in her eyes. 'But she clearly didn't, which was what I'd thought. She left and never returned. Just rang me and told me she'd had an abortion. Apparently, the kid had Down's.'

Clara grunted something in response. She didn't want to hear more; she wanted to hear everything.

'I mean, I'm not judging her,' Jordan said quickly. 'I guess she wasn't ready for it. Or for any baby at all, maybe. I'm pro-choice, I really am. But I was sad. Not for her sake, or even my own, but for the kid's. That it wouldn't get to see the world. Despite everything I know. Despite all that, I cried over a child who didn't exist and would never get to exist. I think about it a lot. What it means.'

'Why are you telling me this,' said Clara. It was less a question than an accusation.

'Because I want you to understand, Clara. Because I think you already do. The others … it's not real for them. Not even for Horst. That's why they're able to take it easy. It's a game for them, all this, these preparations, "the simple life", it's like something out of a storybook. They know as well as you and I do that this is like an episode of some reality TV show which will end in the blink of an eye. Most of them are already sick of it, that's why they've made up all this stuff about Horst's visions and how something's going to happen, soon. Because when it doesn't, they can leave here. Go on with their lives and forget they ever came so close to something genuinely dark.'

'I think you underestimate them,' said Clara. 'I think they like being here. For roughly the same reasons as you and I do.'

'And what are they?' said Jordan. 'Why are *you* here, Clara?'

She closed her eyes. The moment of truth, as it were, if only she knew what that truth was.

'You're here because you love this world,' said Jordan. 'You love it so much it makes you ache inside. You love it so much you want it to exist forever, so much that deep down you believe it will, against all odds, against your own good sense you believe that, you believe it so much you can even imagine putting a child into this world —'

'I've never wanted children,' Clara said. 'I don't see the point.'

Yet another reason why this was a very bad idea, she thought.

'But in theory, Clara, you see what I mean in theory. That's all I wanted to say. We're not so different, you and I. We love the wind but fear the storm. The others, they're in it for kicks.'

He'd come closer to her in the darkness, so close she was dazzled by his head lamp, and then even closer, so the light went over her head and all she could see were the shadows and contours of his face, a mountainous landscape, like the moon.

For He so loved the world, she thought.

There was a gust, a strong one; it tore through them as though they were no more than bones without flesh. They swayed towards each other like grass, and on the other side of the world, at that very moment, someone was writing yet another desperate letter, putting it in a bottle, and throwing it in the sea. Pressing one hand to their stomach and the other to their mouth to stop themselves crying out. Flashing blue in the night.

'Hey, we're never going to find the fucking key,' said Clara, stepping backwards quickly. 'We'll have to just smash a window.'

When they got back to the camp, all the others had either returned of their own accord or been found — all apart from Elif. That didn't surprise Clara. Although two weeks had passed since her return, she still hadn't spoken to Elif, who'd been slinking round the camp like a cat, but was never there when Clara was. If she hadn't glimpsed her out of the corner of her eye a few times, she wouldn't have thought Elif was still on the island, whatever the others said. But then one evening a couple of days previously, she'd passed one of the many tourist restaurants on the high street and caught sight of Elif, curled up in a green plastic chair with her back to the world and a bottle of Quilmes balanced on her fingertip like a basketball. The beer bottle fell and Clara hurried on before she heard it smash on the pavement.

Even now she could recall perfectly the sound of something breaking.

No one mentioned Elif's absence, and actually that wasn't so strange. If the group could be seen as a family, Elif would probably be the neighbour. According to Jordan she was still staying at EcoVillage, and it was unclear what she did each day. Whether a music video had ever been recorded, no one could say. Ever since she'd arrived, Clara had been meaning to go and visit Elif at the hotel, for old times' sake and because she could never quite reconcile herself to the idea that someone was angry with her without being able to understand why. When she saw Elif outside the restaurant and instinctively fled, it was the final confirmation that their short friendship was to all intents and purposes over. But at the same time, Clara felt something suspiciously like longing when she thought of Elif's grinning face, her gangly arms, and irritating habit of calling Clara 'sister'.

When they'd confirmed that everyone was there, that the tents had been taken down and stowed as well as possible in nooks and crannies, that all the fires were out, and all the stars were still, for now, at least, where they should be in the sky, they made their way together up to the reception building with all their rucksacks and equipment. Vedrana bound her hand with a towel and put it through a windowpane. When they'd cleared out enough of the sharp edges, she climbed through and unlocked the door. They threw their packs in a heap and made themselves at home.

Then they sat there — twelve people with nothing in common but the fact that they happened to live right here, right now, which, Clara supposed, was true of all people everywhere, in all kinds of constellations. The smooth tiled floor was cold under her behind, and bursts of ice-cold sea air drew in through cracks in the walls. This house was not built to be lived in. Jordan had done his best to hammer planks over the broken window, but they rattled forebodingly every time there was a gust, and Clara feared it was just a matter of time before they'd come away. In an attempt to heat the place up they'd lit several camping stoves in the middle of the room, and Alicia and Horst were brewing maté for them all. Clara thought about how, as a child, she'd imagined being evacuated. It had seemed so cosy, so reassuring, even though it was probably the exact opposite. You'd gather in a sports hall or a church, ideally a church, and none of the adults would fight, and you'd be wrapped up in woollen blankets and be slowly rocked to sleep by the sound of bombs and grenades. It would be like being in a sleeper train cabin, just bigger, and better.

Maybe it was because she was a grown-up, and responsible for herself, or because she was in the loneliest place on earth, or maybe just because her arse was freezing, but in reality, being evacuated didn't feel the slightest bit cosy. It was just uncomfortable and tedious. And where was Elif? Even though the thought was futile, Clara returned to it again and again. The most likely thing was that she was safe at the hotel, completely unconcerned by the fact that the world was shaking and the sea sucking everything that wasn't securely fastened down towards it. And yet Clara couldn't help regularly going over to the one remaining window and looking out over the empty campsite, which, in the dark, could have been anywhere in the world, could have been a forest. She expected to see Elif padding about out there, like a wolf with bared teeth and eyes as yellow as infected piss. Forsaken by the world, forsaken by God. Or to see her dead, dangling from the heavens, toes pointing to the underworld. She blinked. No. Elif wasn't her problem — didn't she have enough of her own?

Didn't she already have enough lost sisters?

They laid out their sleeping bags on the floor, spread out all the blankets they had, lay down, and listened to the world. One by one, the others stopped moving, until Clara suspected the only ones still awake were her and Jordan, who'd refused to go to bed. He was standing at the barricaded window, had been standing there wordlessly almost the whole evening, smoking and blowing out the smoke through a crack between the planks. No one had had the heart to complain, maybe because his jaw had been so tense and his free hand so tightly wound round his own body, as if to protect it. She looked at him now. One hip hung, as though from a broken hinge, and where his shirt was hitched up, his hip bone stuck out like a shark's fin. She wriggled out of her sleeping bag and tiptoed over to him by the window.

'Give me one.'

He got out his case of ready-rolled cigarettes — Clara had never seen him actually rolling them, maybe he did it in his tent at night when he couldn't sleep — then passed her one and lit it. To her surprise, Clara, who hadn't smoked since she left school, took a proper drag without coughing.

She grew dizzy.

'Hey. That thing you mentioned before ...' said Clara without looking at Jordan.

'Yeah.'

'About … about your girlfriend. Getting pregnant.'

'I know what you meant.' Jordan drummed his fingers lightly against the wall. 'Reckon this shack will last the night?'

Clara inhaled and readied herself.

'So, I've got a sister …'

'Have you? I didn't know.'

'No, I mean, it's been pretty complicated. Between us. But, you see, there are three of us … we have a brother, too … but, so I think that she, I mean, she, like, what you were talking about …'

'She's had an abortion? She and millions more. So, I want to emphasise, Clara, that I'm not accusing my girlfriend of anything —'

'No, no, I understand that. But you're not listening, just let me explain —'

But she didn't get to explain, because at just that moment, a clap of thunder resounded very close to them, completely without warning, without rumblings in the distance, as though the thunder had come into being right there.

'Oh my god! Oh my god!'

Jordan threw himself over Clara, pulling her down onto the floor, crushing his face into her shoulder. In the vibrations from his body she could feel a terror so pure and sharp all her own fears and neuroses disappeared at once.

None of the others woke up, despite the thunder rumbling on over their heads — they slept so peacefully that Clara came to see the thunder as belonging to them — to her and Jordan, and nobody else. He sat pressed hard against her until the thunder stopped, and she held him, not like an adult holds another adult, or even the way an adult holds a child, but like a mortal body holding another mortal body, with no offer of comfort or safety, but with a beating, living heart.

ARCHIVE//: SUBJECT: HEY HOP!

Hello my non-existent sister, it's me again. Since you're not replying to my TOTALLY SINCERE questions about how you're doing after all this, since you seem, SO TO SPEAK, to have DISAPPEARED (which to be honest is a properly pissy thing to do, I mean, intentionally, bearing in mind the chaos the rest of us are in (have I told you Mama rings me three times a day to ask where you are? You can cool it cos I lie and tell her we talk all the time but it's REALLY STRESSFUL, so …)) Okay, there's chaos aplenty. Sebastian seems to be taking it ON THE CHIN, as they say, he's pretty non-committal, as in, he won't commit to anything — I suspect he's either a) in love, or b) depressed, because he sounds weird on the phone, you know, like when he used to get travel-sick back in the day, anyhooo, I miss you. Just wanted to say. I hope you're having a good time wherever you are, I hope you've got someone to hold on to when it thunders. Now I have to run and vomit — don't ask <– funny joke since you never ask anything!!!

xxx M

PS Come home please

Clara was woken at dawn by sunlight filtering in through a knothole in the wall, sharp as a needle in her eye. She strained her ears a moment. It was so quiet. All she could hear was birdsong and breathing. She turned her head away from the sunbeam, opened her eyes. The others were lying along the wall like little stuffed cabbage leaves: Jordan in the middle with his hands folded over his chest, Horst and Vedrana intertwined in an infinity symbol, Siobhan with a stripe of rust-coloured hair over her chapped lips. Clara crawled out of her sleeping bag, carefully stretched out her toes and her arms, and tiptoed over to the door. Her feet, warm from the sleeping bag, stuck to the cold floor tiles and made a little sucking noise each time they released. She opened the door and went out onto the steps.

From the position of the sun, Clara determined that it must be around nine a.m., but her body disagreed — the air felt like a very early Swedish midsummer morning, wet, green, a little chilly, full of the cooing of doves. It was hard to believe a storm had raged through. The palms were as grand as ever, the sea in the distance was turquoise and calm, one or two of the colourful boats from the tourist harbour were already out. The only sign of disturbance was an empty Fanta bottle that came rolling down the slope. Clara followed it with her eyes up to the road where the gravel had already dried and taken on the same dusty texture as usual, and saw that it had come from a blown-over litter bin.

Then Elif came into view. She walked almost unnaturally slowly along the dusty road, then turned off, and kind of rolled hollowly down the slope as the bottle had just done. It wasn't just her movements that made Clara think of rubbish. Her whole person radiated waste, decay, she who'd once radiated wit and impulsiveness. Clara raised her hand in an awkward wave. Elif waved back just as awkwardly. After what looked like a moment's doubt, she headed towards Clara and came to sit beside her on the steps. She pulled out a cigarette, lit it, and leaned back with her elbows on the top step.

'Beautiful morning,' she said, blowing out a plume of smoke. Her mouth put Clara in mind of a keyhole.

'All still alive?' Elif went on, turning her sunglasses towards Clara.

'We evacuated. The others are still asleep in there.'

'Good, good, good. We don't want to die too early. Miss the show.'

Clara sniggered.

'You don't seriously believe that stuff.'

'Maybe not. But I believe in Dakota.'

Clara had absolutely no idea what Elif was talking about.

'Who?' she said, and then, like an afterthought: 'It's all just a big act. According to Jordan, anyway. He's the only one who's "for real", whatever that means.' She made speech marks in the air, but regretted it as soon as she did it — the gesture felt silly, and false. Jordan's fear was for real, she'd always known that, had been drawn to it from the beginning.

'Clarita,' said Elif, stubbing out the half-smoked cigarette on the steps. 'Why did you come back?'

'Why does everyone keep asking that?' Clara said, irritated. 'For the same reason that none of you have left, I guess. Maybe I *like* the act.'

'No, you don't.' Elif stretched out her long legs until they clicked. 'You're one of the most unaffected people I've ever met. Honest.'

'Guess that doesn't say much, though. Seeing as you've lived most of your life in Hollywood.'

Elif grinned.

'Are you angry with me?' said Clara.

'Why would I be angry with you, Clarita?'

'I don't know. Because I took off, I assume?'

'Ha! You and everyone else. Baby, I'm hardened, an old-timer; people die like flies all around me just to get away, people eat my food, take my money, and leave before the body's grown cold, people —'

'I was intending to pay you back,' Clara said, offended. 'For everything. Things are just a little tricky right now, with money and so on —' Elif was on her feet at once, an accusing finger pointed at Clara.

'The money was a metaphor, Clarita! God, aren't words your *thing*? You don't owe me a fucking cent. But if you were wondering, if you were really wondering why I was a bit offended when you left, then I guess I could say that yes, I guess I thought we had some kind of connection, you and I, a friendship, you might say, and when that's the case it's normal to send a little postcard or something when you've gone AWOL, maybe to let a person know you're still alive and doing okay, things that are just plain old fucking manners. But maybe you Europeans aren't into that stuff?'

Clara sat dumbly. Then she said slowly:

'It's more me … who's not into that stuff.'

Elif's hunched shoulders sank. She sat down beside Clara again.

'Alright, alright. I know. I know you're not. Which is fucked up, if you ask me. If I had someone who cared about me the slightest, I'd be texting and calling them every single day, I'd be hiding outside her house with binoculars, I'd be like a stalker in the night, I'd —'

'Am I your nemesis now?' Clara asked.

'Pfft. You can forget it. As you know, that spot's taken.'

Then Clara remembered.

'Dakota Fanning?' she said. 'How are things going with that thing?'

'It's not a thing, thank you very much. But I guess it's been a little up and down.'

Now Elif leaned towards Clara, lowering her voice. Her breath smelled of spearmint and ammonia, of violets.

'On the plus side: she's here. She's here, Clara, here on the island. I know it. She stopped writing to me a few weeks back, but only because she's finally come.'

'Here?' said Clara, instinctively looking around, as though the flaxen-haired Hollywood starlet would turn up any moment. 'Elif …'

Elif raised a hand.

'You think I'm making it up. That's fine, you can believe what you want. But I know. A lot has happened since you left, strange things. Things she thinks are funny. Japes, games, mischief. She's like that. Playful as a child. It's like a game of hide-and-seek. But she's good, she's very good; every time I think I know where she's hiding it turns out to be a dead end.'

Clara didn't know what to say. An image flashed past of the tree plantation, the hundreds of peacock feathers dancing in the wind. There was a pain behind her eyelids.

'Whatever, on the minus side: I'm getting restless. You know I'm a restless soul. I think it's time for her to come out and show herself.'

'I can imagine,' said Clara, searching for something else to say. After years of Matilda going up and down like a yoyo, you'd have thought Clara would've had a fair bit of experience of dancing around another person's delusions, but the truth was she'd always tended to hide from Matilda as soon as she got too intense. That was when Matilda was at her nastiest. 'Love me most when I deserve it least' was a nice proverb to hang on the wall, but hard to follow in practice.

'Anyway,' Elif said, saving Clara from having to say any more. 'She'll turn up as soon as Horst goes blind. He told me himself. And don't ask me how, but that guy's got *powers*. For example, he kept saying you'd come back. And *voilà*! Here you are!'

Clara smirked. 'Yeah, here I am.'

For better or for worse.

'You still haven't told me why?'

'Why I came back? I came to see you, of course.'

Elif slapped her on the shoulder, surprisingly hard.

'As if, you hussy. If we're going to be friends again you need to stop playing with my poor little lonely heart. No one but Dakota would ever cross an ocean for my sake, much less two or three or whatever. So why? Is it Jordan? You want his you-know-what after all?'

Clara felt her cheeks flush in embarrassment and decided to hide behind the truth, or at least the partial truth, the truth that weighed on her most heavily and cried out to spend a moment in someone else's hands.

She took a deep breath.

'Do you really want to know?'

'Tell me. Entertain me.'

'I'm hiding.'

Elif raised an eyebrow.

'The mafia?'

'Worse. You wouldn't believe it. It's like a bad film.'

'I've lived my whole life in a bad film. I *am* a bad film.'

'True,' Clara said. 'Okay. Here goes. The last time I was here ... Right before I left. I found out that my two triplet siblings and I aren't siblings. Or rather, two of us are. The third got swapped at the hospital. I'm absolutely convinced it's me.'

Elif whistled, but Clara got the sense it was less from genuine shock and more because that was what the role required.

'Oh shit.'

'But that's not all. I've also realised that the missing child — I mean, the swapped baby — had still in some ways been a part of our family for a long time. Because. Because ...' Clara had to swallow the lump of anxiety that rose in her throat in order to get the words out. 'Because she happened to be my brother's girlfriend.'

This time, Elif seemed genuinely astonished.

'So your brother ... and your sister, who you didn't know was your sister ... ? Oh shit.'

'So. You see,' said Clara. 'I can't have anything to do with my brother. He can never know, and I don't know how I'd be able to see him without ... You said it yourself, I'm not good at acting. So I'm hiding. That's why I'm here. Because I have nowhere else to go.'

Clara glanced at the door behind them. Still not a sound from inside. Jordan was in there, sleeping. She wondered what would happen when he woke up — would he admit that he'd cried on her shoulder when the thunder struck, sheltering against her shoulder like a little animal in its den? Probably not. But he would know it had happened. It could never be undone, and it changed something between them, opened something up, Clara thought. Though of course, it made no difference. Not as long as Matilda was there.

It was quiet for a while. The only sound that could be heard was the rustle when Elif tore the cellophane off the new cigarette packet and held up the transparent plastic in the air. She just held it there for a few seconds and let it flutter. Clara looked at it, knowing that she should reach out and take it before it was too late, before it fluttered away and caught in the throat of an innocent little gull or fulmar. But she didn't want to. Elif let go and it rose with the wind. They watched it until it was impossible to distinguish.

Elif took a cigarette out of the packet, tapping it on the steps before sticking it in her mouth and saying:

'Families, eh. Ban 'em all.'

'I told you my dad's missing too, right? Probably on the run with a German woman twenty years his junior.'

Elif laughed.

'A ladies' man, eh? Just like mine. Has a new one every other week. That generation, I tell you. Zero respect for the nuclear family.'

'Has? I thought he was dead?'

'No, no, the guy's not dead. Did I say that? It was a metaphor if so. He's alive and kicking.'

'But why did you say he was dead?'

Elif rolled her eyes.

'Duh, cos he's dead to me, of course. I mean, for a long time we weren't in touch. I started talking to him again this spring, but that was the first time since I left home aged fourteen.' Elif waved her cigarette dismissively. 'He's a fucking homophobe and a psycho. Having a son who was coining it in showbiz was cool, but having a son who started looking like a girl and wanted to sleep with dudes was … not.'

Clara bit her lip.

'Elif, I'm sorry …'

'Not that they needed money, really. Dad's been bringing in the bacon since day, you know. He's fucking smart. Brain surgeon.'

Elif drew out the last words meaningfully. Clara wasn't sure what it was supposed to mean.

'I thought you were poor growing up,' she said weakly.

'Tut, tut. Poor kids don't become film stars, it just doesn't happen, does it? The people we lived next to were poor, that's true. My best friend and first nemesis, my Ava, she was poor as a fucking church mouse. But we had a mansion. My dad worked at UCLA. That was about the time

I started looking like this.' Elif swept a hand over her hair. 'He, like, freaked. Wanted to do studies on me. Like some fucking rabbit.'

'What do you mean, studies?'

'So, like, he thought the gayness is in your brain. And if you can find the gay-centre you could put that shit right.'

'God. Elif —'

'So I got out. Then I heard from my mom that he'd been given some cushy job in London.'

Elif grinned.

'Want to know something really sick?' she said. 'Don't get angry at me, I swear this is pretty new info for me too. I think he's your brother's boss. And if you ask me, your brother seems to be on the skids a bit. So you're right,' she went on, thoughtfully, 'it's probably a good idea not to tell him he's been screwing his own sister.'

ARCHIVE//: SUBJECT: ANSWER ME

SISTER SISTER SISTER SISTER SISTER SISTER SISTER SISTER
SISTER SISTER SISTER SISTER SISTER SISTER SISTER SISTER
SISTER SISTER SISTER SISTER SISTER SISTER SISTER SISTER
    SISTER SISTER
    SISTER SISTER
    SISTER SISTER
    ANSWER ME
    i'm going to london, please come too

                              /your evil triplet

It had taken Clara a while to realise the full implications of what she'd discovered in Berlin. There on the floor of the gallery she'd thought of one thing and one thing only. As the darkness and the people had dispersed, as she'd stumbled out onto the street, as the heavens had opened in a downpour as wet and heavy as a dog's tongue over her face, suffocating her, she'd thought of the same single thing, and that thing had been herself. Where she fit in, now it seemed to have been confirmed that she didn't.

It wasn't until a few hours later that she realised that this truth, if it ever came to light, would have decidedly bitterer consequences for Sebastian. Clara had drifted through the streets for hours, Kreuzberg, Schöneberg, up towards Tiergarten, over rivers and roads, and she'd seen Violetta on every corner, on every bus, a reflection in every darkened shop window.

In the end she'd grown tired and gone into a late-night cafe, stretched out on a sofa with big red cushions, and thought about another cafe, in another town, in another time, the first time she saw Violetta.

It was in the innermost room of Cafe Ariman, the one you chose if you weren't intending to move for a long, long time. It was before Violetta got together with Sebastian, probably the first year of high school; they hadn't even met yet, as far as Clara knew. Clara had arrived at Ariman on her own, bought her tall glass of half-coffee, half-milk, and taken it with her all the way to the innermost room. She was going to write a school project on climate change — it was a fairly new subject at that time; that is, the mid-noughties — and she'd hoped to be left in peace. It was impossible at home, because Matilda was in the middle of an episode and spent the whole time running around Clara's room, orating wildly on the second intifada.

But alas for Clara — there was a girl in the best armchair reading Rimbaud with her feet tucked under her and a comically large teacup balanced on the armrest. Clara hesitated in the doorway. Should she sit down in one of the other chairs, which were made of dry old rattan that mercilessly ripped holes in your tights, or should she go to another room? The girl seemed quiet and would probably leave her in peace, but there was something about her manner that made Clara feel inexplicably uneasy. The familiar room suddenly seemed strange. It smelled weird, like rubbish and strong perfume and old books ravaged by damp. Of course, it was impossible that the smell could be coming from the girl.

And yet it was.

Clara remembered thinking it was the smell of death.

Then the girl lifted her head and looked right at Clara. She could still see her there, the way Violetta looked at that moment. Behind her head was the vase of swaying peacock feathers of exactly the same bright blue as her eyes. She was very thin, and quite pretty, and very beautiful but terribly resolute. She had a polo shirt on and a brown bob and very dark lipstick that clashed with those blue eyes. With one hand she held the book, balancing it on her knee, and with the other she reached, almost impossibly slowly, for the cup. She said:

'You can come in if you want. I'm harmless.'

And Clara turned and left, without a word.

When Sebastian introduced his new girlfriend a few months later, it took Clara a while to recognise her. Of course, she looked more or less the same, she was even wearing a polo shirt, but her aura was completely different. The girl Clara had seen in Ariman was a hundred years old. Sebastian's girlfriend was a child. She was giggly, rosy-cheeked, her eyes golden in the midst of all that blue — she was in love, presumably. Even if she recognised Clara, she didn't show it, and Clara didn't say anything either. During the nine years of Sebastian and Violetta's relationship, Clara was often tempted to ask Violetta if she remembered, but always stopped herself at the last moment. To begin with, she was scared of drawing out the walking corpse which she, and only she, knew lurked inside Violetta — and later, when death began to show its face again, she kept quiet in the desperate hope that staying silent would send it back where it had come from.

She hadn't been able to. No one had. Violetta had died, had hung herself in a doorway, and Sebastian had found her there. Clara hadn't been able to send death back through her silence, hadn't been able to save Sebastian from his sorrow. But she could save him from the revulsion, the anxiety, and the shame. She could stay silent now, Clara had thought as she reclined, alone and sibling-less, in a Berlin cafe, hiding between the cushions. She would stay silent until the day nothing was left but her silence, heavy as a stone on the bottom of the sea.

It was Clara who first suspected something was amiss. After the storm and their reunion, Elif had become a more frequent guest at the camp again. In fact, she'd started spending the best part of her waking hours with them, and the group welcomed Elif back into their company just as straightforwardly as they had Clara. She'd even started getting involved in the work — she mainly helped Jordan with the fishing; but today there was no Elif, so Clara had to pitch in and take her place.

Jordan had a new project: lobster fishing. Lobster, he said, had once been a staple food on the island, and even though they had been the victims of overfishing, it was quite possible that there were still a few corpse-eating crustaceans with enormous black claws creeping around the cliffs' gullies. Stranger things had happened than species recovering once they'd dropped out of humanity's line of sight — just look at the coelacanth. Clara had wondered, and also asked, if this obsession with lobsters was a sign of homesickness — Jordan was from New England, after all — but he'd repudiated that in the most explicit terms. 'The people are hungry? Let them eat lobster thermidor!' he'd guffawed, cramming one of his home-made lobster cages onto Clara's head.

But it wasn't until the afternoon that Clara had seriously begun to have concerns about Elif's wellbeing.

Clara sat cross-legged outside her tent, shelling peas into a bowl. Something about Elif's absence put her on edge, but she couldn't really figure out what it was. After all, she'd seen Elif just the night before. Clara ran her fingernail along the pod, letting the small green orbs run through her fingers like a broken string of pearls. Elif had seemed normal, she thought. Totally normal. Maybe a little happier than normal, excited in some way. A fist clenched inside Clara's chest. The fever in her eyes, hadn't she seen that before? The ecstasy of the last burst. Sebastian must have seen it too, but he hadn't been able to decipher it.

Clara tried to quell her anxiety, which she knew was irrational. But it was hard, because Horst had begun circling her with a nervous aura —

he paced to and fro behind her tent like a phantom.

'Horst,' said Clara, tossing the last empty pod into the pile beside her. 'What is it? You seem anxious.'

Horst came out from behind the tent. He was holding his camera. Clara pointed at it.

'Wasn't that missing?'

Horst nodded earnestly.

'It was. But this morning it came back.'

'How?'

'Elif had it.'

'Elif? Did you see her this morning?'

'Yeah. Very briefly. But she wasn't the one who'd taken it. She found it, she said. Last night. She got back to the bungalow at the hotel and there it was. On the table.'

Clara frowned.

'Do you believe that?'

Horst shrugged.

'*Vielleicht*. She said she knew who'd put it there, but didn't want to say more. She said I knew it too, but I don't any more.'

Clara could imagine exactly who it was in Elif's head. But that didn't explain how it had got there, if Elif was to be believed and wasn't the guilty party herself.

'Do you know where she is? Elif?'

Horst shook his head. 'I was coming to ask you the same thing. I have a bad feeling.'

Clara brushed some detritus from her jeans and got up, taking the bowl of beans over to the cooking area. Horst followed her. By the firepit they found a solitary figure.

'Jordan, have you seen Elif today?' Clara asked.

'Nope. She never came to help with the cages.'

Clara looked at Horst, who nodded tensely.

'*Wie beim Schlafen*,' he mumbled, and Clara felt something cold touch her heart.

They set off less than an hour later. Clara and Jordan had wanted to start by searching through Elif's usual watering holes — the hotel, the bars along the high street, the beach in Hanga Roa, but Horst had got his confidence back and insisted they wouldn't find her there. He brandished his camera in the air, shook out his blond curls, and repeated, again and again, with a fervour that made the hair on the back of Clara's neck stand up, that Elif was in danger *somewhere between stone and sea*. So Clara and Jordan gave in. After Clara had asked the others to look in the more likely places, the three of them climbed into the Defender and started their demented search. They would look as long as their energy and the light held out, and if they hadn't found Elif by then, they'd contact the police. They'd search anti-clockwise along the coast, in places where the stone met the sea, and that you could reach without a car. In other words, places viewed as tourist destinations and therefore served by public transport. It was a hopeless, futile plan, but at least it was a plan.

Clara wasn't actually totally convinced that Elif was in danger. Violetta had been a bird, no, something less robust than a bird, a mere feather, blown in the wind. Elif reminded her, more than anything, of a cat: immortal, invincible. There was no similarity, no comparison.

Except that in some way there was. She could feel it in her gut.

And what's more, she thought, hadn't Elif herself said that she'd come face to face with death six times? What happened to a cat the seventh time it fell from a roof? Clara felt uncertain of the exact number of lives a cat was supposed to have, but there was certainly a limit. And hadn't Elif saved her, again and again, even though the stakes those times were so much lower? Hadn't she fished up Clara out of her own personal hell, shown her all the kindness in the world, even if it was in her explosive fashion?

Didn't Clara have a responsibility to repay the favour? Weren't all people afraid deep down, and in need of saving now and then, and wasn't it every person's duty to listen to calls for help, even when they came distorted and indiscernible, like cries under the water?

She looked at Jordan, who steered the Defender with a practised hand, driving out onto the gravel path that ran along the top of the campsite and putting his foot down. She wondered why he was doing this. If he too heard someone calling, and if he did, whom.

They looked and looked without finding her. It was almost night when they took a last stop at Orongo, an old settlement with small round stone houses, where the cliffs on one side plunged three hundred metres into the sea and a scraggy slope on the other led to a peculiar geological formation that most closely resembled the scar left by a bomb or a fallen meteorite. It was, in fact, a crater left by one of the volcanoes that had long ago caused the island to rise up out of the sea. The bottom consisted of wet marshland, a reflective lagoon of freshwater that was the reason the village at the top existed. Aside from providing water, the crater, with its two-hundred-metre-high walls, also offered a favourable climate, shielded as it was from the wind. People had farmed the plateaus within: figs, bananas, mangoes, and guava, not unlike the way people grew grapes on the slopes of Vesuvius. Clara thought, when they got out of the car and she saw the vast hollow, so much bigger in reality than she'd imagined from pictures she'd seen, that there was something beautiful in the way the world's most fertile soil was often to be found in the most violent and inhospitable places, among ash and silt.

There were no trees here now, just water and stone, green, green grass and floating clumps of reeds, a tourist office that had closed for the night, a thin bit of plastic, perhaps from a cigarette packet, that stroked the ground in the breeze and came to rest on Clara's shoe like a second skin. She picked up the plastic and closed her hand around it.

'She can't be down there,' she said, turning to Horst, who nodded. 'She would have been spotted by someone; there must have been loads of people here today.'

'The other side,' said Horst, turning what gaze he had left towards the sea.

'You're joking,' said Clara. 'If she's fallen down there, she's dead.'

Which might well have been what she wanted. Clara shuddered.

'Not necessarily,' Jordan said. 'People used to climb down.'

And it was true. The precipice plunged into the sea, and further out in the water was a rocky islet, Motu Nui, which had once been hailed as a sacred site. Young men used to swim there in order to fetch the first sooty tern egg of the season and bring it back to the mainland. The one who succeeded was named the 'Birdman', and ruled the island and its inhabitants. The ones who didn't generally died.

Clara snorted.

'The ones who succeeded didn't grow up on Sunset Boulevard.'

But Jordan didn't reply. He'd already thrown his rucksack over his shoulder and headed off between the buildings, towards the cliff's edge. A few metres more and the darkness would swallow him, and he would disappear too, maybe down the drop. Clara rushed to grab her torch and shone the blinding light at his back.

'Stay here,' she said to Horst, nodding at the car. 'If we're not back in half an hour, ring the emergency services.'

It was hard to walk without stumbling in the dark, and it was with small steps that they approached the abyss. For the last bit they got down on their hands and knees and felt their way forward to be sure the path wouldn't suddenly fall away from under them. When it did at last disappear, it was because it had been replaced by dry grass. They stopped, letting their torchlight glide through the darkness. There was absolute silence, a great trembling nothing, and then: a scratching sound, as though from a panic-stricken caged animal. Clara got an urge to tell Jordan about when she was a child, and she and Matilda had been invited to a classmate's summer cabin to camp in the garden and cycle down high hills on rusty bikes with no brakes. On the last day, the classmate's mother's boyfriend, a biker called Frans, paid the girls to keep watch outside an outhouse. He was certain that there was a badger living inside, and he wanted to kill it and make paintbrushes from the fur to give to the classmate's mother, who was an artist and painted what Clara thought were beautiful paintings, of wolves howling in the moonlight. Brushes made from badger fur were the very finest, Frans told them, but they cost the earth. Of the three girls it was only Clara who actually saw the badger. She was keeping watch at one door with a broom as her only weapon and instructions to shunt the badger back in if it showed its face. This, Clara realised now, was a crazy situation to put a child in. An angry badger is extremely dangerous — if it bites, it bites hard enough to crush bones. But back then, Clara wasn't scared, not until the badger stuck its ugly snout through a hole in the wooden wall a few metres away. Right before it disappeared into a clump of trees, it looked Clara in the eye, and it was the worst look she'd ever seen. She thought then that that must be how the devil looked, that the smell of the badger was the way it smelled in hell. Frans never got to make his badger brushes, and Clara never told him she'd seen the animal. She only told Matilda, who made Clara swear never to breathe a word about any of it. Mama would make a scene, and they'd never be allowed to play with that particular friend again. Mama was sufficiently sceptical about her as it was, due to her mother's fondness for dream-catchers and common yellow Blends. And Clara had obeyed, but she never went to that summer cabin again, and she still sometimes dreamed of teeth that bit and tore and wouldn't let go until she woke up in a pool of her own sweat.

This time it wasn't a badger making the noise. It was a human, a human lying on an outcrop four or five metres below the top of the cliff edge. It was hard to see properly in the darkness, but the cliff face didn't seem to be completely vertical, in fact it appeared to cast itself down towards the water in cascades, like a frozen waterfall. Clara could understand how it was theoretically possible to make your way right down to the water, even if she couldn't begin to understand how Elif might have thought it a possibility in practice. But it was undoubtedly Elif waving her arms about down there.

Clara pointed the torch down towards where the two white hands were moving in the darkness. On closer inspection, the outcrop was actually a crevice: a cleft in the rock where someone was lying like a broken prima donna.

'Elif? Is that you? Are you okay?' Clara called, so terrified she herself might fall that she was pressing her body desperately against a metal pole — which turned out to be a sign warning people not to try to climb down the wall.

A weak voice bounced jubilantly between stone and sea.

'Clara! Clarita! Is that really you?'

'God, have you broken anything? How did you end up down there? Shall we call an ambulance?'

'Your name means light; did you know that? Light and clarity! Is it really you, Clara?'

'Yes, and Jordan and Horst. We've got some rope, I think? Can you climb up? Or wait, you can't. Jordan?'

He was already one step ahead of her. It turned out they not only had rope, but a whole fucking rope ladder he apparently drove around with in the boot.

'God,' Clara said again, as Jordan fastened the rope ladder to the metal post. 'That's madness. You could fall to your death. And how are you going to get her back up?'

'Carry her on my back,' said Jordan, unconcerned. 'Not like she weighs anything.'

And with that he threw down the ladder, tugged hard a few times on the knot, and vanished over the edge. Clara stood there on her own with the torch. Her heart was racing, and in the minutes that passed before Jordan reappeared with Elif like a sack on his back, her life seemed very, very empty. If Elif took Jordan with her to the grave, Clara would never forgive her, she'd never forgive anyone again.

'What the fuck?' she shouted, once Elif was finally lying on the ground in front of her, a gasping little wisp of a person with grazed knees. 'How did you end up down there? What the hell were you thinking? Were you trying to kill yourself?'

She sank down onto her knees and took Elif's head in her hands. Her sunglasses were gone; they must have fallen into the sea and would end up in the belly of a fish, living there for hundreds of years until the fish died and the flesh rotted and the only thing left was the sunglasses, enclosed in a cage of fish ribs like in a museum display. Elif's eyes were large and wet, but they shone, they shone with a sense of security.

'Ah, Clara ...' Elif mumbled. 'Who cares? You found me! I'll never forget that, never in my life, I swear ... And I'll make it up to you, promise. I have a plan, baby, I have a plan.'

★

They drove home through the night. Clara rested her head against the damp glass and thought about wind turbines. She wondered if it was like with the lobsters, homesickness. She wondered, for the first time, if it was the same way for her as for Siobhan — that she liked this island because it reminded her of home.

They were almost back at the camp when Horst abruptly drove off the road and cut the engine. He said nothing, just sat there with his thin hands on the wheel.

'Horst?' Jordan said carefully.

'Yes?'

'Why've you stopped?'

'It's dark,' he said.

'It's night,' Jordan said.

'That's not what I mean.'

Jordan took hold of the back of the driver's seat and leaned forward. Elif neighed in her sleep, a contented little sound.

'So what do you mean?'

'The last shadows. Gone. Now it's dark. Now I'm blind.'

A single tear ran down Horst's cheek, which was soft and hairless, like the child he almost was, but neither Clara nor Jordan saw it. In the darkness, their hands moved towards one another, as if to ask: what happens now, what's going to happen now everything is coming to an end?

The cicada family is one of the world's largest known insect families, a superfamily with many thousands of sub-groups. Some live in trees and bark, others in burrows under the earth, sucking the sap from roots, and biding their time.

Some wait there, in the ground, for thirteen years, seventeen, hiding so as not to be eaten. Gathering strength and upsetting the balance of the food chain.

And then — a performance.

They pour forth in their thousands, a well-orchestrated resurrection of a million wingbeats. The creatures that had threatened to swallow them whole are now dead, starved, and the few that have survived are unable to deal with the sudden supply; they are swamped by the multitude.

Someone who happened to dig up a dormant cicada from the ground might be forgiven for thinking it was dead.

It looks dead, after all, or at least as if it's sleeping.

Wie beim Schlafen.

But it's not dead. It's just waiting, waiting to be resurrected, to come back in all its shining colours.

The day upon which the world, according to questionable predictions, was due to end in a cloud of fire started like any other day on the island. Clara awoke in her tent, alone and freezing. The morning light came in blue, because the sides of her tent were blue. The sea, Clara thought, as she brushed her teeth under the tap outside the abandoned campsite reception, was blue because the sky was blue. The sky, she thought, as she heated up two cold potatoes in the embers of the others' breakfast fire, was blue because the blue light waves were the most dissolute, the most inclined to flight and jerky movements. The light, she thought, as she washed up her tin plate and waved it in the air to dry, is a compressed force with a beauty that remains hidden until the force encounters an obstacle and shatters around the world. The world, she thought, as she checked the batteries in her torch and fastened her shoes, is a prism.

She felt sure there was some banal lesson in there somewhere.

Though learning lessons, she thought, as she left the deserted campsite and set off on the ten-kilometre walk to Orongo, was pretty overrated. She'd spent her life trying to understand things, because she'd got it into her head that knowledge was the same thing as order, control, superiority. It had been a very bad tactic, she thought, as she saw the first bird of the day fly up from the handlebars of a broken bicycle leant haphazardly against a veranda made hazy by the morning sun on the outskirts of town. She'd never felt more powerless than when she'd got clear answers to vaguely formulated questions. And she'd never felt more in control than now, on this morning, when everything was highly uncertain, highly improbable, and the light, the blue light, danced hysterically around her.

The camp had been empty when she woke, which wasn't exactly surprising. The others had said they'd be leaving early, at dawn. Horst, now completely blind, would drive the stuffed Defender down to the pot-shaped hole in the earth and the others would walk, just like Clara. She didn't think too much about why they hadn't woken her. She both belonged, and didn't. Maybe they'd simply forgotten her. That thought was no longer as jarring as it might once have been.

And she was actually glad to have the chance to walk alone. She liked the metal water bottle banging against her leg, she liked her own shadow, the thought that the sunlight now warming her calves had travelled 150 million kilometres just to be stopped at the last minute from being swallowed by the ground by the fact that it had hit her body. She liked not knowing if her body would exist tomorrow. Deep down she knew, of course, that it would, just like the blackberries would, and the stones and the ocean currents. She wasn't and never would be convinced that Horst could predict anything, least of all the end of the world. But it didn't matter. She understood why people were drawn to thoughts of the end times. It was like with wells and bottomless pits. It was impossible to imagine a fall without end — paradoxically, it was impossible to accept a bottomless hole until you'd hit the bottom.

It was impossible to imagine a world without end until you'd explored the thought, accepting that space was infinite until you'd tentatively reached for its furthermost wall.

It was early afternoon when she reached the location of what Jordan was calling the 'party to end all parties'. Clara was pretty sure that not even Jordan seriously believed the sea would rise up around them and swallow everything, but she wasn't sure of what he hoped deep down. Since Horst's sight had gone and the rest of the camp had started their mad dance towards this evening's apocalyptic vigil, something inside Jordan had seemed to come to life. Clara couldn't tell whether it was the thought of something final that energised him, or just the fact that the camp's loping gait had been shaken up a little.

They'd started building the fire. It was the first thing she saw when she reached the caldera's rim. Of course, it wasn't a bonfire or anything, since that would have been both impossible and in poor taste on an island with such scanty wood resources. Not that that would matter, Clara thought, as she threw her rucksack onto the heap already there beside the old stone houses built around the rim, if they really *believed* that the world as they knew it was about to be swallowed up in a great fire. But in any case, they were calling it a fire, even though it was actually a tree. The last tree, and the first. The burning bush. Clara wasn't clear on the symbolism, but she could see it was beautiful, beautiful just like the crater itself, the crater that had once been a fire-sputtering volcano, and then a garden full of trees, and then a marsh for your wellies to get stuck in, to get stuck and slowly sink down into.

Into the bowels of the earth, the belly of the whale.

They'd found a bit of land on the edge of the caldera that was somewhat stable. The stone circle they'd started to build there was unexpectedly large, maybe four metres in diameter, and the hollow into which the little aito tree would be lowered was very, very small in comparison.

It would be a kind of offering. Afterwards they would leave, climbing back up to the rim of the crater, and wait. They'd eat food and drink marsala. They'd gaze out to Motu Nui and feel the continental plates move under them.

In the beginning, the plan had been to plant the tree out on Motu Nui itself, in a kind of inverted version of the original birdman ritual. Instead of crowning someone king of the island, they'd give it back to nature. It was Siobhan's idea. And from the beginning, Clara had thought it was silly, not to mention rather arrogant, but she'd held her tongue.

But in any case, the idea fell down on its own implausibility. The men who had once upon a time competed to bring back the first sooty tern egg from Motu Nui to Orongo had been training for it their whole lives. The idea that someone would try to get out there with a tree on their back was pure madness. In the end it was Horst who put his foot down. It wouldn't happen that way, he said with the total authority of a blind teenage seer. As everyone knew, the world wasn't going out with a bang, but with a little slurp.

Jordan seemed pleased when she arrived. He was in the middle of shifting a large rock towards the circle, and let her help without a word. When the little monument was ready, an hour or so later, they all climbed up out of the crater and spread to the four winds. Vedrana and Horst lay down on their backs and watched the clouds. Horst had one hand on Vedrana's stomach, and from the corner of her eye, Clara saw her carefully lay her hand over his and stroke her fingertips over the white knuckles. Siobhan ran barefoot between the houses, as though calling her long-dead sheep. Bernie and Grace compared the lengths of their pocket knives.

Jordan, Elif, and Clara wandered along the rim of the crater, down to the beach to go for a swim. On the way they passed the cliff where, a few days previously, they'd found Elif. Since then, she'd fiercely denied trying to take her own life. She'd just spotted something, she said. Something that had sparkled so temptingly in the rocky crevice, as if it were gold. Then she'd fallen, and been saved. Someone had come to look for her; it was unbelievable.

Now she stopped on the rim and Clara got it into her head that she was going to try to fall again just for the chance to experience that moment of salvation one more time. Instead, Elif peered at the sun and let out a contented sigh.

'I can't fucking believe the day is finally here.'

'Are you really looking forward to dying that much?' asked Clara. 'We could have just left you down there.'

'Tsk, who said anything about dying, Clarita? Tonight's the night. She's coming.'

Jordan, who wasn't up to speed with Elif's nemesis issues, looked at Clara quizzically. Elif saw the look and punched him on the shoulder.

'Dakota, dummy. She'll make her appearance tonight, on my mom's life.'

They gathered again at dusk. It fell quickly, as usual, a veil over the eyes — less like dying than being un-born. They lit their lamps and torches, laced their boots, and began the climb down into the great caldera. Horst and Vedrana went first, with the tree — Vedrana carrying the little canopy and Horst the root ball. In the flickering light of a dozen torches, Clara could see how carefully Horst moved his feet over the ground, as though crawling on two legs. Beneath them the light glittered as it caught the streams and pools of the crater's bottom. It wasn't a long walk down, but in the darkness, it felt as though time was standing still, and then moving backwards, into the mother's womb, the primordial soup, outer space.

Clara took a few deep breaths, caught Jordan's earthy scent and realised he was somewhere beside her in the darkness. She thought of the gallery on Kottbusser Tor, how she'd stared so long at her own face that it had ceased to exist and become another. That time, the experience of something otherworldly, inexplicable, had made her panic-stricken. Now it just felt comforting, like burrowing your fingers into sun-warmed soil, feeling your own mortality at your fingertips; not like a threat, but a promise. Water fright, coming night. He that believeth on me shall never thirst. Eternal life. She'd always wondered if their mother had believed in it, really believed in it. I am the resurrection and the life. From thence shall he come. Had it helped her, Mama, when the darkness fell, the belief that this little life isn't the only one, that there was a place where she might get back the daughter who had been taken from her, not once, but twice? She'll come back, Horst had said. Of course, it was make-believe, a coincidence, and a fantasy. But in some ways, he was right. Clara had seen her, looked her right in the eye in that mirror in that gallery, and at that moment she'd been there, blue-lipped but alive, alive in spite of the cold.

And after that she'd seen her everywhere, on every corner, in every leaf that cupped its hand to the rain.

They reached the bottom of the crater. Silently, they made their way between the puddles until they reached the edge of the stone circle. They hadn't really talked about what form the ceremony would take, but still they moved seamlessly, like flowing water, as if they'd rehearsed this thousands of times in a common dream. Jordan walked into the stone circle and took the tree from Horst and Vedrana, lowering it carefully into the hole they'd made earlier that day. The others spread out around the ring with their torches pointed towards the centre. Siobhan, Sytze, and Elif got down on their knees and gently pushed the soil over the root ball. When they were done, they patted the soil with their palms and then stood up, stepped out of the ring, and cupped their hands in the nearest pool, carrying the water back to the tree and letting it run between their fingers. Everyone got up and did the same until the earth round the tree was plump and full.

No one laughed and no one cried and then they walked away together, back up the hillside.

They lit the camping stoves, turned on lamps and lanterns, put on their warm jumpers, and filled up on rice and some kind of strange and not particularly tasty biscuit-type thing with chocolate and orange gelée that Horst produced from his rucksack. Clara sat quietly, listening to the others chatting the same kind of chat as always. She found it somehow touching that these people who were all, on some level at least, awaiting the death of everything, saw no reason to change old habits simply because they would soon be coming to an end. That had to mean something, she thought. That, at the end of the day, the lives we live are the ones we want to have, that they're worth something in all their trivial details.

Horst was sitting beside her. He wasn't saying anything either. Clara looked at him side-on, and realised, for the first time, that he reminded her of Sebastian. The same dark base note in his soul. The same artificial calm. The same startlingly inflated impression of his own importance in the world.

'You're looking at me,' said Horst after a while.

'Do you know you remind me of my brother?' Clara said.

'Sebastian,' said Horst.

'Yes,' said Clara. 'That's his name.'

'I wrote him a postcard,' said Horst. 'He likes Jaffa cakes. And strictly speaking, he's not your brother.'

Clara quickly attempted to rank these three statements in order to determine which she should tackle first, but before she could, Horst went on:

'In some ways I was right. In others wrong.'

'About what?' Clara asked.

Horst smiled weakly, but not sorrowfully.

'Nothing ever really ends, Clara. Everything changes, but nothing really ends.'

He took hold of her wrist; his fingers were warm. He went on: 'I'll admit something: I wanted it to end. *Alles.* The world. Why should it exist, if I couldn't see it? How could it exist? I saw an approaching darkness, and I thought it was impenetrable.'

'But that was wrong?' said Clara.

Horst loosened his grip on her wrist and answered with an almost imperceptible nod towards Vedrana, who was sitting on the other side of the camping stoves. 'She's bearing a child,' he said, placing his hand carefully on Clara's cheek. 'My child. And I want you to know it's a girl. Her name will be Violetta.'

Clara drew the name down into her lungs. Closed her eyes, inhaled. *That's all a person ever has to do.*

'So it was her, after all,' Clara mumbled, full of wonder, opening her eyes. Her gaze was drawn to Vedrana's slender figure, her bright blue eyes, the corners of her mouth, which turned up a little in a contented smile. 'Who was coming. Coming back.'

Horst let his hand fall from Clara's cheek and shrugged in that same almost imperceptible way.

'*Vielleicht.* But it could also have been her I was thinking of.'

'Who?'

Confused, Clara dragged her eyes from Vedrana's stomach, so flat under the black polo neck that it was hard to imagine it held the whole world.

She heard someone call her name.

It was Elif.

She came bounding through the darkness, like a child who's just been given their first bike. Elif dived into the circle of light, and Clara could see she hadn't come alone. Behind her, with calm, leisurely steps, came a woman with long blonde hair and houndstooth shorts, earrings in the form of two glossy blue peacock feathers gaily dangling from her earlobes.

'You see, Clara, you see that I was right? What say you now, huh? What say you now? You see who this is?'

It was Dakota Fanning.

He stood on the edge, or beyond the edge: in the darkness it looked as though he were floating, as though the black water was about to rise up and meet the soles of his feet — the hard, filthy feet that had walked over stones and earth and burning coals, that knew the value of decomposing leaves and uncut grass and a camp fresh with morning dew. As though they were about to walk on water, walk over the sea, away from her.

Jordan. It was almost dawn when Clara discovered he was no longer in the circle gathered round the hissing camping stoves. She'd been busy talking to Elif and hadn't noticed him disappearing. Elif, who'd finally found her nemesis, her better half, her flaxen-haired mirror image in checked shorts. Her sister, her Ava, reborn, resurrected, as though magicked from the air itself.

Magic, Clara had thought. Shakespeare. Hollywood.

Then Elif had told her something even stranger.

'Listen, Clarita. I've got good news. It's *not* you. Nice, huh?'

Magic, Shakespeare, Hollywood.

Because it was Sebastian, Elif had told her. The one who was swapped at birth was Sebastian. Shipwrecked, but not dead.

Elif knew this, because she had contacts. Specifically, contact with her dad, who was Sebastian's boss, and had contacts of his own. Including the siblings' mother. It had taken a meandering chain of telephone calls, threats, and flattery until Elif at last had the information in her clutches. But here it was. She held it out for Clara like a gift, placing it like a golden scarab in her hand.

'And here I was thinking —' said Clara, without finishing her sentence, because she wasn't sure what she'd been thinking. She hadn't thought much.

'Sometimes it's best to just ask, baby,' said Elif.

And Clara had looked up. She'd seen that Dakota Fanning had a kitten on her lap, quite real, with a perfectly real glow round its perfect skull. She'd seen the soaring gulls, the scraps of cloud, the first rays of sun. A world which hadn't ended. Which would, one day. But not today. She'd seen Jordan, a distant speck on the horizon, and she'd gone to him.

But now she hardly dared approach him. Dared not stay there, dared not call out or even stay silent. The slightest sound might make the clouds under his feet dissipate like steam.

Perhaps he didn't exist. If he did, how could he be floating like that, as though hanging in the darkness, crucified against the sky?

All fears are, at base, just the fear of losing something, thought Clara, and opened her mouth.

'Jordan?'

He turned, quite real, with perfectly real earth under his imperfect feet. He was standing on the edge, eyes blazing, pointing down at the rocky cliff.

'What?' said Clara.

'Come,' said Jordan and lay down on his front. 'Come and look.'

She lay down beside him. Beneath them, the rocks dropped away down to the sea. The tidal waters had drawn back and sand was blowing like snow smoke over the damp ground. Sea stars, crab shells, and there: a lone lobster, large, black, slowly, slowly crawling out of a rocky crevice and making for the water.

Every love story, even a love story that started out all wrong, has a chance to be resurrected, innocent and pure, and that was the case with Clara and Jordan's.

Him saying: 'Are you asleep?'

And her saying: 'There's something I have to ask you. It's about my sister.'

V
LONDON

In the window of one of the many music shops on Charing Cross Road was a piano that played itself. On a stool in front of the piano was a puppet of a marmalade cat with its paws floating above the keys. It was vile, absolutely vile, one of the most grotesque things Matilda had ever seen in her life: the glassy eyes, glassy because they were made of glass, the unnatural grimace on the fake cat's fake little face, the piano playing 'The Blue Danube' — blue! — and for the thirty-fourth time since she'd got here, she longed for the cloudy yellow water of the Spree.

This was a despicable city, an absolutely despicable city; Matilda could feel no other way. The Thames, which had looped grey and hard, like cement around her legs, sliced by sharp blades of provocative September sun — *come and get me, you can't catch me!* She'd crossed one bridge after another, felt them rise up at either end and snap shut around her body like great iron jaws. The Empire! The Queen! Their enslavement of India! Their contempt for Europe, for Germany, for Angela! They had so much to answer for, and what did they do? Build towers of glass, nothing but towers of glass, selling themselves to the highest bidder. Matilda rubbed her eyes with her sleeve, turned away from the shop window with its grotesque little cat tableau, crossed the street, and walked with determined steps into Superdrug. By the entrance were stacks of publications bearing non-news, a princess had given birth, what was she called again — Kate? The princess who was so slender the tabloids had feared she wouldn't be able to have children. But now it seemed she'd delivered, for the second time, no less, clever girl — she'd even stood on the steps of the hospital and waved, freshly post-partum but all made up and ready for the slaughter. It wasn't fit to piss on, this damn country. Piss, piss, piss on all your damn countries. Piss on yourself and the little piss in the sea that is your own existence. You shouldn't even exist, strictly speaking, you shouldn't exist. The chances were microscopic. And the possibility of Matilda and Sebastian and Clara existing? Almost non-existent. Twins were one thing, but triplets?

One of them may have ended up in the wrong place, but still, she'd pushed out three, their mother had, and at the same time, too. And not by artificial means, either. There was something almost magical about it. Almost manic. Who was it that said *she* was manic? Was it Billy? Was it his alkie bitch of a wife? Was it Bernarda, the dog, who sometimes came to her in her dreams and yelped so heart-rendingly? Was it the child with the hole between its valves, with the back-to-front heart, who screamed? Was it Mama, who herself had seen the devil, one morning at St Månslyckan? Because it couldn't have been Kathleen, could it, with whom Matilda had sought refuge after fleeing Västerbotten? No, it could have been anyone, but not Kathleen. Kathleen didn't believe in madness, she'd said that herself. She believed only in the cosmos.

There were so many shelves in Superdrug, a thousand at least. Toothbrushes, head lice treatment, make-up, make-up, make-up. She took a few turns around the natural remedies, false eyelashes, electric shavers. Started to feel like a suspicious character, a possible shoplifter or a cokehead. In the end she went over to the shelf she'd come to inspect, holding her sleeve over her nose while her eyes scanned the plastic-wrapped packages. Her sweater smelled of Kathleen. It was Kathleen's sweater. She'd been given it to borrow when she'd gone and rung on Kathleen's door and lied to her very face. Who was it that said she was manipulative? It was true, in any case. She'd lied to Kathleen, about Billy and Siri and all of it. Told her she'd left of her own accord, because he'd hit her, and now she had nowhere else to go. Kathleen hadn't been able to see that the bruises had come from a five-year-old's fist and not a grown man's. An absolutely vile lie, of course, but Kathleen believed everything, the way good people do.

Back in the days when Matilda still kidded herself she could be good if she only applied herself, she would strain every fibre to nurture her credulousness — binding crystals in handkerchiefs and carrying them around in her pockets, saying 'you too', when Billy said 'I love you', even responding to an email from Nigeria, transferring thirty euros to a stranded Italian gentleman who'd had his wallet stolen in Mogadishu, but she never even got a postcard to say thank you. What had that swindler even done with the money? Paid for sex with a minor? Built an international drug empire? Torn out their nearly new kitchen and put in an even newer one with an induction hob and an ice cube maker? Taken their teenage daughter on a trip to London and filled her baskets with cheap jersey tops from Primark, with other children's labour? She'd said all this to Kathleen in an attempt to lay her cards on the table, to display her phoney goodness. To show she'd actually known, the whole time, that all her would-be good deeds had been nothing but an attempt to trick herself into believing she'd been reformed, become someone else, become so good she even believed in the impossible: human dignity. But Kathleen, who really was a good human, if of the naive, American kind, had just tilted her head and said: 'You know what, I think people who send those kinds of emails do so for a reason. Maybe they don't need the money for exactly the reason they say, but they need money, right, otherwise they wouldn't be doing it, if they weren't desperate? If you look within yourself, you'll realise that deep down you really knew that, and that it was kind of you to help where others would have just pressed "delete". It's like with the Syrian refugees. They wouldn't be coming to Europe if they weren't forced to, right? You have to see the big picture.' And Matilda had felt almost nauseous, because that wasn't the same fucking thing at all, how could Kathleen say something like that? But at the same time, she'd been so beautiful, sitting there on the moss-green sofa in full lotus with her glistening red hair in a messy bun and that golden aura that seemed to sort of radiate from the whole of her super-lean body, full to bursting with sympathy, so that Matilda could do nothing but sob in agreement. Just as she'd always suspected, Kathleen's home was a world of harmonious colour. It wasn't only her things — the fabrics and bowls and half-drunk cups of tea — the very air vibrated gently in ochre and amber. Matilda had felt quite safe with Kathleen, completely certain that the colour with no name wouldn't be able to find her there.

But, of course, she hadn't been able to stay, not for any length of time. She'd slept on Kathleen's sofa for three nights, eaten pumpernickel at her kitchen table, applied her Weleda creams, and borrowed her wool sweaters, then she'd felt obliged to leave. Not because Kathleen seemed to want to turn her out, quite the opposite, but because her well-meaning questions and stubborn insistence that she go to the police became harder and harder to dodge. How would she be able to explain to Kathleen that the police wouldn't be able to help her with the problems she had? That you couldn't take out a restraining order on a colour? Kathleen would have understood it metaphorically. She would have started talking about Billy's negative energy. But Billy had no negative energy: he was *the sun* itself. Despite all his failings, despite the fact that he even slept with snuff tucked under his lip, leaving brown streaks on the pillow, despite the fact that he defended his ex-wife in every matter, despite the fact he simulated vomiting every time she listened to First Aid Kit, Billy was still, in contrast to Matilda, a force for good in the world. A force for good in her life. And she'd snuffed it out, with her bare hands, snuffed it out like you'd snuff a candle between your forefinger and thumb.

It was all the colour's fault, but on the other hand, perhaps the colour was her own fault. In order to get to the bottom of it, she'd decided to come here, to track down her brother. Sebastian, who knew things, could do things, about the brain, and about her. Sebastian, who, in contrast to Billy and Clara and the rest of the world, had never judged her, never hated her, despite everything she'd done to deserve it.

Slowly Matilda reached out and touched one of the packets on the shelf, carefully lifting it in her hand. She didn't really have to read the back. She already knew how they worked. Wee, wait. One blue line, or two. Parallel or cross, it didn't matter. Sebastian knew nothing about this yet. She'd told him everything, almost, but not this, nothing about this strange feeling, equal parts dread and hope, which had been buzzing in her body the last few weeks, wilder and wilder and more desperately, like an insect trapped under an upturned juice glass, drunk on the sweetness but also terrified. And nothing about how she'd been through it before, remembered the sweetness, the hope, the tentative feeling of confidence and potential happiness.

She was grasping the packet now, really grasping it, trying to make her feet move towards the till. If only it hadn't been so *blue*. Clearest blue. It was even called that, the brand. Clearblue. It was like a laugh in the face. She checked the other brands, she knew some of them had red lines, too, but there were none like that here on the shelf, everything flashed blue, blue, blue until she couldn't bear it anymore, there was a security guard over there, he was looking at her, looking at her as though she was exactly what she was, a sneaky bastard, someone who couldn't be trusted, someone capable of raising their hand to a child but not sticking around to clean up the mess, someone who didn't deserve what she was beginning, deep down, to feel certain, quite certain, yes, completely certain, she actually wanted, in spite of everything.

And if she didn't get it? If the line emerged alone, without its twin, what would she do then? The guard was approaching her now; his aura was large and round and angrily ice-blue. She put the box back on the shelf, then turned on her heel, and walked out again, out among the cars and exhaust fumes, out into a city that wasn't hers, and a loneliness that was.

Sebastian wanted to talk to Jennifer Travis. No, he *needed* to talk to Travis. What he actually wanted was very much unclear, but as per usual, what he wanted didn't matter. Three days had passed since Matilda had turned up at the Institute, sitting there in Benedict's waiting room with much too little subcutaneous fat, talking about a colour that didn't exist, about another colour that was the colour blue, and about a peacock called Göran.

The thing with the peacock worried Sebastian, almost more than Matilda's assertion that she'd hit her stepdaughter. He quite simply couldn't believe it was true, that last bit — Matilda had always had a tendency to exaggerate, not least her own bad deeds.

The peacock, on the other hand. There was something about that detail that disturbed him. Why? He wasn't sure; he needed Travis's help to figure it out, but when he went down to the lab she wasn't there. Sebastian sighed and sat down on a chair, leaning his head against one of the terrariums. He listened to the rasping sound of fourteen *Zammara tympanum*, a chubby emerald-green cicada variant with wings as fine and shimmering as soap bubbles. He tried to think where Travis could be, but couldn't concentrate. His thoughts were constantly drawn back to Matilda, to her incoherent diatribes about child murder and inherited evil. He'd heard much of it before, though in somewhat different terms — and yet he felt things were different this time, that this was no ordinary phase. Yes, she'd been wound up when she arrived, but since he'd got her home she'd calmed down. He'd asked if she'd been taking her medication, and she'd tersely replied that she had.

So he'd let it go. He'd let her be, let her talk until it had all come out, and then tucked her in on the chaise longue. Observation, thought Sebastian, was the starting point of all serious diagnosis. He would keep Matilda under observation, see how she behaved, see if she really was taking her medication. Once he was quite sure she was stable, he would, possibly, be able to tell her about his appalling discovery.

'Sebastian! I've made an *appalling discovery!*'

The laboratory door slammed shut from within with a bang that sent Sebastian flying into the air. Hidden behind the door was Travis, eyes shining, chewing her lower lip anxiously.

'We can't talk about it here,' she said. 'Come on. I know a secret way out.'

Travis took Sebastian to a gay bar in Soho — the only place she, possibly mistakenly, believed herself safe from Corrigan. Over two White Russians (both belonging to Travis), Sebastian attempted to catch her flowing tears in his hands. He'd never seen Travis cry before, he would have thought her incapable of it, but late shall the sinner awaken, and it turned out Sebastian was a sinner who'd failed to put Corrigan in his place fast enough. Now, it seemed, that bastard had bloody well overstepped the line.

'He — he —' Travis sobbed in the light of the strobe.

'He what? What's he done, Travis, Jennifer? Has he ... has he made a move on you in some, er, way?'

'If you're asking whether he's touched me up or anything, the answer's no,' said Travis and dried her eyes, before immediately bursting into tears again.

'Sorry,' she whispered. 'Sorry.'

'Don't worry.'

'It's just ... It's the cicadas, Sebastian. He wants to get rid of them! For good! No beating about the bush this time — he looked me straight in the eye and said: "The creatures need to go now, Travis!"'

Sebastian furrowed his brow.

'But why?'

'Dunno.' She shrugged. 'A simple display of power, maybe. Or a punishment. Because he thinks I care about them.'

'But you do care about them.'

'Perhaps I do. But that's not why I'm crying, if that's what you think.'

'Of course not,' mumbled Sebastian. Travis raised her head and stared off into a corner, where a young man in leather underwear with the letters USSR printed on the thighs had made his way up to the ceiling with the help of nothing but a pole, and was now doing the most astonishing things with his crotch while gripping the walls and ceiling like a spider.

'How do you think your sister fits in here?' said Travis.

Sebastian jumped.

'Your sister Matilda. It can hardly be a *coincidence* that she suddenly turned up.'

'Matilda? How do you even —'

Travis rolled her eyes.

'I've spoken to Corrigan. He said she's a synaesthete; is that true?'

Sebastian felt a vague discomfort itching under his skin.

'But how does *he* know she's here?'

Travis blew her nose on her sleeve and looked at him with something almost like disdain.

'What planet are you even living on, buddy? Haven't you figured out yet that he knows everything? Or at least everything that happens in the building. God, I thought we'd got past this.'

Sebastian closed his eyes. He suddenly felt very, very tired. He tried thinking about Laura, without actually thinking about Laura. More accurately, he tried to feel what he felt when he thought about Laura, without really needing to think about her as a real person in a real context, since that context, the background, her life just now, was presumably an al fresco cafe near the Plaza de España. He'd long since stopped finding enjoyment in imagining Laura's everyday life. *He knows everything that happens in the building.* The itch grew even stronger. Christ. Sebastian suddenly felt like laughing. How could he ever have believed it was a secret?

'So she is?'

'What?' Sebastian opened his eyes.

'A synaesthete? Your sister?'

'Aha, yeah. Yes, she is. To the nth degree, I'm afraid.' Of course, Sebastian wanted nothing more than to discuss Matilda's symptoms and the potential connections between her synaesthesia and their messed-up family life with Travis, but by this point he'd learned that he had to approach things in the correct order if he wanted to get anywhere in his conversations with her. 'To put it mildly, she has a very complicated relationship with her senses. Primarily when it comes to colour. But Travis, can we focus, please? What exactly do you mean, Corrigan wants to get rid of the cicadas? What reason did he give for it?'

'No reason at all. Rationalisation. Lack of resources. That kind of bull.' Travis took a gulp of her second White Russian, wiped away a little cream from her upper lip, and picked up her phone. 'I don't even know why I'm surprised. He's already tried to set fire to them.'

'Are you really sure of that?' said Sebastian, who'd always doubted it had been Corrigan's doing that the cicadas — and Travis herself — had almost burned to death.

Travis snorted in response.

'Here,' she said, pushing the phone across after primly placing her thumb over the unlock key. 'If you're still in doubt that it was his doing. Here's the final correlate. Or the penultimate one, I reckon. I found it in Corrigan's office, just after he'd told me he intended to suspend my cicada project with immediate effect. He went to the toilet. Let me know he was constipated and would probably be there for at least twenty minutes. It was almost as if he *wanted* me to find it, and that he wanted me to know he wanted that. You get what an arsehole he is? He's playing with us, Sebastian, he has been the whole time.'

Sebastian looked down at the phone. It was a picture of a picture; a poster, it looked like. It was a dark image, grotesque.

'You know what painting it is?' asked Travis.

'It's Goya ...' Sebastian mumbled. For some reason he still wasn't sure of, he felt like he was going to vomit. *What I appreciate about Goya is that he wasn't afraid to paint it black.* How could he have been so blind? Larkin, for god's sake! And Woodman, all the photographs, the way she was hanging there, just hanging there! *Alight here for the Royal National Institute of Blind People.* And the soap bubbles, Laura blowing bubbles one evening, becoming a rainbow in his hand. Frank Auerbach devoting his life to painting Mornington Crescent. Somewhere inside Sebastian, a little snowball began to roll, faster and faster. *Haven't you figured out yet that he knows everything? Or at least everything that happens in the building.*

'Sebastian, hello? Where did you go? The image is called "Saturn Devouring His Son". Do you know why Saturn ate his own children? Because he was afraid of them. Just like Corrigan is afraid of you and me. This is a threat. He's going to destroy us, that's what he's saying. But do you know what I think? I think —'

Now he saw it all perfectly clearly. Now he saw what he hadn't been able to see, hadn't dared to see. That everything was connected, that Travis was right, that Matilda's appearance was not a coincidence, and neither was Clara's disappearance — that not even his insane love affair with the most beautiful, the most tragic woman in the world was. That he'd been so blinded by her smile he'd been incapable of seeing that both of them, he and Laura — no, all of them! — were just pawns in a strange game of indeterminate purpose and an as-yet-unclear ending.

'No. No, Jennifer. Listen.' He slammed his fist on the table. 'This isn't about you or me. Or your cicadas. Or even my sisters; at least, that's not all it's about.'

'What do you mean?'

Around a conference table on the top floor of the Institute, a plate of Jaffa cakes was circulating. By the Plaza de España, a square wine glass fell onto the cobblestones and smashed into a thousand pieces. A dog called Bernarda turned in her grave.

'Laura,' Sebastian whispered. 'It's about Laura and me. We're the last correlate.'

It took Sebastian a good while to explain to Travis what Laura Kadinsky, better known at the Institute as 'Woman Without Depth', had to do with anything. It wasn't until Sebastian swallowed his reticence, leaned across the table, and admitted, in a low voice, that he and Kadinsky had had, and possibly still were having, an *inappropriate relationship*, that the penny finally seemed to drop.

'Aha!' Travis exclaimed, turning her empty cocktail glass upside down on the table in triumph. 'Every mystery worthy of the name has a beautiful woman at its centre. *Cherchez la femme*, and all that. How could I have missed it … ?' And at that moment, there was nothing Sebastian could do but agree, because it was strange. That Laura's sudden arrival in his life had been the trigger for all the world's madness. That so many of the details of the shadow life they shared corresponded to Travis's correlates. That the very moral monkey had reacted so coldly to his attachment to Laura. He'd interpreted it as ordinary moral indignation at Sebastian's poor judgement, the absolute reprehensibility of his sleeping with a married woman in the hope — yes, he could admit it now — that she would one day leave her husband and child and make a fresh start with him. But maybe the fact was that the monkey had simply known something he hadn't wanted to admit. Somewhere in all this he'd believed Laura was the much-vaunted crack that lets the light in, but what if that wasn't the case; it was almost certainly not the case, almost certainly just madness and chaos that slipped through the crack torn by Laura's well-manicured nails in the depressive fog of his life.

Not that he believed that had been her intention. Or had it? The thought was unwelcome, yet he was forced to think it: was there a chance his whole relationship with Laura could have been some kind of *trap*? An act entirely orchestrated by Corrigan? But to what end?

'Sebastian?' said Travis, leaning forward, wiping his brow with the same napkin he'd given her to dry her tears with. 'Has your Laura got any conceivable connection to peacocks? Because I found this, too. Rolled up inside the poster. And I thought it couldn't be a coincidence.'

No, thought Sebastian, and picked up with trembling fingers the broken feather Travis had laid between them on the table — the very tip of a peacock feather, the deep blue eye, nauseatingly intense in the artificial bar light — no, it couldn't be a coincidence.

When Sebastian came home that evening it was to a sister on the verge of drowning in a sea of tears. The sight shocked Sebastian. Matilda was a bellower, not a weeper, and yet here she sat, sobbing in his tiny little bathroom, crying like a child who'd misplaced her most cherished possession. For a while, Sebastian was left standing in the bathroom doorway, a silent witness to something he instinctively sensed was deeply private. She was curled up on the lid of the toilet, legs against her stomach, forehead against her knees.

'Tilda? Tilda, what is it?' he said at last. 'Has something happened?'

She raised her tear-reddened face towards him, and it was her regular face, just puffier, wearier.

'I know what you're thinking, but I promise, I'm not having a relapse. It's the colour, Sebastian, the *colour*. It wants something from me. I thought I knew what, but now I'm not so sure. You know the first time I saw it? When she died. Violetta, I mean. At her funeral. What the fuck does it mean, Basse? Can you tell me?'

But he couldn't, didn't want to.

He made her some food in the little kitchenette, baked potatoes with knobs of butter melting over them and golden sweetcorn from a tin. He apologised for his poor culinary skills, but Matilda ate hungrily. Despite all the things he no longer knew about his sister, it was obviously still true that she preferred food that was the colour of sunshine. Sebastian thought that if she could live on forest resin, on floating amber, she'd probably never eat anything else.

He watched her as she ate. His beautiful, strong sister. He thought about the first time she'd told him about her synaesthesia. It was one evening just after she'd come home from Bangladesh, a year or so before she moved to Germany. She'd read about synaesthesia in a book by Siri Hustvedt, she said, and had realised for the first time what it was, but she'd always had it, as long as she could remember, and probably even before that, because when she'd asked Mama about it, she'd said that yes, Matilda had loved yellow things as a baby, especially the warm-yellow plastic tub she used to put on her head whenever she got her hands on it, which was often, since Matilda, unlike her siblings, was totally unafraid of crawling off, away from Mama's side. She'd always thought in colour, Matilda had said, opening the living room window in what had been their parents' house, and was now Mama's. It was May, and the lilacs were in bloom. Mama Isaksson was in the parish hall, Clara in Stockholm, Violetta curled up inside her own ribs. Matilda had climbed up onto the windowsill, lit an American Spirit, and handed the pale blue pack to Sebastian. Just a year later, Violetta would be dead and Matilda would be forced to swap to the gold ones, even if their filter was too fat for her taste: she couldn't even handle baby blue any more. But anyway, there she was, sitting in the window, her bare toes fluttering like eyelashes in the mild night, telling Sebastian about the wonderful colour palette of Bangladesh and how weird it was to come home to a house their father no longer lived in, but that it didn't surprise her either. Mama and Papa had never really suited each other, Matilda thought; the shades of their personalities clashed. You could see from the air around them.

At first, Sebastian had thought Matilda was high. It turned out she wasn't, because Matilda didn't start smoking weed until she moved to Berlin, and it was then that Sebastian realised Matilda really was a synaesthete and not just a regular hippie like he'd always thought. And what's more, her synaesthesia was multifaceted and hard to pinpoint. Like many colour synaesthetes, it was obvious to Matilda that numbers, letters, units of time, notes and sounds, and even the smallest components of language — the phonemes and the graphemes — had colours. But for Matilda it didn't stop there: feelings had colours too, and people, and physical sensations; even actions had colours, meaning they assumed a much more concrete form in Matilda's consciousness than in Sebastian's. For Matilda, a feeling or thought was something that could almost be touched.

The boundary between her interior world and the world outside was much less sharp than for other people. Sebastian had always thought it seemed beautiful and fascinating, maybe he'd even envied her ability. He'd always imagined her wading through a sea of coloured jewels.

But now he didn't know if it was something to envy.

'Is blue still hard for you?' he asked, when Matilda had put down her cutlery. She answered with a snort.

'Hard? It's absolutely bloody unbearable, seeing blue. It hurts. I mean it, really, physically. Inside my head, as if someone's cutting into my brain. It's so fucking exhausting, you have no idea.'

'But this other colour you were talking about,' Sebastian ventured. 'It's something else?'

'Yes, I told you. It's a colour that *doesn't exist.*'

'But you've seen it?'

'Loads of times. Ever since the funeral. But these last few months, since all this crap with you and me and Clara started, it's turned up more and more often. And everything's got worse, the blue too.'

She fell silent. Then she said:

'Have you thought about how blue her eyes were? It was hard for me to look her in the eye. But you've got to understand, I tried. I really tried, for your sake.'

Sebastian got up from the table and went into the kitchenette again, putting on the kettle just for something to do with his hands. He felt dizzy and nauseous. A new thought had struck him — perhaps that there'd always been a connection there, too, between Violetta's bright blue eyes and Matilda's violent inability to deal with that part of the colour spectrum.

'Tea or coffee?' he said.

'Tea, please. As insipid as possible.'

Over the last few weeks, Sebastian had been forced to reassess so many of the things he'd long taken for granted. Such as the idea that Violetta's death was something that really only concerned him, that the sorrow and the burden had been his and his alone to bear. Yes, he knew Matilda had liked her, in her own way, and that Clara hadn't, and that his mother had watched Violetta's shrinking body mass with worried eyes. He knew that her death had disturbed the already delicate dynamic in their family in some fundamental way, more even than their parents' divorce had. He knew that something had happened just afterwards which had appeared to destroy the last fragile thread between Clara and Matilda. But all this, he'd thought in his foolhardy way — to the extent he'd thought at all during that foggy time in which sorrow had consumed him from within — would probably have happened anyway. The only one whose life had been deeply impacted by Violetta's death, by the fact that she'd once existed and now no longer did, had been him. He was the one who'd loved her! He and only he. He was the one who'd let her down, who hadn't been able to save her. He'd been the one closing his eyes to the obvious in the hope it would go away.

He stopped, dropping the tea strainer into a cup with a clunk. But maybe, he thought, it wasn't only his life that had borrowed its colour from Violetta's. Maybe nothing was as simple or as complex as it looked at first glance. Maybe there were connections linking everyone on earth, in a pattern so intricate it made the billions of nerves in the brain look like the most rudimentary circuit board.

'Basse?' Matilda said to his back. 'I want you to take me on as a patient at the Institute. Or let me see someone else there. I can't live like this anymore.'

He stiffened. Deep down he had probably understood that this was what Matilda wanted, that this was why she'd come. He'd known it the moment she mentioned the peacock, even if he hadn't been able to see the connection then. The connections with everything. Clara, writing about peacocks in her letter. Tilda, Laura, and the Institute. Corrigan. Travis.

And him. The one who had to tie all these threads together, by force if necessary.

Sebastian could understand why Tilda thought the Institute was the solution to all her problems. Just like everyone who sought him out, she wanted to be fixed. Like everyone who sought out the Institute, she thought it was something in her brain that was the problem, something that with the right diagnosis and treatment could be corrected. And maybe that was the case. He, more than anyone, knew that Matilda's brain wasn't quite like other people's. But letting her into the Institute? Giving Corrigan yet another pawn in this strange game that he, for opaque reasons, had decided to stage, with Sebastian as his most important piece? No thanks.

Maybe he was paranoid, but he felt at this point that it was better to be safe than sorry. First, he had to get to the bottom of exactly how Corrigan fit into the picture.

'No,' he said. 'I can't take you into the Institute. It's not possible. Not now.'

Matilda didn't reply. Instead, there was only the sound of a chair scraping against the floor, a door slamming.

He turned around. Only her half-eaten dinner remained. A pool of golden butter slowly congealing into something inedible. He stood there, the cup of tea he'd made for her in one hand, and felt inexpressibly inadequate.

'What do you know about your brother's love life?'

Travis crossed her legs, set down her cracked willow-pattern teacup, and stared determinedly right into Matilda's eyes. Matilda recoiled instinctively. There was something mildly insane in this woman's gaze which, for a moment, made Matilda feel she was looking in a mirror. She'd seen that look before — in photos from the time before Bangladesh.

Sebastian thought she had it again. He wouldn't say it straight out, but she knew that was what he thought — that she wasn't taking her medication, that she'd opened the floodgates and let in the whole world, even though she knew full well she couldn't cope. But actually, Matilda suspected, it was the other way around. It was Sebastian who'd lost his grip. Why else would he trust Jennifer Travis, who, as far as Matilda could judge, couldn't tell her arse from her elbow?

When Travis, a few days after Sebastian had first said no to Matilda being examined at the Institute, had sent Matilda a text saying she wanted to meet up, Matilda had thought — wishful thinking, she realised now — that Sebastian had set her up with a consultation after all. He'd mentioned that Travis was the best they had, and Matilda had been glad that he apparently seemed to take her problems seriously. But she soon realised that Travis had her own agenda. They were meeting in some weird cafe in Dalston instead of at the Institute, and Matilda had been given strict instructions not to tell Sebastian about the meeting. Going behind her brother's back went against all her moral convictions — Sebastian was still the best person she knew — and Matilda had almost blown off the whole business.

But she'd come in the end. Out of curiosity, maybe, or ennui. London hated her, and she hated London. Over the last few days she'd done little but ride the Tube. The Circle Line, naturally, round and round on its yellow tracks. In the Underground it was easier to escape the colours. Easier to imagine she was back home in Berlin, too. If you squinted, the seats looked almost like the ones on the U7 between

Rudow and Spandau. She'd read poems by Philip Larkin, the only book besides academic literature that Sebastian had in his austere home, but they were shit. 'They fuck you up, your mum and dad.' *Yep, thanks, tell me something new.* She spent the evenings trying to convince Sebastian to let her be examined at the Institute. In all honesty, Matilda didn't quite know what they did at that place, and in her conversations with Sebastian she'd got the terrifying impression that he didn't really know either. Did Jennifer Travis? Doubtful, Matilda sensed as she sat there now in a sweaty velour armchair surrounded by dust and potpourri.

'Very little,' said Matilda, truthfully, in response to Travis's question about Sebastian's love life. 'He's quite plainly got something going on with someone, he positively radiates it — his aura, I mean. But I don't know who. I haven't seen anyone this week, in any case. I asked, but he denied it. Glowed magenta, like he always does when he lies. Why are you so interested? You're not in love with him.'

'No,' said Travis, leaning back with a sigh that in a more self-conscious person would have been theatrical. A cloud of dust spread round her head like a halo as her back thudded against the armchair. 'I'm incapable of love. On a purely biological-structural level, I mean. But I admire your brother, and I depend on order, and both of these things put together mean that I require information regarding his sex life. Sebastian has a patient named Laura Kadinsky — has he mentioned her?'

'No.' Matilda noticed, to her surprise, that she wished she'd had something to offer up, some little piece of information she could give to Jennifer Travis.

'She has a problem with depth perception,' Travis said. 'Can only see in two dimensions, and so can't orient herself spatially. But still, Sebastian is wildly in love with her, as far as I can ascertain.'

'Perhaps she has other qualities,' Matilda said acidly.

'What I don't know,' Travis went on, unmoved, 'is whether it's requited, and in that case, what it means. She's married.'

'And?'

'Sebastian doesn't strike me as the type who sleeps with married women just like that.'

'Then you don't know Sebastian. He's a slave to his feelings. And he's loyal, loyal as a dog. Or as a badger, maybe. Once he bites he doesn't let go until he hears the bones crack. And sometimes not even then. You know he had a girlfriend who took her own life?'

'No. I'm sorry.'

'She was anorexic. Hanged herself in the end, when she didn't have the strength to go on living. They'd been together for nine years. Nine years, you know? Sebastian was a child when they got together, and an old man when she finally put an end to it. I know it's terrible, but my first reaction when I found out was one of joy. I thought he'd be free from her, finally. The last years were so awful. He did everything for her, but it was never enough; he couldn't help her, but he couldn't see it. Healthy people don't understand it, that it's not about them, that there are things larger than your relationship to others. But I don't think he's free, not really. But then, who the fuck is? Not me, in any case, and not you, obviously. I should imagine we're both pretty far from nirvana, you and I.'

Travis got up from her armchair abruptly and brushed a heap of scone crumbs from her lap. Her eyes were inscrutable as she leaned over Matilda and quickly stroked her hair. It was only at close range that Matilda could see the real colour of Jennifer Travis's eyes. From a distance they seemed light brown, but now she could see they were actually yellow-gold with streaks of brown. Like amber. And in the centre of each eye — a delicate black pupil in the shape of a million-year-old insect. A mosquito? A fly? No. It was a cicada, one in each eye. Thousands of years of loneliness, times two.

'I want to show you something, downstairs,' Travis said in a serious tone. 'I just have to go and pee first. You might as well go down while you wait.' Matilda followed her instructions, with a sudden realisation that she'd do whatever Travis asked — for no other reason than that she could.

It was hard to know what it was Travis wanted her to see, cluttered with knick-knacks as the lower floor of the cafe was. Thankfully everything was faded, like the pictures in an old comic that had been in the attic for decades, otherwise Matilda would have had a minor brain haemorrhage — that was how it felt when it got too much, as though her brain were about to run out through her nose and down her throat to form a pool between her legs and behind her knees. To empty her completely, like a snakeskin, a used condom, a hat that had fallen off a head and was rolling, alone, down the street. My eyes, my eyes, tomorrow and tomorrow and tomorrow, a horse, a horse, my midriff for the chance to keep my brain — smack, she slapped herself on the cheek. Focus. Don't freak out again, letting your thoughts run away like that.

She let her eyes run across the objects. Somewhere far off there was the sound of a toilet flushing. No people here, it felt like a church, like the jumble sale in a barn in Ånäset where Billy had bought her a ring on their first day in Västerbotten. It was a skull ring, but still, it was a ring and it was round and it fit on her bony, sinewy ring finger and they didn't say all that much about it, mostly just laughed, it wasn't exactly a proposal, after all, but if it was then it was perfect and in the tatty restaurant they'd had butter mixed with Västerbotten cheese, as yellow and gooey as melted sun. But what was she meant to be looking at? The plastic flowers, apothecary's bottles, sconces with pearl screens. The film-star portraits in mahogany frames. A velvet red kippah on a spike. A foetus in formaldehyde. She blinked. The foetus did, blinked, and then Matilda, then she was gone and the jar was empty.

How could she have known it was a girl? How had she seen that in such a short time?

Because it was a projection, of course, she wasn't stupid; she looked at the empty jar with its film of grease. Christ. Soon Bernarda would come lolloping in, too. The skull ring cut into her finger. Footsteps approached like soft, barely perceptible waves in the pistachio-green carpet. One hand on her shoulder, the other pointing — there! She felt her muscles stiffen, her body arcing and flexing and cracking at the unexpected touch of another person. Her skin had become so tight and dry, like the perfumed stationery she used to steal from Clara just because she could. Everything that had meant something to her in life, Matilda thought feverishly, had made her body tense up in an arc, a sliver of moon, a bridge, between earth and sky. Love, the sun, death. Murder? Was that what it was? Yes, maybe. But why was she thinking about that now? Ugh, cry-baby, self-pitying little bitch, said the maybe-baby in her belly, you know why you're thinking that, it's because Jennifer Travis is pointing her unexpectedly well-manicured finger at a box of LPs, a box that is a coffin small enough to contain the sorrow and guilt of the entire world.

'Why are you showing me that?' Matilda whispered.

'Do you recognise it?' Travis asked, almost excited.

'Who even are you?' Matilda asked, still whispering. 'How could you *know?*'

'Sebastian told me.'

Matilda shook her head.

'Sebastian doesn't know. No one knows, apart from J.'

'Who's J?' Travis asked.

'Someone who loved me. Who loved the whole world. I used to call him Jesus. He never told me what he was really called. Just J. Sometimes I think he really was Jesus. He was thirty-three. What are you doing? Are you writing this down?'

Travis had indeed taken her phone out of her pocket and started tapping away at it.

'Have you got anything against it? I have an awful lot of information to keep track of right now; I don't want to miss anything.'

'Record it, then.'

'May I?'

'Yeah.'

She'd never loved J; at least, she didn't believe she had. But she was lonely, and he was sexy, and she loved fucking in the sunshine. It was when she was in Bangladesh. Two years she was there, on the same project — a girls' school outside Jessore. J didn't work there, of course; there were only women at the school. He worked on an agriculture project, the exact purpose of which she never really got to the bottom of. Their affair was short and intense and ended in tears, but while it lasted they laughed a lot, they laughed nearly all the time. She met him when she'd been in Jessore for more than a year, on a training day on sexual violence. That itself was crazy, Matilda thought later, that she'd sat there in a hot, sweaty room, listening to a woman talking about how she'd been raped as a thirteen-year-old and had to give birth to a baby in breech, and all she could think about was the fact that she wanted the man sitting next to her to take her by the hand and lead her behind a hut and fuck her till the sun went down. And that was what happened, more or less. He was an American, well over six feet tall, broad as a fridge. He had brown eyes, like hazelnuts, and a beard that scratched the inside of her thighs. She thought he was from Vermont, or maybe Maine — he was a little unclear on that point, but he talked a lot about the leaves and their colours, how beautiful the fall was where he lived. About children in woolly hats who chucked their backpacks into piles of leaves and rolled around like animals. It was September when they started hanging out, and he missed the air's crisp chill, he said. But that it was worth it, any sacrifice was worth it, when you were doing the right thing. There was a way out, he said, for the whole of humanity, as long as everyone rolled up their sleeves and did some thinking. Some fresh thinking. Our planet is a paradise, he used to say, but we don't make the most of it. He was an uncomplicated optimist, convinced that, at base, humanity was capable of looking past short-term gains — all it needed was a nudge in the right direction. For him, the work they were doing was about that — not doing penance for your own guilt (quite honestly, Matilda didn't think he knew what guilt felt like), but setting a good example. She thought it was simultaneously cute and stupid, but extremely restful. He was good for her, made her feel less bad. And he loved sex and food, and cigarettes and clear, starry nights, and he believed in eternal life. He was kind and friendly to everyone, and when a cicada flew into his room at night and started playing, he took it in his cupped hands and let it out, rather than killing it.

They'd been together — or whatever the word was, they were never that bothered about defining it — for four months when she fell pregnant. Though it was another four months before she realised it. Matilda's periods had been weird for years, her psychiatrist back home in Lund had told her it was stress-related, and she was too busy to notice that it didn't come. Admittedly, they weren't that careful about protection. Condoms were hard to come by and, quite frankly, she'd thought she was the type who wouldn't be able to have children, that nature would have kind of seen to it that someone like her wouldn't be able to pass on her genes. So, after a while, they got a little sloppy, mostly he came on her body, but sometimes inside. Still, she never thought ... He was the one who realised. They'd had a day off, on the same day for once, and had taken the bus to a village by the shore of the Bhairab river. She'd taken off all her clothes apart from her underpants and walked out into the yellowish-brown water. He'd sat on the shore and looked at her in a peculiar way. She'd thought she was beautiful, that that was why. She was beautiful. But her stomach was also slightly rounded, her breasts large and heavy, and between her navel and the waistband of her underpants ran a thin brown line, almost invisible against her tanned skin.

After that it all went very quickly, it had to. Fifteen weeks already, said the doctor they found. She took some time off and flew home. Or, not home; she flew to Stockholm, because she didn't have it in her to explain to her mother, the tender of souls. She didn't want to have her soul tended, she wanted to lie in a white room with machines beeping around her and have a chance to come to terms with the fact that she herself was about to become a mother. That was what she'd thought, anyway. She thought she wanted it, she believed she did.

But then she didn't want it anymore.

Not when they said the child wasn't healthy.

They saw at once that something was wrong with its heart. The doctor drew a picture of it, of the chambers and valves and walls that didn't quite meet, but the only thing Matilda really understood from it all was that the baby's heart was back-to-front, that almost everything in the child was back-to-front, and that it wasn't good. Most of it would still function, they said, but the heart would be tricky. The heart was a problem. Operations would be needed. It would be touch-and-go. The outcome was uncertain, but there was reason to be tentatively hopeful. And there was always abortion.

They told her to think about it, but she said no, she didn't need to think. She decided then and there, before they'd even wiped the transparent goo from her stomach. They thought she shouldn't rush into an abortion, there was still time to think, but no. There was something wrong with this baby because there was something wrong with her. How would she be able to take care of a child with those needs? And suddenly she realised it didn't matter anyway: illness or no illness, she couldn't subject a child to herself. She was bipolar, she knew that. She was also a nasty, egotistical person. So she'd make that sacrifice, she thought, she'd get rid of the baby and do it a favour. She was at eighteen weeks by this point, so she was just in time to do it without applying for permission. She thought she sensed that the doctor felt she was making a cruel, rushed decision, but there was nothing she could say, Matilda had the right to do it. The legal right. And she did it, three days later. She got two pills to swallow to stop the pregnancy, waddled around Stockholm for two days, then went back.

They stuffed more tablets up inside her and injected some morphine into her leg. Five hours later the pains started. They said it would be like giving birth, though not as bad, but of course Matilda had never given birth, so she didn't understand: how much it would hurt, and how it could possibly be worse. When her waters broke she was on her own in the toilet, vomiting into the sink from the morphine. She felt the water running down her legs and was terrified that the baby was going to come right away, it was so little after all, she thought it would just slide out like a fish and land on the floor and then she'd have to pick it up and look at it, or at least step over it to get out. She rang the alarm but it took a quarter of an hour before anyone came; the midwife was busy with a real birth in the next room, a baby who would live and help in the creation of a paradise on earth. She asked whether Matilda felt like she wanted to push. She replied that she felt like she wanted to die. Then the midwife asked if she felt like she needed to poo. Matilda looked at her and felt like she hated her. Which was deeply unfair, of course. And then she felt like she needed to poo and then she pushed, she assumed, and after ten minutes it was as though someone pulled out a stopper and all her innards ran out.

She stared directly into a light as they carried it away. She thought they put it in some kind of box. They asked if she wanted to see it. Then she threw a bedpan at the wall. They asked her if she wanted to know what sex it was. She said no. Then the next day they brought along her notes for her to take home and the notes said what sex it was anyway. It was a girl.

Afterwards she thought about how they'd asked a lot of questions, but not who the father was, and not why she was there on her own, without even her mother, even though she was only twenty-four, without her sister who should have been there to hold her hand. It was as though they thought it would have been impolite or something. Instead they asked if she was in pain, and if she wanted painkillers, and if she was hungry. She wasn't, she was just tired. She was given a drip to make her uterus contract and tablets to stop her milk production, and then they finally left her in peace. And the worst thing, the absolute worst, the thing she returned to again and again when she woke in the night and her thoughts clambered back to that point in time, the point in time when she realised she was rotten to the core, someone who could get rid of a living thing and then tell herself it was for the sake of the child, when really, the whole time it had been about her, that she wasn't ready, the worst thing was the way she felt when it was all over, when the lights were switched off, and the drip machine beeped and the last traces of morphine rocked her to sleep. She felt euphoric. Happy. Safe. She felt invincible.

Of course, the feeling didn't last. The tears came, and the anguish, and then more tears, when she decided not to go back to Bangladesh, or to J. She sent an email, that was all. Told it like it was, that the baby had been sick and didn't exist anymore and that he should forget it all, forget her. She went home to Lund, lived for a while in the big house in Professorsstaden. Then Sebastian's girlfriend died. Then she had a massive fight with her sister, Clara. Then she moved to Berlin and started over. Then she hit a child.

And now here she was.

Jennifer Travis, twenty-nine years old, fluttering butterfly, brilliant beyond a shadow of a doubt but without the merest trace of a soul, felt confused. She hadn't asked for confidences, she barely knew what confidences were, but still, here she was with the shadow of a dead baby in her hands, a dead girlfriend on the wall, and no real strategy with which to handle any of it. When Matilda finished her story and looked at her almost beseechingly, as though awaiting some response, it was obvious to Jennifer that Sebastian's sister didn't have anything informative to say about anything, much less the Francesca Woodman photograph Corrigan — of course it must have been Corrigan — had had hung here.

It was almost funny, thought Jennifer, gently patting Matilda's hand as she'd seen people do on TV, how differently people saw the world. Here they were, sitting in front of the Woodman photo, surrounded by things that were each a portal to a whole world order, and Matilda hadn't even noticed any of it, because another thing, the little coffin, had been the opportunity she'd been seeking to get some things off her chest, just like everybody, at every moment, is looking for opportunities to talk about themselves. For Matilda it obviously meant something that the little white coffin was in this precise place. For Jennifer it was a coincidence, a parenthesis.

But anyway, that wasn't what most astonished Jennifer. The thing that really put her in a thoughtful mood was what she felt when she touched Matilda's hand; to be honest, the same thing she'd felt the moment she first caught sight of her in the cafe. It was a feeling — actually, the sum of several different feelings — that she'd never felt before.

She realised it was *love*.

It was quite evidently love: in spite of everything, Jennifer had examined the patterns of love so many times she could have sketched its many variants and their matrices in her sleep, or by ear, or upside down in an anti-gravity chamber.

This was love, and it was, in its very spontaneity, its unexpected, thunderous arrival, as predictable as death.

Jennifer Travis had read in a poetry book once about love being 'eternally new', but you could feel that way only if you'd never looked up from the detail to see the big picture. Jennifer lived for the big picture, always had.

'What are you thinking about?' asked Sebastian's sister, this woman she appeared to be in love with, even though she'd known her less than an hour.

This was obviously interesting.

This was obviously something that shook Jennifer's whole outlook.

'Come on,' she said to Matilda, pulling her up off the sofa, leading her up the stairs, through the ethereal filth, out onto Balls Pond Road where the pigeons were hopping around in their own shit, and people were queuing up to buy jerk chicken or sourdough toasties for lunch. Matilda stopped behind two kids with colourful elastics at the ends of all their thousands of thin braids and rubbed her eyes. She seemed troubled, by the light, perhaps?

Quite frankly, Jennifer felt bewildered. They stood in silence for a moment, watching the world go by. The buses on Kingsland Road screeched. The plastic bags from Poundland rolled full of air across the pavements like irregular turquoise balls. The espresso machines hissed in rounds. Two drops of rain fell from a solitary cloud above a bench outside Dalston Junction station. A policeman chewed chewing gum. An old woman bought a sponge cake from Déjà Vu Bakery and threw it whole at the birds. A spider crept across the saddle of a bright red bicycle, a fixie that was chained to the element of an abandoned fridge. It's the same world as it's always been, Travis thought. And yet it was new, because *she* was new.

A new person.

No, a person, nothing more, nothing less. A human!

Jennifer almost started laughing. For the first few years after she'd discovered that she wasn't a human being like everyone else, she'd tried to convince herself that it wasn't a question of species, but a question of degree. She'd convinced herself that a human was really nothing more than an algorithm, a blend of mathematics and materials, a beautiful machine. But there was a difference between saying something and really believing it. Deep down, Jennifer Travis had always cherished a belief in the soul, both in theory and in practice.

It was just that she herself had never got one.

In the end she'd come to terms with it. She'd learned to live with being merely a big — and admittedly rather complicated — equation swathed in biodegradable wrapping paper.

But if you can experience love, Jennifer thought, feeling her heart rate quicken, you are experiencing something that really is completely and utterly illogical, that can't be explained as anything less irrational than the wingbeats of the soul.

Matilda nudged her arm.

'Where are we going, anyway?' she asked.

'To the Institute!' Jennifer said confidently. That seemed to make Matilda happy. Which in turn made Jennifer happy. This love business! It was fantastic!

'The Institute? So you're going to examine me?' said Matilda.

'Yes,' Jennifer said. 'It's absolutely essential. But first you have to help me with Kadinsky.'

One mustn't lose one's head, thought Jennifer, hailing a bus, just because one suddenly turns out to have a soul.

At last there came a text from Madrid. Laura wrote: *I had a dream and in the dream you were a beautiful criminal.* He wrote back: *What was my crime?* And she replied: *Loving me when you shouldn't have.* And that was all. Then she didn't write again. And he wished he'd been able to show the texts to the very moral monkey. He thought she would have looked happy for the first time. Relaxed. As though something wrong had finally been put right. It was the past tense, Sebastian thought. The monkey would have been lulled by the grammar. As though Sebastian had put his crime behind him just because Laura had written in the past tense. As though this whole mess would be over if it were true, if it were true that he no longer loved her.

And maybe he didn't. He felt just as unsure about that as he did about whether it had ever been true, that what he'd felt, and still did feel, for Laura Kadinsky, the saddest woman in the world, was love. Love. What a fucking abstract concept. He said this to the imaginary monkey, no, shouted it at the monkey, waving the phone like a maraca: *Love is a fucking abstract concept, you know, love doesn't exist in material form and can neither be weighed, measured, nor judged by eye. How do you relate to something like that?*

But the monkey wasn't there, so who was going to reply.

Madrid. Autumn sun and oranges, azaleas and Velázquez. Laura Kadinsky walked alone through the half-empty galleries of the Prado Museum and was almost happy. Almost. But not quite. Laura Kadinsky was never quite happy, and probably never would be. It was, she thought, as she carefully set down one heel after the other on the cool marble floor, her cross to bear. It wasn't easy to be human when you couldn't even be happy in the Prado Museum.

She breathed a heavy sigh and stepped out into the foyer, where Philip and Chloe were playing hide-and-seek in the staffed cloakroom. Had he bribed the attendant? Laura could only guess. The doors of the main entrance were open to the lush park beyond and Laura sensed the soft, mild evening to come.

'Mummy!'

Chloe extricated herself from what appeared to be a very expensive trench coat and threw herself into Laura's arms. She was hot and excited and Laura Kadinsky was almost happy. Almost.

Later that evening. Chloe had fallen asleep right across the wide hotel bed, and Laura and Philip sat on the balcony drinking wine. The cars buzzed like insects on the street below.

'Philip, I'm sick,' Laura said.

'I know,' he said.

She looked at her husband. She wasn't even surprised.

'So you know. And still you haven't done anything to help me,' she said.

'I thought you were getting all the help you needed,' Philip said.

'What's that supposed to mean?'

But Philip didn't reply. Beyond the dome of fumes and city lights, the stars lit up, one by one, invisible. Philip put his hand in his pocket and got out his cigarillos.

'No one can have everything, Laura,' he said at last, blowing a smoke ring into the night. 'Not even you.'

The first cicada was born of desire. Specifically, from the goddess of the dawn Eos's wish to satisfy her desire, once and for all. Eos loved Tithonus, who was going to die, because he was human and that's what humans do. They die. So Eos asked Zeus to make Tithonus immortal. Be my guest, said Zeus, but because Eos had forgotten to specify that she wanted her lover eternally young, Zeus skipped that detail.

It was a blow to Eos, who found herself saddled with a very old man, an old man who refused to die. He grew ugly, crippled, wrinkly, hunchbacked; he grew smaller and smaller, dried up like an old apple core. In the end he was so little, Eos could hold him in her hand.

Then something fantastic happened.

Eos discovered that Tithonus had been reborn, a beautiful little insect. Like a piece of jewellery. He shone like gold, and Eos was happy after all, given the circumstances. She could carry her lover around in her pocket, put him on a gold chain, and hang him around her divinely beautiful divine throat.

She ran her finger over his glittering carapace.

But then Tithonus unfurled his wings and flew away.

And then there she was again, standing like a quivering exclamation mark. Her shadow fell across his hands, stopping their sleepwalker's movements across the wireless keyboard. Sebastian could hear the very moral monkey bleating in frustration from wherever she was, banging her head against the bars of her vanished cage. Slowly he turned around in his chair and met Laura's gaze.

'I didn't think you'd come back,' he said, without standing up. Laura stepped into the office and shut the door behind her.

'I've got an appointment.'

'But still. I'd been planning to spend the free time playing squash with Benedict. We've got a full squash court on the third floor.'

She sat down on his desk with her hands folded primly in her lap. He remembered that her shoulders were two white shells in which he could hear the sea. He remembered the way he'd pressed his ear against them and heard a heart beating that was neither his nor hers, but the moon's. He remembered that he'd touched the hollow where her skull met her neck and thought it was the most intimate part of the human body, blushing to think she'd let him touch it. He remembered that Laura sounded like a rabbit when she was aroused. He remembered that she liked open fires and high-heeled shoes and the Prado Museum, where he'd never been.

Aside from that he remembered precisely nothing. The three weeks in which Laura had been physically absent from his life melted together into a little marble he could put in his pocket and forget about. She was here and she was beautiful — a little world in miniature, a doll's house to get lost inside, a glossy magazine to flick through ad infinitum. Laura lifted her hands, they were trembling, she fumbled after his face, he brought it closer to her and helped her find her way to his cheeks.

'You've got worse,' he said, ashamed that it made him feel pleased. But why should he be ashamed? Don't we all want to feel needed? Don't we all want our presence to mean something to another?

'Say my name,' Laura asked, resting her forehead on his.

'I don't know if I can help you,' Sebastian whispered, feeling suddenly that he was quite simply going to pieces. 'And I don't know if I can deal with not being able to help you.'

'Just say my name,' Laura said, stubborn.

'Laura Kadinsky?'

She smiled, her face so close to his that he could see her pearl-white teeth and the sorrowful crow's feet in the corners of her eyes. And she replied:

'Here.'

After they'd made love under his desk, quick and efficient and with no extravagances, Sebastian showed her the pictures of her brain he'd spent so much time studying.

'It's beautiful,' Laura said, astonished by the brilliance of the colours. 'Like a soap bubble.'

'It's exceptionally beautiful,' Sebastian said.

Laura straightened her skirt, ran her fingers through her hair, and sat with surprising precision on the chair Sebastian had pulled level with his. She reached out a finger and reverently touched the screen where a mosaic of brain scans formed an intricate pattern that was all of her.

'The problem,' Sebastian said with a deep sigh, 'is that it's also exceptionally normal.'

'You know that's not true,' said Laura, drawing back her hand. 'You know I'm a deeply disturbed person.'

'That doesn't mean you have a disturbed brain, Laura.'

She gave a loud, harsh laugh.

'So what does it mean, then? That I have a disturbed ... what? Soul?'

Sebastian shrugged.

'I don't know. Laura, I've tried. I've stared and stared at these scans but I can't see anything. I can't see what's wrong. From a purely neurological perspective, you're perfect.'

'A purely neurological perspective,' she repeated, affronted.

'As far as I can tell, that is. But I'm just one person, Laura, and honestly, my skills and experience are limited. You're my first genuinely complex subject, and I … I need help. So I was thinking of asking my colleague Jennifer to help. If that's okay with you, that is. She's brilliant, you know, Nobel material …'

'Does she know …'

'No,' Sebastian lied. 'Or, she knows that you … that I … that you function properly when you're with me. But that's all.'

Laura sighed and rested her chin on her hand. With the other she picked bobbles off her wool skirt.

'I don't know, Sebastian. Maybe I'm just hysterical? Philip thinks I am. He thinks it would help if we had another child. I think that seems like a really bad idea.'

'Have you …'

'Told him? Yes. I told him everything in Madrid. Well, not that I'm sleeping with you, but everything else. It was good. We came closer to each other than we'd been in a long time. Then he started talking about me maybe being hysterical, and of course that ruined everything. I told him that hysteria was an unbelievably outdated diagnosis, and did he really think it was my uterus that was causing me to be incapable of relating to anything but a hamster in three dimensions? And do you know what he said?'

'No,' Sebastian said flatly.

'"Yes," he said, full stop. "That's as conceivable as anything, where you're concerned." And he wanted to get me pregnant there and then. I didn't remind him that I have a coil. Now he thinks I'm probably pregnant and happy and he's even more pleased with himself than usual — if that's even possible. And now here you are telling me my brain is perfectly normal. What am I to believe? Sebastian, what am I to do?'

'We have to talk to Jennifer,' Sebastian repeated, banging his fist on the table in an imitation of agency.

Laura saw it and her heart bled out over her blouse. She realised that she liked the fact Sebastian was a person who tried but failed. That he, just like she, was someone who stumbled on the finish line over and over but still managed with touching dignity to get up and continue.

'Okay,' she said, placing her hands around his clenched fist, which reminded her, more than anything else, of a freshly baked croissant. 'Okay, let's talk to Jennifer. But you have to tell her everything. I can't bear to live without witnesses any longer.'

The day after Sebastian's and Laura's flesh had been reunited, they stood outside the door of Travis's office. Sebastian clasped Laura's hand. It was so very cold, as if the blood didn't quite reach her fingertips.

'Ready?' he asked.

He looked at her, saw her silent nod as she carefully rearranged her facial features — becoming someone else, someone harder.

He let go of her hand and knocked on the door.

'Sebastian! And … Laura Kadinsky, I take it?'

Laura put her hand out politely, but Travis didn't shake it; instead she waved them inside and shut the door behind them.

'Exceptional timing. I was just telling Matilda it would be fun to meet the woman in question, and now here you are, right on cue.'

Sebastian's eyes had been on Laura's outstretched hand, but when he heard his sister's name, he looked up. And there, in a chair beside Travis's desk, sat Matilda, hugging her knees with electrodes on her hands. She rested her head on the knees and gave Laura a curious look.

'What are you doing here?' Sebastian asked, casting a severe look in Travis's direction. They'd agreed, hadn't they? That Matilda would be kept out of this for the time being.

'I've taken your sister on as a little side project,' Travis said cheerfully. 'On her own initiative, I must add.'

'Does Corrigan know about this?'

'I assume so. I haven't told him, but that means nothing, as you know. So, to what do we owe the pleasure? Laura Kadinsky, here in my office … The Woman Without Depth.'

Laura wrinkled her nose in displeasure.

'That's what they call you in the canteen,' Travis said. 'But don't be upset. I didn't have a soul for a long time, and I get along quite well.'

She looked Laura up and down and then walked around her body as if to check she had a back side.

'For a correlate she's surprisingly vacant,' she muttered. 'But I'm still glad you brought her.'

Laura looked at Sebastian quizzically, and he felt obliged to intervene.

'In all honesty,' he said, taking a firm grip on Travis's arm, 'I'm not progressing that well with Laura's case. In fact, I'm getting nowhere. *That's* why we're here. Her history is clear, as, to some extent, is the ... er ... treatment method. But the underlying causes escape me. And the treatment is becoming less and less effective. In other words, the resistance of the pathology is increasing, to put it one way, and, well ... we need your help, Travis. I need your help. Cards on the table, full access to the case notes, all you need to do is help me, and everything's yours.'

'Cards on the table? What does that mean?' Travis said, shaking off Sebastian's hand.

'What he's trying to say is that we're sleeping together,' Laura said, drumming her fingers on the shade of Travis's desk lamp. 'There, I said it. Can we move on now?'

'Pff, we know that little detail,' said Travis, with a glance at Matilda. 'And as far as case notes are concerned, I have them. You really should find a better password, Sebastian. Really.'

Sebastian and Laura looked from Travis to Matilda, then at each other, then out of the window. There was a bang as a bird flew into the windowpane and fell like snow to the ground. Laura jumped.

'You get used to it,' Sebastian said, raking a sweaty hand through his hair. It was always hot in Travis's office, owing to the fact that she kept three of her most valuable cicadas in a terrarium in the corner. There was a soft whirring. Sebastian looked once again at Matilda, who was still sitting there by the table, quietly observing.

'Travis,' he said slowly. 'Have you dragged my sister into this?'

'This is partly about your family, Sebastian, so it didn't feel beyond the pale. And on top of that, I'm in love with her.'

'Unrequited,' Matilda filled in. 'Just to clarify.'

'Isn't that good news?' Travis said, taking Sebastian's face in her hands. Laura muttered something inaudible. Matilda laughed. Sebastian felt dizzy.

'I'm a human being, Sebastian! With feelings! Isn't that wonderful?' Travis crowed, before letting go of Sebastian's cheeks, going back to her desk, and sitting down.

'Fabulous,' Sebastian mumbled in confusion. 'But what were you saying about Laura's notes? Have you been looking at them?'

'Since day one, Sebastian,' said Travis, taking the electrodes off Matilda's hands. 'But I wasn't really interested until you came up with the idea that you might be the final correlate. Matilda has been helping me. Her relationship with colours is genuinely *exceptional.*'

'My sister is a synaesthete,' Sebastian said to Laura. 'She's recently invented a new colour. You could say. She can see a colour that doesn't exist.'

'That's so childish,' said Laura. 'It's not even possible.'

Matilda cleared her throat. 'Can you stop talking about me like I'm not here? And as far as the colour goes —'

She was interrupted by a loud, happy laugh, almost a warble, from Travis. Laura had leaned across the table to take a look at a picture — a Francesca Woodman, of course — that Travis had taped to the edge of her computer screen, and a sliver of gold had fallen from the neck of her blouse. It was the necklace that had made Travis laugh like a bird with a beak full of worms — because dangling from Laura's pale throat was an eighteen-carat gold cicada, a *Cicada orni*, with its chubby stripy body and the most delicate of golden wings. Laura clutched the necklace and hissed:

'What is it?'

'Where did you get that?' Travis asked, not taking her eyes off the clenched fist in which Laura hid the pendant.

'I was given it by my husband. What does that matter?'

'When?'

'A few weeks ago. He bought it for me in Spain. He's the kind of man who thinks women should be given jewellery at regular intervals. I tend to think so too, so I accepted it. In spite of everything.' At this point Laura shot a look at Sebastian, who was also struggling to tear his eyes from her hand. There was something in the way she held the pendant, as though it were the sensitive skull of a newborn baby. Strength and gentleness. Boundless care.

Travis leaned back in her chair and raised her eyes to Laura's part-perplexed, part-offended face.

'Do you know you have one of these in your brain?' she asked.

'A what?' said Laura, instinctively bringing her hands to the sides of her skull.

'A cicada. Like the one you have round your neck. Like the ones in the tanks there. The world's most beautiful insect, if you ask me.'

'In … in my brain?' The blood drained from Laura's face. 'L-living inside?' she said with the back of one hand pressed against her mouth.

Jennifer Travis laughed.

'Are you crazy? I don't mean a real one, you know. An insect in your brain? Good god, even Sebastian would have noticed if you had an insect in your brain. I mean the pattern. Look at this. You too, Sebastian.'

She opened a cupboard behind her and tossed a heap of fMRI images on the desk. Sebastian reached for the pile and ran the tips of his fingers over the scan at the top.

'I've looked at these so, so many times, Travis. If there's something you've seen, tell me straight out; I'm not going to see anything new in any of these pictures.'

'I'm sure you're right. The problem is that I don't think you've looked at them together.'

'Of course I have,' Sebastian muttered bullishly.

'Okay, okay.' Travis held up her hands and nodded at Matilda, who dutifully stood up, picked up the pile, and walked over to the empty wall.

'Of course you've looked, compared, perhaps. But not in the right way,' Travis said. She cleared her throat and went on: 'It's actually very simple, unbelievably simple. After all, the number of combinations of sixteen parts in a four-by-four grid is limited. Then, of course, we had the correlates, which sped everything up a bit … but still, Sebastian, Sebastian. Still.' Travis tucked her hair behind her ears and looked over at Matilda, who'd begun to put the pictures up on the wall in a four-by-four square.

'Matilda was the first person to see it. It's yellow, you see, and you know how she is with yellow, am I right. She's drawn to that shit like a fly to the very same. So, she started playing around a bit, and —'

Travis made a sweeping gesture at the same moment Matilda put up the last two colourful scans of Laura's brain, and a short silence sliced through the room — not even the cicadas were singing. Then there was an astonished squeak from Laura, a bewildered whistling from Sebastian's nostrils, a contented gurgle from Travis. A window blew open and the cicadas in the corner started chirping louder than before, perhaps because of a recognition so subtle it could be characterised as animal magnetism.

Because unfurling on the wall was a pattern that had taken wing. The ordinarily flickering images of the brain's wave motions, caught and frozen in sixteen moments no longer than the blink of an eye, moments separated by days or weeks, now created an aurora of colour on the wall. The rapeseed-yellow field representing aspects of Laura's brain activity — in other words, aspects of the only thing that actually separated Laura from a dandelion or any other form of less soulful living matter — together formed the contours of a cicada with outstretched wings, identical in every detail to the one she wore round her throat.

'It's incredible,' Matilda said. 'Cool, right? I think it's her prana. Her life force, I mean.'

'Call it what you like, it's there,' said Travis.

'But what — what does it mean?' Sebastian asked, taking a step towards the wall, which seemed to him to be almost fluorescing.

'Fuck knows,' Travis said. 'But I'm starting to think you're right in that you and Laura are the final correlate.'

The only person who didn't say anything was Laura. Her lack of reaction made the other three turn in one movement towards her. She was backing towards the door, and had one hand on the door handle and the other locked, once again, around her necklace. She looked like she did when she was about to cry, Sebastian thought.

But instead she tore open the door and ran out.

Two seconds passed before he heard a crash, and a shriek. When they came out into the corridor, they found Laura sitting on the floor —

blood was pouring from a cut in her forehead and one of her shoes had gone flying. Beside her was a cage, in the cage sat a monkey, shrieking.

It was the very moral monkey.

'I tripped over that,' Laura said in a faraway voice, waving vaguely at the cage. 'Why did someone put it there?'

It wasn't until Sebastian crouched in front of Laura and brushed the hair from her forehead that she felt the pain and saw the blood. It was dripping between her outstretched fingers like water in a cave. She gently touched her forehead with the fingers of one hand, found the gash, and pressed her fingers against it. When she realised that the pain wasn't primarily coming from there, but from her heart and her self-image, she finally stopped crying.

'Oh, Sebastian ... It's over. Is it over? Say it's not over,' she whispered quietly so the others wouldn't hear.

'Hush, don't speak. There, there. Come here.'

He drew her in close, laying the uninjured part of her face against his white coat. She felt him press something, a handkerchief maybe, hard and determinedly against the cut on her forehead. They sat like that for a while, and when she looked up the others were gone, as was the monkey in its cage. Sebastian helped her get up, without letting go of the handkerchief.

'Come on,' he said. 'Let's get you a plaster.' Laura took the handkerchief and he helped her to his office at the other end of the corridor. How many times had Laura walked, reeled, run, or staggered towards that door? Would this really be the last time? It seemed unthinkable, like going on holiday and being unable to imagine being in any other place. You know, of course, that soon you'll come home and that when you do the days, or weeks, or even months that have just passed will shrink down to a little parenthesis, nothing but a crack in time.

Sebastian helped her into a chair and went to get a first-aid kit from the cupboard. Laura automatically looked around for the monkey, but it wasn't here either. One of the others must have taken it somewhere. She breathed a sigh of relief — she'd never liked that monkey, or the way it stared at her like she was a war criminal. Sebastian returned with the first-aid kit, took out an antiseptic wipe, and set to cleaning around the wound, where the blood had just begun to congeal. It stung, and she gripped the edge of the chair to stop herself batting away his hand.

'You should get this stuck together,' he said, concerned. 'It's quite deep.'

'Just tape it up,' said Laura.

'You'll have a scar.'

'So much the better. It will be a reminder of our bitter end.'

Sebastian stopped wiping. His hand slowly dropped to his side and hung there like a wet rag.

'Why do you say that?' he asked.

Laura didn't answer the question. Instead she looked out of the window. Dusk was beginning to fall. Soon the moon would rise over the buildings, like a big yellow cheese. Or maybe it would be a different shape. Maybe it would have eyes and a mouth, like in Chloe's picture books, and the moon would smirk. Maybe it would turn its back and there would just be one big crater, a sinkhole, a magician's hat. Nothing felt impossible anymore, and nothing felt possible. Maybe God existed. Maybe she really was a happy person.

She turned back to Sebastian, who was still standing there, dismayed and insanely beautiful in the half-dark. She suddenly felt the urge to ask something that had been gnawing at her for weeks.

'Have you saved my messages? My emails?'

'Yes.'

'Good. I can't bear the thought that nothing of this would be left. It would feel like it had never existed.'

'Why does it suddenly feel like you're bidding me farewell?' said Sebastian. He sounded wonderfully desperate. 'Are you?'

'Do you have copies of what you sent to me as well? I haven't saved anything, as I'm sure you can understand. With Philip in mind. It's Adultery 101 that you can't be sentimental.'

'I don't want to say farewell, Laura.'

'Me neither. I want it to go on like this forever. You and me and an eternal life in between. But it's not me, not us, who gets to decide, don't you understand that?'

She reached out to take his hand and raise it to her forehead again, but he backed away. She couldn't interpret his expression, couldn't read his body, never had been able to, she realised now. Perhaps she'd never really wanted to. He was at his most beautiful when he moulded himself around her trembling hands. Now, as he pulled away, drew up his shoulders, averted his eyes, he was like a stubborn child who's realised for the first time that they don't have to do what they're told. It drove her crazy and it drove her to despair. She pressed her hands against the sides of her head and made her voice as small as possible — she knew from her training with Chloe that the best way to win over someone who's in revolt against what they perceive as an autocratic attitude is to bare one's throat. She almost whispered:

'You saw it, didn't you? What was in my brain?'

He turned around. She held out the gold pendant she wore round her throat.

'This. This is in my brain. Don't you get what that means?'

'No,' Sebastian said. 'Do you?'

'It means I should stay with Philip. Or at least that that's what I'm going to do.' At this point her voice cracked, and she herself didn't know whether it was for real or an act. Maybe both. Sebastian said nothing. She continued. 'You once asked me what I was most scared of in the whole world, do you remember that? It was at a bar. You were wearing a light blue shirt and had shaved for me. We'd eaten noodles that tasted of nothing, because all we could think about was touching each other's wrists. You had that measuring tape you were always winding round your hands and you asked me what I was most afraid of in the whole world.'

Sebastian said nothing, but she could see that he remembered, of course he remembered.

'Do you remember what I answered?'

'Not being in control,' Sebastian said, but he still refused to look at her.

'It was true then, too,' said Laura. 'But it's only now I realise I'd already lost it. Maybe I'd never been in control, maybe everything that's ever happened to me has been nothing but the consequence of some kind of sick game I've been a pawn in.'

When she said this Sebastian jumped, as though she'd kicked him.

'That's madness,' he said. 'Delusional. Completely crazy. What are you trying to say? That none of this has been real? Is that what you're saying?'

'I don't know.'

Sebastian snorted. Why did it sound like he hated her, when just now he'd sounded like he couldn't live without her?

'You don't know?' he said, darkly.

'I have a cicada in my head!' Laura shouted, but it sounded more like the whining of a dog. 'It's written in my brain, don't you see? I can't cut loose, however much I want to. From Philip or anything else. The life I've chosen is the life I chose for a reason, and I'll never have another. I thought you could save me, but you can't save me. And still I want you to save me!' These last words came out as a shriek, that turned into weeping, that turned into her falling, sobbing, from her chair and lying flat on the floor with her hands over her eyes. There was a throbbing from the cut on her head, and from between her legs; there was a fluttering all over her body as though from thousands of black butterflies. Then she felt Sebastian's hands on her forehead again. He was taping the wound. One day the wound would heal and the scar would look like a cicada, but that was a way off yet — right now it was still a battlefield, a bloody mess with notched edges made of sorrow.

'If you want to walk that way, I'll walk this way,' said Sebastian. It sounded formal, almost borrowed. But where could she walk to, when she could barely even crawl?

'I don't want you to walk that way, I want you to say my name.'

'Laura Kadinsky … What on earth are you doing?'

She smiled faintly. Looked down at her own hands and saw how they'd found their way in under his bloodied lab coat, the way they were making their way towards the axle around which her world turned.

Just one last gasp, she thought. Just one last gasp of air.

While Sebastian was taking care of Laura, Matilda and Travis were taking care of the very moral monkey. Travis was really on one, and thought it was of the utmost importance that they 'get the monkey to safety', without specifying how, where, or why.

In the end they decided to take it back to Travis's house. Together, they carried the heavy cage out of the Institute, out onto Queen's Square, past the hospital where all the world's sorrow and fear dwelled, past Bloomsbury's shuttered edifices, the houses where no one lived, the hotels with their polished brass door knockers and night porters crouched smoking behind bins, past the gothic spires of St Pancras, all the way to King's Cross where they boarded a bus to Honor Oak. Travis, who was leading, steered the cage up onto the top floor of the double-decker, and together they put it on one of the front seats, so the monkey — who they couldn't be sure didn't tend towards travel sickness — could see out. Then they sat down on the other side of the aisle.

Matilda still wasn't absolutely sure what kind of monkey it was. When she found out it was a creature with an apparently perfectly calibrated moral compass, she was exuberant. Wasn't this what she'd been searching for all this time? A secular confessor? A little flame of hope blazed through Matilda's inner darkness and lit her up with a warm, yellow light at the thought that maybe it wasn't too late to teach her inner angel new tricks after all.

'What's it called?' she asked, reaching over to the cage so the monkey could grip her finger. Like a newborn baby, she thought, feeling a familiar ache spread from the base of her spine.

'Nothing,' Travis replied. 'We don't name our lab animals.'

'Not even informally?'

'It'll have a number, but I don't know it. You'll have to ask Sebastian.'

Matilda removed her finger from the monkey's grip. There was a definite ache in her lower back. She swallowed the lump that spontaneously formed in her throat. Goddamn fucking typical.

'I'm going to call her Bernarda,' she said, letting her hand fall back onto her lap. 'All living things deserve a name.'

Had she given her back-to-front baby a name? No. But perhaps it wasn't too late, thought Matilda sadly as the bus swayed across Blackfriars Bridge. She decided that Jennifer was a name as good as any, a beautiful name actually, a name that suited someone who wasn't really like everyone else.

When they reached Bermondsey, Matilda helped Travis carry the cage up to her flat. After a little vacillation they decided that Bernarda should live in Travis's bedroom so she wouldn't feel lonely. Matilda knew she should head off, it was almost evening and this wasn't her home, but she was having difficulty tearing herself away from the monkey, who, improbable as it was, actually seemed to *like* her. Matilda was sitting on the edge of Travis's bed with Bernarda on her lap when Travis came in with two cups of tea and a bunch of bananas.

'I think you're wrong about this monkey's moral compass,' Matilda said. 'She doesn't seem to have any problem with me, and I'm pretty rotten.'

Travis neither laughed nor protested. Instead she looked like she was giving the matter serious consideration.

'Maybe,' she said after a while, 'I'm blinded by love. But I'd say you're not half as rotten as you think. That's my observation.'

'I should go,' Matilda said, lifting Bernarda down from her lap. 'It's getting late.'

'You can stay here if you want. I've got a spare room.'

'Hmm,' said Matilda. 'I don't want to be any trouble.'

'It's no trouble at all. I want you to stay. Ideally for fourteen months.'

'Why so long?' Matilda asked, perplexed.

'According to my calculations, that's how long it will take for me to conclude, with statistically significant margins of error, that you are guaranteed never to fall in love with me. Then I can get on with my life without that inhibiting "what if ..." feeling that underpins so many popular romantic comedies and which, I presume, on the basis of its popularity as a trope, must have some foundation in reality.'

'I don't know if I can stay for fourteen months,' Matilda said.

'No matter. Every day makes a difference. I'll go and make the bed, then we can have something to eat.'

While Travis was making up the spare bed for her, Matilda went into the kitchen. She wanted to help out, so she opened the fridge. There were eggs and milk. In a cupboard there was flour and salt. One-one-two, Matilda thought, and started making pancake batter.

It was just as she'd put the first dollop of butter in the pan and watched it melt, warm and yellow, that her pocket vibrated.

She pulled out her phone, saw the little flag on the email icon, and without knowing how she knew, she knew.

She took the pan off the hob.

SUBJECT:
clara__isaksson@koolaid.com

Tilda,

The world didn't end. Someone said it was going to, yesterday night, but I never believed it, not ever. The world just goes on and on. In one form or another there will always be a new day. Whether it will be liveable I don't know. Probably not. But as long as there's life, there's hope, as they say, and there's life. There's life in a cliff's narrowest crevice, that's my evaluation. And you don't need to be blind to see that.

Sorry. I should get straight to the point, but I'm no good at it, as I guess you know by now. I should say sorry, I guess. For not replying to your emails, to start with. And for what I said, you know when. You were horrible but I was worse. I didn't mean what I said, but also, I did.

I don't know if you'll ever be able to understand it, how I experienced her death. It was like the last thread snapped and everything we were spilled out all over the floor. And of course, I was right, though the floor wasn't a floor but the whole world. I don't know if you ever think about her. I don't mean what happened to her, and to Sebastian and to us, but about her as a person. Who she was. Why she did what she did. I can honestly say I haven't, not really. I was always a bit scared of her. And I've always been scared of you, even when I've longed for you.

I know you think I'm not interested in having a relationship with you. It's not quite true, by which I mean it's not true at all. I actually went to look for you. It sounds stupid because you've been there the whole time, but that's how it is. I looked for you in Berlin, but you weren't there. I've looked for you here, in the loneliest place on earth (I'm on Easter Island

461

again, in case you hadn't figured that out already). I looked for you in a man I thought had been yours, but he was mine instead, as it turns out. His name is Jordan. I'm afraid you'd like him.

Whatever. I saw a lobster yesterday. It was as big as a cat and the sun rose and the cliffs glowed pink and someone was saved and someone came back and someone turned up in miraculous fashion. I know it sounds freaky, but it was the most complete moment in my life. I just wanted to tell you. That this isn't just some whim. I'm not afraid anymore. So I'm going to come and find you, for real this time.

/C

And then in the end came the blood. The aches had spoken their truth. It was slow, thick, and sticky, a coating on her labia rather than bleeding, but that was how it always started, it was normal. It was when Matilda and Travis had finished their pancakes and said goodnight. She was sitting on the made-up guest bed, which had the same creaky springs every guest bed has had since time immemorial, and took off her tights. She felt the damp patch on the cotton, the rounded smell of sour blood.

It could be a miscarriage, of course, but she knew, as she had the thought, that it wasn't. She wasn't in any particular pain. She wasn't afraid. Just sad. And … disappointed? She took her feelings in her hand and touched them the way Kathleen had taught her. Yes, she felt disappointed. She cried. The tears fell on her underpants. Fucking fucking fuck. For the second time in her life she'd lost a child who'd never existed. And she'd lost Billy, Siri, her life in Berlin.

She cried until her pants were wet through, then she took them off and rolled them into a little ball. She wanted to hide them somewhere not even her third eye could see, but she knew that was impossible. She put them on the side of the bed.

She lay awake a while and waited for more blood. It came, but it was perfectly ordinary blood, no clots, no cramps, nothing that even came close to the pains she'd experienced when she gave birth to the baby she wouldn't have been able to — no, wouldn't have wanted to take care of. The girl who was so sick. Jennifer. But with her hand on her heart, and here she literally placed her hand over her heart because she always used her body like a highlighter, it hadn't mattered that she was sick, the girl. Matilda had been looking for a way out, and she'd found one in the doctor's furrowed brow.

She didn't want children, not back then, not with J, not on the other side of the globe. That was the truth.

But now! Now it was another matter. She'd thought it was the same but it was different. She wanted to have children with Billy! She wanted a girl or a boy, or for that matter a little pony foal, who'd blow bubbles in the playground on Weichselplatz, who'd fly kites on Tempelhof and go to a Kindergarten and guzzle Apfelmus and say 'Lecker!' and have a big sister who loved dolphins. She wanted to go to Kathleen's prenatal yoga and have her baby in a birthing pool, a living baby who cried when it was born and didn't end up in a box, end up as ash. And she could have had it, not just yet, apparently, but later, next month, next year, whenever. But instead she'd struck a child and run away. Fucking fucking fuck.

She picked up her phone thirteen times before sunrise, with the intention, the impulse, to call Billy and beg for forgiveness. To tell him everything: about the abortion, the colour, and the fear. About Bernarda the dog, and Bernarda the monkey. About the evil inside her, the emotional mark of the devil that for some reason had been burned into her at the same moment she was born to an unknown woman and became the final, wholly unnecessary addendum to her brother and sister. Taking another child's place. Would she have been someone else, if the mix-up had never taken place, or was her darkness hereditary? Billy would have laughed at a question like that. Get it together, he would have said. She wanted to hear him say that. Now!

But she couldn't. Not because she didn't want to, or dare to, but because she didn't have the right. She had no right to try and force her way back into Billy and Siri's life. It was only a couple of weeks since she'd taken off, but it felt like years. The impulse to call became weaker every time she picked up the phone. It was a kind of exposure therapy and, at last, she was able to put it down alongside the balled-up pants and drift off. It was possible — not probable, but possible — that she'd be a better person one day. Maybe she already was. But until she knew, until she was certain, she wouldn't move a muscle. Clara, her beloved, hated sister, had finally, finally got in touch. Clara was coming, Clara would find her. She'd wait for Clara. She'd stay in London, she'd help Jennifer with anything she asked, she'd get to the bottom of the colour fluttering in her brain.

More than anything, she'd leave Billy and Siri in peace.

If she did all that, if she did it right, then maybe one day before the end of time, she'd be worthy of a child.

Jennifer Travis's flat was a spacious two-bed in a well-kept Georgian house in Bermondsey. The door wasn't locked, and Sebastian entered without knocking. It was a week since the very moral monkey had been found and — like Matilda — made a new home with Travis, and Sebastian had come to say hello, both to his sister and the monkey.

The flat was neat on the inside, too, clean verging on pedantic, which surprised Sebastian, who'd always pictured Travis's home environment as an unsanitary inconvenience. But maybe, he thought, hanging his jacket on a shiny silver hook, this was the only way she could function, with her home an ordered midpoint around which her mind could follow its capricious paths. The only signs of disorder were his sister's things, easy to identify since they were the only objects not in their right place. A dirty rucksack tossed under a chair. A mustard-yellow top with baggy sleeves flung over a weeping fig. The flat smelled of camomile, and something a little acrid and animal that Sebastian immediately recognised as the very moral monkey's scent. He pulled the door closed behind him, placed his shoes on the shoe rack, and went in.

In the bright living room, Sebastian found Travis and Matilda doing yoga. They sat opposite each other in lotus pose, like yin and yang: one thin and dark-haired, the other blonde and curvy; two smooth brows and four hands resting on the same number of knees. It was a sight that made Sebastian both happy and sad. He'd witnessed this scene before, in the house in Professorsstaden. It was a few months after Matilda's first breakdown; she'd just started her medication, but she was fragile, so very fragile. Clara had taken care of her, in a way that Matilda had honestly never taken care of Clara. She'd done it even though she was scared; he knew she'd been scared. Of Matilda's unpredictability, her bouts of rage, the times she woke Clara in the middle of the night to tell her how she'd just read on the internet that it was unhealthy to sleep with too many mites in your bed, and wouldn't it be a good idea to get all the sheets in the house and wash them, right now, wouldn't that be a good thing for everyone involved?

He'd forgotten, but remembered now, that it was Clara who'd got Matilda into yoga. Who'd prodded and pleaded and teased and bribed until she'd convinced Matilda to sit cross-legged and count her breaths. Who'd taught Matilda silly mantras that had made Matilda laugh until she cried, and finally calmed her down.

Where was Clara now?

Sebastian had got an email from her, just like Matilda had. She'd written that she was coming. But when? It didn't say. And how sure could they even be that the email was from Clara? He knew what Travis would have said if she'd known about it.

He cleared his throat cautiously as he stood there in the doorway. Travis and Matilda opened their eyes in a single movement.

'Sebastian!' Travis twittered. 'To what do we owe the honour?'

'We'd agreed I would come by today. To see the monkey.'

'Bernarda,' Matilda said. 'She's got a name now.'

'Bernarda,' Sebastian said. 'Like our dog.'

'Like our dog, yes. But I'm not going to kill her, if that's what you're worried about.'

Travis swatted Matilda on the arm. 'Oof! Isn't she silly? I think she's silly. She's a wonderful person, your sister, did you know that?'

'Yes,' said Sebastian.

'Sort it out, you two,' said Matilda.

It was a while before Sebastian got to see Bernarda. First, Travis wanted to tell him about the latest development in the war against Corrigan. By shuffling various papers here and there and invoking a clause or two in the contract outlining the rights, responsibilities, and authority granted to the Multi-talents (for such a thing apparently existed: when Sebastian displayed scepticism, Travis dug it out of her desk; it looked unquestionably authentic, even if the signature at the bottom of the page looked worrying like it was written in blood), Travis had succeeded in getting Corrigan to push back the cicadas' expulsion from the building, but now all opportunities for respite were exhausted and Corrigan had set a precise date for when the devastation would occur: the twenty-fourth of

October, three weeks thence. It was very unclear what would happen to the cicadas after that point, but Travis was not hopeful. She was anticipating a genocide. It was possible the rarest would be embalmed and donated to the Natural History Museum (there was a paucity of cicadas in their collections, Travis thought), but on the whole: a bloodbath. Her voice trembled a little as she said it, and Sebastian saw Matilda lay a comforting hand on her thigh. But, Travis went on cheerfully, she and Matilda had a plan. For a rescue operation. She held up sketches and calculations, timetables and maps.

'What are you going to do with them then?' Sebastian asked cautiously. 'I mean, where will you keep them?'

Travis shrugged.

'Here, I guess. To begin with, in any case. Then we'll see. I'm considering starting an independent research project. This flat is worth a tonne of money. I could sell it and buy myself a lab somewhere. Wales, maybe. There are some crazy cheap houses in Wales. And sheep. I like sheep, don't you?'

'I'll be sure to come and visit,' said Sebastian, and thought that, in spite of the practical issues, this was actually one of the best ideas Travis had ever had. She needed to get away from the Institute — they all did.

For a while, all three lost themselves in thoughts of Travis's new life as a sheep farmer and maverick self-financing applied neuroscientist, then Travis raked together the papers spread across her living room table and changed the subject.

'Kadinsky,' she said.

Sebastian jumped. 'What's up with Laura?'

'She's married.'

'Yes,' said Sebastian glumly. 'I'm familiar with that fact.'

'And her husband is called Philip Kadinsky?'

'Yes. Why?'

But Travis didn't reply, just let out a thoughtful little *hmph*.

'Out with it,' Sebastian said, but he'd lost her. Travis made an absent gesture.

'He's famous, right? A great talent. Maybe even what one might call a Multi-talent. That was all I was thinking. Nothing important. But I must say I find it a little frustrating. That we've reached the final correlate — in other words, you and Laura and your little *liaison dangereuse* — but we don't seem to have got to the end of this game. It bothers me. Where's your sister, for instance? Still missing!'

Sebastian looked over at Matilda. Clearly, she hadn't told Travis about Clara's letter either. It was for the best, Sebastian thought, shaking his head slightly in Matilda's direction — Travis was already sufficiently close to overheating.

'Whatever,' Travis went on. 'Carry on doing whatever it is you have been doing with Laura Kadinsky. She's a correlate, I'm absolutely certain of it.'

'And here I was thinking she was a person,' Sebastian said. 'How wrong of me. Where's the monkey, then? I want to see her.'

'Hey, don't be upset! Do what you like, of course. But it would be good if you didn't end it with her for a while. We're *this* close to cracking it, I promise. Bernarda's in the bedroom. To the left, off the hallway.'

The door of the cage was open, and the monkey was sitting on the windowsill, half hidden by the curtain. Sebastian was struck by an unexpected tenderness when he saw her — he'd missed her mute companionship. Perhaps he was fooling himself, but he thought she seemed glad to see him too. The corners of her mouth kind of turned up, and she tugged a few times on the curtain.

'Hi,' Sebastian said, entering the room. He sat on Travis's neatly made bed and reached out his hand. The monkey immediately jumped down from her nook and climbed up onto his lap. He gave her a few banana chips from his pocket.

'Whereabouts were you, anyway?' Sebastian asked, even though he knew he wouldn't get an answer. 'When you were gone. Who had you? Was it Corrigan?'

The monkey looked away. Sebastian couldn't tell if that meant yes or no.

'I missed you, in any case,' he said, and the monkey smiled again. Sebastian glanced towards the door, trying to figure out what Matilda and Travis were up to. From the living room he could hear Matilda's voice, gentle and soft: *The light in me bows to the light in you.* It sounded like they'd resumed their yoga session, but Sebastian still lowered his voice: 'I wanted to ask you something,' he whispered. 'I need some advice. It's about Laura.'

This time, the monkey didn't react with her usual distaste at Laura's name. Instead she climbed down and sat on the ground in front of Sebastian as if getting ready to listen. Sebastian said:

'I don't know what to do. I love her, in some ways. And I think she loves me, in her way. Maybe it started as a game, maybe Corrigan has something to do with it — I don't know. I don't even know if it matters, as long as she needs me.'

He looked at the monkey, whose expression didn't change in the slightest.

'But we can't …' he went on tentatively. 'I mean, I know there are other things to take into consideration. That you don't like. And maybe it's wrong. That she's married. Has a child. I know it's wrong in some ways. But even if I ignore that, there's … there's something deeply problematic in what we're doing, you know?'

The monkey nodded, slowly, expectantly.

'I thought I was good for her, but now I don't know. And she was probably good for me, for a while, but now … We can't care for each other's sadness, you know what I mean?'

The monkey nodded again.

'So I should leave her. But then what will happen to her?'

The monkey no longer looked happy. She started moving anxiously around the floor, jumped up on the windowsill again, looked out. Sebastian followed her gaze, but saw only cars, sky, birds.

'Should I not leave her? Is that what you're saying? That it's my responsibility to stay? She says she can't live without me. But I don't think she can live with me, either.'

Sebastian fell backwards onto the smoothly stretched covers. He could have fallen asleep right there. He wanted to fall asleep. Father, remove this cup from me. Then he heard the monkey lollop across the room with her long, nimble hop. He raised his eyes to the door. The monkey was hanging, her fingers around the door frame, toes towards the underworld.

He looked at her. She was a monkey, she was a woman, she was grotesque, she was gorgeous, she was his greatest love, and a gaping wound, she was his sisters, his responsibility, she was his curse, she was his comfort, she was his madness, she was his mainstay, she was a woman, she was a monkey.

And for the first time, the monkey opened her mouth and spoke.

Really spoke — or at least that was how Sebastian remembered it later, that the monkey had opened her mouth, and words had tumbled out like sunbeams through a chink in thick autumn clouds, what their mother always called *angel's light*, a sudden, unexpected gift from above. He knew it wasn't possible, and yet it was. The monkey opened her mouth and spoke to Sebastian, and what she said was this:

It was never your fault.

It took him almost two hours to get to the cafe on Balls Pond Road. He walked as though in a dream, not even needing to use his phone for directions, and maybe he took a wrong turn on the way or maybe he was just slow, blind in one eye. But in the end, there he was, standing before the blue wooden door with its dirty glass, the chime that sounded like a great bell's toll as it struck the door frame. The cafe was empty except for the waiter who was leaning halfway across the bar with eyes closed and ears full of music. Sebastian walked right past him without a word.

In the basement everything was set out as though in a museum. It was quiet — too quiet. It was the bubbling sound from the aquarium that was missing. Otherwise it was all much the same. Well, apart from the stool — a collapsible stool with carved wooden legs and a triangular seat of worn brown leather; soft, he saw it was soft without even having to touch it. He knew because Violetta's father had had a similar one in his office, leant against piles of magazines and journals, years' worth of *Res Publica* and *Månadsjournalen* and *BLM*.

The stool was right in front of the picture.

He sat down on it.

He moved the stool closer to the image.

He touched the picture with his fingers, rested his head against its cold surface.

He pushed his hands against the wall, for his legs were shaking so.

He bit his lip hard, till his mouth filled with blood.

Till his memory filled with blood.

He'd bought her a ring. It was silver, since he knew gold would make her feel like a circus monkey. He walked to her apartment; it was on Grönegatan, just a studio apartment, but with parquet flooring, window niches, and an old-fashioned bathtub with feet — she'd rubbed the parquet with sandpaper to distress it, she'd developed photos in the tub so many times the chemicals had eaten rings into the enamel, had vomited into the heart-shaped toilet bowl so many times the vomit had eaten rings into the enamel — of the bowl and of her teeth, on her nails and on her hands. She loved that apartment, thought it was beautiful. He thought it was sick, wanted to take her away from there, he wanted them to get married, maybe, move in together, certainly; he wanted to save her, to save them both.

He opened the door to the apartment with the key she'd very reluctantly given him. It felt like overstepping a boundary, but she hadn't answered the phone in three days, not since she'd pressed a worn measuring tape into his hands as they sat on the steps of the Wrangel Library.

He called her name, there was no reply, he pulled aside the curtain separating the little entranceway from the apartment's only room, and he didn't scream. He didn't scream, and he didn't drop the little silver ring he held in his hand, there wasn't a sound.

Now he screamed; quiet and restrained, but a scream nonetheless.

He'd just stood there, staring. The double exposure, one girl's body in another's, one beautiful in its way, the other ugly. The imitation of a death that didn't belong to her, but had still become hers. The way she hung there, just hung there, like the blind photographer in a story he hadn't read, as though she were sleeping, sleeping with her eyes open. *Wie beim Schlafen.* Afterwards, when he'd studied the image carefully, he could see how much effort she'd put into the detail.

The naked legs under the nightshirt.

The stool and the shadow it cast.

The lamp cord she'd been forced to move, from the edge of the image to its centre. The closed door.

On the door was a Post-it note, and on the note it said: nothing.

The most painful thing was that she'd failed.

Because it wasn't a beautiful scene.

It was abhorrent.

Someone who's never seen a dead body can never imagine the difference between that lifeless body and one still full of vitality. It's not at all true that she looked like she was sleeping, he thought now — there was a stiffness in the arms and legs he'd never seen in her before, not even when she was at her thinnest. When she slept, her body was always soft, her contours loose, vulnerable in some charming way. In death she was hard as bone, rigid as steel.

And yet so weak.

The person hanging in the doorway between the kitchen and the single room of the apartment on Grönegatan was no longer a person, but a thing, a dead rag. The wide-open eyes were bloodshot and swollen, the mouth open like a fish, the rope cut into her throat and made the loose skin under her chin bulge out to the sides, flapping like gulping gills. The shirt she was wearing — it was one of his, a pale blue, threadbare thing — had sweat stains ingrained under the arms. At the moment of death, she'd both pissed and shat herself, and it had run down her legs, drying on the almost fur-like hair covering her thighs and calves.

But the worst thing was her arms.

The photo she'd loved, the photo she'd sought to imitate, showed a living woman, a woman strong enough to hang from a door frame by her fingertips.

What physical strength it takes to hang from a door frame without assistance. Violetta would never have managed it, not while alive, much less when dead, and she'd known that. To make the right Y-shape, she'd wound scarves around her wrists, long enough to allow the fall from the stool, and then nailed them to the frame. Or the other way around: she must have nailed them first and then tied them, perhaps first measuring the scarves' length precisely with the measuring tape that had become her noose. She was always precise, and yet still, everything ran through her fingers. In that, as in much else, they were the same. Darkness and light. She couldn't handle it.

But he could. That was where they differed.

He could live with stumbling through life like an unhappy coincidence. He could live with not being in control — to be honest, he liked it. He liked being a mirror for the wishes and desires of others, there was a freedom in it: going with the flow, having no agenda, making other people's joy and misery his own. For Violetta it had been another story.

Had she known? Maybe. There'd been things she'd said, things he hadn't understood but which now seemed strangely clear-sighted. Her obsession with their common birthday, which he'd merely accepted, with a romantic notion about destiny. Her reserved, almost hateful relationship to his sisters. Her absolutely disproportionate rage the time he'd gone out into the garden, borrowing her father's raincoat and hat without asking; the way she'd gone completely white when he came back in, and screamed at him to never ever pretend to be someone he wasn't again. He'd thought it was the double exposure itself that had scared her — that for a moment she'd seen him as someone else — but maybe it was more about the fact that it had been her father's clothes he'd been wearing.

The way she'd sniggered when they'd been flicking through an old photo album and he'd said she looked like her mother when she was young. 'It's more environment than inheritance,' she'd said.

Her father's study, the way Sebastian used to lie there on rainy days, reading copy after copy of *National Geographic*, the crystal-clear memory of one of those afternoons, when he'd felt he was being watched, and looked up to see her there in the doorway, shoulders sorrowfully drooping. 'Don't stop,' she said, 'you fit so perfectly there.' And then raised her hands to her face and clicked, as if taking a photo.

But he could be reading too much into it. She'd been a strange bird in so many ways; so much of what she did was peculiar and irrational. Perhaps he remembered these things so clearly because they happened to fit in with his life's new narrative. Maybe there were other moments, other points that could be arranged in a totally different pattern.

In any case, Violetta had been deeply unhappy. She'd been unhappy when they met and had only become unhappier over the years.

It was never your fault.

It hadn't been his fault.

He'd thought it was, that the responsibility for her happiness lay in his hands, because that was where she'd put it. She'd said so often that she wouldn't be able to live without him, and he'd believed her. In the end it wasn't enough. She couldn't live without him, but she clearly couldn't live with him, either. She took her own life. And nothing he could ever do, for himself or anyone else, would change the fact that she'd taken a part of him with her into the grave. He might have hated her for that, if it hadn't been the same thing as hating part of himself.

For the last time he looked at the image of Francesca Woodman's living body, the photograph that Violetta, for some unfathomable reason, had loved to death.

His first love, his great love.

His sisters' sister, his shadow twin.

You have a dream and in the dream the world is ending. You're standing in front of the building site next to Paddington station and you can see the construction workers with their helmets of glass. Over their heads floats a banner that says: *All harm is preventable.* They turn and mouth the words: You know that it's not true, and you know that it is true.

You have a dream and in the dream you're riding horses in a lush valley in Eastern Europe. It reminds you of someone else's dream you once saw on a theatre stage.

You have a dream and in the dream a cat is playing a keyboard. It's wearing a turquoise shirt and tinkling 'Nearer, My God, to Thee'. You have a dream and in the dream you are the cat, and everyone is looking at you.

The leaves clutched at the branches, almost desperately. It was October, the month of leaf fall, *the fall* — since she was a teenager Laura Kadinsky had insisted on using the American word rather than the British *autumn*. The value of words, she thought, wasn't a question of culture so much as world view and temperament. *Autumn* was a beautiful time of bronze and children in new wellingtons, *fall* a time for sorrow and sanction and boredom. A time to hide, to go under. Of course, Laura didn't want to *go under*, she was much too captivated by herself to imagine a world in which she didn't exist, but she wanted it to *be over*. The fall. The suffering. The lust and indolence. Under, over (she thought about Sebastian), there were always things to wonder over (she thought about God), there was a way out of this limbo, she just needed to find it. But how could she find a way out when she never went out, when she couldn't even find her way to her own kitchen without pressing her palms hard against the walls. That was the question.

Philip thought he'd found the answer in a Swiss clinic. After the trip to Madrid, when Laura had finally opened up about her problems (but not about her affair), Philip had sprung into action with characteristic verve. To Philip there was no problem that couldn't be solved, no sum of money that couldn't be wasted if it might lead to something good, and he'd invested time, energy, and many nights' lost sleep to find an expert he thought might be able to help Laura. The expert in question was a well-regarded neurosurgeon named Stockhausen (yes, like the composer, said Philip delightedly), with a clinic in Schaffhausen (what wonderful symmetry, said Philip delightedly), who had agreed to see Laura and Philip at the beginning of November. Philip had planned it all — they would travel by train, he would read Thomas Mann, Laura would have a hat box. They'd spend three weeks at the sanatorium, as he called it, Stockhausen would swing a pendulum in front of Laura's eyes and take her pulse with two fingers on her wrist. Then he would operate, and Laura would be well.

She'd told him repeatedly that she didn't think it was quite that simple. After all, she'd been the subject of several months' highly detailed investigations at one of the world's leading neurobiological institutes, and the only thing they'd come up with was that she had a cicada in her brain. 'I'm sure they're very good at LICS,' Philip said, taking a big bite of his chilli. 'But the Swiss are better. They're always better.' Laura had nothing to say to that. She knew much too little about Switzerland.

The trip was still three weeks away. Laura was staying in the house as much as she could. Since the break-up with Sebastian two weeks ago, her condition had worsened further. That's how she thought of it: as a break-up rather than a desertion, an abandonment, because she appreciated the fact that the phrase included the word 'break'. That was how she perceived it, that she had been broken, they had both been broken, the laws of nature had been broken: laws that say bodies that are drawn to each other should be together. But a break-up is generally mutual. Two people sitting in a bar late at night, a worsening headache, beer gone warm and flat, someone raising their eyebrows and saying: *so then, maybe it's time we broke up?* and the other nodding in response, and thinking: *what a relief he said it, I'm starting to feel pretty tired.*

That wasn't what had happened. Sebastian had got up and left and she hadn't seen it coming. She'd rung him all afternoon and he hadn't answered. In the end, she'd gone round to his house and stood out on the street, holding her handbag above her head as shelter from the rain. She'd thrown stones at his window until he'd let her in. And then he'd said it: *We can't take care of each other's sorrow. It was never my fault. Go home, Laura, go home.* She hadn't gone home, she'd lain down on his bed for the last time. *Go home, Laura, go home*, he said afterwards.

And so she did.

She hadn't thought it was for real. Not this time either. But it was. She'd rung fifty-two times and got no reply. Then she'd stopped, not because she wanted to, but because her hands were no longer capable of picking up her phone.

It helped only moderately that Essie the Escapist, as if by magic, had returned at around the same time. One evening during dinner, Philip, who for once had been there, had suddenly stiffened and got a wild look in his eyes, that special mad glow that almost always meant his eardrums had caught some kind of aural dissonance. Without a word he'd got up from the table and gone out into the hallway, and when he came back he was holding a wet, gaunt-looking Essie in his cupped hands. Or at least, a hamster who looked very much like Essie. The markings were in the right place, the whiskers were just the right length. But Laura wasn't convinced — she knew Philip was a man fully capable of finding a hamster identical to his daughter's escaped one, starving it, drenching it, and then setting up an elaborate homecoming, just to please said daughter. The problem with fantastic men, Laura had thought as she sat there with an ecstatic Chloe cuddling her hamster (which was wrapped in a very expensive towel), and feeding it Cheerios, is that you forget in between times the great acts of which they're capable. You fail to adjust.

Her suspicion that Essie wasn't really Essie but an interloper was reinforced by the fact that she, just like everything else in Laura's life these days, was entirely two-dimensional. On the other hand, that applied, as previously mentioned, to everything in her life, so perhaps it wasn't the hamster who was the interloper, but Laura herself. Aside from Essie, Sebastian had until recently been the only reliable link between her and the third dimension, and now she didn't even have access to him.

A few days after the break-up, the final thread had been cut. She'd received a call from the Institute. A woman by the name of Tiffany Temple had informed her that changes had been made to the research groups and that from now on she'd be seeing a scientist by the name of Dr Childs, instead of Dr Isaksson. This Dr Childs' assistant contacted her numerous times to book a first meeting, but Laura never went.

What was the point?

Instead, she stayed at home and watched Sebastian on YouTube. On the whole internet there were only two films of Sebastian. In the first he was a mere detail, one face among many. It was a recruitment film for LICS, one of a series of films that had been floating around the internet during the time Laura had become aware of the Institute. But this was one she hadn't seen. Or had she? Was it possible her eyes had once drifted across Sebastian's face and it had left her quite unmoved? She doubted it. He had such an insanely beautiful mouth, it was almost impossible to bear. And yet it wasn't Sebastian's face that had cut through reality like a knife, opening up a hollow in which she could rest. It had been his voice when he first said her name, the name that was only half hers.

She was born Laura Violet Barnes. It struck her, long after it was already too late, that she'd never told him that. Perhaps it all would have ended differently if he'd known that in a sense she shared a name with the woman he talked about in his sleep, the one he must have felt an ineffaceable love for. Neither had she told him that she'd once had a goldfish she fed to death. Nor that the first person she'd kissed had been the girl next door whose dad Laura used to fantasise about when she saw him cutting the grass in their communal garden, a kiss she now realised was all about projection and the proximity principle, but which had felt, when it happened, like love. Nor that she, like all children, had found comfort in the scent of clean sheets, and still spent far too much money on fabric softener. Nor that she hadn't had any siblings, or that her fundamental belief that the reason for this had been her parents' realisation that Laura was such an exceptional child no sibling could ever compete for their love had been unimpaired by her mother's revelation that she'd developed polyps on her ovaries shortly after Laura's birth.

There was so much she'd never told Sebastian, so much he'd never asked. He'd never been interested in who she was before she became the one he fell in love with. He'd loved her as she was, but he hadn't known what it was he loved. Maybe that was why he never managed to decode her heart, maybe that was why he didn't understand what he was missing.

And Philip? He knew where she came from, but never where she was at that moment. As though he saw her with a kind of time delay, her soul a silhouette in the background. It struck Laura as unpleasant, bordering on dizzying, that you could be loved by two different people at the same time, but for such different reasons.

She didn't watch the first film that much; it wasn't sufficiently enjoyable, or sufficiently painful. Even if she froze the image just as his face flickered past, if she swallowed her awkwardness in the eyes of the implicit observer who'd forever accompanied her, the audience of one for whom she played out her life, and allowed herself just to sit and stare at the outré curve of his lips, his high Scandinavian cheekbones, to call forth the sensation of him saying her name with ludicrously round vowels, even that could sustain her inner masochist for no more than a quarter of an hour, give or take a few minutes. After all, he didn't speak. And what's more, Laura was understandably fed up of flat, still images after spending almost a year with almost no depth perception.

The other film was much more lo-fi.

In it he was extremely young, barely more than a child. It took her days to find it, because his name wasn't in the video metadata, though his dead girlfriend Violetta's was, and in the end that was how she found it. He was sitting on a stool in a kitchen with a guitar on his lap, his long legs crossed like a girl's. He had a fringe back then, and it kept falling into his eyes. Behind him in the window niche, there were pots of pelargoniums with a pale shade of pink Laura had never before seen in pelargoniums. A girl was filming, she was speaking Swedish, presumably — it was Violetta, presumably — at one point you saw her hand flicker past — if you paused you could see she had slender fingers and nails painted turquoise. She laughed a lot. The whole film was leading up to Sebastian playing a song on the guitar. At first, he didn't want to, or at least he made out as if he didn't. The girl egged him on, alternating between begging and teasing. In the end he started, with the same voice he still had, though brittler, more childish:

If you walk away I'll walk away
First tell me which road you will take
I don't want to risk our paths crossing some day
So you walk that way, I'll walk this way ...

In the second verse, the girl's voice joined him, turning the song into a duet; husky and melodic and a little distant, even though she was closer to the microphone:

And the future hangs over our heads
And it moves with each current event
Until it falls all around like a cold steady rain
Just stay in when it's looking this way …

The first time she saw the film was the first time she realised Sebastian could play the guitar. He was actually pretty good at it, or had been at the time he was a barely grown boy-calf with long, slender legs, pale of nose and in love with an angel. Sebastian's evident musicality disturbed her, because it created a connection between him and Philip — one that wasn't *her* — and she didn't want one to exist, she wanted them to continue to exist in parallel but sharply differentiated universes.

She could no longer go into Philip's little study, because in there were two guitars made by Alhambra, the same make, she'd noted, as the guitar Sebastian was playing in the film. She thought a lot about that guitar. It was a classical guitar, not a pop guitar, so what was it doing in the hands of a teenage troubadour? Was it the girl's guitar? Could she play flamenco, like Philip sometimes did when he was horny and Laura didn't want to fuck?

But it was Sebastian playing. The more she watched the film, the more convinced she became that the guitar wasn't really there, or at least that it hadn't been the day Sebastian and his girlfriend had decided to record a melancholy duet — instead, she decided it was a projection of her own subconscious, a detail that had been created by the cicada in her brain and that had changed the passage of time, like a false memory. It had to be so, however improbable it seemed — how else could you explain the fourth, languorous verse that always made her vomit tears:

And Laura's asleep in my bed
As I'm leaving she wakes up and says
'I dreamed you were carried away on the crest of a wave
Baby don't go away, come here …'

Matilda was beginning to grow impatient. Weeks had passed, several weeks, since Clara had issued her promise to find her, and still she hadn't been found. And yet, she was finding it relatively okay, living and waiting.

For example, she was no longer struggling so much with the colour, even though it was now pretty much everywhere. It had seeped into the fallen leaves, into the cracks in the pavement, into the waxy skins of the apples and the bulging amaryllis buds on Jennifer Travis's windowsill — but it didn't scare her anymore, not really; it didn't make her eyes hurt. Okay, it was quite irritating. It woke her up in the night sometimes, floating clump-like in the dark room, as though it wanted to tell her something. It sat beside her at the breakfast table, poking her in the side. It was a tenacious bastard, a mosquito bite that wouldn't stop itching — but it didn't drive her to distraction. Travis had got nowhere with her questionnaires and fMRI scans and pretty diagrams, but that didn't seem to matter. Matilda knew what it was, the colour, probably always had done. She knew it had something to say to her, and that sooner or later it would tell her what.

She just had to wait, to quell the restlessness in her soul.

One day in the middle of October, the colour accompanied Matilda and Sebastian to a museum. Sebastian wanted to see an exhibition of Goya's portraits at the Tate. 'Why in holy hell do you want to do that?' Matilda had asked. 'You've never been interested in art.' He replied that people change and she hadn't argued, because of course she wanted it to be true.

She didn't like the paintings. It was as though he — Goya, that is — had dipped his brush in darkness in between each stroke, mixing all the colours with black. Her own colour didn't like them either. It galloped through the exhibition rooms and she followed willingly. She drank coffee and ate cake in the cafe while Sebastian finished looking round.

It was a black forest, and she was homesick.

★

Afterwards they walked along the river (which was still really bloody ugly, Matilda would never stop thinking that). When they reached Westminster, Sebastian stopped and climbed up on the wall that faced the petrol-fume-grey river, sitting with his back to the water and his legs dangling down towards the pavement. Matilda was pretty certain that was illegal. In this country everything was illegal. No damn way was she breaking any rules. The old Matilda, the one she was trying so hard to shake off, wouldn't have cared. But she was trying hard to be someone else now, someone who respected rules and regulations, who didn't murder dogs or hit innocent children.

But just this once, she thought then. What does it matter? Maybe people can change, but not to the extent that you can't occasionally allow yourself a relapse. She wanted to sit next to her brother and dangle her legs. The only thing she wanted more was for Clara to be there too, sitting on the other side of Sebastian, shouting: 'WATCH OUT!' when his arse got too close to the edge.

She braced her foot against the wall and heaved herself up.

'I miss her,' Matilda said, looking at her feet. It was good to be honest. It was good to say what you were feeling. *Communication.* These things were worthy of praise, all of them, morally right, Bernarda had confirmed it — the monkey Bernarda, that is, not the ghost dog. She'd always thought she was good at it — communication — since she talked so goddamn much, she'd thought of herself as an open book. But if that was the case, she wouldn't end up in the situations she did, would she? She hadn't communicated with Clara, not really. Nor with J. Not even with Billy. The only person she'd ever seriously been able to talk to was Sebastian. He was special that way, in many ways.

Sebastian was quiet for a while, picked up a chestnut from the wall, and threw it over his shoulder, down into the Thames. The fall was so long Matilda never heard a plop; it was as though it went on falling forever.

'Clara?' he said then.

'Yeah, dummy. Who else?'

Sebastian shrugged.

'I think she misses us too,' he said. 'I think it's just hard for her. Not knowing, I mean. Which of us it is.'

'That's not the only reason,' Matilda said.

'No. But it's part of it. I think.'

'Honestly,' said Matilda, winding the sleeve of her top around her hand. 'Who do you think it is? I won't be upset if you tell me.'

'Why would you be upset?'

Matilda snorted.

'Stop it. Everyone knows it's me. It's okay, I'm okay with it. Honest. But it would be nice if Mama could just say it, so that we could get it over and done with. I've tried to force it out of her, but she flatly denies it.'

'If it doesn't matter to you, why are you so determined to find out?'

'Because I've decided to try and live honestly and sincerely, Basse. But I can't do it on my own. Honesty is worthless if it's unilateral. For example, Billy was always honest and sincere to me, he was true. But what the fuck good did that do when I was always keeping things from him?'

'What kind of things?'

'All the stupid things I've done.'

'There aren't that many things, are there?'

'You don't know the half of it.'

Sebastian fiddled with the buttons on his coat.

'Okay, if you really want to know. I really don't think it is you, Tilda.'

She laughed.

'What, you reckon it's you? Mama's golden boy? Hardly.'

'Why not?' said Sebastian.

'Because you're the only one of us who's normal!'

'Maybe I come from a normal gene pool, unlike you. No, but seriously. If it's me. Would it change anything? Would it make you feel differently about me?'

She replied without a moment's hesitation.

'Never. You're my brother and I love you.'

Saying it felt like cheering. Saying the word 'love'. Kathleen always said: *The word is the messenger of the heart.*

She turned to face Sebastian and squinted into the sun. She noticed now that he'd started getting small wrinkles at the corners of his eyes. She saw how tall he was, a head taller than her. Than Clara. She saw how blond he was. How soft his contours were, aside from the sharp lines of his cheekbones. She saw the colour circling his head, his hands lying folded in his lap, his long, flat feet. Her own feet had beautifully curved arches. Clara's too.

'Sebastian,' she said slowly. 'Answer me honestly: do you truly believe it's you?'

But Sebastian didn't answer. 'Have you had enough art?' was all he said. 'If not, you can come tomorrow night. One of my patients is having an exhibition; I promised I'd go. Travis is coming too.'

The colour floated above his head, a ring around another ring that was magenta-coloured, the colour his aura took on when he was lying or avoiding something.

But she couldn't be certain. Maybe it was just the autumn sun, making his hair look like it was on fire.

Nothing ever ends, but everything ends.

That's why soap operas are the only true narrative form, and the soap bubble the only true art form.

Nothing goes under, the world is a wonder.

A month to the day after the world didn't end, it was the private view of the first solo exhibition by Subject 3A16:1, known as 'Toilet Baby', real name Esmeralda Lundy. The exhibition was called 'Mirror Images', and it was held at the Whitechapel Gallery. Sebastian arrived early, accompanied by Matilda and Jennifer Travis. The plan was to leave the opening before it got too crowded; specifically, before the gallery started overflowing with people from the Institute. Neither Sebastian nor Travis had any great desire to come face to face with Corrigan over a cheese platter.

It was one of those London evenings when the smog and the street lights and the humid miasmas thrown up by the Tube through vents in the streets and alleyways make the city feel like a nineteenth-century pastiche. It was unusually warm for mid-October, and the Christmas decorations already being hung in cafe windows underlined the surreal feeling of being completely lost in space and time.

The fact they'd come early had apparently made no difference at all. The gallery was already crammed with groups of people standing, mouths agape, Prosecco glasses clasped between index finger and thumb, before the paintings. The only thing that set this opening apart from all the other openings happening at that moment in Whitechapel and the world was that, instead of the usual hum of voices, a deafening silence hung over the room. Even Matilda, who had very little experience of visual art and even less interest in it, could understand why. The three-by-three-metre oil paintings that covered the walls were *pure light* — and, at the same time, pure darkness, both extremes at once. The strangest thing about these images was not that they were magnificent (they were magnificent) or technically brilliant (they were technically brilliant) or even outmoded (they were outmoded, not least in their choice of motifs — a lot of rearing horses and pious men in kaftans and curvy naked women with tiny pieces of fabric draped over their arms), but the fact that for some reason they made you want to *cry*; tears as large and glittering as diamonds.

Jennifer Travis whistled. 'It's just like at the Tate,' she said, snatching a glass from a passing tray.

'Or the Prado Museum,' murmured Sebastian, who hadn't forgotten Laura's predilection for the painters of the Spanish Baroque and their followers.

Not even Matilda seemed unmoved.

'Wonderful colour palette,' was all she could muster.

There was a constant influx of people through the front door, and they were forced to move further into the gallery. Sebastian — who, after all, had played a certain role in this success story — cast his eyes about for Esmeralda's heavily made-up face. It was one of the few but significant disappointments of his career so far that he'd never got full access to her brain: soon after they'd started the tests, she'd been snapped up by an agent, given a big studio on the South Bank with a view of the Thames, and, by her own account, had no time to ponder where these sudden talents had come from. Sebastian suspected, however, that Esmeralda's reluctance to open herself up to testing was less about lack of time and more about fear. He'd seen it in her eyes, the way she avoided his gaze when he'd started talking about genetic mutations and crossed synapses. 'You mean it's like a bug in a computer, or something?' she'd asked. 'Yeah, you could say that,' he'd replied, and watched as she pursed her bright red lips till her lipstick cracked. 'And if you do all these tests on me, and find the bug, what's gonna happen then, eh?' He'd asked her what she meant, though he understood really — someone who finds something broken will sooner or later want to fix it, no one knew that better than Sebastian, and Esmeralda Lundy didn't want to be fixed. She'd been given an unearned gift, and she'd do whatever it took to avoid having to return it.

So Sebastian had let go of Toilet Baby, despite the fact that Corrigan had got very upset and started roaring about 'the price of science'. But when it came to it, Sebastian realised as he caught sight of Esmeralda in the midst of a sea of camera flashes and canapés, he wasn't particularly interested in the science. He was interested in grace, in whatever form it manifested itself.

He was just about to push his way through to congratulate Esmeralda when he felt something cold and wet spreading across his crotch. For a confused moment the world went fuzzy — he started thinking he was sleeping and that he'd wet the bed again, even though these embarrassing episodes had stopped the very moment he'd bid farewell to Laura Kadinsky. But then he felt someone daubing the leg of his trousers with a paper napkin. On his knees in front of him was a man with wild hair and long, graceful fingers, engaged in rubbing frenetically at a patch of spilled Prosecco on his leg. Piano fingers, Sebastian thought, before he was suddenly struck by the absurdity of the situation and jerked back. The man got to his feet and swept his mane of hair out of his eyes, a broad grin spreading across his face.

Sebastian recognised him immediately, recognised him from all the thousands of pictures he'd googled his way through whenever jealousy had taken over his mind and body.

It was Philip Kadinsky.

Sebastian looked around for Travis or Matilda, for anyone who could save him from this doubly challenging conversation, but they'd disappeared without a trace.

Laura and Philip arrived at Whitechapel Gallery in the company of Emma, who, to Laura's great astonishment, had left her TV producer husband and started dating a Czech concept artist she'd met at the Kassel biennial. Emma had spent the whole taxi journey there talking about it: *the coincidence*, she'd wittered, *can you imagine the coincidence!* To add to it all, the Kassel biennial wasn't actually a biennial at all but a quinquennial, it only took place every fifth year, and what were the odds of them bumping into each other and falling hopelessly in love in Kassel under those circumstances? Enormous!

Laura had wanted to protest — the odds were no higher than the odds of them running into each other and falling hopelessly in love in Regent's Park or in Tenerife or anywhere else: love, in contrast to lust, was always a coincidence, and since she had no idea which of these enormities this particular case turned on, she'd held her tongue. The only reason she'd agreed to get into a taxi with Emma and go to her protégé's first exhibition at all was that Philip had shown such uncharacteristic enthusiasm for the invitation. He, who would never usually lower himself to nagging, even with Chloe, had practically implored her to agree to the two of them going — let's get out and about, do something together, drink bubbly, live it up! He hadn't used those words, of course, but that was the content. Faced with this sudden enthusiasm, Laura could do nothing but capitulate. Somewhere in her shrivelled soul maybe she felt a certain longing for art, any kitsch nonsense at all, really, anything at all that was already flat, and that she could escape into and maybe never come back from, and from what Emma had told her about her wunderkind, she actually did sound rather promising.

She moved slowly through the gallery space. She was alone. The fact that she was able to make her way through without the support of Philip's arm was due entirely to the number of people thronging around her. Laura thought that, together, they were a little like a forest. She'd read, in a popular science book about the emotional life of trees, that just like humans, trees need one another. You might have thought that a single tree would do better than one forced to share water, nutrients, and sunlight with others, but it seemed that wasn't the case. Single trees can't grow particularly tall, or they fall at the slightest autumn storm. Trees that stand together can resist winds of almost any strength. If a tree is struggling, those around it help by channelling nutrients and water to the sick or damaged individual. Not because trees have a moral consciousness, but because they themselves want to survive. Every gap in the tree canopy is a danger to be avoided. Crowd injuries in people work the same way — as long as everyone in the crowd is standing, no one will die, but as soon as one person falls, so does everyone around them, like bloody rings on the water, like the children who were trampled to death at Bethnal Green station in 1976. Laura didn't want a responsibility like that on her shoulders, so she stayed on her feet, progressing slowly through the mass of bodies by leaning on one shoulder after the other. It wasn't easy to hit the target, but if she missed the shoulder she'd aimed for, her hand always ended up landing on another. There was a comfort and a beauty in it which Laura could only vaguely sense, somewhere on the periphery of her limited emotional spectrum.

Laura wanted to get through the crowd because she'd seen something when she and Philip had first set foot in the gallery, a painting that vaguely reminded her of something that had once been important to her. It was more of a feeling than a fully formed thought — it had been such a short glimpse before her vision filled completely with people, Prosecco bubbles, Philip's rough stubble as she peeped gingerly out at the world from her refuge behind his cheek. Now Philip had abandoned her, and with a determined bewilderment, she found her solitary way back to that picture. Seeing it had felt like stroking a child's soft cheek, feeling its perfect roundness, the defencelessness of sleep. Laura couldn't really explain it — after all, her biggest problem was her inability to understand her own emotional inducements — but in some way, she felt a responsibility for that painting.

As if it was there specifically so that she should see it.

As soon as she was in front of it, Laura recognised the painting. She didn't even need to look at the plaque to confirm the painting wasn't an original but a skilfully produced replica of a painting she'd looked at dozens of times in art books and exhibition catalogues — but still never really *seen*. Just like many romantically inclined art enthusiasts, Laura was of the opinion that every meaningful artwork possessed a quality that lay beyond words, that there was an essence that could only be perceived and never described. This applied not least to portraits, that superficially banal art form. 'What's the point of portraying one human being when there are six billion of them?' This question had been posed by a pedantic guy with oversized front teeth and oversized pretensions when Laura was studying art history at university.

Without putting her hand up, Laura had replied: *Because behind every face is the shadow of another, and another, and another.*

Clara Serena Rubens was the first-born daughter of Peter Paul Rubens. In 1616, he painted her portrait — Clara was five years old at the time and had hair the colour of melted butter.

Round cheeks, a distinct cupid's bow, chubby fingers onto which she like to put Cheerios, to her mother's horror.

'Do you know the artist?' asked the man who was quite clearly Philip Kadinsky, raising one eyebrow towards the ceiling.

'Yes, yeah, in a way,' Sebastian mumbled, troubled.

'I don't,' Philip said. 'I know her agent. Friend of my wife's.'

'Aha.'

'That's my wife over there. In front of the painting of the child.'

'Ah, right.'

'Pretty nice, wouldn't you say?'

'The picture? I guess.'

'Laura. That's her name. My wife.'

'Oh.'

'You don't recognise her?'

Sebastian filled his mouth with Prosecco, then immediately started coughing.

'I mean, she's your patient,' insisted Philip. 'Or was. For quite a long time, if I've understood correctly.'

Sebastian pretended to search his memory.

'Laura, Laura … Kadinsky? Yes, of course, I see now. That it's Laura. How is she?'

'Not particularly well,' Philip said and drained his glass. 'You could say you failed.'

Yes, thought Sebastian. I failed. *But it was never my fault.*

'A little odd, I think,' Philip continued. 'That you didn't recognise her. As I understand it, the treatment was rather … intensive.'

Sebastian coughed again. 'Aha, I mean, yes, of course I recognised her,' he said, feeling his cheeks flush. 'But confidentiality, you realise, it's paramount. You see. You have to keep information where it belongs. I can't go around talking about my volunteers to anyone who asks.'

'That may be, but I'm her husband. Not a particularly good husband, which I'm sure Laura has already told you, but nonetheless.'

Philip leaned forward.

494

'I want to know how you did it, Isaksson.'

'I don't think I understand what ...' Sebastian squirmed.

'Making her happy!'

'I ... I mean ...'

'Don't look so terrified. You don't need to go into detail. I don't want details, I'm not a masochist. You didn't prescribe her anything, I know that, and the idea that it would have been enough to ... never mind.'

Philip backed away again, turning to look at Laura. Sebastian reluctantly looked in the same direction. She was standing in front of a reproduction of Rubens' Clara — reaching out to touch it, and at that moment, Sebastian saw something very strange: her hand was steady, her gaze soft, and when her hand touched the canvas, it landed just where Sebastian realised it had been meant to, every time, landing like a caress on the child's round cheek.

'You must realise I love her dreadfully,' Philip said. 'She's crazily difficult to live with, but then, so am I. All I want to know is how I might make her happy.'

'I didn't do anything,' Sebastian mumbled, not taking his eyes off Laura.

'Hmm.'

Sebastian turned his head and looked Philip straight in the eye.

'I didn't do anything; I let her decide. That's all.'

'Hmm,' said Philip Kadinsky again, and at once he looked elated. 'Why didn't I think of that?'

Laura pushed her way through the crush. She was going home. Home to her house, her beautiful things, home to the magnolia, the bed, and the sheets that always smelled of fabric conditioner. Home to Chloe's soft round cheeks, the birthmark behind her left ear. Was it still there? What if it had disappeared? When did she last blow raspberries on her daughter's tummy? When did she last open her eyes and see, really see, what was around her?

Laura Kadinsky was selfish, spoiled, and shallow. She knew that, beyond a shadow of a doubt. But she was no better or worse than anyone else. She was who she was — woman, wife, mother, scenographer. Almost happy, which, when you thought about it, really thought about it, wasn't that bad. Not bad at all, considering genuinely happy people were often pretty stupid.

Laura was in such a hurry to get out of the gallery she almost didn't notice how easy it was to find her way. No fumbling, no stumbling, no face-plants. She got to the door without causing a single accident, for herself or anyone else.

Just before Laura left the gallery, she caught sight of a face in the crowd, a reflection in the glass doors. She jumped and turned around — it looked like Sebastian's face, because it was Sebastian's face.

And yet not.

What was he doing here? Why was he standing there next to her husband, a spectre in Philip's shadow? Why wasn't he more beautiful?

Maybe he was no better or worse than anyone else. Maybe he was just who he was — soap bubble, passing fancy, someone she'd loved once.

Laura pushed open the door and walked to the Tube station without so much as a wobble.

Sebastian was in a cold sweat after his encounter with Philip Kadinsky. At the same moment Philip had taken his eyes off him, he'd taken the opportunity to sneak off, and now he needed to find Travis and Matilda, he needed to find them right away. Meeting Laura's husband was bad enough — being forced to talk to Laura herself was more than he could bear. Maybe he didn't love her anymore, maybe he never had, but a single look had been enough to rekindle that old desire to run his fingers along her throat, to let her bite his arms as though he were a loaf of freshly baked bread.

The brain is plastic and can be retrained, but the body wants what the body wants. There's not much you can do about it.

He found Matilda in one of the gallery's furthest corners. She was standing with her back to the room, face upturned towards a painting. Sebastian put his hand on her shoulder. She didn't move.

'Have you seen Travis? We have to go.'

Matilda was still motionless. He took a firmer grip on her bony shoulder and turned her to face him. Her face was mottled with tears, but she didn't look sad. Calm, rather.

'What is it?' he asked. 'Tilda, why are you crying?'

'Look,' was all she said.

Sebastian looked up at the canvas. To begin with he had difficulty focusing anywhere; the image was messy, like a hell scene from Breughel or Bosch — *that bloody two-bit joker*, as he'd once heard Laura giggle. It made Sebastian think of his mother's giant jigsaws. She puzzled her way through their whole childhood, motif after detailed motif, never fewer than two thousand pieces. She had a special table for it in a corner of her study. Sebastian never actually saw her sitting there — when would she have had time to, with three children and thirty thousand souls to tend? Still the motifs emerged, bit by bit. With hindsight, Sebastian realised she must have done the puzzles when they'd gone to bed, but for several years he'd regarded it as something almost magical, the way the pictures just kind of grew, from the centre (in contrast to most people, their mother started not with the edges but with the middle of the image). She only did art puzzles, never those tacky pictures of the Golden Gate Bridge at night or alpine peaks and edelweiss; she never hung them on the walls in the hallway as proof of her own endurance. One day the picture was complete, the next it was gone. The boxes were stacked in crates and borne up to the attic.

One image he particularly remembered was Breughel the Elder's 'Tower of Babel', maybe because it was one of the few times she'd chosen a biblical motif. That was the image that came to mind as he followed Matilda's finger in the air. The painting in front of them depicted an enormous building in cross section. A hospital? It was a hospital, *higher than the handsomest hotel*. In it, there were paperbacks, tea for sale, pale, vain, conciliatory flowers. The number of faces in the picture — dying, newborn — was overwhelming, but he soon saw the detail that had caught Matilda's attention. In a corner, by the maternity ward, there were three children and a dog — or more precisely, three girls and a Newfoundland. One of the girls had her arms round the dog's neck, the other two were sitting beside them, holding hands. They were wearing party dresses with lace collars and red tights, because it was Christmas.

Not that that was apparent from the painting as a whole — that it was Christmas, that is — but it didn't need to be. Sebastian knew, because he'd seen that very portion of the picture before. It was just that, on the photo that had stood on the piano in the living room in Professorsstaden, he was the one with his arms around Bernarda's neck.

'Three girls,' Matilda whispered. 'It *is* you, isn't it? Who was swapped.'

'Yeah.'

'I was drawn to this picture, immediately … *the colour*, Sebastian, can you see it?'

'No.'

'It's totally fucking magical. And it's everywhere, even in her fur,' Matilda said, briefly touching the painted dog. 'I used to think the colour wanted to hurt me, but it doesn't. It wanted to free me. Kathleen always says: *the way to freedom is through the senses.* I've never seriously understood what she meant before.'

'Who's Kathleen?'

'My yoga teacher. How long have you known?'

'A few weeks.'

'Why didn't you say anything?'

'Because I ... because I didn't dare.'

'You didn't think I'd be able to handle it, did you?'

'No,' Sebastian answered honestly. 'I didn't.'

Once again, Matilda held out a finger, this time touching the girl's pale face, the bright blue eyes, the straight little nose.

'Who's she?'

'You know who it is.'

'She looks so sad. Like a shadow.'

He laid a gentle hand on her shoulder.

'Tilda, we have to go. We can talk more later, I promise. But I can't stay here.'

Matilda jumped, as though she'd just remembered something important. When she turned to Sebastian, she looked worried.

'Jennifer's gone,' she said. 'She took off.'

'Why? Where?'

'She talked to your boss, what's his name ... Corrigan. And then she went completely mad. He's changed the date, apparently.'

'The date?'

'For the removal of the cicadas. Seems like it's going to be tomorrow?' Jennifer said. And then she took off. I was going to go after her, but then ...' Matilda made a sweeping gesture towards the painting.

This wasn't good, not good at all. Sebastian quickly went through the possibilities in his head. Most probable was that Travis had gone to the Institute — such were the mechanics of love and obsession.

'The Institute,' Sebastian said. 'She must have decided to put your rescue plan into action early.'

'But that's not going to work! Not in a single night. We were going to ship them out over a week! And she's on her own. Without a car. We were going to hire one. I was going to drive. I was going to *help* her.'

Sebastian shook his head in despair.

'If you want to help her, first we have to find her. If it's really true that Corrigan's got it in for her, you never know what might happen. Have you got any better suggestions for where she might be?'

Matilda exhaled. Her gaze had returned to the painting.

'No,' she said. 'I haven't.'

And just at that moment.

A voice. From the other side of the planet, from right up close.

'Tilda? Sebastian?'

They already knew before they turned around that it was Clara who'd come, Clara who'd finally found them.

They took a taxi to the Institute, the siblings in the back seat and Jordan up in front. Clara was sitting in the middle, like she always used to in the family's old Volvo V70. Sebastian on the left, Matilda on the right, Violetta a ghost in the rear-view mirror. When people are reunited, thought Clara, they often claim afterwards that *it was as though no time had passed*. It was, like most claims people make, both true and false. The fact that she and her siblings could sit here, packed together like this, as though no time had passed, depended on one thing alone: that time had passed.

That they'd changed and stayed themselves, become more themselves.

They barely spoke during the journey. Clara couldn't quite understand why they were going to Sebastian's workplace, or why they were in such a hurry to find this woman, Jennifer Travis. But it didn't matter, they had time now, time to be in a hurry. Talking could come later, or not at all. Just now, she thought, it was enough to close her eyes and inhale — the familiar smell of car and darkness, the familiar smell of Sebastian (milk) and Matilda (honey).

They stopped in front of the main entrance to the Institute. Sebastian paid the taxi driver, led the others round the back of the building, and told them to wait while he went to show his ID to the security guard. The plan was apparently for Sebastian to go in on his own and then let in the others via a fire exit. It was cold, and Clara was shivering in her thin windcheater. Jordan offered to put his arms around her, but she declined.

Instead it was Matilda who, without asking first, wrapped her in her bony embrace. It felt unfamiliar — Clara couldn't recall Matilda ever having hugged her voluntarily.

'Sorry,' she whispered into Clara's hair.

'For what?'

'Sorry I'm your sister.'

Clara felt her tense muscles soften.

'It's okay. Sorry I'm yours.'

'I can't get my head around you going to the other side of the world to get away from me.'

One day, maybe, Clara would explain. How it had actually been the exact reverse. One day, maybe, they'd laugh at it. *Me? And him? Good god, Clara, wouldn't it have been easier just to answer my emails?*

But what's easy isn't always the same thing as what's possible; at least, it wasn't the same thing for Clara. Maybe Matilda would never be able to understand, but that was okay. You could still love what you didn't understand. The sea. Space. Another person.

'You went first,' said Clara. 'Bangladesh, Berlin.'

'But that was to save the world. Well, the first was, anyway.'

'And I went to see it ending.'

Clara crept further into Matilda's embrace. 'Whatever,' she mumbled into Matilda's sharp shoulder. 'Now we're here. In the same place.'

'The mothership would be so damn pleased if she knew.'

'The lambs gathered.'

'But who's the shepherd?'

Just then, the door opened, and out popped Sebastian's head.

'Let's split up,' said Sebastian, when he'd corralled the others into the building. 'You and I will have to take one of the others each, Tilda, since we're the only ones who know our way around. Clara and I will start at the top, you and Jordan from the bottom. Start with the lab, here, take my card, the code is 11772792. Remember it?'

'No.'

Sebastian dug a piece of paper out of his pocket, scribbled down the code, and pushed it into Matilda's hand.

'See you at my office — you can find it, right?'

'Think so. But hey — is this really necessary? Us splitting up? We'll find her anyway, no?'

Sebastian shook his head.

'You've only seen a fraction of this building, you have no idea how big it is. And jumbled. And illogical. The only person who really knows the place is Travis, and that's only because her brain is an even more complex structure, if that's possible. So yeah, it's necessary. Go on, we'll start up there. And take the stairs. Travis likes stairs.'

With a defeated gesture, Matilda nodded to Jordan that they should go. Sebastian and Clara went in the other direction, to a door that led to the outer stairwell.

They started climbing in silence. Clara must have got used to uphill terrain on Easter Island, thought Sebastian, because she took the stairs two at a time, while he came panting along after her. After thirteen or fourteen flights of stairs they came to a landing with four doors and an empty lift shaft.

'What now?' asked Clara.

Sebastian leaned against the wall, catching his breath.

'I don't know, we'll have to take our chances.'

'Not down there, in any case,' said Clara, staring down into the empty hole. 'That's a health and safety risk. Don't you have a health and safety officer at this workplace?'

Sebastian laughed. 'This workplace is a bloody madhouse, Clara.'

His sister smiled silently.

Clara, thought Sebastian with a moment's gratitude. Back. Clara, who'd been so kind to him after Violetta's funeral, even though he'd rejected her attentions, the same way he'd rejected everyone who didn't want anything from him. In many ways it had been easier with Matilda — she'd cried and raged and demanded answers from him. How could he not have realised his own girlfriend wanted to die? Why hadn't he had her hospitalised? Was it true she only weighed forty-four kilos? And what the fuck was that weird colour floating above her coffin like an evil aura? Clara had come to his defence, but he hadn't wanted to listen. Matilda had said terrible things to Clara, too; he couldn't quite remember what, had probably been too taken up with his own inner noise.

'What did Matilda actually say to you? After the funeral that time?' he asked now. He looked at Clara, who was sitting with her legs dangling down into the lift shaft.

'Don't you remember?' she asked, seeming genuinely surprised.

'Everything from that time is blurry.'

'She said I was pathetic. That I was a coward and a little mouse, and a load of other things that were true.'

'But why did she say that?'

'Because she was upset, I guess. Because Violetta did what she did, to you. She's always loved you the most.'

'I find that very difficult to believe.'

'Why's that? There's nothing to say you have to love all your siblings equally. It's not as if you choose them.'

'But that's exactly why,' Sebastian protested. 'That's exactly why you have to love them the same. Because it's the only thing you have in common — that you're siblings. Because it's special.'

'How special? We're just three people who happened to grow up together.'

Sebastian said nothing.

'I didn't mean it like that …' said Clara. 'I just mean that family is something different. Than blood. That was all I meant. I didn't think it was a particularly controversial opinion these days. I forgot you've always been a bit conservative.'

She was teasing him. And it made him happy, but he wasn't yet ready to let go of the subject he'd just embarked on.

'Is that why you haven't spoken to her since then?' he said. 'Tilda? Because of what she said?'

Clara laughed, a curt laugh that stopped as quickly as it had started.

'No. God, no,' she said then. 'It wasn't Tilda's fault.'

'No? She seems to think so.'

'I know,' said Clara. 'But she wasn't the worst. That was *me*. You weren't there, it was later that evening, you were asleep, Mama too. I came into the kitchen and Tilda was sitting there doing a crossword. A fucking *crossword*. No idea why I got so upset about that, but I did. It just felt so trivial. Unfair, somehow. You know the way she's always been so fucking worried about the world and injustice and genocide and god knows what. But as soon as there was a crisis at home, it was as though it didn't touch her. Unless she was the crisis, that is, which quite frankly she mostly was.'

'You know that's not true,' Sebastian said. 'You know she cared.'

'Well, now I know that, yeah. And then too, I guess. But it didn't really matter, there was so much I wanted to say to her that I'd never said and it was as though I suddenly thought I had a chance, know what I mean?'

'So, what did you say?'

'All kinds of things. Quite a lot of it was true. But quite a lot wasn't. For instance, I said ... I said ...' Clara drew a deep lungful of air. 'I said it would have been better. For everyone, for the family, I mean, for you. And for me. If she'd been the one who'd taken her own life. I asked her how she could have been mentally ill for a decade but never even tried.'

Sebastian said nothing. Those words coming out of Matilda's mouth? Maybe. But Clara's? It was almost impossible to believe.

'You understand there was no way I could look her in the eye after that?' said Clara. 'I mean, I wanted to, but it ... I just couldn't. I thought it would work out in some way, I just had to wait. So I waited. But she moved. And then ... I don't know.'

Clara shrugged.

'It hasn't always been easy, being her sister. As I'm sure you'd agree. But it turned out to be harder not being her sister. But I was still so angry. At her. Because she'd made me say all that. Because she'd hurt me over the years in so many small ways that should have more weight together than a few throwaway words, and yet didn't, and so it was suddenly *me* who was the awful one. It was as though ... I've always thought we were so different. And suddenly we weren't.'

'Are you still angry?' said Sebastian.

'No. Not at her, anyway. And not at you, but then, I never have been. I'm not even angry at Violetta, though perhaps I should be. I was so afraid of her, the whole time you were together. It felt like she was a great fucking hole of darkness that was going to devour my whole family, but I never got why. As if she'd taken my place before she'd even come into our lives.'

'Clara, there's something you need to know —'

Clara stopped him by raising a hand, a dark shadow against the wall behind her, lit by the hazy light coming through the window from the street.

'Sebastian, I know. You don't need to say it. I figured out that Violetta was the missing link in our family a long time ago, long before Mama even sent that email.'

'What do you mean? Are you trying to tell me you knew that Violetta and I'd been swapped on the maternity ward?'

Clara laughed, a short laugh that echoed in the empty lift shaft.

'Of course not, that would be absurd. I just mean that she filled a void in our family, and when she died it broke. Papa and Mama got divorced, we all moved to different places. We needed her. Or you did, in any case. Then, when Mama sent that email, and told us all that stuff about the mix-up and so on, well … I mean, I didn't expect it. I really didn't.'

She laughed again, that quick, almost weightless laugh.

'I thought it was me? Can you imagine. How self-obsessed can you be? But I guess I thought it would explain a thing or two. Why Matilda and I had such a hard time with each other.'

'I never thought it was me,' Sebastian said. 'Not really. How blind can you be? It was Travis who saw it. Not me.'

Clara reached out a hand towards Sebastian and touched his cheek.

'Imagine how hysterical I was when I realised it was Violetta? Like —'

She raised her eyebrows and grimaced, and suddenly he realised what she meant.

'Clara, ugh! No! God!'

Then he said: 'But how did you know? That it was her?'

'Have you ever looked in the mirror a long time, I mean a really long time? Just stared?'

'No?'

'Don't do it. You never know what you might set off. Does Tilda know?'

'Yes.'

There was a pause. Then Sebastian said:

'We should look for Travis.'

Clara swung her legs up onto the floor, stood up, and brushed the dust off her trousers.

'A family is just a system like any other, Sebastian. It's there to give us a feeling of safety and stability. But it's a system that means nothing unless it's filled with something of value. Love. Trust. Things like that. Anyone can be your family, as long as those things are there.'

'You sound like Tilda when she was poly.'

'She isn't anymore?'

'Don't think so. She seems pretty fixated on Billy, but I think it's over.'

'Shame. He seemed good.'

Clara was standing in front of one of the doors, with her hand on the handle. She pushed it.

'Coming?' she said.

He looked at her back. It seemed straighter somehow.

'You're different to how I remember you, Clara.'

She said, without turning around: 'I've seen the loneliest place on earth, Sebastian. And it wasn't lonely at all.'

Then she opened the door, and together they continued the upward climb.

At the same time, Matilda and Jordan were feeling their way along underground. Of course, Matilda had been to the lab with Jennifer several times, but it was hard to find the way in the dark. Should've brought a fucking head torch, or at least an inner light, should've had a more powerful third eye. This Jordan guy's presence bothered her, like a piece of straw under her foot, cracks on your heel that start itching just as you're falling asleep. Why didn't he say anything? And what the fuck did he want with Clara? He seemed totally fine, actually totally fine brother-in-law material, but what did she know. If he ever hurt Clara in any way at all, she was going to kill him. Ow, fucking hell! Matilda walked straight into a wall, felt her nose crumple, her chin scrape against stone and plaster.

'You okay?' Jordan whispered.

'Why are you whispering, arsehole?'

'I thought this was a covert thing.'

Matilda rubbed her chin with the sleeve of her jumper and snorted.

'The only person who might be down here is Jennifer and she *wants* to be found, believe me.'

'You seem to know her well.'

Matilda snorted again.

'Not really. It's just that she's like a newborn baby.'

She reached into her pocket and dug out her phone, turned on the torch, and held the flat, glowing rectangle under Jordan's chin. The light streamed like a halo around his head, the shadows from his eyebrows ran like tears over his cheeks. It looked macabre, the way he was smiling.

'You remind me of someone I once knew,' she said.

Jordan grinned.

'Really?'

'His name was J and he was really good at fucking.'

'Ah, can't be me, then. I'm mediocre at best.'

'Most people are.'

Matilda turned off the torch and they stood silent in the darkness.

'I really want to be the one who finds her,' Matilda said at last, quietly.

'Then we should carry on looking.'

The door Clara had chosen led to a new stairwell. After a further twenty-two floors they reached a door, which in turn led out onto a roof terrace Sebastian hadn't even known existed. They looked around, confused, at the empty, black space — there didn't appear to be any other way back into the building than the door they'd just come from.

Clara walked over to the edge and leaned over the waist-high wall. Floating up from Russell Square came a car alarm's lonely cry, the fountains' distant hissing, the soft murmur of a mother's blood circulation in a newborn's ear. Clara closed her eyes and went on listening. The wet smack of trainers, a dog's paws on the parquet on the first sunny Sunday just before Easter, a cicada's whirr among the azaleas outside Pablo Neruda's house La Chascona. A bucket full of stars poured out into the sea, landing with a hiss one by one. Sparklers stuck in generous portions of baked Alaska on New Year's Eve '96, '97, '98, '02, and for the last time in '07. She looked at the dark-windowed house fronts that reared up like cliffs on the other side of the abyss, impenetrable fortresses of the rich, heard the restrained cries of a diplomat's wife biting her knuckles, locked in a bathroom with double washbasins and soap that smelled of cedar and lemon balm. She thought about Elif, who'd stood on the edge of an abyss and dreamed of being not a bird, but a person worth looking for. She thought about Jordan, all his failings and shortfalls, and all his love. She thought about Violetta, who'd died and come back to life. About Horst, who'd lost a sense and lost his mind and yet still left the battle victorious. What were they doing now? She didn't know, and that was okay. She was here now; her life was here now. She thought of the earth, which would still exist long after the last human had bought their last bottle of sparkling water at the last airport before the last flight to the last white sandy beach. She heard a rumble from the earth; it was the Underground, it was the lava and the magma, it was the uprising, it was the snotty phase of a cold, it was grace.

And then suddenly, like a battle cry: the vibration and cheerful trickling sound of a mobile phone.

'Clara!' whispered Sebastian from the other side of the roof. 'There's a door here, I think it leads to the directors' corridor. Come on.'

Clara waved the phone she'd just pulled out of her back pocket.

'It's Mama!' she shouted.

'Mama?'

'Ringing me. I have to answer.'

'Call her back!'

'But what if she's unhappy or dying? I'll be right there.'

'You'll never find me.'

'I'll find you, Sebastian. Go.'

Behind the door there was a dead space, a square-metre-sized overflow of dust and feathers and forgotten phone numbers and anniversaries and suppressed trauma and the odd vicious impulse, disarmed and stuffed in a box without a key. At the other end was yet another door, and beyond the door, a corridor, and beyond the corridor, another corridor, which was the very corridor in which Sebastian had once, many months ago, stood and collected himself ahead of his first meeting with Corrigan. This time, the directors' corridor was dark; the only light was what came in through the windows, and crept in diagonal stripes across the floor and up the walls — it looked like the clumsy footprint of an enormous bird, maybe a raven, maybe a peacock or a fulmar.

Sebastian walked carefully down the long, elegantly decorated corridor, aiming for the door at the other end. He tried to read the names on the doors as he passed, but the times he managed it, they meant nothing to him. It wasn't until he was nearly at the end of the corridor that he saw one door was ajar, with compact, almost fluorescent darkness spilling out. Sebastian counted the doors, consulted his internal map, and calculated that it was Corrigan's office.

He swore quietly at Travis's carelessness. Breaking in to your own workplace was one thing, but breaking in to the office of your ultimate boss was grounds for dismissal, and possibly criminal. Travis would do just fine in prison, he had no doubt about that, but he himself had no major desire to get banged up for aiding and abetting. He crept up to the door, listening in the silence, and hissed through the crack:

'Travis? What are you up to?'

The wheels of an office chair scraped across the floor. A monkey squawked. A lamp was lit.

'Isaksson? Come in, please. I've been waiting for you,' Corrigan said, throwing the door open.

Matilda and Jordan felt their way on through the passageways, past laboratory after laboratory. Matilda listened carefully to see if she could distinguish the whirring of the cicadas — the muted vibrating sound that Jennifer insisted on calling a song, though to Matilda's ears it sounded like nothing so much as a motor engine. She'd said as much to Jennifer once. As always, Jennifer'd refused to be offended, and had instead chosen to interpret the statement metaphorically. *The engine of the world, yes, yes.* Matilda listened, but didn't hear any whirring, though there was a faint tinkling sound, a few solitary notes trilling through the air, each one a little drop of coloured light, yellow, green, purple. She watched the blue note float away, dissolve in the air, and disappear. It didn't hurt.

'Is that a piano?' Jordan said.

'Sounds like it.'

'Can that Travis woman play the piano?'

'Doubtful. But I don't know.'

They moved towards the sound.

'It sounds like "Nearer, My God, to Thee",' said Jordan.

Matilda didn't reply, because now she'd spotted the source of the music. Through the glass that divided one of the laboratories from the passageway outside shone a weak, bluish light. They put their foreheads against the glass and peered in, and there, on a stool in the middle of the room, sat a cat at a keyboard, pressing the keys, one clumsy paw print after another. Jordan whistled.

'What the hell do they do in this place, anyway?'

'I think,' said Matilda, slowly moving her head back from the glass, 'that not a single fucker knows.'

Just then came a crash, and a laugh, followed by a crash, and a laugh, and a crash, and a laugh, in a pattern so simple and perfect that not even Philip Kadinsky could have found fault with the intervals, and over the symmetrical bass chord rose a murmur and a whir, a revving motor, the murmur of the sea in the shell Jordan had brought in his pocket all the way from Easter Island, and which now, with a clinking like the sound of an exploding lightbulb, fell to the concrete floor.

Matilda tugged at Jordan's arm and they ran through the darkness towards the sound.

They found Travis sitting cross-legged on the floor of her lab, hands resting on her knees with her palms facing upwards. *Sukhasana*, thought Matilda, and at once felt a longing as sharp as physical pain for that simplest of things, the purity of the body inhabiting the world, even when it — the world, the body — was crumbling or being resurrected, whichever was the case. Death and rebirth, thought Matilda, and what the fuck was she up to, this crazy, beautiful person?

It was, actually, Matilda realised when she looked around, quite obvious. Along each wall, and on all the tables and benches, the terrariums that had once held Jennifer Travis's cicada collection were wide open — empty, gaping cubes of glass. The black plastic covers lay scattered about, some cracked, others whole, all shimmering like black sheets of code in the light of hundreds of flickering fluorescent lights. The air was thick with wings, layer upon layer of rainbows, fish scales.

Jennifer, who'd been sitting with her eyes closed, opened them suddenly, swept the hair from her face, and smiled with cheeks as round as a hamster's.

'The light in me bows to the light in you,' she said with her hands over her heart, raising them to her forehead and nodding slightly. 'How lucky you came. I need some help with the windows.'

Jordan and Matilda looked around them in confusion — they were in a basement. But Travis wasn't lying. Up by the ceiling along each of the walls was a row of narrow windows that Jordan managed, with some difficulty despite his height, to open. A delighted Jennifer Travis began to catch one flying insect after another in her cupped hands, before casting them up towards the narrow vents. They flew from her palms like confetti. Every single one managed to get out.

'Are you sure that's a good idea?' Matilda asked. 'Do you really think they'll survive?'

Travis stopped, one hand reaching for the night outside the window, and said nothing, as if she were considering matters. Then she said:

'You know what? It's actually not possible to determine everything with complete certainty. Sometimes you just have to do what your instinct tells you.'

Blinded by the sudden light, Sebastian had to hold the wall for a moment so as not to fall over. Corrigan guffawed as he took him by the arm and led him into the office, seating him in a black leather armchair.

'Bernarda ...' said Sebastian, because there she was, curled up on a bookshelf. When Sebastian said her name, she immediately jumped down and climbed up into his arms.

'Who?' said Corrigan.

'The monkey. How did she get here? She should be in Bermondsey.'

Corrigan shrugged. 'Fuck knows, Isaksson. Guess she took the bus.' He went over to a filing cabinet and got out a bottle of cognac, two glasses, and two cigars. Sebastian would rather have been treated to coffee and Jaffa cakes, in the name of tradition, but he didn't feel it was quite the time to complain.

'Strictly speaking, Isaksson, you shouldn't be here either. It's contrary to regulations.'

'Sorry,' he said, taking the glass Corrigan was holding out, 'but I'm looking for Travis ...'

Corrigan lit a cigar and flopped down behind his desk with his feet up. 'I know, I saw her a while ago. Snuck down to the bug lab. That is to say, if she found it, what with the rotations and all. Come on, have a puff.'

Sebastian caught the cigar and made a valiant effort to light it despite Bernarda's apparent displeasure. The cigar smouldered, then went out, before finally flaring up with a dirty, fleshy glow. He puffed a little and began to cough. It was nothing like cigarettes.

'I ... Why were you waiting for me? And how ... how did you know I was coming?' he said between fits of coughing.

'I told you, I saw Travis. You almost always move about as a pair. So I assumed you'd turn up. I must have been sitting here for three minutes, just waiting, so maybe we should get to the point?'

'Ah, yes, okay.'

'So?'

'I'm not sure I know what the point is, sir,' Sebastian admitted, setting down the cigar in an enormous glass ashtray Corrigan was holding out across the table.

'Of course you don't,' Corrigan replied. 'That's the problem, isn't it? You think there's a question you need to find the answer to, but you don't know what the question is. What does that tell you, Sebastian?'

'About?'

'About the question.'

'You're asking about the question?'

'You're asking me if I'm asking about the question? The answer is yes.'

'I don't think I'm quite with you, sir.'

'Look here, Sebastian: if you have a question, but you don't know what the question is — do you really have a question?'

'Maybe? You're wondering what the question is, which is a question in itself.'

'Of course. But is it an important question?'

'Pardon?'

'Put simply, Isaksson: a question that can't be formulated can't in all honesty be called a question, since, strictly speaking, it doesn't exist. That's what I'm trying to make you see. But perhaps you're not philosophically minded.'

'I suppose I'm not, no.'

'You and Travis, you've been up to something.'

'Yes. Though I'm not sure what.'

Corrigan roared with laughter.

'Seems she isn't, either.'

At this point, Sebastian felt moved to protest.

'Well, Travis seems to ... She had some thoughts about ... about the activities here at the Institute. What they're actually for. Whose agenda they're serving. I think that's been the question, for her. And for me too, maybe. In part, at least.'

'What they're for? The activities?'

'Yes?'

'But that's perfectly obvious, Sebastian.'

'No, I don't think I would say that.'

'They're not *for* anything, of course!'

'I'm not sure I follow —'

'In the beginning, yes. In the beginning there were grand plans, ambitions, the full whammy. You know I was involved in setting up the work here? No, of course you don't, it was confidential. It was at the request of the old lady herself. She's been through a lot, I can tell you. World war, fallen empires. Seen everything first-hand, the intrigues, what goes on behind closed doors. The human factor, which always has a much bigger impact on how things turn out than we'd care to believe. You could say she's developed a certain interest for the human psyche over the years. The mechanisms, so to speak.'

'Excuse me, but are you talking about —'

'About the Queen, Isaksson, I'm talking about the Queen, naturally. Her Majesty. We go back a long way, you know; she turned to me. The brief was very, er, brief: "Corrigan," she said, "I want you to figure it out."'

'Figure what out?'

'The whole palaver. The meaning of human existence, the existence of the soul, the universe's final denouement, whether humans are born good or evil, all that stuff.'

'You were going to do that?'

'This guy called Kadinsky was in on it too. Young whippersnapper at the time, barely out of short trousers. Started out in literary studies, I believe, but a savagely talented man. Nothing he can't do. Perhaps you've heard of him — Philip Kadinsky? Wrote a few decent operas, too, if I recall rightly.'

'I know who he is, yes. His wife has ... been one of our subjects here. But I suppose you know that.'

'Kadinsky's wife? What the devil? What was wrong with her?'

'Honestly? I don't know. I never got to the bottom of it.'

'No, of course you didn't. The vast majority of people have something wrong with their heads. It is, so to speak, the default position for humanity, and the fact is, it's very seldom something we would view as pathological. What I'm trying to get at here, Isaksson, is that over the last few years I've come to certain conclusions that rather derange this whole project, so to speak. In contrast to you, I've been clear what the question is throughout, and now that I have, in some way, found the answer, there's no reason to continue, no reason at all, as I see it.'

'What was the question?'

'Whether there was a system in all this madness.'

'And is there?'

'Of course not. If there was, it wouldn't be madness. On the other hand, Isaksson, there is madness in believing in the system. You are perfectly free to quote me on that, so to speak. Just look at Travis.'

'I mean, I have actually been wondering … Travis thinks … you know, the cicada puzzle?'

'Travis's little hobby, yes, yes.'

'She thinks you have something to do with it. That it's you who's, well, behind it all?'

'Why on earth would I be?'

'To … freak her out, I guess?'

Corrigan laughed again.

'As if she needed any help there! Oof, Isaksson, cicadas, cicadas … Did you know a cicada can't sing if the air temperature is below twenty-five degrees Celsius? They're very human that way.'

Corrigan took a deep gulp from his brandy glass and gazed out of the window.

'But you haven't answered my question,' Sebastian insisted. 'About whether you had anything to do with the puzzle.'

'Have you ever asked yourself whether the puzzle even exists, Sebastian?'

'Whether … No?'

'What I'm trying to say, Isaksson — touché, I know: a rather telling example came up just now, with Kadinsky and his wife, who, presumably unaware of each other's involvement with us here at the Institute, have been living side by side, sharing a bed and bodily fluids, been as intimate as two people can be, well, you understand, I'm sure. A coincidence? Most people would say no. It's too improbable. In this city of millions, this world of billions, how could it have been a coincidence?'

'Though I think he knows that she —'

'Perhaps he knows, perhaps he's always known, or not. The point is that we humans are rational creatures, or at least we want to be. We want to believe that there's an order to things, no? To the world? The idea that it could be just the reverse is terrifying.'

Sebastian felt a shiver run down his spine.

'But listen carefully now, Isaksson: there is no order. The whole damn thing is just chaos. When you've stared at as many brains as I have, you understand that. It's just a goddamn mess in here,' he said, rapping on his skull, 'a goddamn mess in every goddamn skull that's ever strutted around this earth. Synapses form and burn out faster than you can blow out a candle. The little lightbulb switches on, and poof, it explodes. The rest of the world is just a reflection of that.'

'But ...' said Sebastian. 'The correlates? Travis's correlates, the ones she found ... And Laura ...'

He bit his tongue, but it wasn't really necessary. Something else had caught Corrigan's attention. With a bang he snapped his chair upright. He stood up and crossed to the window in a couple of long strides.

'Well, I'll be damned, Isaksson. I'll be damned, how beautiful,' he said, pressing the lit end of his cigar against the windowpane.

It really didn't matter that it wasn't particularly beautiful. The shimmering insects, the way they rose towards the heavens like a ragged curtain, a clattering blind that made the street lights and TV-lit windows flicker. It was a grotesque performance, terrifying; a dark firework display of flesh and shell.

But still. They whirred like a motor.

It didn't matter that it wasn't beautiful, or ugly, that it was impossible to define as either one or the other, that it wasn't possible to allocate and classify, demarcate and survey, pigeonhole, arrange in rows, that Sebastian couldn't tell what it was he felt as he watched them — pure fear or sheer joy. It was like a Goya painting, at once grotesque and radiant.

Sebastian let Bernarda slip down from his lap and went to stand silently beside Corrigan. The realisation that they were, in spite of everything, still just two strangers who happened to be standing next to each other, staring out at the same magically tragic view, immediately made Sebastian feel very, very alone.

But also happy.

Because really, he wasn't alone. He had sisters. He had a monkey who liked banana chips and Harriet Löwenhjelm poems and had just come over to clutch at his knee. He had two unhappy love stories behind him and who knew how many ahead. He had a knack for making other people feel seen, he had a heart, he had a hundred and fifty thousand kilometres of nerve fibres in his brain that could be retrained, all life long.

And he had a friend who, at that moment, came rushing out through the main door of the Institute, threw her arms up into the air, and started dancing in a cloud of wings and scuttling feet.

'Travis, Travis, Travis …' Corrigan chuckled. 'Whatever will she do now?'

But Sebastian didn't have time to answer, because from the corridor came the sound of feet and, presently, Matilda and Jordan came into the room.

What the hell, thought Matilda. Even that crafty little monkey creature had found her way here. Sebastian was standing at the window with Bernarda hanging off his leg. He leaned down and scooped her up onto his hip.

'We found her,' Matilda said, out of breath. 'Jennifer. We found the lab. She let them out.'

Sebastian nodded at the window.

'I know. Look.'

She walked over to the window. There was a red-haired man next to Sebastian. He turned around, but didn't introduce himself. It wasn't necessary. She realised it was Sebastian's boss.

'Badger summer,' he said.

'Sorry?' said Matilda.

'Isn't that what you call it? A summer that never seems to end. An Indian summer.'

'I've never heard it called that,' said Matilda, a little irritated. She wanted to watch Jennifer's show in peace. It was so beautiful. She'd never thought insects could be beautiful, but they were.

Corrigan nodded at the cicadas. 'They're singing now, but it's going to rain tomorrow. They'll all die.'

'Alright,' said Matilda and sat down on the desk. 'Can you be quiet now? I want to talk to my brother.'

Corrigan raised his hands in a conciliatory gesture.

'No problem, no problem! My work here is done.'

He wiggled his eyebrows in a way Matilda couldn't interpret. Then he flung himself down on the black leather sofa and pulled a cushion over his head.

Matilda had just managed to relate how they'd gone about finding Travis when the door was once again thrown open and in came Clara. They turned their heads towards her, all apart from Corrigan, who seemed to have fallen asleep. Clara looked excited; she waved her phone and glittered at Matilda.

'Papa!' she shouted. 'I mean Mama, Mama rang. About Papa. Papa's come back!'

Bernarda did a somersault. Sebastian blinked rapidly three times. Matilda furrowed her brow.

'Papa?' she said. 'Is that really something to celebrate?'

'You don't get it,' Clara said excitedly. 'He was with Billy.'

Bernarda did another somersault. Matilda blinked rapidly three times. Sebastian furrowed his brow.

'My Billy?' Matilda said slowly.

'Yes! And Siri. They're at Mama's house. All of them.'

'But how … ?' said Matilda.

Clara shut the door behind her and went and sat down beside Matilda on the desk. She took Matilda's hand, stroking her thumb across her knuckles.

'But, like, what do you mean? Why are Papa and Billy with Mama?' Sebastian interrupted. 'I don't get it.'

Clara squirmed a little.

'I mean, I don't know exactly *how* … but it's something to do with Billy's ex-wife? Käthe, was that her name? I mean, apparently Papa knows her and —'

Matilda laughed abruptly.

'Papa and Käthe? But that's madness.'

'Whatever, Billy's at Mama's house, because he thought you might be there and he wanted to see you, so he went there. So, that's what's happened.'

'He went there with his ex-wife who just happens to be Papa's latest fling?'

'I don't know if that's the exact situation … but yeah.'

Matilda laughed again, she laughed because it was so absurd, but also, she realised, from sheer, pure joy. Billy had been looking for her! And he'd found her, via a detour, he'd found her and he was waiting for her, at home in Mama's house in Professorsstaden. And Siri was waiting for her, Siri who she loved, even though she had no right to.

'Don't cry, Tilda,' said Clara.

'I'm not crying.'

'Yes, you are.'

'No.'

'Yes.'

'Shut it,' Matilda said, but heard herself that she didn't sound that convincing. When she'd finished crying, she dried her eyes with the sleeve of her top and sniggered.

'Fuck, what a crybaby. You'd think someone had died.'

She clapped her hand to her mouth. Someone had died, someone whose memory still hung in the doorway, casting its shadow over Sebastian's face.

But Sebastian just laughed. He laughed, Clara laughed, Matilda laughed, the very moral monkey who was now called Bernarda laughed.

They laughed till it was almost morning. Then Matilda opened the window, climbed up on the windowsill, and took a packet of yellow American Spirits from her pocket.

'Wish we had some ice cream,' she said, tossing the packet to Sebastian. He climbed up beside her. Clara and Jordan sat on the floor.

'Know what?' said Matilda to Clara, nodding at Sebastian. 'Our brother's seeing a married woman. A full-scale affair, hotels and hanky-panky, the whole package. You wouldn't have thought it, would you?'

'Was seeing,' Sebastian said, flicking ash over the rooftops. 'It's over.'

Matilda put her head on his shoulder.

'Sorry,' she said. 'I didn't know. Are you sad?'

He shrugged his free shoulder.

'No,' he said. 'Just tired.'

'To be honest, she seemed pretty tiring,' Matilda said. 'High maintenance, so to speak.'

She felt Sebastian snicker a last, tired, but happy laugh.

She saw Clara's head on Jordan's lap, she saw that she was at ease.

She saw a nine-week-old foetus on the other side of the earth, who'd just decided to be a girl named Violetta.

She saw Violetta finally let go of the door frame, gather up her shadow and creep out of the room.

She saw the colour, it was a firework display in the sky, it was a star, it flickered for a moment, one last farewell, and was gone.

And down on the street, she saw Jennifer Travis, still running along the pavement, her arms stretched up to the lightening sky, her lab coat flapping like golden wings.

They'd met like this so many times before. He in the doorway, she on the sofa, the night a roller blind outside the window.

'You disappeared,' Philip said, casting his overcoat down by her feet on the sofa.

'Three hours ago,' Laura said. 'Where have you been?'

'It took me a while to notice.'

'Three hours.'

'Okay. It didn't take three hours. Maybe one. But I didn't have the courage to come home.'

'Why not?' said Laura, trying to act as if she wasn't fishing.

'I was afraid you wouldn't be here.'

'What would you have done then?'

Philip shrugged and grinned.

'Marry Giselle, I guess.'

She picked up a sofa cushion and threw it at him.

'What?' Philip laughed. 'Chloe already knows her. It would be better than me marrying a twenty-three-year-old ballet dancer, wouldn't it?'

She let her head fall back against the sofa.

'I've been offered a job,' she said. 'In Madrid.'

'Madrid?'

'Yes. Just one performance, but still. Lorca. *The House of Bernarda Alba*. At the Teatro de la Zarzuela. I want us to go.'

'But what about Switzerland?'

Philip sat on the coffee table, folded one leg over the other, and started untying his Italian leather shoes. They were extremely well polished. Laura loved well-polished Italian leather shoes.

'Fuck Switzerland,' she said. 'I don't need Switzerland if I can work.'

Philip took one shoe off and threw it over his shoulder.

'Okay,' he said.

'Okay?'

'Okay. If that's what you want. We'll move.'

'But your things? You're going to be given a title and all that.'

'Ah,' said Philip, throwing the other shoe over his shoulder. 'The Queen can wait. Let's go if you want to.'

He leaned forward and kissed her forehead. Then he got up and went out to the kitchen.

'Drink?' he shouted.

Laura said nothing for a moment. Then she shouted back:

'I was lying. I haven't been offered a job in Madrid at all.'

'Okay.'

'I just wanted to see what you'd say.'

He put his head through the door.

'I said yes.'

'Do you still say yes?'

'Yes.'

He came back with two gin and tonics and held one out to her. Laura looked around the house at all the things that suddenly seemed to jump out from the walls, surrounding her with their three-dimensional cosiness.

'We'll have to rent something furnished,' she said. 'We can't move all this.'

'If you say so.'

'And put Chloe in a private school. They have dreadful schools in Spain, I've heard.'

'It's lucky we're rich,' said Philip.

'Bloody lucky,' said Laura, taking a gulp of her gin.

'Want to fuck?' said Philip.

'Yes, please,' said Laura.

And in the bedroom, between clean sheets, wrapped in the scent of fabric conditioner, Laura Kadinsky lay with her legs over her husband's shoulders, and saw her feet standing out against the wall — bony, solid, and very, very real.

You have a dream.

In the dream, you're an atonal piano.

You see a colour. It floats in front of your nose. It's a colour that doesn't exist. It's a colour that exists.

You wake up, see the soap bubble.
    See it burst and immediately give birth to a new one.

The world's going under, the world is a wonder.

THANKS

Johan & Harriet.
Mama & Papa.
Håkan, Elise, & Linda.